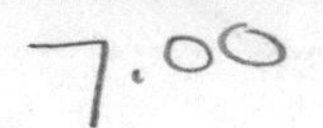

THE BOOKSELLER'S DAUGHTER

THE BOOKSELLER'S DAUGHTER

PAM ROSENTHAL

KENSINGTON PUBLISHING CORP.
http://www.kensingtonbooks.com

BRAVA BOOKS are published by

Kensington Publishing Corp.
850 Third Avenue
New York, NY 10022

All Kensington titles, imprints and distributed lines are available at special quantity discounts for bulk purchases for sales promotion, premiums, fund raising, educational or institutional use.

Special book excerpts or customized printings can also be created to fit specific needs. For details, write or phone the office of the Kensington Special Sales Manager: Kensington Publishing Corp., 850 Third Avenue, New York, NY 10022. Attn. Special Sales Department. Phone: 1-800-221-2647.

ISBN: 0-7582-0445-0

First Kensington Trade Paperback Printing: January 2004
10 9 8 7 6 5 4 3

Printed in the United States of America

To Michael Rosenthal and Ellie Ely

PART ONE

Chapter 1

Provence, July 1783
Six years before the French Revolution

The rule at the château was never to hire a pretty servant. And yet there was no denying that the copper-haired girl serving tea in the library this afternoon was pretty. Clumsy too: if she continued rattling that Sevres cup and saucer she was going to spatter hot tea all over the Viscomte's impeccable white stockings.

Bored with each other's company, the family of the Duc de Carency Auvers-Raimond directed keen eyes in the girl's direction. Sevres was shockingly expensive; a servant who broke a piece could expect to be punished—even, or especially, a servant as pretty as this one. The cup rattled more loudly. The family waited in dreamy stillness for the shivering crash of china on the parquet floor.

But none came; only a few faint beige drops of tea marred the Viscomte's shins, for at the last possible moment, he'd put out a long, deft hand and rescued the cup from immanent destruction.

"Thank you, Marianne," he murmured.

She managed a curtsy, lowering her eyes from his and blushing beneath the freckles scattered over her cheeks.

Teatime finally over, she made her way back to the kitchen. A narrow escape; catastrophe barely averted. No broken china to sweep up, and—more importantly—no punishment to anticipate. The Comtesse Amélie had only glared at her. Ah well, a glare was nothing. What one had to look out for was the Comtesse's scowl, the Gorgon-face that meant a thrashing was in order.

She wouldn't be hurt and she wouldn't be fired. No servant would be fired today; there was too much work to do. All right, she told herself, she should be glad of the work then. Because her job was the main thing, wasn't it? Her job, her salary—surely these things were more important than the fact that *he* had clearly forgotten he'd ever seen her before.

Yes, of course. *He* was of no importance whatsoever.

Though it rather pained her to admit that she'd recognized him the instant she'd entered the room. The set of his shoulders, the dark gleam of his eyes: she'd known him immediately. No wonder she'd stopped breathing properly; of course she'd rattled the china.

And, she warned herself, if she continued thinking of him so . . . so *physically*, she was still in danger of dropping things—this time the whole damn tray. She hurried into the kitchen, laid down the delicate tea things, and tucked her thick curls into a cap, to protect them against soot and grease.

Be honest, she thought. *Admit the whole truth and be done with it.* She winced; the appalling, humiliating fact of the matter was that since last December she hadn't let a day go by without thinking of him.

Thank you, Marianne.

And thank you, *Monsieur le Viscomte.* Even if you don't remember that my name is Marie-Laure and *not* Marianne.

She pinned a stained apron to the front of her dress. One couldn't expect an aristocrat to know a servant's proper name.

Heaps of work awaited her in the scullery. A mountain of pots to wash, a bushel of onions to peel and chop. Plenty of distraction from her troublesome thoughts. She took a heavy knife and sliced off the tip of an onion. Predictably, her eyes filled with tears. *Well, of course,* she scolded herself. *What else could one expect, from such a strong onion?*

There would be a banquet. A chandelier of Bohemian crystal

had been installed in the mirrored dining room; tomorrow evening thirty guests would feast under its light in celebration of the Viscomte's visit.

He'd arrived only this morning, together with his mother the Duchesse. No one among the château's army of servants knew what had brought about the sudden family reunion.

"The Duc's illness could have taken a turn for the worse," Jacques, the Duc's valet, had speculated that morning at breakfast. "The doctors looked graver than usual, last time they visited."

"Perhaps they're selling off some property," someone else suggested. "*That* will usually bring a family out of hiding, to clamor for their share. Or perhaps it's time to find a wife for the Viscomte Monsieur Joseph."

It would have to be a matter of some import, everyone agreed, to pry the Duchesse away from the convent that had been her home for the last few years.

"Of course, the Duc was always a wretched husband, even when he had his wits about him." Nicolas, the château's general manager, prided himself on his knowledge of the family's history. "Joked in public that the Duchesse was a prune in bed. Had a list of mistresses as long as your arm, and you couldn't keep him away from the maids and village girls." Which was why, now that the old man was too enfeebled to have a say in things, his daughter-in-law tried not to hire pretty servants.

But even Nicolas hadn't known Monsieur Joseph's whereabouts these past few years. There were rumors of duels, prison, exile, even a sojourn in America.

"America?" Marie-Laure was an enthusiastic supporter of the recent revolution in the English colonies. How wonderful, she thought, if Monsieur Joseph *had* joined the Marquis de Lafayette in the fight for American independence. How worthy. And how utterly improbable that a member of this nasty, spoiled family would do any such thing.

The group in the kitchen would have been pleased to gossip the morning away but Nicolas hustled them off to work. And so all Marie-Laure had learned of the Duc's younger son was that he'd been his father's favorite and hadn't visited in more than a decade.

But *I* know something that Nicolas doesn't, she thought, putting aside the last onion and moving over to skim the foam from the veal stock. I know what he was doing last winter. He was smuggling forbidden books into France. And cheating booksellers. Well, at least he cheated me and Papa.

Of course, last winter she hadn't known who he really was. But she'd suspected he wasn't what he seemed. She'd liked that about him.

The sights and smells of the busy kitchen dissolved into the steam rising from the stockpot. She was in a shabby, beloved room—with books, books everywhere.

Home.

Home had been the seaside city of Montpellier, beyond the Rhône to the west. She could hear a wind howling outside and boys hawking the latest scandal sheet through the streets. The boys shrieked like seagulls.

Read it and shudder! Read it and weep!

Horrible! Incroyable!

The Baron Roque murdered over his solitary luncheon, blood in the crème brûlée, the killer still at large!

She remembered thinking, that day in Montpellier, that she wouldn't weep for the Baron, a gross, self-important man whose footmen had carried him everywhere in an ornate litter. She'd hated the way he'd leered down her dress whenever he visited the shop, thrusting his bulk between her and the bookshelves, so she'd have to brush against him as she passed. But she might sigh just a bit for the loss of a customer. There had been few enough of them lately, and that afternoon the spiteful wind—the mistral, it was called—seemed to have blown away every customer from the Vernets' bookshop.

She'd urged Papa to stay upstairs in bed: his weak heart and swampy lungs had been making him cough. And even without any sales or customers, she'd been busy climbing up and down the ladder, rearranging the overcrowded shelves. She'd piled and sorted the books, category by category, onto the spare bed in the kitchen.

It's going to storm outside, she thought. For at dusk she'd lit another candle, and now a sharp wind had blown it out, plunging the shop into darkness.

But it wasn't a storm. It was the tall figure who'd banged open the door and whose broad shoulders obscured the twilit sky behind him.

"Vernet?" he demanded, as she fumbled to relight the candle. His voice was raspy. "I have business with Vernet."

Odd that she hadn't been frightened of him. He'd been dirty and desperate-looking in the flickering candlelight, swathed in a ragged cloak with a greasy bandanna holding an eyepatch in place. His visible eye had glittered feverishly above hollow, unshaven cheeks and haughty cheekbones. But perhaps she'd simply been too pleased to be frightened: as he took off the heavy pack he'd worn under his cloak she could see that it contained books.

New books! Winemakers must feel like this when they taste the first Beaujolais of the season.

And not just any books—by the look of him, he was carrying books smuggled from Switzerland. The French censors had banned just about everything even mildly disrespectful of the status quo, from philosophy to smutty anecdotes of court life at Versailles. Any bookseller who wanted to keep up with the march of ideas had to depend on illegal consignments from foreign publishers.

Too bad Papa wasn't here to smell the new ink, and leather bindings as the books were unpacked.

"But he needs his sleep," she told the smuggler, "and so I'll sign for them, Monsieur."

"And I'm to depend on the accounting and ciphering abilities of a girl." He sneered, and she felt herself gathering up every bit of her five-feet-and-almost-half-an-inch in haughty response.

"You are." She nodded curtly as she drew the curtains and locked the door. Trading in smuggled books was illegal, even if everybody did it. She needed to be careful. If only he weren't so tall, she thought. If only that one visible eye weren't so black and luminous. Was he really sneering, she wondered, or was that a sort of grin?

"And a girl," he added (perhaps it *was* a grin), "with ink-stained fingers."

She didn't know whether to laugh or scowl or blush, as this ragged, half-starved fellow fastidiously wrinkled his nose (not a bad nose, actually) at the lingering stains she'd gathered from writing in the ledger and in her journal. Confused by how to respond, she compromised by shrugging her shoulders.

"Well, Monsieur, of course you know that 'the most compelling of encounters is with a woman's provocative imperfections.' "

He gaped and she wondered what in the world had made her say that. The ornate phrase came from her favorite novel, *A Libertine Education* by a pseudonymous Monsieur X. But this fellow probably couldn't read much beyond the titles on the books in his pack.

She'd always found it rude when people flaunted their reading, and now she'd done it herself. Well, he'd unsettled her by the suddenness of his arrival, the intensity of his presence. The small, cluttered room didn't seem to contain enough oxygen for the two people occupying its space.

She caught her breath.

"Please sit here, Monsieur."

She dragged her father's armchair toward the desk. Perhaps he'd seem less overwhelming if she wasn't peering up at him.

She sat on a stool and cleared a space for the new books, dipping her pen into the inkstand while he reached into the pack to pull out the first volumes. His chair rattled; Papa usually propped up its broken leg with a volume of English plays. But Marie-Laure was too impatient to bother with details.

Briskly, she began checking off the titles he pulled out of the pack, new ones and reorders, with Monsieur X's book among them. She glanced with pleasure at the marbled endpapers of one new edition and had to restrain herself from stroking the heavy cream pages of another. What quick, elegant hands he has, she thought absentmindedly.

But surely there must be more copies of *Anecdotes of Madame du Barry* in his pack.

"Just two copies?" She frowned. "But we wanted six. Word has been spreading, and we've taken four orders for it already."

He shrugged.

"And that's all, Mademoiselle," he announced, leaning back, coughing and stretching and scratching his neck. Marie-Laure thought belatedly of the lice setting up housekeeping in the chair's torn upholstery. And then, as what he had said began to sink in, she forgot about the lice completely.

"That's all? But that can't be all. What about Monsieur Rousseau's *Confessions?*"

Customers had been demanding it for months.

He slouched back into the chair, shrinking down into his cloak, his bony knees in their uncouth trousers poking forward. The toe of his left shoe was held together with a rag.

"Short print run," he muttered. "Sorry."

She didn't believe him. And a sickening certainty rose inside of her, like a bad taste, all the way up from her belly.

"You came here last, of course?" she asked softly.

"Of course not," he snapped. "Different fellow covers the route to Nîmes."

"Don't be stupid," she replied a bit more loudly now, and with exaggerated, condescending patience. "I meant, of course, that you came here to my father's shop after you went to all the other bookshops in Montpellier.

"And I'd wager ten livres," she continued, "that Monsieur Rigaud has gotten everything *he* ordered. And maybe even a little more."

She knew she had him, by the guilty look that crept over his face.

Rigaud. Marie-Laure could hear his suave, insinuating voice. "Take it from me, my boy, Vernet won't care about the Rousseau. He's eccentric, you know, a bit of a specialist." He'd probably slipped him a few extra sous, too.

The smuggler raised himself weakly in the armchair. He winced, and she was glad of it. She hoped she'd made him as guilty and uncomfortable as possible.

"You can always complain," he muttered, "to the directors in Switzerland."

"We will," Marie-Laure said grimly. The *Société Typographique de Neuchâtel* accounted for their shipments of illegal books as meticulously as they did their legal ones.

And that should have been the end of it. She should have signed for the truncated shipment and sent him on his way.

But instead she heard her voice rising.

"We'll complain to them, but right now I'm complaining to *you.*"

Worse and worse. As though his presence somehow shined a bright light on worries and frustrations she usually suppressed.

"Well, you can see, can't you, what any idiot can see? That we're poor, that my father has a weak heart, that we're always in danger of losing customers to that predator Rigaud."

She couldn't seem to stop.

"And that *I* wanted terribly to read the Rousseau and now who knows when I'll be able to."

She looked him full in the face, at least the part that wasn't obscured by the eyepatch and bandanna, and the cloak muffling him up to the jaw. He looked squarely back at her out of his good eye. Well, it was really a series of looks in quick succession—guilty, angry, amused. For a confusing split second he even looked distinctly lustful, before his features let go of something, like a carnival figure removing a gaudy mask to reveal the wan face beneath. She paused, frozen in bewilderment, while his eye rolled back in his head and he collapsed in a dead faint, tipping over the shaky chair and scattering books onto the floor with a crash.

The peas, Marie-Laure!

She blinked. How long had she been lost in her memories?

"You'll need to shell them quickly." Robert, her young colleague in the scullery, tugged at her arm.

Of course. The Duc's family had to eat tonight as well as feast at tomorrow night's banquet. Robert had been turning a row of ducks on a spit in the fireplace.

Once her fingers began popping the peas out of their shells it was easy to return to that winter day in Montpellier.

* * *

Was he dead? she'd wondered. Not that she'd cared a whit for his safety. But the police would be out, investigating the Baron's murder. She shuddered, imagining a police inspector finding a dead smuggler on their floor.

His visible eyelid fluttered: no, not dead, thank heaven. She bent over him. Blood seeped through his filthy cloak, staining her apron. She pulled the cloak away. His trouser leg was soaked. He was bleeding, she thought guiltily, all the time I was shouting at him.

The front door rattled; had she forgotten to lock it? No, it was only Gilles. She listened gratefully to the sound of her brother's key turning in the lock.

Gilles wouldn't finish medical school for another year, but he'd always had a doctor's personality—confident, observant, eager to take command and send everybody scurrying to do his bidding.

"Light the lamp, Marie-Laure, for God's sake." Her bossy brother chased her away from the man's side and took her place. "Are there any clean rags? Water heating on the hearth? Bring your sewing basket. And what's left of the brandy."

The lamplight shined on Gilles's carroty hair and cast deep shadows in the hollows of the smuggler's cheeks. Marie-Laure heard cloth ripping; first the rags and then the bloody trousers. She watched Gilles's clean, economical motions and listened to his running commentary.

"A wound to the thigh, near the artery. I might need a tourniquet." None of the rags were long enough. He glanced about for something to tie around the top of the thigh to stop the bleeding. "Your fichu," he said. The long linen scarf was crossed in front of the low square neckline of Marie-Laure's dress and tied at the back of her waist. She undid it while Gilles continued to poke and prod, mopping up blood as he went.

"Better, better, not so bad as it looked at first," he murmured. "Not the artery anyway, but there is some infection that I'll have to clear out before I sew him up." He took out his small, sharp knife.

"Odd," he said now, almost to himself. "It looks exactly like a dueling wound."

There were really two wounds, he explained. And the more recent one—perhaps from a fall on a rocky path through the forest—had caused the older one to reopen. The older one looked like a dueling wound, though of course it couldn't be. Gilles supposed it was the result of a knife fight somewhere, perhaps a brawl at an inn. But certainly not a duel; only aristocrats made ceremonies out of their brawls.

The peas were cooking beautifully with a bit of bacon on top of the stove, and Marie-Laure was back in front of the tub of greasy dishwater.

There were no more ink stains to worry about anyway; endless hours of dishwashing had taken care of that. Her hands were red and chapped, with burns here and there from the stove and fireplace. She was no more a bookseller now than he was a smuggler.

She supposed she should have recognized right off that he wasn't the sort of person to deliver illegal books. Especially given the evidence of his dueling wound. And the eyepatch.

She'd threaded a large needle with strong thread and handed it to Gilles.

"Now feed him some brandy," he said, "so that you can hold him still while I sew him up."

Gently, he rolled the smuggler from his side to his back. They'd need a good clear space to work in. A pile of books was in the way. Marie-Laure reached across the man's face to push them aside. A button on her sleeve caught in his bandanna, pulling the eyepatch askew.

She flinched, expecting a hollow socket. But he opened his eyes just then, both of them equally beautiful. And for a moment she forgot Gilles's instructions and simply gazed into a pair of fathomless black eyes. Eyes that had locked onto hers for a heart-stopping instant this afternoon in the library.

"Quickly, Marie-Laure." Gilles's voice had been urgent.

"Oh . . . yes." A bit dazed, she took the man's head into her lap.

"Drink, Monsieur," she said, uncorking the brandy and putting the bottle to his lips. "My brother is going to take care of your leg, but it will hurt a little."

He smiled up at her, a magical flash of white teeth and finely curved lips punctuated by ironical little lines at his mouth's edges. The smile was slightly asymmetrical and all the more eloquent for it. *Life is amusing, isn't it, Mademoiselle,* the smile seemed to say, its mocking, crooked gallantry tugging at her heart.

" 'The most compelling of encounters . . .' " he whispered hoarsely, before putting his mouth to the neck of the bottle.

He held tightly to Marie-Laure's hand while he gulped down the brandy. She kept hold of his hand after he passed out, while Gilles cut and sewed, whistling through a broken front tooth and cursing in a comforting monotone. The man's lips quivered; lines appeared and disappeared at the corners of his mouth. But he'd drunk enough brandy to prevent him from regaining consciousness.

"He's got a bump on the head from falling. And he's chilled and damp and has a bit of fever from the infection. But mostly he's suffering from loss of blood and lack of food," Gilles concluded. They were tidying up now, scrubbing up the blood and piling the illegal books behind a false partition in the kitchen wall.

"Odd about the eyepatch," Gilles said. "But he might have had an inflammation that has recently cleared up."

She must have murmured some vague assent.

"And look at this." Gilles opened the man's shirtfront. A small signet ring of silver and onyx hung from his neck on a greasy string.

"Stole it, I suppose, perhaps at the same time he got the leg wound. Took it off some aristocrat, by the look of it. Well, good for him, anyway."

He'd worn the ring this afternoon, on the little finger of the hand that had taken the rattling saucer from her.

"I think he'll sleep through the night. He can't move around easily on that leg, so I don't think we're in any danger from him. I'll stay down here in the shop tonight, though, just to be sure. There are some anatomical drawings I need to look at anyway.

"And calm down." Gilles smiled. "You were a perfect assistant and he'll be fine."

Gilles proposed they move him to the spare bed in the kitchen. But that bed was covered with books, in an intricate order Marie-Laure wouldn't want to reconstruct.

"What about my bed?" she asked.

And when Gilles raised his eyebrows and leered suggestively, she slapped him. "And *I'll* sleep upstairs in *your* bed, idiot."

Marie-Laure's bedchamber was really just an alcove off the kitchen, overlooking the patch of garden behind the house. It smelled of rosemary and lavender; she liked sleeping beneath herbs she'd hung from the ceiling beams to dry. She helped Gilles pull off the man's clothes and clean him up a little before they squeezed him into one of their father's much-mended nightshirts. It was a quick, businesslike operation; Gilles needed her help but he was hardly going to let her linger and gape at the fellow. She hadn't had to gape, though. She'd worked calmly and capably while the lines and shadows, angles and volumes of the sleeping man's body imprinted themselves upon the deepest, most vulnerable spaces at her core.

He'd been painfully thin and covered with scratches. His long muscles were stark and sinewy, too close to the bruised skin but powerful-looking nonetheless. Her inner eye had followed their lineaments, tracing their elegant diagonals from broad shoulder to narrow waist to . . .

She lifted a large, grease-encrusted skillet into the water and scrubbed furiously at it. Bad enough that the dark, heavy sex at his center had troubled the margins of her dreams all these months. She was damned if it would interfere with her waking life.

She hauled simmering water from the fireplace to the basin, poured it in, and plunged her hands into it. Too hot. Too painful. Good.

The water cooled. The memory grew bearable.

* * *

Gilles had gone upstairs to see to Papa, leaving her to fuss with quilts and pillows. She'd stared down at her bed for what seemed like hours, finally turning away to gather up some clothes to wear the next day. She fumbled with the garments stored in the chest, taking forever to choose a dress and even longer to find a blue ribbon for tying back her hair. Finding a pair of stockings that didn't need darning became a major undertaking. Her threadbare stock of aprons and fichus was pathetic, she thought.

But finally she had no choice but to turn—with infinite slowness—and look at him again.

The rising moon cast shifting light upon his hands and cheekbones. She wanted to touch him but she was afraid—afraid to wake him, and afraid of what he'd awakened in her. So she simply studied his face as though a schoolmaster had told her to memorize it. She considered how much she liked an aquiline nose on a man, when it was narrow and delicate, with flaring nostrils. She wondered how she'd missed the vulnerable notch at the center of his upper lip. She examined the slight widow's peak above his high forehead and the tracery of his eyebrows, admiring the graceful arcs dispassionately, as though they were the vaulting of a cathedral.

His black hair fanned out upon her pillow. Well, it would have fanned out, she thought, if it had been clean. It would gleam and catch the light's rainbows like a jet black silk fan, if it were clean and brushed. She imagined washing his hair, drying it gently with a linen towel, brushing it until it crackled with electricity. She'd loop a strand of it around her hand like a skein of black silk embroidery thread.

Her breath caught in her throat as though she'd been jolted by the imagined electricity of his hair. Her gasp became a moan and then a long shudder, leaving her face hot and her thighs weak and trembling. She fled the room, to take care of Gilles and Papa.

The water in the basin was cold and greasy. Time to empty it and start fresh with hot water from the hearth. Time to forget about him and the naive, impressionable girl who'd stood staring at him—was it only a few months ago? Just a night coach's ride from here?

No matter. That girl was no more herself than the heroine of a book she once might have liked to read. In another life. When she'd had books to read. Before he'd blown out the candle and changed everything.

Chapter 2

His valet tossed the tea-stained silk stockings onto the back of a chair, atop this afternoon's coat and breeches. Glancing at their reflection behind him in the mirror, the Viscomte caught sight of his own bemused smile as well.

Well, of course he was smiling—who *wouldn't* smile, he thought, after this afternoon's encounter in the library? Her image glowed in his mind's eye: flushed and tremulous, all freckles and bright hair and round little breasts like quinces.

Astonishing. How in the world had she come to be serving tea in his father's château?

Hardly noticing what he was doing, he stepped into the breeches the kneeling valet held out for him. Obedient and absentminded as only someone who's been bathed and dressed by others all his life can be, he extended his arms, lowered his head for the gauzy linen shirt with intricate tucks at the shoulder.

But now he shook his head. No, not the pink waistcoat with fussy gold embroidery. The dark red velvet was better, a little soberer.

"And just brush my hair straight back into its queue, Baptiste. Don't try to make it curl."

He'd been kept (he loathed the word, but had to admit that it was accurate) for the past several months by a woman who liked to see him dressed like an organ-grinder's monkey. He hadn't had any choice: she'd paid for the clothes; the only garments he'd owned when he'd arrived at her country house had been those bloody smuggler's rags.

On occasion, however, she'd indulged him by costuming him as he preferred, in simpler and darker garments *à la mode Américaine.* Men dressed with refreshing plainness in America—he'd learned there to appreciate a style and set of manners that made few distinctions between statesman and tradesman. Of course, it was one thing to admire, even to affect, a style. He could still revert to type when affronted or threatened: his eyebrows would rise and his lip would curl with the best (well, the worst) of his class. The epitome, he knew, of a spoiled, parasitical, French aristocrat. A veritable Baron Roque.

So he could hardly, he chided himself, afford to feel superior to his benefactor Madame de Rambuteau. She'd played intermediary between him and his family during his sojourn abroad. It had been she who'd written, telling him to come back to France if he wanted to see his father again. Together they'd planned his return in the letters they'd exchanged. He'd found a way to sneak across the border; she'd sent a coach to fetch him in Montpellier.

She'd enjoyed caring for him while his leg healed and his family sorted out his legal status. His bad condition and ragged clothes had excited her, allowing her a safe bit of rebellion against the memory of a stodgy husband. It had been easy for Joseph to regale her with tales of seedy encounters and narrow escapes. She'd kept her looks, too; it had been easy to make love to her.

Not, he supposed, that her looks had really mattered. He'd kissed her dimpled little hands and pretended there were ink stains on the fingers; slid his fingers through her long pale hair and imagined it glowed like copper. And when he'd tongued her breasts he could almost taste freckles sprinkled across them like powdered cinnamon.

Tolerant, worldly, realistic, she must have understood that it wasn't really *she* he'd pleasured so dutifully every night and afternoon. But Madame de Rambuteau was wise; she took what life offered and didn't waste time yearning for the unattainable.

A quaint version of the unattainable, he supposed. A shopgirl, no, not even that anymore—she was only a servant now. *His* servant—well, his family's, anyway. Unattainable only if you followed the idiosyncratic code he'd adopted almost fifteen years ago. The powerful mustn't exploit the powerless. Terrible things might happen otherwise. Terrible things *had* happened once.

But could anything so terrible happen if he touched her glowing cheek or patted her little derrière as she passed?

Yes, damn it. They could happen and probably would.

He wouldn't touch her and that was final.

No matter how difficult it was going to be. Much more difficult than it had been last December.

He'd awakened in a panic just before a wintry dawn with absolutely no idea where he was. *A year of exile and hiding can do that,* he'd thought—a year of sleeping in palaces and hovels, depending on how well his charm and his skill at gaming had served him. He sniffed: rosemary and lavender. And something else, spicy as cinnamon, tart as lemon. A woman. The sheets of her bed smelled like *her.*

Memories flooded back: the endless afternoon, the pain, the dizziness, the growing fear that he'd never get back to the inn where he was supposed to wait for Madame de Rambuteau's coach. Someone had jostled him in the street—someone in a furious hurry had knocked against him yesterday and from then on his leg had hurt like the devil.

What awful work to be a book porter, he thought; if he ever had to sneak over the border again, he'd certainly find another way. Smuggling was hard and dangerous, even if a month ago it seemed like an opportunity to bring worthy and interesting literature into France.

Trudging over rocky paths and hiding from border guards had been grim rather than romantic. The fall he'd taken had almost finished him off. But worst of all was facing all those difficult, demanding booksellers yesterday—what had that pushy fellow's name been? Ah yes, Rigaud, Rigaud who'd wheedled the last copies of Rousseau's *Confessions* out of him when he'd been too weak and dizzy to care.

Still, he'd made it back into France, all in one piece and without his creditors or other enemies knowing. With any luck his family would pay off his creditors and placate any enraged husbands who might still demand satisfaction.

He leaned back on the lumpy pillows, breathing rosemary and lavender, lemon and cinnamon as he contemplated the last and most difficult bookseller, the girl whose bed smelled so sweet and spicy. His mouth twisted into a lopsided grin as he remembered how furious she'd been to discover that he'd shorted her father's order. She clearly wasn't just a shopkeeper, though she'd impressed and rather annoyed him with her competence. She was a *reader:* she'd even quoted a passage from Monsieur X's memoir. And had he imagined it, or had her ink-stained fingers lingered for an extra moment over the pages of that particular book?

Ridiculous to have been so enchanted by those fingers, he thought. But not so ridiculous to have been stirred by eyes like turbulent Paris skies. And by a wide, determined mouth that was clearly capable of passion.

And then—ah yes—the freckles. Bronze and copper as tiny autumn leaves, they scattered themselves across her glowing cheeks, drifting down her neck and chest like faint clues on a treasure map and disappearing tauntingly into the snowy linen tied across her breasts. When she'd untied the fichu it had been worth all the pain, all the terror of being weak and wounded. If only he'd been a little more clearheaded. If only he could remember whether there were three or four of those freckles on the breast that had been so close to his face when she'd leaned over him and knocked away his silly eyepatch.

"She's engaged," the little bulldog of a brother had announced when he brought him a bowl of bread and coffee in bed.

"Well, all but engaged, to someone who understands, as we all do, that her head is altogether too full of books and stories, and that she needs looking after.

"It's a good deal for everybody. She'll get to stay in the book trade. She'll be an asset to Rigaud—I suppose you met him yesterday?"

The Viscomte must have betrayed some consternation, for the fellow had laughed merrily.

"No, of course she's not engaged to old Rigaud—what could you be thinking, old fellow? Her sweetheart is Rigaud's nephew; my dear friend Augustin has been crazy about her since we were kids. He and Marie-Laure will run Rigaud's shop when Augustin's uncle gets too old. It's a profitable business, unlike this one."

A good deal. A profitable business.

And was she also crazy about the nephew?

"And if you so much as touch her, my friend," the brother had added, "I'll tear your leg back open."

He hadn't touched her. Well, if you didn't count lying in her lap and squeezing her hand as touching her. He hadn't touched her as he'd wanted to, in any case.

And—half a year later—it seemed that she hadn't married the nephew.

He'd liked Gilles, who chatted amiably and volubly now that he'd made it clear—man-to-man, so to speak—that Marie-Laure was off limits. He'd been amused by the fellow's directness and impressed by his devotion to his family, his sweetheart Sylvie, his friend Augustin. And his work.

"Best work in the world. I've always wanted to be a physician. I hung around the university's medical school when I was a kid and did errands, just for the chance to learn bits and pieces here and there. Lucky for me that my father—the best father in the world—figured out a clever way to pay the school fees."

Work you love and the best father in the world. And that sister as well. Lucky for you indeed, Gilles Vernet.

He couldn't help but feel bitter and jealous after Gilles had clomped off to school. Though you wouldn't think that Joseph Dupin, Viscomte d'Auvers-Raimond, would have reason to be jealous of a shabby, carrot-haired student.

They were a family of nobodies, he told himself: middling people of no consequence, history, or property. Banal, petty tradespeople with not a hint of wit or style: they were, quite simply, not his equals.

And she was the worst of them. Just look at the silly crayon portrait of her hanging by the side of the bed, he thought. The artist couldn't have been without talent, for he'd gotten the eyes right: that wonderful, changeable blue-gray wouldn't have been easy to capture. But why had he given her that rosebud of a mouth? And—how dare he not show the freckles? Perhaps the portrait had been conceived to please young Augustin Rigaud, a man for whom the Viscomte felt an unreasoning and absolute dislike.

"Monsieur Joseph, they tell me that supper will be late. An hour at least."

"That's all right, Baptiste, I'm not hungry. Why don't you go ask the other servants about a girl called Marie-Laure? Marie-Laure Vernet. Or perhaps Marianne." His sister-in-law liked to address her servants by names of her own choosing.

"Find out when she was hired and where she works. And if she's managed to hide herself from my father."

Hideous to contemplate his father pawing at her. But how *had* she kept herself safe from that lecherous old goat? If she had.

"And don't forget the rosemary and lavender for my room." Since last winter he hadn't slept a night without the two herbs perfuming the air.

Chapter 3

Supper's lateness wasn't merely due to the preparations for tomorrow's banquet. There'd also been an argument between the chef, Monsieur Colet, and the wife of the Duc's older son—Madame la Comtesse Amélie, better known to her servants as the Gorgon.

Marie-Laure had found the proceedings vastly entertaining. As usual, Monsieur Colet's kitchen had produced a masterwork of a meal, from the hors d'oeuvres and foie gras to the ducks and glazed shell of beef. But for dessert the Gorgon had insisted on a towering confection of spun sugar, though the day's weather was far too humid for the spinning of sugar. Monsieur Colet had shouted and sputtered at his employer as only a master chef—one who was entirely indispensable—could do.

He'd been even more voluble after the Comtesse had stalked away in defeat. He'd paced and declaimed, waving his arms and thundering about idiot bosses who knew less than drooling infants about running a kitchen and hadn't the savoir faire to appreciate his strawberry tart properly anyway. It wasn't until Nicolas opened a very old and dusty bottle of the Duc's Chateauneuf-du-Pape that the chef ceased his tirade and waved his minions back to work.

And so supper had finally been served, both upstairs in the dining salon and downstairs in the dessert kitchen, a dry, sweet-smelling room where baking supplies were stored and the servants took their meals. Marie-Laure squeezed onto the edge of a bench at the long table and picked at the food on her plate, glad at least to stop working for a while. And to have a moment—while the argument between Monsieur Colet and the Gorgon was recounted with great hilarity—to remember more about her first meeting with the Viscomte.

The next morning had started out pleasantly enough. She heard conversation downstairs; the tone was companionable, though she couldn't make out the words. He must be feeling better.

Papa was better too: sitting up in bed, eyes bright behind octagonal Franklin-style spectacles, engrossed in a pamphlet about the Americans' victory (with French help, of course) over the English General Cornwallis.

"You must check on the smuggler," he told her. "Poor fellow, doing his part to bring brave and original thought to France."

She nodded abstractedly as she straightened his bedclothes and opened the window to let in some air. Reluctant to face the man who'd caused her to . . . well, to feel *that* way last night, she looked around for ways to make Papa more comfortable.

But nothing presented itself and Papa needed his coffee. She couldn't hide up here all morning. And anyway, she told herself on the stairs, doubtless he'd seem quite ordinary this morning; last night's emotions had probably only been a trick of the light, a mood shift brought on by the mistral. Peasants, after all, believed that a strong mistral could drive you mad.

He was lying on his side. At first she'd thought he was asleep, but as she came a bit closer she could see that he was staring fixedly at the crayon drawing that hung next to her bed.

"Monsieur?"

"He left off the freckles," was the odd, abstracted reply. "He got the eyes right. But the mouth is completely wrong. What could you have been thinking?"

For a moment, she wondered if he were delirious. And then she began to laugh.

"But it's not a picture of me, Monsieur. It's my mother when she was my age. It's . . . well, it's not me at all."

Looking up from the portrait, he laughed too.

"No," he agreed, "it's not you at all." His voice was still hoarse but not as raspy as it had been yesterday.

"She was pretty, wasn't she?" Marie-Laure asked. "She died when I was twelve."

He nodded, his expression sympathetic, respectful. Such a mercurial face, Marie-Laure thought. More human, more playful than the fiercely sculpted visage she'd contemplated while he'd slept. This morning he seemed quite friendly. And almost boyish: she judged that he was in his late twenties—perhaps five years older than Gilles or Augustin, but less serious-looking, less settled, as though he'd never quite found his place in the world. She cut him another slice of bread, and some cheese as well. He wasn't as formidable as she'd feared; he was simply hungry.

She brought Papa his breakfast upstairs, and then came back down to eat, while she and the smuggler talked.

Well, mostly she talked. About everything and nothing. About Papa's passion for America, Gilles's vocation for medicine. About how Papa had taught her and Gilles to speak English after Mamma's death: he'd thought they could bear their grief better in the beginner's phrases of an unfamiliar language, and he'd been right. She was fortunate now, she told him, to be able to read the novels of Richardson, the plays of Shakespeare, and the humorous essays of Ambassador Franklin in their original tongue. And particularly fortunate to spend her days surrounded by the books she loved so well.

Of course, she added quickly, she was also lucky to have Gilles and Papa. But sometimes—she'd hesitated a bit here—it was difficult to explain, but sometimes she wished she could be somewhere, anywhere but within the walls of the city where she'd been born. Sometimes she dreamed of Paris or Peru, Persia or Philadelphia, someplace new and different, where she could find whatever it was that was missing from her life.

She paused, abashed by her volubility. She hadn't meant to rattle on like that; no one could really be interested in her petty confidences. But his steady black gaze had seemed to encourage her. If he'd found her tedious he'd certainly hidden it well.

She corrected herself: eyes couldn't really be black; his eyes must really be a very dark brown. But she felt blackness when she looked into them; she felt something undefined, restless, unfinished. A hunger, as though he could swallow her words and thoughts whole.

He bit his lip as he propped himself higher against the pillows; it must hurt him to move his leg, she thought, disconcerted by the sudden thrill of sympathy she felt.

What she'd experienced last night hadn't been a trick of the light.

She looked away from his face and then quickly looked back: better to stare at his face than his shoulders straining at Papa's old nightshirt or his hands grasping her quilt. Especially when all he'd noticed about her were her least favorite features, her freckles and less-than-refined mouth. Oh, and her ink-stained fingers. Charming.

"You're indeed fortunate in your family," he said. "Your brother's very fond of you. He warned me that if I touched you, he'd rip my leg back open."

But you have touched me, she thought. *You lay in my lap and squeezed my hand. Of course you don't remember any of that.*

But Gilles had remembered. Damn him and his protectiveness anyway.

"My brother takes his responsibilities very seriously," she replied.

"But did he also tell you how he happens to have a broken front tooth?" She raised her arm and made a fist, showing that she knew how to put her shoulder behind a blow. Gilles had taught her to fight like a boy and she'd been better at it than he'd expected.

The man laughed.

"No," he said. "He didn't tell me that. He told me that you read too much, that your head was crammed with books and stories, and that you needed looking after.

"And he also said that you were as good as engaged to his best friend."

Marie-Laure blushed. She made a noncommittal gesture, sort of a nod but a little like a shrug as well. One didn't have to explain *everything.*

The silence between them grew awkward.

"That book," he asked now, nodding at Monsieur X's memoirs on the little table next to the bed. "I've delivered quite a few copies to booksellers. Is it interesting?"

She nodded eagerly, glad to talk about anything besides being as good as engaged.

"Oh yes," she said, "you should try it sometime. Well, that is, if you, uh, enjoy reading."

He did a clever imitation of her nod and shrug combination.

"What's it about?" he asked.

"It's a satire," she replied, "on the aristocracy, and on the corruption of life at court." The author had charmed her by his readiness to laugh at himself. He'd also—though she didn't usually dwell on it—excited her by the sly sophistication with which he recounted his amours.

"What happens in it? What's its . . ." He searched for the proper word. "What's its plot?"

"Ah, well," Marie-Laure began, "let's see . . . there's a young military officer, an aristocrat but a poor one, posted at Versailles. And he's immediately taken up by a very elegant lady."

"And then?"

Belatedly, she realized that the opening episode was one of the raciest in the book. "The lady was the mistress of the Baron Roque, the gentleman who was murdered yesterday, you know," she said.

He shrugged. "Yes, but what *happens?*" His dark eyes were mischievous, daring her to continue.

"Well, the Baron would receive his mistress in a bedchamber the size of a ballroom. So there would be room for a small orchestra, off on one side, playing sweet airs while the mistress entertained the Baron in bed.

"What's usually done, according to Monsieur X, is to hire blind musicians. But the Baron was different. His musicians saw everything, having been sworn to secrecy and also knowing that during the Baron's travels he'd had his bodyguard educated in the cutting off of hands.

"And when the mistress began secretly to visit Monsieur X in his much smaller apartments, well, she'd become used to music, you see, and so she'd often break out in song, when . . . aroused."

She felt her cheeks grow hot under his keen gaze.

"But I wouldn't want to spoil the story for you, Monsieur," she said quickly. "So you must read it yourself, to find out what happens next." And too bad, she thought, if that embarrassed *him.*

He didn't look the least bit embarrassed. He nodded and settled back against the pillows.

It seemed that it was up to her to pick up the thread of the conversation.

"He wounded the Baron in a duel," she told him, "later in the book. It's rumored that this actually happened, along with many other duels and skirmishes—even a brief imprisonment. It's said that the author insulted so many people that he was forced to flee abroad." Well, it didn't embarrass her to say this, anyway.

"Monsieur X gets away with a lot," he said.

"Yes and no," she answered. "His love affairs always end with what he calls a slightly metallic taste, when the artificiality of the liaison overwhelms the pleasures. He says it's the way of the world. His book is a chronicle of love's impossibility."

She stopped to take a breath.

"Well," he said, "if I were to look at a book I might try that one. You have a talent for summing up a man's beliefs in a very few words, Mademoiselle."

She wasn't sure if that was a compliment.

"Do you agree with the author's conclusion?"

And she certainly hadn't expected to be asked for her opinion.

But since he *had* asked . . .

"No," she said, "I don't. Of course I'm no authority, especially compared to Monsieur X. But no, Monsieur, I don't believe that passion is based upon artifice, or that real sympathy or constancy is impossible between lovers."

He was nodding slowly, smiling his devastating crooked smile; she guessed that he approved of her sentimentality, her optimism.

She cleared her throat.

"And furthermore, I don't think that Monsieur X really believes it either."

His eyes froze, his smile turned angry.

"I should think that if an author says he believes something, a reader ought to accept him at his word."

Marie-Laure frowned. These were difficult ideas to explain.

"I think," she said slowly, "that an author sometimes leaves out bits and pieces—things that were too difficult or painful to think through all the way. And somehow, with Monsieur X, I think there's another story there, one that happened perhaps before the book began."

"So," he said sharply, "you're telling me that when you read a book you read what the author *didn't* write, as well as what he *did.*"

Put that way she had to admit that it sounded far-fetched.

"Well, it was just a thought."

"Not much of one." His voice was frigid and his eyes glittered like black ice. How in the world, she wondered, had she come to be discussing the art of letters with this fellow? And what gave him the right to criticize her so high-handedly?

"Your brother is right," he added. "You do read too much for your own good. But at least you should stick to what's on the page."

Absurdly, she felt as though she were being dismissed from her own bedroom.

"Perhaps I'm tiring you, Monsieur." She stood up with as much dignity as she could muster. She wore an old pair of Gilles's breeches under her dress, for climbing the bookstore ladder, and she smoothed her skirt clumsily down over them. "Well, I must be getting to work and so I'll leave you now. And—there's no rush of course—but please do remember to sign this receipt for the books."

What had all *that* been about? She'd liked him so much before the conversation had taken that turn. Still, there *was* work to be done. Disciplining herself to maintain an unhurried pace, she quit the room. The shop's doorbell was ringing. It was time to open up for business. And that had been the last she'd seen of him until this afternoon in the library.

Chapter 4

Baptiste returned to the Viscomte's chamber just before it was time to go down to supper.

"She arrived last May, Monsieur Joseph. Works in the scullery. Recommended by a woman in Montpellier—her brother's sweetheart's mother is Nicolas's cousin."

Joseph shrugged, a bit befuddled. But after all, he thought, why *shouldn't* common people take their family connections as seriously as aristocrats did?

"In May, Baptiste?"

"*Oui*, Monsieur, just two months ago, while we were at Madame de Rambuteau's, and you were making . . . your recovery. Martin, in the stables, fetched her off the night coach. Said he'd felt sorry for her, she'd looked so thin and pale and tired. Of course everybody looks awful after that journey, but Martin says she was sick before she came here. Typhus. His sweetheart, Louise, shares Marie-Laure's bed, you see."

"You spoke to Louise?"

"She's away, Monsieur, at her mother's funeral. It's she who usually serves tea in the library. She's got a bit of a harelip, you know, so the Duc's not interested in her. Sometimes it's Bertrande who serves the tea—well, *she's* fifty if she's a day. But Bertrande has a sprained wrist, due to an unfortunate argument she and Nicolas . . ."

"Yes, I see, Baptiste."

Typhus, mon Dieu. *And then she came here. Pale and tired-looking enough to be hired despite the chateau's rule, but growing prettier and healthier every day, until . . .*

His father hadn't seemed to notice her this afternoon. But Joseph suspected that his father was capable of more coherence—and more guile, too—than people generally thought. I get that from him, he thought, that flair for playacting. For certainly no one in the library could have suspected that *I'd* ever seen her before.

He was sure of his performance. He'd been calm, amused, distant—even while his heart had swooped in his breast like a hawk ranging the thin mountain air.

He'd turned from the bookshelves and there she'd been, cup and saucer in hand. The girl who'd held him in her lap, who'd sat at his bedside and confided her impatience with a circumscribed provincial life. The girl who'd thought she understood Monsieur X—and who'd struggled so charmingly to tell Monsieur X's lewd story.

The heroine of the new story he'd been scribbling; the object of several months of tumescent fantasies.

Oh, and the girl I rather insulted as well. Don't forget that part, Joseph. He'd been nasty and patronizing, simply because she'd read Monsieur X's book a bit too perceptively for his comfort. Of course, he'd intended to beg her pardon before he'd left. But Baptiste—who'd been searching the streets for him—had arrived with Madame de Rambuteau's coach while Marie-Laure had been out at the market.

Perhaps, he'd thought then, it had been just as well. For his response to her had been so strong (how touching she'd looked when she'd stalked out of the room, head high, back straight and proud) that he might well have given in to temptation and risked a broken tooth of his own.

But to find her here this afternoon! At first he hadn't been able to believe it. He'd needed to look into her eyes. No wonder she'd almost dropped the cup and saucer—the gaze he'd directed at her had been the most charged he could muster. Of course, once he'd ascertained her identity, he'd been obliged to feign disinterest.

But then, what could he have done? Ravish her in full sight of his family? Or—far more inappropriate—shake her hand and ask after her father's health?

One could hardly breach the rules of conduct between master and servant, noble and commoner, all based, he thought, upon some noodleheaded assumption of aristocratic superiority. You're bathed and dressed, fed, flattered and—if you like—serviced by your inferiors.

The thought made him dizzy: part of his brain swooning with images of intimate conversation with her; the other part wanting only to drag her into a dark hallway, raise her skirts, and get it over with quickly. Take what he wanted and move on; liberate himself from his complicated feelings for her. Assert his right to her as some of the worst of his peers might have done—the vile old Baron Roque, for example.

"Time for supper, Monsieur Joseph."

"Thank you, Baptiste."

"I know how to get to her room, by the way, Monsieur Joseph. She'll be the only one sleeping there tonight, with Louise away."

"You know I don't take advantage of servants, Baptiste." *Hypocrite, you've thought of little else for an hour.*

"No, Monsieur Joseph."

"Well, not for a very long time anyway."

"That's true, Monsieur Joseph."

His eyes strayed to the notebooks spread out on his desk. Boyish yearnings and libertine cynicism cobbled together with a bit of wit and a lot of salacious detail. Rather a pathetic little body of work, really. And the story he'd been writing these past months, about the sultan and the gray-eyed harem girl—embarrassing stuff, especially under the current circumstances.

"But . . . Monsieur Joseph?"

"What *is* it, Baptiste?"

"Well, when I was sniffing around for information down there, I kept bumping into your father's valet Jacques. And Jacques was asking a lot of the same questions I was. Especially about where she sleeps."

If it had been any other girl, he might have been amused. The rule about keeping pretty servants away was his sister-in-law's invention, a straitlaced and rather spiteful way of imposing authority over an anarchic household. *Let the old man do as he wants,* he might have thought. *Let him live as he always had—selfishly, reprehensibly—in the little time left to him.*

If it had been any girl but this one.

He hadn't a clue what to do. But he knew he was going to do something.

"Suppertime, Monsieur Joseph."

He supposed the food was quite good. His parents had always set an excellent table, even as his father's debts eroded the family fortune, weeds choked the château's moat, and the mistral blew shards of slate off the roof and stone from the battlements. He sipped his soup, a chilled sherried consommé with morels. He was too agitated to taste it, but he suspected that it was splendid. All the food was probably splendid now that his sister-in-law was in charge of things. She'd brought an immense dowry with her, along with an ironclad determination to restore the family to its former glory. There were plasterers and carpenters everywhere, busily transforming the rough-hewn thirteenth century château to a mini-Versailles.

An easier job, Joseph thought, than making an elegant gentleman out of Hubert. His brother—six years older and a head shorter—had never been much for social graces, or even simple table manners. Joseph watched a tall, muscular footman refill his plump brother's wineglass and then his soup bowl. Hubert proceeded to slurp one and slop the other; his lace cuffs would be a multicolored marvel by the time the meal was done.

"And do tell me all the news of Madame de Rambuteau." Amélie leaned solicitously toward him, the better to hear what he might say, and to give him a closer look at a not-unreasonable bosom. She had sharp greenish eyes and pointed features, excellent height and carriage, and no family to speak of. Her father's title had been all too recently purchased, with an obscene fortune bled from sugar plantations in Haiti. His sister-in-law was rather a joke with the family's oldest intimates—Madame de Rambuteau had entertained him more than once with her devastating parody of the lady's arriviste affectations. "Ah, well," his mother had sighed this morning in the coach, "she was the best we could find for Hubert."

He hoped that Hubert was less inept in bed than he was at table. But he doubted it: his own particular theory was that while a hearty and gourmandizing eater was a good lover, a helpless glutton was not. All of which made him more sympathetic than he might otherwise be toward the Comtesse Amélie, this high-strung, energetic woman whom the marriage market had placed in such an awkward position. If only she wouldn't take out the frustrations of her situation on her servants. He'd seen the way she'd glared at Marie-Laure this afternoon, and heard the cold, threatening tone in which she'd ordered "Marianne" to serve the family their tea.

She was still waiting for an answer from him, bosom still thrust under his nose.

"Madame de Rambuteau is gracious as ever," he told her. "She spoke often of you, too, and the pleasure she takes in your company."

She returned a gratified (if somewhat surprised) nod. "She must have been sorry to have to let you go."

He smiled. "Actually, Madame, my departure was most felicitously timed. Well, perhaps just a *trifle* belated . . ." He turned toward Hubert, hoping to slip in a barbed reference to all the anxious months spent waiting to hear that it was safe for him to venture outside of Madame de Rambuteau's protection. But Hubert had sunk blissfully into an enormous wedge of beef and seemed quite oblivious to the conversation.

Joseph caught the misdirected anecdote in midair and gracefully tossed it to the table at large. "Because toward the end of my stay she conceived an intense desire to learn to play the clavichord, having been quite profoundly moved by the work of a young virtuoso who'd performed for us one evening. In fact, she'd been so enamored of the gentleman's, ah, fingering, that, quite unbeknownst to me, she'd entered into a passionate correspondence with him, and had finally convinced him to stay a few months with her, for an extended course of instruction."

It was true. Madame de Rambuteau liked variety. She would have tossed him out in a few weeks even if he'd had nowhere to go. Well, at least it made a story you could dine out on. A pity, he supposed, that he thought of eating with his family as "dining out."

The anecdote was a success, anyway. His father rewarded him with a high-pitched giggle, and even his pious, overbred mother allowed herself a bit of a guilty smile. As for his sister-in-law, she was virtually transported by his performance, laughing heartily enough to set her bosom heaving and—was it possible?—thrusting it even farther forward.

"It will be delightful to share your wit and spirit with my guests tomorrow evening. And so we must all get plenty of rest tonight, to be *fresh* for the festivities. . . ."

He nodded absently. *What was his father planning tonight, and how could he be stopped?*

But she hadn't finished with what she was saying.

"And so *I*, at any rate, will be abed *quite* early, all safely tucked away between sheets perfumed with heliotrope. And I *know* my dear husband will be getting a much-needed rest as well."

Her instructions couldn't have been clearer if she'd posted them on a cathedral door. *Not tonight, Hubert. Tonight I'm hoping for a visit from somebody with a little wit and spirit.* Poor woman, she seemed to think this was how such things were done.

He might have blushed for her if he were given to blushing. His mother had rolled her eyes to heaven, and his father—impossible to tell what he was thinking, but his small blue eyes shone with keen malice. Hubert shrugged. Even the footman—rather a good-looking fellow, Joseph thought, and oddly familiar, as though he'd once seen him in a dream—seemed a trifle mortified.

He supposed it was up to him to put an end to this. Feigning an ostentatious yawn behind a fluttering hand, he murmured, "I fear this morning's coach ride was too much for me, Madame. A long sleep sounds exactly like the prescription I need. You're a wise physician."

She bowed her head, her smile threatening at any moment to

become a nasty scowl. Baptiste had told him that her servants called her the Gorgon.

The silence at the table continued halfway through the strawberry tart, which was good enough, in any case, to claim everyone's attention.

And then there was a crash.

A much louder crash than the one he'd averted this afternoon in the library, it seemed to carry with it a sense of inevitability, as though everybody had been waiting since then for *some* crash to happen. It sounded quite beautiful really, as expensive lead crystal does when it shatters. The Duc had chosen to drop an enormous faceted decanter full of old brandy. It wasn't a decanter Joseph recognized—Amélie must have brought it with her.

Bravo, Monsieur, got her *there,* Joseph thought. But he'd savor the moment—and the look on her face—later, at his leisure. Now it was time to act.

For the Duc's move, planned to get him away from the table early, had been slightly miscalculated. He'd dropped the decanter a bit closer to his leg than he'd intended, and Joseph could see that a few shards of glass had penetrated his calf, drawing a little blood through the stocking.

"Monsieur!" He jumped to his feet. "Monsieur, you're hurt!"

The old man threw him a furious look. "Not a bit of it," he snarled. "I'm fine. Just need to wash off this brandy I've spilled on myself. If you all will excuse me."

Joseph was at his side, pulling out the glass, perhaps a little more roughly than was quite necessary. "Can you walk, Monsieur? Or should I carry you? That's right, lean on me, good, good, we'll get you to your room, perhaps call the doctor . . ."

What was the handsome footman's name? Ah yes, Arsène. "Arsène, can you help me get the Duc to his room? Thank you, thank you. . . ."

The anxiety in his voice sounded convincing even to himself. Well, this gambit had better work.

"I'm perfectly *fine,* Joseph," the old man sputtered.

"Of *course* you are, Monsieur, and very brave as well." He and

Arsène strong-armed the struggling, protesting Duc from the room and up the corridor to his bedchamber, where Jacques was just laying out a handsome dressing gown. *Vain old coot; it was what he'd planned to wear when he made his visit to Marie-Laure.*

"A bit of a mishap, Jacques. A bit of a different evening than perhaps he'd planned. He needs to be put to bed, after you give him a good long bath and soak that leg.

"And you will stay with them, Arsène, that's a good fellow, in case he needs any help? While I, um, while I, go, uh . . ."

Arsène was looking at him strangely. Well, he supposed his act was wearing a bit thin. His powers of invention certainly were. And as he couldn't think of anything else to say, he simply quit the room without finishing the sentence. Where the devil was Baptiste?

Luckily, he was in Joseph's own room, seeing to his linen.

Joseph tossed off his coat. August was so unbearably hot in Provence. And he didn't have much time before his father got back on his feet. But at least he knew what he was going to do—in its general outlines, anyway, if not in every particular. He grinned.

"Quick, Baptiste. Take me to where she sleeps. And not a word out of you."

Chapter 5

It was as hot and airless in her little garret bedchamber as it had been in the kitchen. *Go to bed,* Marie-Laure told herself, *go to bed and get some sleep.* At least she'd have the mattress to herself tonight, and for once she'd be free of Louise's snoring.

But instead she paced the tiny room as though pursued by fleeting images and fragments of memory. She needed only to blink to set his image shimmering at the margin of her vision. In some ways he'd changed enormously since Montpellier: the legs that had flopped around in ragged trousers were graceful and well turned in fine faille breeches; the lanky frame that had slumped in Papa's armchair stood poised and balanced, legs angled in a dancer's perfect fourth position.

And yet in the essential, infinitesimal particulars—a torque of muscle at the small of the back, a whimsical tilt of the head, a few loose strands of silky black hair escaping from the velvet ribbon at his nape—in every way that mattered, he hadn't changed at all.

Why had he undertaken to act the role of a smuggler? Had it been a sort of holiday from the poise that an aristocrat puts on along with garments of velvet and lace?

She could only suppose he'd done it for the adventure. Yes, she decided, he'd smuggled the books across the border as a reckless, dangerous diversion. And—she set her mouth in a hard line—she probably hadn't been the only woman to help him.

She thought of the banquet she and her colleagues in the kitchen had been preparing. All the noble families of the region would be here tomorrow, bringing daughters decked out in pearls and plumes, towering hairdos and skirts so wide they'd have to skitter sideways through the doors like crabs. She hoped he'd choose one quickly and take her far away.

Of course, last December she'd merely shrugged when she'd come back from the market and found him gone, leaving only a receipt initialed with an *X*.

Good-bye and good riddance, she'd told herself. He was nothing but a drain on her emotions, a useless distraction from her perfectly acceptable life.

Which continued, busy and bookish, innocent and safe. The holidays came and went; when Augustin kissed her under the mistletoe at the Rigauds' extravagant New Year's fete, she flashed a sidelong look at his dreadful cousin—the one who'd been flirting with him all evening—and smiled modestly.

Papa ceased his coughing, though Gilles had given her a sober assessment of his condition. But he seemed well enough; she enjoyed their days together as winter became spring.

The *Société Typographique de Neuchâtel* sent replacement copies of the short-shipped books, with their apologies. The squint-eyed, bandy-legged porter who brought them had been most polite and respectful.

She even caught up on the sewing she hated; it was something to do with her hands when Augustin came to call in the evenings. She smiled at him over the sheets and towels she hemmed and embroidered—for the future.

And then Papa died and she became ill. And suddenly she had no future.

In the end, it hadn't been her father's weak heart that killed him. It was typhus, doubtless contracted at a ratty inn during the spring book fair in Lyon. She and Gilles nursed him for two weeks, bathing him with alcohol, feeding him broths when he could take them, trying not to squabble with each other. Papa rarely was conscious, though she once heard him muttering a few cryptic phrases to Gilles: "Rigaud" and "taken care of" were all she could make out.

Her own illness waited politely until after the funeral. She collapsed and lost consciousness, awakening drenched and exhausted a week later to see a pale, relieved Gilles at her side. She'd passed the crisis, he told her in a shaky voice.

Only to encounter the real crisis.

For when Augustin came to her bedside and at long last proposed a formal engagement, she didn't murmur the expected "yes" but stammered a tearful "no."

She was as surprised as everyone else. What more could she possibly want, Gilles and the Rigauds demanded. But what she wanted—*who* she wanted—was too preposterous to be admitted, even to herself. So she simply wept and shook her head, looking dimwitted and disagreeable, until they explained her financial situation to her and left her to contemplate it.

The house and books were mortgaged to Rigaud. It had been foolish of her, she thought, not to realize where Gilles's school fees had come from. Gilles owned the furniture, such as it was; the sale of it would support him through his last year of medical training. But except for sentimental knickknacks (she'd insisted on keeping Papa's spectacles as a remembrance), Papa had left nothing to Marie-Laure. Well, there was nothing to leave; there hadn't had to be. The Rigauds had wanted her even without a dowry, Augustin because he loved her and Monsieur Rigaud because she'd be an asset to his business.

You could say that Papa had mortgaged his daughter to pay for his son's education. But that would have been putting too calculating a face on it. Papa had thought she'd be happy with Augustin and the paradise of books he'd someday inherit. Marie-Laure knew he'd intended the best.

Whatever face you wanted to put on it, though, the fact was that she was destitute. She'd have to live with Gilles after he set up a practice and married Sylvie next year. But in the meantime?

The job in the scullery was the best solution, even if it proved how far she'd come down in the world. Still, she thought, at least she'd gotten to see something of the world outside the city walls of Montpellier.

Of course she missed her family. Gilles's regular letters weren't very satisfying; he'd never grasped that writing might be more than a vehicle for the communication of facts.

But what she missed even more was life among the crowded bookshelves. She ached for intellectual stimulation, and for something else as well: like all true booksellers, she felt herself incomplete outside of a community of book lovers. Tedious day-to-day work is a small price to pay for the joy of matching a book with its ideal reader; slender profits don't matter when readers hurry back to tell you how much they loved your recommendations. Marie-Laure's customers had relied upon her, rewarding her with their confidences, their respect and trust.

A servant, on the other hand—well, she'd known that a servant wouldn't command anyone's respect. But it had still been a harsh thing to experience, immediately upon her arrival at the château.

Exhausted by her journey, she'd been handed over to the Gorgon's poking and prodding, her furious scowls and angry mutterings that "Marianne" was prettier than Madame Bellocq had let on in her letter of recommendation. Marie-Laure had almost been fired on the spot for daring to correct the lady about her name.

What had saved her—though she hadn't know it then—was the tantrum Monsieur Colet had thrown the day before, threatening to quit if he didn't get more help. So Madame Amélie had to satisfy herself by slapping "Marianne" several times with a folded fan and commanding her to stay downstairs in the kitchen.

Luckily, she liked the kitchen. And she liked the other servants, too—except for one crude fellow whose advances she'd had to fight off her first week. She'd managed quite well, though, first using her fist and then—for Gilles had also taught her some dirtier techniques—her knee, which had left him howling in the corner of the storeroom.

The rest of the household staff had treated her with a certain degree of formality. At first she thought it was due to her success in the storeroom, but little by little she realized she'd always be an outsider here. For everyone else had grown up in tiny Provençal mountain villages, sharing superstitions and secrets forged by isolation and blood feud.

Wisely, Marie-Laure didn't pry. Respectful of the sudden silences that sometimes greeted her entrance into a room, she was awarded a grudging approval in return. She was different, people decided, but not a bad kind of different; one or two of them even approached her and shyly asked her to teach them to read. What mattered was that she could be trusted in the unceasing silent war between servants and masters. The welts she'd received from the Gorgon's fan sealed her acceptance into the world downstairs.

What she liked best about this downstairs world was its undisputed ruler, Monsieur Colet. Marie-Laure had always enjoyed cooking. After Mamma's death she'd almost memorized her copy of *The Modern Kitchen;* she'd been comforted to see it here, on Mr. Colet's shelf. And when the chef caught her looking at it one morning before work, instead of punishing her he quizzed her on it, nodding approvingly as she recounted its sound principles.

A generous teacher, he encouraged her to learn all she could from his example. He'd even suggested that she become a cook herself rather than live with Gilles and Sylvie. A paid servant, he'd told her, was always better off than an unpaid one, which was what a spinster sister would be, even with the best of brothers.

Marie-Laure was still pondering his advice, as well as some tentative, secret plans of her own devising. For if she could earn an independent living here in the middle of nowhere, why couldn't she also do so in a city—one with theaters, cafés, and bookshops? A cook, even for a bourgeois family, could make a decent living. And maybe, if she were a good enough manager, and if she sacrificed and saved her money wisely . . . maybe she wouldn't have to be a cook forever.

And so, she concluded, things really hadn't turned out so badly. The smuggler-Viscomte hadn't really cheated her; it was time she stopped blaming him for unwittingly teaching her what physical arousal was all about. Grimy, exhausting, and déclassé as her life now was, she was lucky to have escaped a passionless marriage.

Perhaps she'd find someone else someday: someone who'd stir

her desires without confounding her affections, someone with the Viscomte's magnetism but without his rude emotional volatility. And—as long as she was wishing—someone of her own station in life. Yes, she told herself firmly, she'd find that someone someday. The same *someday* she was done with washing pots and back in the world of books and letters.

She nodded, as though she'd been persuaded by impeccable logic rather than stubborn optimism. Well, if no one else was around to remind her of what was just barely possible, she'd simply have to do it herself.

Time for bed, she told herself. Tomorrow would be a hard day. But just one more thought before sleep. She sighed and shook her head: even *she* couldn't convince herself that this last thought was a logical argument. It was only a slim, rather pathetic hope, a final little request to the fates. *Please, oh please,* she whispered to whatever powers might be listening, *please make his visit a brief one.*

She'd just reached to loosen her dress when someone began a thunderous pounding at her door.

Chapter 6

In future years Marie-Laure would never be quite sure what had really happened during the next moments. Of course she'd recall it with vividness and clarity, joy and delight. But she'd never truly be able to separate perception from imagination or distinguish memory from surmise. For how could she possibly have experienced every astonishment, decoded every sign, interpreted every wonder of that first embrace?

He'd mumbled something when she opened the door and looked up into his dark eyes. *Pardon me, Mademoiselle Vernet, I'll explain all this later*, was what she thought she heard; perhaps he'd also said something about "danger" or "protection." But the only words she could be sure of were "Mademoiselle Vernet," the only emotions she'd be able to swear to were giddy delight and delirious elation—silly, selfish relief and prideful vindication, in truth—that he hadn't forgotten her name after all.

He wasn't wearing his coat or waistcoat. She'd caught a quick glimpse of his hips and thighs in pearl gray velvet breeches. The lights and darks of the velvet, illuminated by her flickering candle, revealed rather more than she was prepared to admit she'd understood.

Nonsense, she'd think later. *Of course* she'd seen the bulge between his legs. After all, she wasn't a child or a fool—the velvet was definitely stretched by the tumescent flesh beneath it. And even if she'd been embarrassed to bring it to consciousness upon first observation, there could be no doubt of what she'd felt a moment later, no mistaking the urgent press of him against her own hips and thighs. And no use pretending that she hadn't been thrilled by it.

The weave of his linen shirt had grazed her chest and shoulders; his hand cradled her breast. She'd gasped with surprised recognition: somewhere, in some secret place at her center, she'd wanted his hands on her breasts ever since she'd watched him pile books onto Papa's desk.

Was that the sound of cloth ripping? It was hard to discern behind the sound of her heartbeat and her breath, hard to concentrate with his mouth against hers, opening it, probing and teasing it with his tongue.

His other hand was tight at the small of her back. Well, it had been tight at first. Yes, she was sure of that. He'd held her closely—for a moment. And . . . she was *pretty sure* of what had happened next, *almost certain* that his hand had loosened, had become more adventurous. It had moved downward, slowly but confidently lingering over the curve of her buttock, while it gathered her skirt and petticoat out of the way. And as for where his hand was poised to go next, and where he might put his fingers . . .

She'd marvel, later on, that she hadn't been shocked or frightened by how indecently he was touching her. But wasn't she also caressing him under his shirt at the back of his waist? How could she take offense at his wandering hands, when her own hands were touching him everywhere she could reach? She could feel the ache starting up in her belly, the trembling, like that night in Montpellier. . . .

Such a jumble, such a torrent of sensation. And such a mystery, for she couldn't think how they'd come to be in each other's arms in the first place. It didn't seem quite accurate to say he'd "swept" her into his arms—or, for that matter, that she'd "rushed" into his embrace. If there had been a crucial gesture, a shy or importunate first touch, she couldn't specify what it had been or who had made it. The embrace had simply . . . happened, like a bolt of summer lightning.

It ended just as quickly.

The door rattled. She realized with a start that nobody had locked it. But who else could possibly be coming here at this hour?

She blinked in the sudden glare of another candle. A short man had flung open the door. He wore a quilted satin dressing gown, open at the front, his wattled neck purplish against the ruffled shirt below.

The Viscomte took his hand from her breast. He dropped her skirt but kept an arm around her waist. She tried to pull away from him and discovered that she needed his help to keep steady on her feet.

She heard laughter. High-pitched, ironic, and oddly affectionate. The Duc's crazy laugh.

"But I thought you were too much the egalitarian to take advantage of a servant, Joseph." The old man was shaking his head in mock exasperation.

His mouth hung slackly, but his small blue eyes were sharp, even proud.

"The first pretty girl they've hired in ages," he sighed. "Well, the race goes to the swift, no denying that." His narrow, bluish lips curled into a satyr's grin.

"But I'm glad you learned something during your time away. About seizing . . . dammit what's the expression? Seizing the moment? No. Ah yes, seizing the time, that's it." He laughed again. "Or seizing . . . well, whatever there is to be seized." He leered at Marie-Laure's torn dress and the bit of breast it revealed.

"I'll beat you at chess tomorrow though," he declared. "Cold consolation, but at least I'll get you there.

"You could have latched the door," he muttered before he slammed the door behind him.

But he wasn't gone yet. His laugh rang out again. "You're here too, Hubert? Too bad—little Joseph has beaten us both. You'd better try a visit to your wife instead and see if you can finally make us an heir. Maybe if you're good she'll reward you with a whiff of heliotrope."

His disconcerting high-pitched giggles receded down the corridor with him.

And I, Marie-Laure thought, *have been playing a role in a comedy entirely beyond my own devising.*

Joseph dropped his hand from around Marie-Laure's waist. At least, he thought, the illness hadn't robbed his father of his spirit. He grinned, savoring the nastiness with which the old rascal had spat out the word *heliotrope.*

But it was a guilty pleasure; he tried to suppress it. And merde! Who'd have predicted that sluglike Hubert would grope his way to her room as well?

He looked down at the girl at his side, her flushed face a study in embarrassed bewilderment, her arms tight around herself as she endeavored to hide the tear in her dress. Her eyes were wide and startled, shading from gray to blue and then to gray again as she sought to understand what had happened.

He clenched the hand that had caressed her breast, the hand that wanted desperately to hold and caress it again. His hand could probably deliver a treatise in natural philosophy on her breast's size and shape, softness and firmness, its nipple hard as a cherry stone between his fingers. He wasn't sure what had transpired, but it had been as though his hands and mouth had known exactly where to go and what to do—as though, unbeknownst to *him,* they'd been planning this for months.

The embrace hadn't gone as he'd intended; he'd planned something a great deal more polite yet also more theatrical. Something to signal to his father that she was taken, but to reassure her that it was all a bit of an act.

He certainly hadn't intended to become so absorbed by the encounter, so caught up by the banal fact of desire. *Mon Dieu,* he thought, *I must have terrified her.*

But she hadn't seemed terrified.

What had she thought he'd meant, he wondered. And, for that matter, what had *she* meant during that moment she'd been in his arms?

He must have taken her by surprise. Perhaps she'd been half asleep when she'd come to the door. Yes, he told himself, there'd been that dreamlike quality to it, that sweet trustingness. It had felt familiar, inevitable: they'd reached for each other like longtime lovers in the middle of the night.

Not, he supposed, that any of it mattered. The moment was past, whatever he or she had intended. What was important was that he'd succeeded in protecting her.

He handed her a shawl hanging from a nail in the wall. She took a deep breath, smiled ruefully, and wrapped it around herself.

"Thank you." Her voice had a tremor in it.

He shrugged. "It's nothing."

"No," she said in a firmer voice, holding out her skirt with her free hand as she curtsied, "it's everything." She laughed. "Because if you *hadn't* come and put off Monsieur le Duc like that, I would have had to punch him. Which would at the very least have cost me my job."

He laughed too. But his relief, he realized, was laced with disappointment. In truth he would have liked her to be a little more flustered, even overwhelmed by what had passed between them. As he had been.

Doubtless, he thought now, all the surprise had been on his side. He'd so wanted her to want him that he'd imagined all sorts of things once he'd had her in his arms. But really, he told himself, it was better that things had worked out this way. And it was clever of her to have figured it out so readily and to have gone along so enthusiastically.

"My father would have looked most unducal with a broken front tooth," he said.

Flushed and breathless, separated by a comfortable twenty inches or so of space, they smiled at each other like actors taking their bows after a successful performance.

"I apologize," he said, "for tearing your dress, Mademoiselle Vernet, but I needed evidence that my father would find absolutely convincing. And not having time to arrange things with you beforehand, I worked for economy of detail."

Liar, he chided himself. Of course he'd had absolutely no intention of reaching so hungrily and oafishly for her. He adored buttons and laces, intricate hooks and eyes; deftly undressing a lady was one of his specialties. But the provocative little rent in the fabric of her dress—shorter than the length of his thumb—*had* turned out to be an eloquent piece of stagecraft. It was a clear message in his father's code, communicating impatient, proprietary desire: a master wouldn't admit to impediments like a servant's clothes. A master *would* simply rip away whatever was in the way of his pleasure, before tossing her on the bed, raising her skirt above her face, and . . .

But that was his father's idea of a tumble with a servant, not his. Of course it wasn't. He'd torn her dress as a clever theatrical gesture. He'd done what he'd needed to do, and it was time he left off this useless self-scrutiny.

She nodded thoughtfully.

"But your brother." She frowned. "Had you thought that the Comte Monsieur Hubert would also be here?"

He hadn't. And he couldn't have foreseen his father's nasty comments, echoing down the corridor, in the wing where all the servants slept. He grimaced. She was right to be worried; by morning every servant and peasant within a league of the château would know the story.

And since they were probably already laughing at Hubert's evident inability to get his wife pregnant, this latest round of jokes would hardly help matters. Poor, prickly Amélie, already so insecure of her authority, would imagine sneers and snickers every time a servant bowed or curtsied to her.

And she'd blame it all on Marie-Laure.

"No," he said, "I hadn't thought that the Comte would be here. Nor about the, uh, complications for you. I would imagine," he added, "that even under the best of circumstances my sister-in-law wouldn't be the easiest person in the world to work for."

"She said I could be dismissed for lewd behavior." Marie-Laure's voice wavered.

"Don't worry," he said, "I'll make sure that doesn't happen." A little courtly politesse was all it would take, he thought. "But I'm afraid I can't transform her into a pleasant employer."

She shrugged and he felt a bit abashed. "Pleasant" conditions of employment obviously weren't uppermost among her concerns right now.

"Don't worry," he repeated, "I promise you won't lose your job. After all, it's the least I can do for someone who saved my life."

She wished he were not being so courteous, so understanding of her situation. She'd vastly prefer it, she thought, if he were as ill-tempered as he'd been last winter, when he'd lectured her about reading what wasn't on the page. *That* unpleasant man might well have taken physical advantage of her. If *that* man were here with her, the only emotion she'd have to admit to would be outrage.

But as things stood—with him being so kind, and smiling so affably—well, there was no getting around it: she knew how enthusiastically she'd responded to *his* caresses. No evading responsibility: her body had been suffused by the same desire she'd felt the night she'd watched him sleep, only—even worse—this time without any of the guilt or surprise.

He *must* have felt how much she'd wanted him, she thought, no matter how tactfully he now chose to ignore it. Well, she supposed she'd just have to ignore it as well. Like him, she'd have to pretend it hadn't happened that way at all.

"We could hardly let you die on our floor." The words came out a bit more sharply than she'd intended. "And anyway, it was my brother who saved you."

"I hope he's well," the Viscomte said. His polite disregard of her bad manners felt like a reproach. "And is he still studying medicine?"

She nodded slowly.

"And your father, I trust his health has improved? And what of the bookshop?"

"My father died last May, Monsieur Joseph. As for the bookshop," she added, "well, Papa was rather in debt, as it turned out."

He grimaced. "Something we have in common. Our fathers' being in debt, I mean. But I'm sorry about the loss of your father, Mademoiselle. It seemed to me from my brief stay in your home that you were a very loving family—which, as you can see, is something we do *not* have in common."

She looked away.

"And you didn't marry your brother's friend after all." He sounded almost accusing.

She shook her head. "My father didn't leave me a dowry." Which was true enough, if not the real reason she hadn't married her brother's friend.

The real reason she hadn't married her brother's friend nodded sympathetically.

But he wasn't addressing her properly, she thought.

"Pardon me, Monsieur Joseph, but perhaps you shouldn't be calling me 'Mademoiselle,' " she said. "Now that I work for your family, I mean. Perhaps you should be calling me . . ."

". . . Marie-Laure." The lines around his mouth deepened as the sounds issued from his lips.

Oh yes, much better, she thought. Especially the way his tongue had rolled itself around the final *r.*

"Marie-Laure," he repeated firmly, "Marie-Laure and *not* Marianne. And you don't have to call me 'Monsieur Joseph' when we're alone together. 'Joseph' is fine."

"But I might forget myself and call you, uh . . . 'Joseph' when others are around." *What a soft, liquid sound it had when you said it slowly.*

"In fact," he said thoughtfully, "now that we're lovers, it might be effective if once in a while you forgot yourself in public and did simply call me Joseph."

"Now that we're *what?*" Her voice rose a full octave; so much for soft, liquid sounds.

"In effect, I mean." His eyes danced with pleasure above his smile. He looked like Gilles, she thought, describing a new and wonderful medical procedure.

"Because now that they've noticed you, the only way to keep my father and Hubert out of your bed is to convince them that you're regularly in *my* bed.

"But we can do that easily enough," he continued. "We'll just have my valet bring you to my room every night."

He rattled the door, producing a muffled expletive from the

other side. "In fact the rogue's spying on us right now, through the keyhole."

"Don't strain your eyes, Baptiste," he called.

"And anyway," he added quickly, "I promise you won't have to worry about what happens between us. Because, as my father has already rather crudely informed you, I do *not* take advantage of servants."

After all, he assured himself, it *was* the best way to keep his father and brother away from her. And he certainly did owe her his protection; the nightly charade he'd proposed was nothing more than a simple expedient for maintaining her safety. It had *nothing* to do with what *he* might want.

All right, not *quite* nothing. All right, so he wanted to see her again. Well, what of it? He'd promised not to touch her. He *wouldn't* touch her. They'd simply talk, as they had in Montpellier. Of course, he'd be more polite than he'd been in Montpellier. And he'd call her by name—"Marie-Laure" instead of "Mademoiselle."

Marie-Laure. He could taste the deep velvet tone of its final syllable.

"Well anyway," he said, "you're welcome to visit, Marie-Laure, if you also think it's a good idea."

"It probably is. A good idea, I mean," she stammered.

She began again slowly. "Yes, Joseph, I think it would be a very good idea—just to be on the safe side. Thank you." She gave a little nod and smiled gratefully.

My God, he thought, *it's hot in this stuffy little room.*

But *would* it be such a good idea, she asked herself, to spend every night in his presence? Especially when he was proving so witty and sympathetic.

Every ounce of her common sense said no.

Spend every night behind closed doors with an aristocrat? Have you gone quite mad, Marie-Laure? Her common sense tended to speak in Gilles' voice.

But if I don't, *I'll be at the mercy of two other aristocrats.* This in her own firm inner voice. *Two rather disgusting aristocrats,* her inner voice added.

And at least this *one had promised not to touch me.* (*No matter how much I might* want *him to . . .)*

Her common sense was unconvinced.

Her inner voice tried a new argument. *After all, it's not a question of what I might want. It's for my safety. It's in the service of keeping my job.*

Her common sense shrugged and left her to her own devices.

Well, she could always change her mind. Later, when she was free of his distracting presence. She'd think it over carefully when he was gone: for surely he'd be leaving in a moment.

Though in fact he didn't seem to be making any motion toward opening the door. In fact, he looked rather awkward, as though he didn't quite know how to end this interview.

"And so," he said, "I'll see you tomorrow night. Sleep well."

"Yes," Marie-Laure answered, "and you too."

He didn't move. Should I thank him again, she wondered. Another curtsy, perhaps? Some additional word or gesture was needed, it seemed, but she had not the slightest notion of what it could be.

"Don't forget to latch the door," he said.

She shook her head. "No. Well . . ."

He opened the door slightly and then shut it again, suddenly looking very young. Quickly and in a low voice, he said, "You were right about Monsieur X, you know. About the story that happened before the book began."

What in the world was he talking about?

It came to her all at once, in a rush of delicious understanding and unrestrained laughter.

His shoulders stiffened. "Well," he said, "I don't know if it's really as funny as all *that.*"

She struggled to hold back her laughter.

"Perhaps not," she said, "but it solves one of the two riddles that puzzled me for months. The first riddle, you see, was how a mere book porter could have ordered me about in such an imperious, aristocratic fashion."

"And the second?"

"Why he should have been so excessively interested in Monsieur X."

He smiled sheepishly. "An author's vanity," he murmured.

She returned the smile. "You're a wonderful writer, you know. And I am—or *was*—one of your most devoted readers.

"I suppose I'm still a reader in spirit," she added.

He nodded. "Of course you are. You're probably the most astute reader I've ever had."

"Will you tell me how you came to write the book? And what you're writing now? And how it felt when . . ."

He laughed, putting up a graceful hand to stem the torrent of demands.

"Yes, yes, of course. But gently, one question at a time. I'll tell you everything. Beginning tomorrow night.

"And thank you for the compliments."

Swiftly, he turned on his heel, ran down the corridor, and disappeared around a corner.

She watched the empty air that had stirred in his wake, before shrugging, latching the door, and quickly removing her clothes.

And so it would be quite all right to visit him, she decided. It would be a literary matter and not a personal one. After all, a bookseller—and someday she *would* be a bookseller again—ought to know everything she could about her authors.

But for now, how nice it was to have the bed to herself this once. And so, stretching her limbs as far over the mattress as they'd reach, she fell into a sound, happy sleep.

Chapter 7

She would have to get through a very long day, however, before the night's visit.

It would be a day of jokes and teasing; the story of last night's bedroom farce had spread like a forest fire whipped along by the summer mistral. If *she'd* been confused by the night's events, Marie-Laure thought, she seemed to be the only person who had. Everybody else in the château seemed to know exactly what had transpired. And everybody wanted to talk about it.

The servants' breakfast coffee was particularly strong and plentiful this morning. It had made them giddy and loquacious, animated by wild hilarity over the Duc's insulting remarks to the Comte Monsieur Hubert.

It wasn't surprising that they'd love any story where the Gorgon got the worst of it, but Marie-Laure was nonetheless disconcerted to find that she was the story's heroine, and that everybody "knew" the Viscomte was her lover. They were pleasant and funny about it, though—all except for the Duc's valet, Jacques, whose advances she'd once repelled, and Arsène, who maintained his usual prudish rectitude.

"Got to keep your strength up." Nudging each other and grinning, they'd handed thick slices of bread and butter down the table to her. "A master who's been plying his trade in bed all night—it's the only trade *their* breed ever learns—can sleep all the following day. But a servant has to work, same as always."

Or—today, anyway—even harder than always. For it would be a day of unrelenting labor in preparation for the banquet.

"Well, you're young enough to miss a little sleep," Nicolas told her, as he chased everybody off to work, "so I'm sure I won't have to worry about you dozing over the pots and pans. But I don't want to see you sighing and dreaming about the handsome gentleman when you should be working."

She shook her head. She wouldn't correct their misapprehensions: the more convinced everyone was that Joseph had claimed her services, the safer she was from his father and brother. She smiled and blushed, which seemed to be all that was expected of her.

But when Bertrande slipped into the scullery to hand her some dried herbs in a small folded paper, Marie-Laure had to restrain herself from giggling.

"You make a tea with it," Bertrande told her. "Drink it every day; it'll keep you from becoming pregnant.

"Well," she added sheepishly, catching the skeptical gleam in Marie-Laure's eye, "it's better than not trying anything, because I doubt that *he* cares to bother. . . ."

Marie-Laure thanked her and brewed the tea. In this case, she thought, although never before or again, the herbs were going to be one hundred percent effective.

"How was she, Joseph?"

Suppressing a shudder, Joseph struggled to find an acceptable response to his brother's question.

He supposed Hubert was trying to be sporting about it. If only, Joseph thought, his brother's mouth weren't so wet—he found it distracting, the way it glistened in the midday sunlight.

He'd already spent an hour this morning with Amélie, assuring her that his dalliance with a servant was nothing out of the ordinary. It happened, he'd told her, in all the best—all the *oldest*—of aristocratic families. Yes, it was regrettable, he'd sighed, but what could one expect from a hot-blooded, weak-willed young noble like himself?

Of course, he'd murmured, were it not for his duty to his brother, he might indulge in a more sophisticated pleasure—with a more elegant lady. But surely, Madame—he'd leaned across her on the sofa, his legs elegantly disposed beneath him, his nose practically in her bosom again—surely, she understood the loyalties an ancient family conferred upon one.

She'd come around easily enough: in fact, it had been rather *too* easy to make her to stop pouting, especially after he'd promised to enchant and delight the guests at tonight's banquet. He'd been glad to be summoned to the chess game with his father, where there'd been some challenge to losing the game and still keeping it interesting.

And now he was expected to hunt rabbits with his brother.

The field was overrun with the creatures. The dogs seemed to enjoy sniffing them out, and Hubert loved shooting at them. Two manservants carried the guns and a growing bag of little furred bodies.

Feigning total concentration on his marksmanship, Joseph raised his musket to his shoulder, took aim, and squeezed the trigger. Perfect. Just close enough to be a convincing miss.

Another silly private game, he supposed, but he didn't feel like killing innocent creatures today. Hubert caught a big one, and the dogs set off happily to fetch its carcass.

Hubert gave a satisfied nod and turned back to their conversation.

"And last night's prey?" he asked. "Was she eager? She looked like a hot, enthusiastic little thing. Or did you have to force her, make her scream?"

If his mouth gets any wetter, Joseph thought, *he'll be drooling along with the dogs.*

"They pretend they don't like it, you know." Hubert was clearly proud to share this information. "Especially when you push them down and force them to . . ."

The end of the sentence was almost lost in a torrent of giggles, while the servants pretended to busy themselves with dogs and equipment.

Joseph felt as though he were back in school. But he should have known to prepare a story, he thought. Like many gentlemen, Hubert was still an overgrown schoolboy; half the pleasure of an amatory triumph was in the telling, the other half in the listening.

What made it worse was that these sniggering conversations inevitably took place with servants at one's elbow, like pieces of furniture. Most of his fellow aristocrats were unconscious of the implicit cruelty, but the cleverer of them liked to exploit it. The Baron Roque, for example, was famous for enlivening his dinner parties with tales of gross debauchery and then—during the cheese course—announcing that the woman whose lovemaking he'd described in such detail was the daughter or wife of one of the footmen in attendance.

Hubert was growing impatient.

Joseph sighed. "She was . . . delicious."

"And?"

"And"—he glanced at a tip of velvety rabbit ear poking out of the bag one of the servants carried—"very . . . innocent." He thought of the present King's grandfather, Louis XV, who'd kept a private brothel, stocked with young women he'd hunt like game animals through field and forest. The Deer Park, it had been called. *Those* were the days, his father liked to say.

Hubert chortled. "She probably begged you to break her in. How many times did you have her?"

How to put an end to this vileness? He breathed deeply, as though beginning a juicy confidence. Hubert grinned in anticipation.

"Baptiste is bringing her to my room tonight."

Hubert was nearly panting.

"And *so,* Monsieur le Comte"—Joseph bowed suddenly and gracefully from the waist—"I'm sure you'll excuse me if I don't squander my powers in chatter, which sometimes, you know, diverts a gentleman's energy from the act itself."

The servant carrying the rabbits broke into a coughing fit to cover his sputtering laughter, while the one with the muskets maintained a look of fierce reserve. It took Joseph a minute to place the second attendant—ah yes, Arsène from last night's dinner, dark-haired today without his powdered footman's wig.

Well done, Arsène. It must take some force of will not to snicker at us.

But where had he seen him before? Montpellier, perhaps? No, that was ridiculous: booksellers didn't employ footmen.

He turned back to his brother.

"Or don't *you* find that talk can be the enemy of virility, Monsieur le Comte?" he added softly.

Hubert shrugged as though he hadn't understood the innuendo, but his red-rimmed eyes were icy.

"Of course, Joseph. Save your powers, your famous charm. We haven't formally inquired yet, but rumor has it all the young ladies we've invited to dinner tonight have pretty good dowries attached."

"And if I'm not inclined to search for a wife just now?"

"Oh, but you are. You're pining, you're dying, you're *desperate* for a wife."

"Not at all. I came to visit our father, and I'll be off again as soon as . . . it's all over."

"Merde." Hubert missed a shot. He handed his musket to Arsène to reload. And when he spoke, after a pause, it was in a soft but authoritative voice.

"I'm not as stupid as I look," he said. "And Amélie, whatever else she might be, is damned intelligent, almost as intelligent as her bourgeois father's lawyers. She's as heartless, too, and as intent on getting what she wants. You made a mistake, Joseph, getting on her bad side."

Joseph shrugged. She'd seemed easy enough to get around this morning.

Hubert reached into a capacious pocket and drew out a pair of documents.

"You can have them. I've had copies made for you. But I'll keep the originals, with the official seals on them."

The first document enumerated the money he'd spent paying off Joseph's creditors and bribing those angry husbands.

"The specifics don't matter—I'm sure you don't remember, never even attended to the petty costs of your adventures. But what does matter is the total amount of money you owe me. This is a bill, Joseph, due six months after our father's death, whenever that may be."

Joseph scanned the second document while Hubert brought down two more rabbits. They were little ones, babies really, he noted, some part of him registering their pathetic smallness in the dogs' maws while the cold legal words took shape in his mind. The baby rabbits had doubtless been driven frantic by the loss of their mother's protection. He felt his cheeks grow hot as he struggled to keep his voice soft and even.

"So if I don't pay you I could go to prison?"

"Shows a concern on my part, don't you think, for the general morality? The King's agents congratulated me on my public-spiritedness. I'm doing my bit for France by trying to teach Monsieur X some decent behavior. You've had a good time all these years, Joseph, but you're going to be profitably married, just like the rest of us.

"And yes, I do need the money. Odd, how once you get money you find that you need more of it. But you'll learn. Even with your reputation, your looks and bloodlines ought to buy somebody as good as Amélie anyway."

Joseph felt a chill seep through his bones despite the merciless midday sunshine.

"You can't," he muttered. But he knew all too well that Hubert could. Joseph wouldn't be the first young nobleman locked away for the supposed public welfare with the King's seal on the lettre de cachet his family had secured. He thought of the Comte de Mirabeau—eight years in and out of prison at the whim of a hateful father. And if the Marquis de Sade's mother-in-law continued to have her way, *that* gentleman would live out the rest of his life in the Bastille.

He struggled to concentrate on what his brother was saying. "It was good of you to make this visit," Hubert continued. "Not a day went by last winter when the old Duc didn't regale Amélie and me with pronouncements of how overjoyed he was about the imminent return of his favorite son.

"Too bad the lawyers took so long with their subtleties of phrasing or you might have been able to return sooner. But *I* couldn't help but enjoy the old coot's frustrations when I'd tell him he'd have to wait a bit longer."

Couldn't help but enjoy it. Yes, I can imagine.

"Is he really as ill as your letters said?" Joseph asked.

Hubert threw him an aggrieved look. "Would I lie about a matter of such import? Speak to his doctors yourself if you wish. Of course, if you absolutely can't bear the idea of marrying, you could probably get away right now—cross the border back to the shabby adventurer's life you were living. But you won't."

He's right, I won't. I've committed myself to staying with our father through the course of his illness.

"You needn't hurry to find a fiancée, after all," Hubert continued. "Our inquiries to the marriage brokers have been most perfunctory as yet. Personally I'm delighted to have you here—saves me from having to listen to the old goat's stupid rants at dinner and tea. After he dies, of course, we'll need your quick cooperation."

Joseph aimed, fired several shots in quick succession, and watched the dogs retrieve the limp little bodies.

"Good work, little brother. You're a quick study. And no doubt you'll plug the little kitchen slut just as efficiently tonight."

Would this afternoon never end?

"She's *not* . . ." he began furiously. But what *was* he to say exactly?

Hubert smiled. "What was that, Joseph?"

"Nothing, Monsieur le Comte. Nothing at all."

The workday in the kitchen had been regularly punctuated by Monsieur Colet's tantrums, the latest one being over the crayfish tails.

"Too small! They'll be lost in the dish! It's a disaster!" It took all of Nicolas's wheedling and cajoling (and a very fine Côtes du Rhône) to get things on back on track.

Marie-Laure knew that the tails were only a garnish. Tucked around the outside of a large dish, they would form a scalloped edging for a thick sauce, holding slivered sweetbreads, mushrooms, truffles, foie gras, and cockscombs. Upon which would be laid the squabs, braised with slices of veal, ham, and bacon, covered in diced sweetbreads, truffles and mushrooms, and topped with a heart-shaped slice of puff pastry.

"And *how* many such complicated dishes will we be preparing today?" Marie-Laure whispered.

Her fifteen-year-old workmate Robert beamed. "Twelve. Twelve, Marie-Laure." Robert had often been hungry as a child. Working in this kitchen, he often said, was like being paid to go to heaven.

Of course, the twelve dishes didn't include the soup, the vegetables—even Monsieur Colet was satisfied with the beautiful young peas and artichokes and asparagus they had to work with—and the salads. Not to speak of the delicate little hors d'oeuvres. And as for the desserts . . .

But there wasn't time to begin contemplating the desserts. Robert and Marie-Laure had to race to keep up: to clean the pots and pans the rest of the staff kept dirtying, to split and de-fuzz more than a hundred baby artichokes. To chop and scald and peel and stir, wherever they were needed. But even as Marie-Laure's hands flew and her head began to ache, Joseph's image drifted toward her through the steamy air. Here was his smile and the taste of his mouth; there, the arcs of his hands and the outline of his hips.

And here was . . . a huge cleaver sailing through the air and landing in a wooden dresser. It marked the opening salvo of Monsieur Colet's next tantrum. This one was directed at Arsène, who was getting in everybody's way, on his way to the meat locker to hang up a ridiculous number of freshly killed rabbits.

The crash caused a huge dessert soufflé to fall. And so, as Monsieur Colet proclaimed to everyone's delight, the ruined soufflé would have to be eaten by the servants. The idiot guests would simply have to make do with the strawberry, raspberry, and apricot tarts, the heaps of meringues and macaroons studded with almonds and pistachios, the molded marzipan cakes in amusing and sometimes indecent shapes and colors, the chocolate-covered eclairs and profiteroles filled with crème anglaise, the towers of fruit topped with hothouse pineapples, and the fantasia of molded milk and water ices flavored with fruit, coffee, chocolate, coconut, and candied violets.

They could hear the guests' carriages clattering over the drawbridge. Nicolas inspected the footmen's livery, clucking about a grease spot here, a bit of tarnished braid there. The troop of them finally marched up the stairs, each carrying a more impressive platter than the last.

And marched back down, for more food, more wine. A lot more wine, Nicolas called out. The banquet was a success.

The guests had only come, he explained later, out of respect for the Duchesse's ancient pedigree and curiosity about the Viscomte's reputation. But they'd stayed and enjoyed themselves. The food had been a triumph and the family had risen to the occasion. Even the Duc had behaved quite respectably, contributing a witty anecdote of life and manners at Louis XV's court.

"So the Gorgon's finally been accepted into the local gentry," Nicolas concluded. "Let's hope at least for a bit of relief from her everlasting demands."

"And now, Mesdames and Messieurs," he added, opening another bottle of wine and passing around the flat but still delicious soufflé, "it's our turn to celebrate."

But Marie-Laure slipped away early, carrying a jar of lemon water that Monsieur Colet had given her for washing away kitchen smells—it seemed that even he was interested in her supposed adventure with the Viscomte.

She scrubbed herself. Not bad.

She pulled off her cap. Her room's cracked mirror couldn't tell her much, but she thought that her hair had regained the thickness and luster it had lost to the typhus. She brushed it vigorously. She didn't have any ribbons, so all she could do was force a few strands at the sides into spiral tendrils, continuing to brush it while she waited for Baptiste's knock at the door.

And when the knock finally came Marie-Laure could feel a collective sigh rising from the servants' dormitories down the hall: everybody who wasn't still carousing in the dessert kitchen had been waiting along with her.

Chapter 8

Returning Baptiste's silent smile and nod, she followed him down the stairs and through an unfamiliar corridor, all silvery stone that the Gorgon's plasterers hadn't covered over yet. Their footsteps echoed as though from afar. She felt surprisingly calm, oddly without volition, mysteriously removed from the physical space she occupied. Perhaps it was the effect of a long, fatiguing workday, but she felt as though none of this was really happening. Or—more precisely—that it was all happening to somebody else. To a character in a play perhaps; yes, it was all happening to a breathless ingenue who just happened to be named Marie-Laure. While *she*, the *real* Marie-Laure, watched the drama's progress from a cheap hard seat in paradise, the rows at the very top of the theater.

Baptiste stopped in front of an arched doorway and turned a large iron key in the lock. He opened the door, delivered an ironic bow, and—since Marie-Laure's legs seemed to have forgotten how to move of their own accord—gave her a little shove inside a very bright space.

Someone must have lit a lot of candles. Her eyes needed time to adjust from the corridor's dimness. She thought she could discern large shapes of furniture; there was something shiny to her left—a glass-fronted bookshelf, perhaps. But in fact the only sense organ she could truly rely on was her nose. She stood still, breathing rosemary and lavender while Joseph's image took shape and substance at the other side of the room. He was leaning on one of the posts of a large, curtained bed, grinning mischievously, and wearing slippers and an embroidered dressing gown.

His grin made everything real again.

He winked. "At last," he said. "At last some intelligent conversation."

That insouciant wink guaranteed his sincerity. She didn't know how she could be sure of it, but she was.

She could tell that he hadn't lied about his principles last night. No matter what else might transpire between them, he wouldn't take advantage of a servant.

All right then. They'd have a conversation.

Well, *that* was a relief anyway.

Of course it was a relief.

Sorry, Baptiste, she thought as the door closed behind her. Sorry we won't be giving you anything to peek at tonight.

Still, she found it difficult not to stare at his enormous bed.

Happily, he seemed to understand, for he motioned her to a cushioned window seat and drew up an armchair for himself, partially obscuring the purple velvet bed curtains from her line of vision.

"At least I won't topple out of *this* chair. No broken legs, you see." He smiled and so did she, until both their smiles began to wear thin and it became clear that one of them was going to have to say something else.

They settled, as though by mutual consent, on literature as the safest topic of discussion. Marie-Laure hadn't spoken about books or writing for some months now. But encouraged by the interest in his eyes, she soon found herself rattling on as though she were back in the shop.

"And so I must admit," she concluded, "that Monsieur Rousseau's memoir rather disappointed me, even while it fairly overwhelmed me with its honesty and . . . and greatness of soul. But it was a very *aggressive* honesty, a very *prepossessing* greatness."

He knit his brow. "You're a severe critic."

"For a scullery maid, you mean."

"No, that's not what I mean at all. I stand by what I said last night. You're a reader worth having, an extraordinarily clever one."

She stared. But he'd said it without irony or affectation.

"And you're right," he added. "I hadn't thought of it in quite that way, but Rousseau does betray a streak of egoism, doesn't he? As though he were using all that honesty and humility to bludgeon his readers into submission."

She laughed. "Yes, yes, you've expressed it perfectly. Well, of course, as an author yourself . . ."

But—just as she'd been about to turn the conversation to him and his writing—she was seized by an enormous yawn.

And it had been going so well, Joseph thought.

Of course it had been rather a physical ordeal to have her so close by and yet so off limits. But it had also been delightful.

She'd been timid at first. Well, to be honest so had he—but he was a better actor, and able to hide his nervousness. And he'd had a good sharp opening line to deliver, one he'd honed and polished throughout that endless banquet.

Mon Dieu, what a dreary affair *that* had been, with only the excellence of the food to make up for all the vapid witticisms and clumsy double entendres directed at him—not to speak of the fluttering eyelashes of half a dozen predatory provincial demoiselles. He'd endured appraising stares from potential fathers-in-law and sidelong glances from their wives, a few of them clearly hoping there might be a little something in it for *them* as well. He'd worked *hard*—smiling, smirking, bowing, and gesturing.

All the while trying to concoct the perfect welcoming remark to make to *her*. Something brief and witty: friendly, unprovocative, and just a bit sly and unexpected.

On the whole, he'd thought that his greeting had come off rather neatly, and that he'd done a good job nudging the conversation around to literature in general and Rousseau's *Confessions* in particular. Given how deftly she'd dissected his own writing last winter (but *that* he'd be sure to steer her away from) he'd been sincerely eager to hear what she thought of the book all literate France was discussing.

He'd engineered an abstract, cerebral conversation, to bridge the chasm between their all-too-separate social positions. A meeting of minds—to distract attention from their all-too-present bodies.

And very successfully too, he'd thought. Not that she hadn't also been marvelous to look at. Wonderful that way she had of casting her eyes about for just the right word, all the while curling her legs under herself and snuggling into the window seat's cushions. Her bright hair seemed to reflect the light of all the room's candles, while her eyes glowed with subtler inner lights—her immersion in the subject's complexities, of course; her joy in matters of the intellect.

Until her yawn had put an end to all that by showing him just how fatuous his perceptions had been.

A good thing his olive complexion didn't show blushes. But he felt a deep chagrin at his thoughtlessness.

How could he not have noticed how exhausted she was? Her hand was trembling; the skin below her eyes was blue.

How could he have imagined it tactful to ignore what she'd been doing all day? As though physical labor were something shameful, regrettable.

Anyway, what *had* she been doing all day?

All he knew was that she'd helped prepare the large, formal dinner—the excellent meal that he'd been quite happy to eat. And that she worked in the scullery.

But what did they actually do in a scullery? He believed—though he wasn't sure—that they washed pots there. Food *was* cooked in pots, wasn't it? Or was it pans they used down there? Pots, pans—what did it matter? He probably couldn't tell one from the other anyway.

He had only the most distant notion even of how an omelet was prepared. One simply sat at table and food appeared, lightly veiled by its pastry shell, or fragrant and blushing atop a pool of raspberry sauce—as cunningly and elaborately arrayed as a woman dressed to meet her lover. And as silent, as secretive about the mysteries of preparation.

He stared at the girl in the window seat. Her skin was pale

under her freckles. She raised a chapped hand to her mouth, endeavoring to stifle another yawn and failing miserably.

"But you're tired. You've been working all day. Cooking that dinner must have taken a lot of effort."

She shrugged. "I didn't really *cook* it."

"Well then, doing . . . ah . . . something, whatever it was. And I've kept you up so late, with all this conversation."

"It's been lovely to talk to you. I don't get opportunities like this any more."

"Still . . ." He felt abashed for having thought *he'd* worked hard, bowing and simpering and charming the family's guests. He'd thought himself magnanimous to be so unmindful of her inferior station. And such a hero and martyr too, for not touching her.

Damn his self-centeredness—it seemed that he'd also misinterpreted those longing glances she'd been directing toward his bed. He'd thought she'd been imagining the same thing *he* had.

"You need to sleep. I'll have Baptiste take you back to your room. Or . . ."—*well, she* would *be more comfortable*—"would you like to take a little nap here? You really *can* trust me, you know," he added.

"I know."

"Because I *never* . . ."

"Take advantage of servants. Yes, you mentioned that." Her voice was quiet, but that slight curve of her mouth, he thought, might hint at irony.

"Well, perhaps I will lie down, just for a little." She uncurled her legs from beneath her. Her left stocking had a little tear in its weave, near the ankle.

His bed was high off the ground. Perhaps he should lift her onto it. *No, better not.*

"Just rest for a while," he whispered, as she sank down onto the pillows. She sighed and stretched her legs, searching for the perfect posture.

"Just . . . rest." The tiny catch in the fabric of his voice, it seemed to him, reflected the rip in her stocking. But she hadn't heard him; she'd already fallen asleep, barely moving—except for the gentle rise and fall of her chest—all the next hour, until he wrested his gaze from her and whispered to Baptiste to wake her and lead her to her room upstairs.

A blush suffused her face as early morning sunlight slanted through her bedroom window and memories of the preceding night rushed back to consciousness.

Had she really fallen asleep in his bed? How sweetly awkward, how chastely intimate the evening had been.

You really can *trust me, you know.* It seemed she could, which was a good thing, she supposed.

Well, of course *it's a good thing.* (She heard this thought in Gilles' insistent voice.) *It's a very good thing indeed that he's so decent. You're lucky to have his protection, Marie-Laure.*

Even if the evening wasn't anything like her dreams of visiting Monsieur X's bedchamber. Nor the way anyone else in the château had imagined it.

Well, damn everyone in the château then. Damn them and their lecherous fantasies too. Anyway, she thought now, there was at least one person here who'd be glad to know the innocent, virtuous truth.

Her bedmate Louise had returned from her mother's funeral late last night, while Marie-Laure had been in Joseph's room. Of course Louise knew where Marie-Laure had been: her fiancé, Martin from the stables, would have told her the whole story when he'd fetched her at the inn.

Louise was pious and believed in the sacraments. She and Martin, as she'd told Marie-Laure, were waiting until they could afford to marry. She'd been asleep when Marie-Laure had come back to bed last night (there was no mistaking her loud snore), but Marie-Laure had thought she'd detected Louise's disapproval even in sleep, from the way she'd scrunched herself up and turned her face to the wall.

She wasn't sleeping now, though. Marie-Laure couldn't hear any snores from Louise's side of the bed. Only—just as insistent, somehow, in its silence—a regretful, intensely pitying stare.

Louise's sorrow about Marie-Laure's sins would be even more

difficult to bear—unearned as it was—than everybody else's lusty, unbridled fantasies.

She reminded herself that the whole point of her nightly visits to Joseph's room was to create an illusion. She tried to convince herself that an illusion wouldn't be much good if even one person knew the truth.

She turned to face her bedmate. Louise had huge pale blue eyes, fringed with long black lashes. If it weren't for the harelip that deformed the lower part of her face, she'd be a beauty. The lovely eyes were solemn, troubled. Marie-Laure hugged her.

"It's not what you think, *chérie,*" she whispered.

And quickly, while she and Louise dressed, she explained the situation as well as she could.

"I'll tell you more later," she promised as they hurried down to breakfast. "But you can't tell a soul. No, not even Martin. Absolutely not."

It might have been a mistake, she thought, plunging her hands into the washbasin after breakfast. But she wasn't sorry; she needed to confide in someone and with luck, Louise wouldn't tell. All the servants loved to gossip about their masters, but they were closemouthed with their own secrets and loyal with each other's. Marie-Laure had been reminded of this a week or so ago when Arsène, who'd been solemnly explaining something to Nicolas (it seemed to have something to do with his family) immediately became silent and chilly when she entered the dessert kitchen.

The pace of kitchen work had become bearable again. After the preceding few days it felt almost luxurious: only the curate and the magistrate were invited to dinner tonight.

"We'll stew the rabbits," Monsieur Colet had said. "Cuisine *ordinaire* for the local flunkies."

Marie-Laure held up a faceted crystal goblet and watched it bend a sunbeam into a rainbow.

No dreaming of the handsome gentleman, she reminded herself, as Nicolas passed by on his way to go over accounts with Monsieur Colet. But she wasn't dreaming—at least not in the way Nicolas would have thought. She was happily sifting through thoughts and insights that had lain dormant for months.

Books and stories were the things she loved best in the world. She'd spent most of her life talking about them; doing without such talk these past months had felt like starvation. How fantastic to have found someone with the same enthusiasms—someone, moreover, who'd done something as splendid as writing and publishing his own story. She knew from his wonderfully constructed phrases that he shared her reverence for writing; she would have felt honored to meet him even if he weren't so . . . wonderful in other ways.

Someone to talk to, listen to, learn about.

Of course, there were *some* things about him—some physical things—that she probably knew too much about already.

But in other ways he was still an enigma. Even through all her exhaustion and confusion last night, she'd clearly discerned how prickly he was about revealing certain thoughts and opinions. She would bet a year's wages that he was avoiding some aching memory or troubling experience. Well, she supposed that it was his business and not hers.

Back home in Montpellier, she'd sometimes stay up all night to finish a particularly interesting book, just to see how it all came out; she'd drift through the next day in a happy haze fitting the pieces together. He'd said she was a clever reader; maybe she was just an especially persistent one.

Shrugging, she turned her attention back to the crystal goblets. He'd penned an elegant, many-faceted memoir, but Marie-Laure was surer than ever that there was one story he hadn't been able to put down on paper. And whether it was her business or not, she knew that she wouldn't be satisfied until she knew what it was.

Chapter 9

As the summer wore on, Joseph was to learn a great deal about clever readers—or at least about the very clever one who visited him every night. He quickly learned that she was an eager listener, one who caught every detail and examined it for flaws and inconsistencies. She knew her subject, too—he couldn't help but feel flattered that Marie-Laure had all but memorized some of Monsieur X's stories. And she was endlessly, shamelessly inquisitive: having utterly disarmed him with what she understood already, she'd look at him with large, clear, innocent eyes and ask yet another devilishly simple question.

"And what did you do then?"

"But why did the Prince become so angry?"

"Was she pretty?" "Was it expensive?" "Did it hurt?"

Her attention was a goad, a stimulant. In different circumstances he might even have found it an aphrodisiac. *Stop that*, he told himself, *stop that right now*. But it was certainly amusing, even invigorating, to talk to her; her gaze made him feel quite eloquent. It made him voluble too—sometimes rather more so than he wanted to be.

He tried to limit himself to safe, impersonal subjects. Anecdotes of life at court were good choices, he thought, because the material would already be familiar to her. And not just to her: all of

France—literate or not—were quickly becoming authorities on the royal family and their ridiculous, money-draining excesses. Marie-Laure shook her head at the glitter and corruption and laughed at absurdities like the Queen pretending to be a shepherdess, carrying a beribboned crook and tripping about the palace gardens with her flock of perfumed sheep.

He lingered as long as he could on such things. After all, the facts of daily life at Versailles—the spectacular entertainments and inexorable maneuverings for power and influence—were amazing in themselves, the scope and size of the place fabulous beyond imagining. "I was told," he said, "that there are six hundred apartments there. For members of the court, you know."

Luckily, she didn't demand to know how many of those apartments he'd actually slept in—or *not* slept in, which had more often been the case. He'd once attempted to tally it up for himself and had been a bit shocked by the result; if asked for a numeric reckoning of his nights at Versailles, he'd appear rather like a male Scheherazade, with a thousand and one tales to recount.

He sometimes felt like Scheherazade in any case, telling a different story every night in order to avoid—well, not his own death of course, but *something* deadly, something filthy and obscene and untellable.

What had she said last winter? . . . *an author sometimes leaves out bits and pieces—things that were too difficult or painful* . . . Damn her perspicacity anyway!

In their early meetings, he tried to tell her about everything but himself.

But every good storyteller—and he was a very good one—adorns his narrative with at least a few personal details. Anyway, he comforted himself, she already knew a lot of it from his memoir. Though it was different, somehow, telling it face-to-face.

Telling it to such a pretty, eager face, with such a quick mind animating it.

The pleasure of writing the book, of course, had partly been the fun of boasting about his numerous conquests. While the art of it (if art there were) lay in a single sad irony: that when all was said and done he hadn't conquered anything or anybody. Love—or the lack of it—had always conquered *him* in the end.

He'd never been the sort of person who needed much sleep. And so at Versailles, it had been his custom to return to his apartment at dawn and spend an entertaining hour or two scribbling down the pleasures and the woes of the night's adventure. Writing had made him feel clean and powerful, his pen racing to tell the world his story—or at least the parts of it that his wit could encompass. But now, faced with an audience of one, he was less sure of what he really *did* have to say.

Looking into her eyes—and trying to avoid looking at her hands, her shoulders, her breasts peeping out of the top of her dress—he could only wonder how petty, how frivolous, how exceedingly shallow and trivial she must find him.

Because—right now, in his own mind—the dashing young courtier that he'd been two years ago seemed trivial indeed: a silly, randy, young beast, strutting through mirrored corridors like a turkey cock, prowling the huge château like a fox in a gilded henhouse. His affairs had been exciting, diverting—even more diverting when they'd been cold, selfish, and a bit cruel. But there'd always been a sameness to them. As though he'd been trying to fill some deeper need . . . But he wouldn't speak of *that.* Not right now. Wouldn't even take the time to wonder about it. Another time perhaps.

Right now, he had something else to tell her. Something he was purely and simply proud of.

"Well, you see," he added casually (wondering immediately if his tone had been *too* casual), "Lafayette and the rest of us were considered glamorous heroes when we returned from America, and so it was easy . . ."

Her face lit up.

"So you *did* fight in America after all."

Of course. He should have thought to tell her sooner. He'd almost forgotten how devoted she and her family had been to the American cause. She already knew the names of the battles: Brandywine, Valley Forge, Barren Hill; he held her spellbound for a pleasant few nights, describing what it had been like to fight in them.

Which led them to a discussion of the philosophies and thrilling new ideas at the heart of the American revolt. For she was familiar—at least as familiar as he was—with the words that had lit the sparks of the conflict. Her father's shop had specialized, she told him, in the writings of the great revolutionary thinkers, Messrs. Jefferson and Franklin in particular. And pamphlets, too—piles and piles of brilliant, incendiary pamphlets—even those of the Englishman Tom Paine.

"Papa used to say that if the Americans could accomplish all that—and *they'd* started out as mere Englishmen after all—just think what the people of *France* could do if they set their minds to it. Just imagine how simple, to unseat those useless, petty aristo . . . Ah, but I beg your pardon, M-Monsieur . . . uh . . . Joseph. Of course I didn't mean *you.*"

He'd laughed gallantly and waved away her apologies. "No, of course you didn't mean *me.*"

But the moment stayed with him, keeping him tossing and turning for hours after Baptiste had taken her back to her garret room. It was as he'd suspected all along. She *didn't* respect him. She thought him spoiled, selfish, petty. . . .

Petty. What a vile word, Marie-Laure thought, to describe someone so intelligent, so delightful—and so heroic (fighting in America, no less) as well. She spent all the next day regretting what she'd said and wishing she'd thought before speaking. But she'd become so involved in the discussion that the words had simply slipped out, as though she were back at home, voicing an opinion at the family dinner table. "Petty" was Papa's word for an aristocracy that lived selfishly and thoughtlessly off the industry of the rest of the nation. Papa, Gilles, the Rigauds—everybody at home had used such words, and much worse ones too.

And *their* ways of talking had been mild and measured, cultured and polite, compared to the pungent antiaristocratic invective employed every day in the dessert kitchen.

"They're devils," Arsène insisted flatly. "Every one of them."

"Though in truth I wouldn't mind working for the devil if he were a fair and generous employer," Bertrande had replied.

"Which *they* manifestly are *not,*" Nicolas had added, "but still, they do have the dignity of their position."

"*Ah oui?*" Bertrande had laughed. "Well, it's not the most dignified part of them that we see when we empty their chamber pots."

Bertrand's bon mot had of course led to a series of jokes about which part—or which *parts*—of the aristocracy Marie-Laure was likely to see during her nightly visits, always accompanied by uproarious laughter. As usual, she simply blushed and kept her counsel, though in truth she was becoming a bit tired of it all.

Still—she thought of the Gorgon's meanness, Monsieur Hubert's childishness, the Duc's malevolent rants—in some ways her colleagues had described their masters with perfect accuracy. How could one not feel contemptuous of grown people who were so spoiled and thoughtless?

As if by tacit agreement, though, the servants were relatively gentle in their treatment of the Viscomte. For he at least *tried* to remember to say *please* and *thank you*—to treat you like you might have some feelings of your own, as Louise had put it.

And now, Marie-Laure thought, *I've insulted him myself.*

Not that he'd really care what a scullery maid thought of him.

And yet he did seem colder and more distant for the next few nights, abruptly ceasing to speak of America and beginning a series of linked erotic stories instead. Amusing, rather wicked stories whose plots turned upon which lover could most thoroughly demolish the other's amour-propre.

He didn't narrate these stories, preferring to act them out as little dramas. She marveled at his acting skill. Yes, he told her modestly (a bit *too* modestly perhaps), amateur theatricals had been all the rage at Versailles; he'd been invited to play the male lead in one; the Queen, of course, had acted the female lead.

Anyway, he continued, such stories as he was telling these nights lent themselves well to dramatization, didn't she agree?

She supposed that she did agree. In any case, he was certainly effective, both as himself and as a series of haughty ladies, whispering endearments ("I shall await you breathlessly") and then appending cynical asides ("and you'd better be as good as they say you are, Monsieur"). Mincing and simpering, he managed to look absurdly effete and thrillingly handsome at the same time—his black eyes burning in a livid face that the candlelight had turned white as rice powder.

But even as she laughed, she wondered why he'd want to present himself in such an unflattering mode. It was almost as though he wanted to punish himself—and her too, by making her his witness.

Or perhaps the message lay buried in the prologues that he used to set the scenes. He always insisted on the same point: every woman he'd seduced had been a great beauty, a well-married noblewoman or a notorious courtesan—"which comes to the same thing, you know"—a woman of lofty station, "higher than mine, if possible; I made it a point of pride never to take advantage of a woman of lower birth than myself."

He reiterated these words as though they constituted a principle of egalitarian virtue. And she supposed that in some ways they did. But they hurt nonetheless.

Yes, yes, she wanted to scream. *Yes, I know, Monsieur. Yes, you needn't repeat yourself. For you have made it purely and absolutely clear—transparent as crystal—that you would never lower yourself to touch someone like myself.*

Or that if you did—when *you did, because you* did, *you know, even if* you've *forgotten that you* did *touch me—it was only to protect me. Your embrace, your kisses—yes I know, they were nothing but amateur theatricals. No real passion (well, except on my part); on* your *part it was simple generosity: the benevolence that any liberal aristocrat might extend to a worthy commoner. Nothing more than a momentary instance of noblesse oblige. It was only . . . charity.*

She was beginning to think that her nightly visits weren't worth the anguish they caused her; she might prefer taking her chances with the Duc or the Comte Monsieur Hubert (for surely they'd have forgotten their moments of lustfulness by now). But just when she didn't think she could bear it, he left off the erotic stories as abruptly as he'd begun them.

"Because I've been awfully rude," he said to her one night, "monopolizing the conversation and not giving you a chance to tell me about yourself.

"And anyway," he continued—how lovely, she thought, to see his mischievous grin again—"I'm tired of hearing myself talk."

But she didn't have anything interesting to say, she protested. Her life at home . . . well, he'd already seen the drabness, the sameness of life back home in Montpellier. Days in the bookshop, meals with Gilles and Papa. And Mamma, of course, when Mamma had been alive.

"You saw your parents every day."

"Well, we could hardly help it, could we? You know how tiny the house is . . . um, was. There was barely room for the books, not to speak of the people. We children were always under foot, giving Mamma and Papa headaches. And worse, sometimes . . ."

She had to smile here.

". . . oh dear, I'd almost forgotten. You see, there was a period when Gilles and Augustin were mad for scientific experiments. And they used *our* kitchen, of course. The Rigauds' cook had already chased them out of her domain, but Papa believed in encouraging children's intellectual curiosity, and Mamma believed in the wisdom behind Papa's eccentricities. . . ."

She laughed and so did he. The evening passed quickly and pleasantly. He was a charming listener, she thought later, his quick nods and sudden smiles inspiring her to turn the silliest of domestic mishaps—bad smells and exploding kettles—into knockabout comedy.

She searched her memory for more stories to tell him. He seemed to enjoy hearing them, and she found it soothing to remember Mamma and Papa so happily. And if there had been a note of wistful envy in his comment that "you saw your parents every day," he made sure never to show it again.

Once she even confided some of her plans for the future. He didn't say a great deal, but at least he didn't laugh at her. "Yes," he said quietly, "I think you'd be able to accomplish that. Well, you're a very impressive girl, you know, Marie-Laure."

They became comfortable together, so comfortable that by late August they sometimes simply spent the evenings reading books from his shelves, each of them illuminated by a different halo of candlelight, both of them isolated in their own worlds of the imagination—separated and yet bound together in an easy intimacy.

Every so often one of them would break the silence, commenting upon a passage or even reading it aloud. They argued sometimes, but more often they found themselves in agreement, for they both preferred wit to sentimentality and liked a spare style instead of a florid one.

"You'll enjoy this," he or she would say. And the other *would* enjoy it, too. They laughed sometimes at this uncanny ability to know what each other would like. It was almost a shared instinct, a miraculous correspondence of taste and sensibility.

And yet she'd failed in her quest to discover his hidden stories; in truth he was as much of a stranger as he'd ever been. She was as confounded by his moods now as she'd been in Montpellier, as ignorant of his real emotions as when she'd first begun visiting his room.

A frighteningly attractive stranger, of course: most attractive, perhaps, during these quiet, companionable, readerly evenings, when the sudden flare of a guttering candle on his cheekbone would cause her belly to tremble and her thighs to tighten.

She tried to suppress her body's unruly behavior. But as this quickly proved impossible, she could only endeavor not to become too accustomed to his presence.

These nightly meetings wouldn't go on forever. The Duc would die soon enough; nowadays everybody knew just how ill he really was. And then—well, the gossips in the dessert kitchen agreed that the family would marry Joseph off as quickly as they could, especially since some spectacular offers had recently arrived from Paris.

She tried not to listen to these discussions, but the provisions of the marriage deals—fabulous one-time gifts and princely yearly allowances—lodged unpleasantly in her thoughts nonetheless.

And so now when she visited him, another shadowy entity seemed to materialize in the bedchamber. Was it the inescapable presence of his future wife? More likely, she thought, it was simply the dark shape of his impending departure.

Watching him turn a page or smile at a well-constructed sentence, she'd be seized with sudden vertigo, as if the space of the room were reshaping itself, the short distance between armchair and window seat expanding to become an awful, unbridgeable chasm. The few feet of warm empty air between them could have been the span of an ocean. Because any distance was too long, she reflected, when it interposed itself between two physical bodies that oughtn't to be separated at all.

Bodies that should be touching each other in every way it was possible for bodies to touch.

Not that she could be entirely sure what she meant by such a thought. Of course, she had a few of her own ideas: a few regular nighttime fantasies, accompanied by a host of fascinating questions about how certain acts were actually managed. But how absurd it was, she told herself, even to wonder.

Nothing would come of her lurid imaginings. Nothing except some momentary excitement, followed by sadness, loneliness, and (she blushed here) some very unpleasant physical frustration.

The worst thing, Joseph thought, about these recent weeks of chastity—the longest interlude he could remember—was that everybody thought it quite the opposite. His father took envious pleasure in observing that "at least *somebody* in this house is being satisfied," before launching into another highly embroidered story about his own long-past conquests. And just yesterday, Hubert had looked up from a letter from a marriage broker with a sharp laugh. "Hah, Joseph, *this* one settles enough on you to buy you a *proper* mistress. It'll keep you out of kitchens forever."

"And if it's kitchen grease that stirs his blood?" his father had retorted from the depths of the rattan wheelchair he occupied these days. "Leave the boy alone. He amuses me in the daytime and pounds his little scullery girl at night. There have been worse arrangements in this château."

It wasn't as though Joseph lacked for other opportunities. Flirtatious notes from local ladies arrived with numbing regularity, and he'd heard that the girl plying her trade at the village inn wasn't bad either.

The local ladies presented more complications than he needed, especially during all this tiresome matchmaking. And so he'd turned his thoughts to the girl at the inn, deciding to ride down to the village and get a little relief from her.

He brought protection; not, he supposed, that she'd expect a customer to care about that sort of thing. But he did care: there was always the possibility of disease—and of other dangers as well. And so he'd put several protective sheathes—the best quality he knew how to find, made of pig's bladder—in his waistcoat pocket, just to be ready.

He sat down at a table and ordered a glass of their terrible brandy. The innkeeper could see, though, that he hadn't come down the hill for a drink.

"She'll be ready in a wink of an eye, Monsieur le Viscomte," he'd said, "I'll just go give a yell for her to finish off the fellow she's with. And then she's all yours."

A wink of an eye. Finish him off quickly. Ah yes, very appealing indeed.

He threw some coins onto the table and had galloped halfway back up the hill by the time the innkeeper came out to the courtyard to see what had become of him.

Weeks had slipped by since then. It was the somnolence of life in the country, he told himself. You simply let the weather, the season, the movements of peasants and crops, lull you into a bovine tranquility.

And if he found himself looking forward to each evening with growing eagerness? If he could hardly finish Monsieur Colet's tarts or glaces because he wanted to get back to his bedchamber and scribble away at the story with the gray-eyed heroine and then pace impatiently while listening for her steps in the corridor? Well, what of it?

The physical discomfort was considerable; he hadn't contained himself in this manner since—well, for many years, anyway. Still, he found himself wishing that this frustrating and yet oddly delightful interlude would never end. He'd convinced Hubert to widen the search for a wife, to write to marriage brokers in Paris as well as Provence and Languedoc. Waiting for responses by post would at least slow the process down. Hubert had agreed: a well-married brother-in-law in Paris accorded perfectly with Amélie's plans for social advancement. And now that the Parisian offers were coming in—well, they were so ridiculously detailed that they'd take forever to evaluate.

Meanwhile, there was his father to amuse. Or to distract, for the doctors said that the intermittent pain gnawing at his belly and joints would only increase. Poor old man, with so little to be proud of, so little to comfort him. Hubert and Amélie were pointedly bored by everything he had to say and only interested in what they'd inherit, while the Duchesse—who once had loved him passionately—was only good for wringing her hands and praying over him.

And so it was left to Joseph to devise entertainments: the chess games he won only as often as necessary to remain a credible opponent, the feigned interest in his father's rambling, disjointed stories. He even did magic tricks: as a boy Joseph had spent a week—and all his pocket money—persuading a carnival magician to teach him to make a deck of cards do his bidding and to pull gold coins from behind people's ears. He'd put the card tricks to use at various gaming tables over the years, and he was gratified to discover that he could still make coins appear.

He insisted that the Duc breathe some fresh air every day. So unless the mistral kept them inside, they took a daily walk through the château's gardens, Joseph's tall figure looming over his father's wheelchair.

The centerpiece of all his efforts was a restaging of a comedy the old man had once written and paid a small fortune to have produced at a theater near Versailles. He'd proudly shown the manuscript to Joseph one day; he remembered its hackneyed lines more clearly than what he'd eaten for dinner the night before. Perhaps they could produce it again, the Duc suggested, for the neighboring gentry; perhaps Amélie's carpenters could build a little theater here at the château.

"Perhaps," Joseph had replied, "but let's start with something simpler." He'd taken the manuscript and prepared his own little presentation: at afternoon tea in the library, with the family as audience and himself variously draped in old sheets and curtains, taking all half dozen roles.

"And Marie-Laure, it was absolutely so dreadful that even *I* could tell what a bad writer the Duc was," Louise reported in an awestruck giggle. "But Monsieur Joseph, well, *he* was something to see, the way he changed his expressions and posture for each character. He seemed to become all those different people—one after the other, as though he'd been possessed by their spirits.

"And when he took a sword and played both sides of a duel—once he even made me gasp in fear for him, well, for *one* of him, anyway, and the Gorgon threw me one of her scowls. But anybody could see how happy it made his father to watch him."

Marie-Laure thought of the rehearsal Joseph had staged for her just the night before, whirling about the room in a precisely choreographed duel against his own shadow. He'd been unaccountably nervous about this performance, and so she supposed she was glad it had gone off so well. She'd be sure to congratulate him tonight, though she doubted that he'd care. He was probably more interested in his impending marriage, which had been the overriding topic of conversation this evening at the servants' dinner.

Not that *she* cared about such things. Why should she interest herself in the trivial doings of the tedious family who happened to pay her salary? Why should *anybody?* France was a big country: wasn't there anything to think about besides the nobility's everlasting maneuvers for marriage and position? Anything else for the servants to chatter and squabble over as they took their meals?

Because it was official. The family was choosing between the final candidates—the two ladies in Paris.

"Well, the offers just dwarfed everything they got from *this* region." As always, Nicolas was proud of the extent of his knowledge.

"And it'll be the Marquise de Machery," he added firmly. "Her family is richer, and I overheard the Viscomte laugh and tell his brother that she's an old friend of his. From Versailles, I believe he said."

From Versailles? Marie-Laure kept her eyes fixed on her dinner plate. The meat was unusually tough this evening, she thought. If she didn't chew it carefully she was likely to choke on it.

Bertrande snorted, fairly bursting to tell what she'd overheard yesterday at tea. "Friend or foe, it doesn't matter a whit. The only thing that matters is how much the lady's family is willing to pay for a husband.

"The Marquise's family has offered—this is only for Monsieur Joseph's monthly *clothing* allowance, mind you—a sum that would feed my entire village for a year."

Her self-satisfaction was tinged with resentment. "That's aside from the dowry itself, of course. The Marquise is fat, though, and bookish. Monsieur Hubert said she was a regular blue-stocking. . . ."

Nicolas laughed. "And the other lady is skinny, and suffers from convulsions. But, in both cases, the money's the main thing."

"The Viscomte won't be leaving right away, though," he added. "He'll stay with the Duc for as long as, um, it takes."

The conversation trailed off. None of the servants was looking forward to the day, not so long in the future, when Monsieur Hubert became Duc—and the Gorgon assumed even more power than she had now.

"Anyway," Bertrande had remarked to Marie-Laure as they'd cleared the table, "it's a good thing you're drinking that tea. The family wouldn't enjoy an unwelcome visitor right now."

Marie-Laure had shrugged breezily. "Nor would I. I do have my own future to think about, you know, even if there's no marriage broker looking after *my* affairs."

Damn Bertrande anyway.

And damn the Marquise de Machery, who'd been at Versailles and whose family fortune could have fed half of Provence. And who liked books as well. Somehow she hadn't expected that he'd be marrying a woman who cared for books and reading. She tried to tell herself that it didn't matter. But it did matter; somehow it mattered terribly.

Well, damn Joseph too.

But she was only wasting her energy on him. *Stop it,* she told herself. *He's not a part of your life; he never was.*

Soon he'd be no more than a swirl of memory and yearning, locked tightly away in some secret, untouchable compartment of her thoughts. As tightly as she'd locked him away the first time he'd left her.

Of course, there would be more memories to lock away this time. But she'd manage. She lifted her chin. She'd manage quite well, thank you. She *did* have a future—the future she'd once described to Joseph.

It would seem a lot more possible in December, of course. Because in December, there would be twenty livres, her first half-year's wages. She would save as much of it as she could. And she resolved again to pay the strictest attention to Monsieur Colet's lessons and techniques, always thinking how to adapt them for the sort of small city household that might hire her to cook for them. The château, she thought, had been a fine first step outside the confines of a sheltered childhood. But soon it would be time to move on to a city—Nîmes, perhaps, or Avignon.

A city where she could visit bookshops on her afternoon off, keep up with what people were reading, exercise her professional eye for bindings and typefaces. She vowed to save every *sou* she was paid. And once she had her next job, she'd cadge a few additional sous each month from the household accounts. For Monsieur Colet had taught her *that* as well: petty grifting, he insisted, was as much a part of a cook's repertoire as a good béchamel sauce. She'd been scribbling figures and estimates on bits of scrap kitchen parchment and the totals were modest but reassuring: in a few years she would have enough to open her own bookstall.

It wouldn't be much, of course: just a few square feet near the marketplace; she'd never be able to afford a whole shop. But she'd be surrounded by stimulating urban hubbub and more importantly, she'd be a bookseller again, a citizen of the republic of letters. Most important of all, she'd be away from this oppressive world of petty servants' gossip, adults reduced to squabbling children, careening between the pride and resentment bred of living in the shadow of their masters' lives.

She opened the door at the first sound of Baptiste's knock, ignored his surprise at her curt, unsmiling nod, and followed him swiftly down the silent late-night corridor.

Chapter 10

On the whole, Joseph congratulated himself, his performance had come off quite well. His father, at least, had watched with rapt attention, laughing, cheering, sometimes even reciting along, thrilled to see his words acted out after so many years. His father had thought it a huge success.

And his father's response was what counted, wasn't it?

Of course it was.

After all, nobody else cared.

It would have been foolish to expect Hubert or Amélie to understand how much work he'd put into the little show. And fatuous to hope that his mother might steal a moment from her prayers to witness her younger son's few poor talents in action.

But in fact he *had* expected something. Sadly, secretly, in some unsophisticated place inside of himself, he'd wanted them all to laugh, to admire and enjoy. Perhaps even to appreciate his kindness to the old Duc.

The truth—much as it humiliated him to admit it—was that he'd wanted their attention. Attention or something even better: their understanding, their encouragement.

What had Marie-Laure said? *Papa believed in encouraging children's intellectual curiosity.* He wondered what *that* would have felt like. Having spent the greater part of his early years with no one but servants and a very boring tutor to talk to, he supposed he'd never know.

His parents had often been at Versailles, Hubert away at school. From time to time his mother or father would come home for a visit, and the servants would get very busy, cleaning, cooking, and cursing; eventually he'd be summoned, usually to be shown off for guests: a precocious prattling toy, his hair painstakingly curled and a miniature sword dangling from his side.

He'd almost never seen his parents together; they had separate interests and pursuits—and separate guests, like the series of gorgeous ladies his father had entertained.

"Your little boy's adorable, Alphonse," a lady would coo. "Sweet as my lapdog."

"If he were smaller," one of them had added, "I'd borrow him to wear on my arm like a bracelet."

He'd always known quite well that these ladies were his father's mistresses—the servants' jokes about them were easy enough to understand. And while he hadn't liked the way they'd fawned over his father, he'd certainly preferred the mistresses to the priest who came to give his mother religious instruction. He'd hated his mother's tremulous humility in Père Antoine's presence, her long eyelashes casting shadows over her flushed cheeks, her red lips parted in what she must have supposed was devotion.

He'd wanted to kill Père Antoine. But he was too afraid of him to dare misbehaving. So he simply recited some verses he'd memorized, bowed, received the priest's hurried commendations, and backed away, staring at the large, ivory, manicured hand laid so possessively over one of his mother's small white ones. "And now, my dear Madame, we will sequester ourselves for your, ah, confession. . . ."

The double doors would close upon the tableau of his mother kneeling on an embroidered stool, the priest looming in front of her, his hands invisible under the even folds of his heavy silk gown. It looked as though she were worshipping at the foot of a black marble pillar topped with alabaster, a look of smug anticipation cleanly carved into the priest's cruel, handsome face.

Joseph would try to find a hiding place after Père Antoine's visits. He didn't really mind the servants' jokes about his father's playmates, but he didn't like hearing what they had to say about his mother's confessor.

He'd been less a child, he thought now, than a house pet—clever, pretty, and pathetically eager for affection. A witness to things a child shouldn't witness, he'd been brought in to confer innocence on the proceedings. He'd been quite a valuable little asset, all in all.

And now he was going to be sold to the highest bidder.

Which had *really* been what they'd wanted to talk about this afternoon at tea. His father had barely begun to applaud and to call out his bravos when Hubert launched into his own song of praise—about the two potential wives from Paris.

The lawyers, he announced, had deemed the Machery offer a better one.

"But they advised us not to play our cards too quickly," Hubert continued. "Keep them bidding a little longer; we can probably squeeze another thousand out of them. Amazing, isn't it, what those old bloodlines of ours are worth?"

He grinned sourly as he poured a bit of Armagnac into his tea. "Especially when a lady's main charm is her family's money. Of course, the Machery family is a pretty ancient one too. But I guess nobody wanted that fat old Marquise without a fortune attached to her."

His wife chose to ignore the opening part of his comment.

"I've heard that their house in Paris is magnificent," she said. "The art, the furnishings . . . it will be a delight to be received there."

"Especially," she turned to Joseph with a sisterly smile, "because we shall be seeing *you* surrounded by all that splendor. We'll come to visit you and your wife often, dear Joseph."

And so it went. Hubert relishing the money, Amélie the family connections, his mother nodding and smiling, promising to produce the precious necklace she'd been saving all these years for Joseph's bride. Worn out by the excitement of seeing his play, his father snored in his wheelchair.

I was a damned fool, Joseph told himself, to expect anything else. From *them,* at any rate.

He paced his room, too agitated this evening even to write.

And if he were to try to describe his feelings to Marie-Laure? Never.

It would mean opening the Pandora's box of his emotions—anger, petulance, and confusion would come flying out; she'd see what he *really* was like inside—and how powerless he was over his destiny. Better to keep a tight lid on all that, maintain a little dignity.

And anyway, her life had its own challenges. Remarkable how strong-willed she was; she actually intended to work her way back into the world of bookselling, all from the pittance they were paying her to scrub and scour the pots.

"I'll sell Papa's spectacles too," she'd told him one evening. "They're good ones, from Amsterdam; I know they'll bring in something. Of course, then I won't have them to remind me of him—but I'll know how proud he'd be if he could see me through them, and that will be just as good."

How extraordinary that he could admire her as he did, even while wanting her so fiercely that it went beyond pain. It wasn't supposed to work like that, he thought.

Hearing her describe her plans for the future, he'd begun to make some of his own. Not as brave as hers, but creditable enough. Jeanne de Machery was a good friend. If he had to marry someone he didn't love, she was the ideal candidate; she had her own complicated life, her own secret reasons for marrying. They'd joke about their situation. They'd be honest with each other. They'd have civilized conversations over breakfast, reviewing the latest talk at the political salons, where the best of the Parisian upper classes argued about how to make France a better, fairer place. And then they'd part for the day, each in pursuit of separate interests—they'd part, knowing that they wouldn't see each other until the next day's breakfast.

He'd renew old acquaintances, join Lafayette's antislavery society. He should have done it years ago; having fought for the rights of the American colonists, he had a responsibility to work for the freedom of their black slaves. He'd reconnect with the people he'd disappointed at Versailles: returning from America a hero, he'd squandered his glory by becoming a fop and a libertine. All because of some obscure angers and long-ago shames that shouldn't matter any more.

He'd be all right, he thought, once he was gone from here and mercifully free of his family.

Gone from here and—most likely—never to see Marie-Laure again.

He stopped pacing, to allow himself to feel the pain of that last thought.

Well, at least he could be proud that he'd stood by his principles. He hadn't taken advantage of her, hadn't harmed her. As once he *had* done, to another innocent . . .

He raised his chin. *Listen. Aren't those her steps in the corridor?*

He dove into the armchair, hurriedly opening the volume on the table. A collection of American political writing; the editor had chosen to call it *The Pursuit of Happiness.* Rather an annoying phrase, he thought, when one was being denied the freedom to pursue one's own marital happiness.

But the ideas in the book were still interesting and worthy of discussion. Yes, he'd keep the conversation to books and ideas tonight. A peaceful, intellectual evening would be best.

The only problem with this scheme was that *her* mood was anything but peaceful or intellectual. He could see it as soon as she walked through the door. The exaggerated straightness of her back, the tilt of her chin, the flush in her cheeks and opacity of her usually limpid eyes gave her away immediately. She looked as she had last winter, when he'd told her she should stick to reading what was on the page.

"Are you tired?" he asked hopefully. "Have they worked you too hard in the kitchen?"

She shook her head.

"I'm used to the work," she said, "and today was actually rather pleasant.

"We learned how to make madeleines," she added. "Fashionable little teacakes, Monsieur Colet says they're quite the rage among the gentry. I imagine you ate a few of them this afternoon."

He hadn't eaten anything.

"My father enjoyed the performance," he offered.

She nodded. "Louise told me."

"The maid who served the tea and cakes," she explained with rather exaggerated patience. "The girl with the misshapen mouth."

"I know who Louise is," he answered quietly.

His jaw tightened. *Of course* Marie-Laure knew how his show had come off. An aristocrat's life was always a performance, acted out in front of the same merciless audience who washed your soiled linen. What other entertainments did servants have, after all?

He was usually so conscious of that all-seeing gaze, too. But somehow he'd managed to trick himself into forgetting that *she* was part of that audience.

And that she obviously knew about his family selling him on the marriage market. Perhaps even about their threat to imprison him.

His stomach clenched. In the kitchen they would have been discussing his marriage, as well as making the same kinds of scabrous jokes they'd made about his mother and Père Antoine. Marie-Laure had doubtless laughed at the jokes—and at *him* and his ridiculous situation too. Perhaps, since she knew him so well, she'd even contributed a few bon mots to the proceedings.

She relaxed against the cushions, her breath coming more evenly now as her muscles uncoiled. She watched the candlelight cast shadows on his cheek. One of the candles flared suddenly; the smell of the singed wick prickled her nostrils.

He looked sad, tired, perhaps even a bit angry. She regretted that she hadn't thought to say something nice to him.

For he *had* been a dutiful son all these weeks, sensitive and imaginative, caring and devoted. Even Gilles, who thought all aristocrats were heartless parasites, would have applauded the loving consideration Joseph had shown his father.

She'd say something now.

Something comforting and encouraging.

But as soon as she opened her mouth to speak, she could feel the words coming out all wrong.

"And your intended wife," she heard herself saying in a sharp, querulous voice. "The Marquise de Machery. Does *she* like acting and theater?"

If she'd rehearsed all day, she thought, she couldn't have chosen a worse question to ask him. She watched in horrified fascination as his mouth compressed to a thin line and curved downward into a sneer. His face became a mask of aristocratic hauteur, his black eyes suddenly gone cold.

"Yes," he said, "she does like actors." His voice was calm, emotionless. "She's rather a patron of the theater, in fact, and has got some intimates in the Comédie-Française."

He shrugged.

"Well, she knows actors *and* actresses, of course. Which will be rather a help to me when I look around for a suitable mistress. Because I'll be able to afford the best . . ."

"I suppose so," she said.

"Don't interrupt," he replied quickly. "It's impertinent for a servant to interrupt."

She stared at him.

"Yes, I'll buy the most expensive mistress I can find. Of course, you and the rest of the crew down in the kitchen already know about the fabulous clothing allowance I'll have. It's almost as good as the King's brother's. And if we hold out a little longer, wait for a better settlement, who can say what riches they'll shower on me and my family? Quite impressive all in all, don't you think?"

He's dueling with his shadow, she thought.

She opened her mouth to reply but no sound came out.

"It's also impertinent," he told her, "not to answer when your master asks you a question."

She took a breath.

"And what," she asked, "will you actually *do* with your life in Paris?"

He raised an eyebrow. "An aristocrat doesn't *do* anything, Marie-Laure. But I thought you already knew that. An aristocrat simply *lives*, brilliantly and gracefully, wasting his time and spending France's money. You told me that yourself—told me how selfish, how petty . . ."

"Stop it," she cried. "You *know* I'm sorry that I said that. It's just something Papa used to say, a general observation about the aristocrats who patronized our shop. But Papa hadn't met you. And you're *not* like that."

"On the contrary," he snapped. "Your esteemed Papa was quite right about me. Because I'm *exactly* that selfish and petty. Worse, if truth be told—but that's a story I think I'll keep to myself.

"And I'll go on being that way. I'll enjoy it too. I'll buy the most expensive mistress in Paris, and when she cheats on me I'll dabble in more esoteric pleasures—but only as a diversion—and then I'll toss her out and move on to the next, even more stunning, mistress. I'll eat good food, drink expensive wine, sleep with beautiful women on perfectly laundered linen. No fleas in *my* bed, thank you."

She gasped.

Now you've done it, Joseph. Badly phrased, that comment about fleas. Everybody knows that typhus is spread by flea bites. And typhus killed her father.

She was trembling.

He looked down at his hands and discovered that they were shaking as well. He balled up his fists.

Should he apologize?

No, he was still too angry. Too ashamed. Too paralyzed by the skewed emotions that had seized him.

Whatever he was feeling, though—at least it wasn't desire.

You're a liar, Joseph. Mixed in with all the other uncontrollable feelings was the strongest desire he'd ever felt for anyone.

She was sitting up very straight, and staring at him with eyes that had dulled to the color of lead. Her freckles were dark on her pale cheeks.

He stared back at her, feeling his face contort, his entire body stiffen with rage.

No, not only with rage. It wasn't rage that was doing its work, down there between his legs.

It was humiliating. It was—*mon Dieu,* it was fantastic. And she was so close by, just a step or two away. He need only grasp her shoulders . . .

She was speaking now, in so low a voice that he had to lean forward to catch it.

"Yes, perhaps he was right about you after all. And perhaps I was wrong. Wrong to like and trust you and to hope that you might earn a place for yourself in the world. Like my papa did. Or Gilles or Augustin. Or any decent, ordinary man I might love."

She'd slid off the window seat and was standing in front of it. He could probably reach out an arm and pull her to him. But he didn't. He sat still, his hands still balled into fists.

"Any *man,*" her voice was disdainful, "with the self-respect to try to make the world a better place than he'd found it. But I guess *you* wouldn't know about such things. And I'm only sorry . . ."

Her voice caught. She paused to collect herself, but she continued to stare at him with eyes like storm clouds.

He hadn't known her eyes could look like that. There was heat lightning behind the clouds.

You've lost her, Joseph.

You never had her, idiot.

"I'm sorry," she said, "that I ever left my old way of life. Sorry I ever met you. Or wanted you."

She looked away for a moment.

She had *wanted him. He* hadn't *merely imagined it. And now he'd ruined any chance he had of . . . of* what, *Joseph?*

"They'll put me in prison if I don't go along with this marriage." The words slipped out before he could stop them.

She touched his shoulder. So quickly and lightly that he didn't believe it was happening.

"I know," she said softly. "I'm sorry, Joseph."

And then she was gone.

She couldn't remember how that awful night had come to an end. Or even how the next day had begun. But she didn't suppose there'd been anything special about it; everything must have gone as it usually did.

Baptiste must have led her back through the dark corridors and up the stairs. She must have tiptoed into her garret room, slipping silently into bed beside a snoring Louise.

The sun must have risen this morning, she thought. She and Louise must have washed and dressed. She suspected that she'd drunk some coffee before getting to work, though her throat was so clogged with unshed tears that she couldn't have eaten anything.

She saw his taut, white face in the bottom of every pot she scrubbed.

Why had he wanted to hurt her so deeply?

And why had she responded so harshly? It should have been obvious how aching and needy he'd been, how furious and alone. At the moment when he'd most needed comfort she'd responded by telling him that he wasn't a man that she could respect. He'd never want to see her again.

Well, he shouldn't have made that horrid joke about the fleas. He shouldn't have pretended to be everything she loathed—and everything he loathed as well.

The next pot had so much grease burnt onto it that it took all her concentration to get it clean. She grimaced with bitter satisfaction as she put it aside to dry.

Of course, she thought now, it would be stupid to delude herself about who had actually set the evening's combative mood. She remembered her stiff posture, the aggrieved look on her face as she'd marched into his bedchamber, her curt answer when he'd asked whether her work had been too hard.

But that was different. I was angry at him because he's leaving me. And I didn't want him to know how much it hurts.

I've ruined everything, she thought as she brushed her hair that evening. *He'll never want to see me again. It's hopeless, impossible. Baptiste won't be knocking on my door tonight. Or ever again.*

She continued, nonetheless, to brush out the tangles, to toss the ringlets down her back. *I'll go to bed in a minute.* In five. In ten. She smoothed her skirt and straightened her apron.

Baptiste's tap was so soft she couldn't hear it at first. Belatedly, she flew to open the door.

Monsieur Joseph's apologies, Baptiste told her, but he'll be spending tonight at his father's bedside.

For the Duc's illness had taken a definite turn for the worse.

Chapter 11

He remained at his father's bedside for the next three nights and days, with the Duchesse, who wept continually, and Monsieur Hubert, who dozed over his brandy-laced coffee. The Duc was in pain a good deal of the time. He was angry and rebellious—especially, according to his valet Jacques, when the Duchesse would begin the next round of prayers for his soul.

"He told them he wasn't interested in the next world, that he was too angry at *this* world, which had never admired him and never would."

"Well, *I'll* admire him," Jacques told the group in the dessert kitchen, "if he leaves me a year or two's wages, to tide me over while I look for a new job. For I can already see that bitch Madame Amélie sizing up my skinny arse and wondering who else will fit into my livery breeches—to save her the expense of buying somebody else a new pair this year."

Nicolas nodded. "We're going to see a lot of changes around here, once that harpy takes over."

"Those she doesn't fire," Bertrande added dolefully, "to replace with staff from her parents' mansion in Avignon."

If any servant were likely to be replaced, Marie-Laure thought, it would probably be the irksomely pretty scullery maid whom the

Duc and his older son had tried to visit—to everybody's great amusement.

And if by chance she weren't fired, there would be the new Duc's advances to worry about. She knew she could defend herself; well, she'd made forcemeat of Jacques, hadn't she? Fighting off Monsieur Hubert would be easy: he wasn't very big and he was usually drunk. But the pleasure of seeing him with a black eye (or worse) would be short-lived. She'd be dismissed instantly, and without her twenty livres half-year wages. She could only hope he'd lost interest in her by now.

In truth, though, she was grateful for these worries, for they were more bearable than the dumb, dazed panic that engulfed her whenever she tried to imagine her life without Joseph in it.

The funeral was adorned with every pious detail money could buy: the army of paupers carrying candles, the deafening tolling of church bells. The servants followed at the back of the procession, all of them maintaining a very sorrowful demeanor, until it was time to scurry back to prepare the sumptuous supper the new Duchesse had ordered for the local worthies who'd attended the ceremony. All Marie-Laure had seen of Joseph was the back of his head, towering above the other members of the procession, just behind the coffin.

"He'll stay for a month of mourning," Louise told her, "and then he'll escort his mother back to the convent."

"And then?" Marie-Laure prompted her.

"And then," Louise hesitated, "oh, just some legal business that they're working on . . . I don't really understand it, these nobles are always petitioning the King for something . . . imagine my family petitioning the King not to conscript my brothers to build his roads during the harvest season, when they're really needed on the farm. Oh yes, *we* might as well petition to raise the dead or stop the mistral. I don't know anything else, Marie-Laure."

"Yes you do," Marie-Laure said. "What is it?"

Louise's voice dropped to a harsh, sad whisper. "They've decided to settle it quickly. He's going to Paris, with Monsieur

Hubert—I mean the Duc—and with the new Duchesse too. He's going to be married."

Marie-Laure nodded, her face expressionless, her chest as tight as if it were bound with steel bands.

"Come to bed, Marie-Laure," Louise said.

But she found the air in the little attic room impossible to breathe—and Louise's snore absolutely insupportable. She slept fitfully, trying not to fling herself about the bed. And at the first gray dawn, she stole down the stairs and across the fields to the river, where it would be cool.

She stood on the hillside and looked down at the water. It was not really so much a river at this point as a brook, gurgling as it swept over the rocks in its path. The autumn sun was just beginning to show over the eastern hills, its slanted rays outlining each needle of the pine trees and illuminating the little yellow leaves of the poplars.

About a mile to her right, the brook met up with other streams, and the river widened, flowing through fields and farmyards, past barns and hayricks and noisy squadrons of ducks and geese. Marie-Laure turned to the left, through a small wood, where the water formed pools bordered by ferns. A large, flat rock overlooked one of the pools. She'd sat there and dreamed away many a spare moment; it would be a good place for weeping as well. This morning, she intended to weep until she couldn't weep any more.

The path through the woods was stony and narrow; she had to watch where she stepped. Tiny lizards skittered from rocks that the sun was just beginning to warm up. *The sun will be shining on my own rock,* she thought.

She'd discovered this spot during her first month at the château, reveling in the stillness and solitude before hurrying back for breakfast and the day's work. Not recently, though; these past few weeks she'd been staying so late in Joseph's room that she could barely drag herself out of bed in the mornings.

The fluttering wings of a startled grouse distracted her attention; she almost slipped on a loose stone. Her rock was just around the bend. She steadied herself and hurried toward it.

To discover that someone had gotten there before her.

Wide shoulders strained against his dark waistcoat; his silky black hair threatened to escape from its queue. When he turned at the sound of her footsteps she could see that his eyes were moist and his mouth freighted with grief.

"Oh," she stammered, "I'm so sorry. I don't want to bother you."

He tossed a stone into the stream, skipping it lightly across the water's surface.

"No," he said, "please stay. There's room for both of us, I think, if I move over a little. Yes, there, voilà, please stay."

She slipped timidly beside him. Yes, if she situated herself very carefully there would be just enough room. She concentrated on the slender margin of space between his body and hers; she gazed at his profile, dark against the sunlit water, and at a stray wisp of black hair fluttering in the breeze. Her attention thus monopolized, her only problem was remembering to breathe.

They sat silently as the sun crept higher and the water's surface turned from silver to palest gold.

"I'm . . . I'm . . ."

"Sorry," one of them, both of them, stammered.

"I . . ."

". . . was rude, thoughtless . . ."

". . . didn't mean to hurt you . . ."

". . . that night."

She couldn't identify which words had issued from his mouth and which from hers, but it didn't seem to matter.

Another stone skimmed across the pond, four hops before it dropped below the surface.

"My father taught me to skip stones," he said, "on a spring morning, right at this spot."

He rose abruptly, startling a rabbit that had been watching them from the underbrush.

"Let's walk," he said, reaching down a hand to help her from her seat. "Shall we?"

Silently, in single file, they threaded their way along the sun-dappled path. But she had no memory of beginning to walk; she had no thoughts or feelings at all except in the hand he'd held, his touch rippling along her nerves' trajectories. And when the forest path widened to allow them to walk side by side it seemed the most natural thing in the world for him to take her hand again. They stepped into the clearing.

"I thought I had nothing but bad, angry memories of him," he said. "But now that he's dead, I'm suddenly recollecting other things."

He reached into a pocket to scatter some breadcrumbs for the ducks.

"Mostly he was away. But there were a few weeks once . . . I was seven . . . he and my mother were both visiting the château, and I got scarlet fever. And astonishingly, my mother sent the maids away and stayed with me all night. Do you know, it was the only time I've ever seen her with her hair tumbling down her shoulders, not combed and puffed, powdered and swept up. I thought she looked like a saint, and I remember my father standing behind her, stroking her hair. And she reached up and held his hand, while she continued to smile her sweet, worried smile at me."

His voice, which had been soft and bright with wonder, shaded into dark irony.

"I suspect that my father was reading Rousseau at the time, and that it had inspired him to give the domestic life a try. Perhaps he wanted some novelty; he'd sampled every other pleasure. He even told me to call him 'Papa,' though I'd been raised to address him and my mother as 'Monsieur' and 'Madame.'

"And when I was well enough to walk outside, he and I would come here, and feed the ducks, and talk. It seemed to me that we discussed everything I'd ever wondered about—from the heroes of history and mythology (he had a harebrained notion that our family could trace our lineage from both Charlemagne and Aeneas), to whether you could train a duckling to follow you around as though you were its mother."

The sun, rapidly climbing in the sky, shone brightly down on the hayricks. Marie-Laure could see peasants at work, dotting the hilly fields around them. She'd miss breakfast if she didn't hurry.

"And so, while I know as clearly as anyone," Joseph said, "that he was a fop and a scoundrel and a wastrel and a failure—and rather a buffoon in his later years as well—I can also remember those walks by the river, and our talks, and . . . and skipping stones. And that spring, when I was seven, *I* thought"—his voice began to tremble—"that he was the wisest, funniest person in the world."

She looked up at him, losing herself for a moment in the sorrow of his eyes, and then they both looked away, walking on in bashful silence.

"I can imagine," he added, "how it must have hurt him for the only person who'd ever admired him to renounce and desert him.

"He was also kind to my mother that spring," he added a few moments later. "I know, because she dropped her everlasting praying for a while, and some of her other interests as well. For about a month, her confessor didn't come to visit us. And my father didn't bring his mistresses home either—though I think he still ran after servants and the girls from the village."

"Did your mother know he was doing that?" Marie-Laure asked.

"She must have," he said. "But you see, I think that she actually loved him. That month was as close as she ever came to having him for herself; my guess is that she simply decided to cherish that little bit of time together with him, and to forget all the rest."

"Do you think that was stupid of her?" she asked.

"I don't know," he answered. "I couldn't make that decision for someone else."

They stared at each other, his eyes bright with unspoken questions, hers shining with a new confidence.

The path took a fork. She pressed his hand, guiding him away from the river and toward an empty barn. They stopped and peered in, at the dust motes turned to gold by sunbeams streaming down through a hole in the roof to the straw heaped on the floor.

"You have to get to work," Joseph murmured.

"Not quite yet," she lied, leading him inside.

His kiss was gentle, tentative at first. She put her arms around his waist, and he sighed and pulled her to him.

"I promised myself I wouldn't do this," he whispered. "I've driven myself half mad with my resolve not to touch you. And there's still time to stop. Are you sure it's what you want, Marie-Laure?"

Never surer of anything. But she'd show him. Reaching her hands to his shoulders, she gently moved him backward and onto the pile of straw, dropping to her knees beside him. Lucky she'd worn Gilles's breeches so often, she thought, because if she knew nothing else about this business, she knew the pattern of the buttons, and how to undo them. Just one more little pull, *voilà*, and . . .

"You're sure?" He put his hand on hers to stop her from going any further. "You have to say you're sure."

The words wouldn't come. His hand was tight about her wrist; in another moment he'd pull himself away.

Peasants shouted in the fields. Flies buzzed. Life hurtled on.

"Yes," she whispered.

"Ah." He removed his hand and she pulled open the last button.

"Yes yes yes yes yessss."

Her last *yes* shaded to a gasp of surprise. She hadn't quite expected the length and breadth of flesh suddenly freed from his breeches. Naively, she supposed, she'd pictured something more decorous, less rampant. Less thrilling. On sudden impulse, she leaned over to kiss the dark, purplish head atop the long, erect shaft—like a delicious wild mushroom, she thought, swollen after a rainstorm. She licked a salty drop of moisture from its tip, and traced a slow, adventurous finger along the sort of seam on the shaft's underside, watching awestruck as he continued to grow and harden.

He made a throaty, incomprehensible sound, abruptly pulling away from her and sitting up.

Her boldness disappeared; she froze with embarrassment.

"Oh no," she gasped. "Oh, I'm so sorry. Oh dear, did I do something terrible? Perhaps people don't actually *do* such things with their tongues, but you looked so . . . so lovely, and I just wanted . . ."

He'd taken something out of his waistcoat pocket. It was whitish, translucent. She watched in fascination as he rolled the sheath down over his penis. Ah yes, Gilles had explained that to her. He'd made it sound quite the manly self-sacrifice too.

And it's a sacrifice for me as well. Timidly, longingly, she touched the stretchy stuff that contained his flesh and separated him from her.

"It's important, Marie-Laure . . ."

Though hardly foolproof, Gilles had warned her. Still, it was good of him to think of taking such precautions. She should probably thank him for it.

But there wasn't time to thank him; there wasn't time to say anything, because now it was she who lay on her back on the straw, and he who was rising above her, his hands lifting her skirt and parting her legs. It was happening very quickly now, the pressure of his thighs on hers, his entry into her, his mouth on her mouth, her cheeks, her neck. It was moving so fast, it was taking too long; it was lovely, it was confusing; she felt a marvelous opening and grasping somewhere inside. And then pressure, too much pressure. And too soon, only pain.

He held her tightly, licking the tears from her face.

"Oh, my dear," he said, "I wouldn't have planned it that way for you, but you took me rather by surprise, you know."

"*I* . . . took . . . *you?*"

He nodded.

"I've never been seduced quite so expeditiously before. It was all I could do not to make a complete fool of myself."

He sat up, smiling at her astonishment. "Such a determined mouth," he murmured, tracing her lips with his little finger and smiling as her lips parted and the tip of her tongue became visible.

Light as thistledown, he touched the tip of his own tongue to hers.

"And yes," he added, "people *do* do such things with their tongues. They do it all the time, though not nearly so charmingly as you did. But you'll see."

She managed to return his smile. "Well, I didn't think it would be quite so easy. After a month of your very decent and honorable resolve not to touch me, after all."

He laughed. "And after all the time we've spent together in one or another bedchamber. Well, maybe it needed to happen on neutral territory."

He'd undone the white cravat from his neck and was gently wiping the blood from her thighs. "Careful, don't move, or you'll get blood on your skirt. Yes, it's all right, nothing stained—somehow we managed to get all the cloth tucked out of the way."

He leaned over and kissed the spot he'd just cleaned. It was a new sort of kiss, she thought, her eyes widening and her lips beginning to tremble. So light, and yet so lingeringly present. He lifted his head, smiled ruefully as he scanned her face.

"I was selfish a few minutes ago," he said. "I couldn't stop myself—well, after all those weeks of stopping myself, you know . . . I didn't give you time, didn't help you be ready.

"And so I fear I've given you the wrong idea of what it's all about. It's not about a gentleman driving into you as though with a battering ram. Well, not entirely. It's also about what you're feeling right now. But next time—next time you'll see." He kissed her along the insides of her thighs and she shuddered with wonder.

She reached her hand to caress his bare throat, almost drunk with the pleasure of touching him whenever she wanted to, now she had the right to, now that this was no longer a fiction. She tucked an unruly lock of hair behind his ear.

He'd rolled the sheath off himself and wrapped it in a handkerchief. She touched him curiously. His penis was smaller, more relaxed now but still energetic—it jumped and twitched to the touch of her fingers, especially as she became bolder and began to trace the shape of the dark sac at the base of the shaft.

She smiled to draw a long, trembling sigh from him, before he lifted her hand from between his legs and brought it to his lips, kissing each of her fingers in turn.

"I've got a little time before I have to get back," he said. "And you? When do you have to get back?"

She grinned, almost proudly, as she rose to her feet. "Oh," she said, kissing the top of his head, "I needed to be back at least an hour ago."

He grasped both her hands.

"I love you, Marie-Laure," he said. "My God, all those evenings together and I've never told you I love you."

"I love you too." Telling him was almost as thrilling as touching him, hearing it from his lips as wonderful as kissing him.

"Tonight," he called, as she began to walk, a bit unsteadily, up the road and back to the kitchen.

"Tonight, *mon amour.*"

Monsieur Colet was furious and Robert was deeply disappointed in her. One simply was not late (more than an hour late!) for work in the kitchen.

She could, she supposed, have made up some sort of excuse—she hadn't been feeling well, or (perhaps more convincingly) that Monsieur Joseph had been most importunate this morning and insisted she stay with him. But she didn't. She remained uncharacteristically silent, not wanting to disturb the delicate balance of emotion and sensation within herself by saying anything at all.

Her punishment was to stay after supper and scour the fireplace's iron heat reflectors. It was filthy work, and it gave her no time, before Baptiste came to get her, to change her dress. All she could do was get the grease and soot off her hands and run a brush through her hair.

Baptiste's expression was the same as ever—knowing, reserved, with an ironic edge that intended no harm.

She nodded cordially. Did she look any different, she wondered? She could tell as little from Baptiste's face as from her own reflection in the small, tarnished mirror. But she must look different. She *was* different.

Everything was different now.

Chapter 12

He wore the same embroidered dressing gown and slippers he'd worn all the other nights she'd visited him. But while he usually kept the gown open, revealing his shirt and breeches, tonight it was tightly sashed around his slender waist, and Marie-Laure knew he had nothing on beneath it. His hair, loosed from its queue, fell to his shoulders. His lips curved slightly; the curves and hollows of his neck shimmered as he breathed; his opaque black eyes glittered like those of a wary forest animal.

She walked slowly toward him, stopping before she quite reached him. Overwhelmed by his stillness and abashed by her shabby clothes, she was suddenly mortified by the streaks of soot on her stockings.

How lovely his dressing gown was, she thought; its dark gray velvet was embroidered in sinuous patterns of purple and metallic gold. How sad that she had nothing beautiful to wear when she came to him.

He shook his head. "It doesn't matter, Marie-Laure. Truly it doesn't."

Had her thoughts really been so transparent?

But then he must also know how much she wanted him.

He reached behind her waist to unhook her dress, gently lifting it over her head and tossing it onto the floor. Her stays tumbled off when he tugged at the knot in the laces; her petticoat floated after them. Clearly, he was as familiar with the ties and fastenings of her clothes as she'd been with the buttons of his breeches. When he knelt before her to take off each shoe, to slowly unroll each stocking, she put her hands into his thick black hair, letting it trickle through her fingers like water as he bent to kiss each instep.

He rose quickly, moving back a few steps. She willed herself to keep her eyes open and her hands at her sides, as his eyes slowly traveled up and down her naked body, his mouth curving into a broad smile.

"Oh yes." It was more a breath than an utterance, a mist of warm air like a veil around her flesh. She could feel the shape of her body—the roundness, the hollows—in the movements of his eyes and the currents of his breathing. It felt rather a nice shape: too short in stature, of course, but quite all right on the whole.

Of course she knew that she was pretty. People had always told her so; clearly it hadn't only been her cleverness about books that had attracted a certain percentage of Papa's small clientele. In consequence, she'd always been a bit contemptuous of her appearance, preferring to dismiss the subject, and pretending not to care.

She cared now, though; she wanted to be pretty, for him.

He put out an arm, to lift her to the bed.

"No," she said.

He raised his eyebrows.

"Not yet."

The corners of his mouth twitched.

She reached for his sash, made a lucky guess as to what sort of knot he'd tied, and pulled gently.

He shrugged his shoulders out of the heavy velvet dressing gown, kicking it out of the way as it fell to the floor.

He stood easily, his weight lightly balanced on slender, muscular legs. His face was alight with mischief. Could she survey his body with the same ease and boldness she saw in his eyes?

Could she move her eyes casually and confidently over his shoulders, his torso? Or would she simply gape, dumbfounded, at the taut lines of his muscles, the tracings of fine black hair on his belly? At his flat pink nipples and the heavy sex rising from the thick wiry darkness between his legs?

She couldn't pretend to be casual; it was all too new, too astonishing. Her eyes widened and a gasp escaped her parted lips.

"*Mon Dieu,*" she whispered, "how beautiful you are."

"And you, Marie-Laure, and you." He was whispering too. He'd come closer; his chest just grazed the tips of her breasts. He pushed her heavy hair behind her ears, holding it at her nape while he brushed his lips against her earlobe. His other hand traced the curve of her spine, lightly at first, but holding her with increasing firmness, slowly pulling her to him. She could feel the insistent swell of him against her belly. She pushed back shyly, rotating her hips forward and back, to stroke him. How nice it felt, to move like that.

But now he was lifting her up; she wrapped her legs around his waist, moaning softly at the feel of his penis arched along the furrow of her bottom.

She thought he'd hurry, she'd imagined him as eager to get on with it as he'd been this afternoon. She remembered overhearing jokes Gilles and his friends made, about there being a moment when one was not able to wait any longer.

But Joseph seemed quite capable of waiting.

He carried her to the bed, sat down beside her, reached for something on the bed table, and handed it to her. Another of those sheathes, she realized.

"This time," he said, "*you* put it on me."

Which meant that she could touch him there, she realized. She'd wanted to since he'd taken off his robe. But her experience this afternoon had made her shy. Was there a decorum, she wondered, about where you could put your hands, a sort of dance pattern to what you might touch first and what second?

Or—an astonishing thought—was everything simply and gloriously permitted? Was it all right to do whatever you liked? Whatever gave you pleasure and—how thrilling—however you could give pleasure in return?

She examined the thin membrane, deciding that one put it on

as one did a very delicate stocking. Slowly and gently, she stretched it over the head of his penis.

His lips trembled as she smoothed it down over him. Lovely to make that happen, and it was wonderful, too, how he continued to swell at the touch of her fingers. But how sad to have to hide him away like that.

"Lie down," he told her.

There was a heavy candelabrum on the table. He moved it closer to them, and opened the bed curtain wider.

"I want as much light as possible," he murmured. He brushed his lips against her breasts, her neck, her belly. It took her a moment to realize that he was tracing the path of the freckles on her skin, and trying to kiss every one of them.

She would have laughed if her quick, ragged breath had allowed her to.

"I've wondered about this for so long." He smiled before bending his head again, his tongue lapping at all the little coppery spots on her body like a cat eating up spilled cream.

He worked his way downward. Marie-Laure had just a few freckles near her belly and thighs, but he paid special attention to each one, his silky hair flowing against her skin in the wake of his lingering, inquisitive kisses.

He moved upward now, his lips traveling to her breast again, his rough cat's tongue flicking the nipple. She could see his wide, naked shoulders above her; she arched her back to try to touch the length of his trunk, the heaviness of his sex, with her trembling belly. She felt a stab of longing between her legs, just before (but how had he known to do it just exactly then?) he parted her thighs with his hand, opening and exploring her, caressing her with small, patient, delicate strokes. In her mind's eye, she saw his hands—his long, strong, slender fingers. She felt them moving, searching. Stopping now. And suddenly all her senses converged upon a single point, her world, her universe, balanced upon his fingertip.

"Ah, there you are," he murmured as her flesh stiffened to meet him, his finger a tiny torch setting her center aflame while the rest of her body seemed to melt, to moisten, like sugar bubbling in a copper pot. She heard herself moan. She knew she was ready.

He lowered himself onto her, his thighs around hers and the hair on his chest prickling her breasts. He raised himself again, his hands cradling her hips and lifting her as he entered her.

She could see anxiety in his eyes. He didn't want to hurt her this time. He wanted it to be delicious for her.

It is *delicious*, she tried to whisper. *Yes, yes, I'm beginning to understand*, she tried to call. But her whisper became a gasp and her call a sigh. And the gasps and ragged, wrenching sighs grew deeper with every confident arc he traced within her.

He rose above her onto his knees, onto his toes it seemed, before each thrust; she strained to open, to widen, to grasp and contain the entire miraculous length and thickness of him before each slow, teasing stroke outward. But oh! he went so far away each time, almost, it seemed, to her vulva's swollen, wet outer lips. As though he wanted to repeat the moment of entry—as though every time might be the first.

She allowed herself an instant of exquisite panic that he might leave her empty, starving, gasping with desire. *Oh no he won't*, she told herself stoutly. *Not if I have any say in the matter.* She wrapped her arms around him, grasping the small of his back (it had been so lovely to touch his skin there, that first night in her attic room). She held him, she pulled him closer, moving her hands down over his lean, thrusting buttocks and squeezing him to her. Greedily. Gracelessly. Shamelessly. She watched his anxiety fade, she saw joy rise in his eyes, a mirror of the joy that he could see in her own.

Faster now. Somehow he must have taught her to move in time with him, to take active part in this arching dance, this high-spirited gallop, this intricate weave of pleasure and desire, desire and pleasure.

A whimsical twist to his mouth, and suddenly the world turned upside down and she was astride him, her breasts bobbing in his hands, her entire body, it felt, filled with his rising sex. She blushed to be so visible; she tried to hide behind her hair, all tangled now into wild, tight, sweaty, copper coils.

He held her breasts more tightly, catching the nipples between his fingers. He arched his back and thrust harder. And suddenly she was past caring what he could see. Let him see—let him know—every inch, every iota of her, let him hear the deep moans, the gasps, the greedy, bestial growls issuing from her lips, rising from the volcanic tremors (but he must be able to feel them too!) at her center. She threw back her head and cried out; she heard him cry out as well, before he pulled her down to his wet, salty-tasting chest, his heart (or was it her heart?) pounding wildly, his arms hard around her, both their bodies drenched, trembling, exhausted—as if they'd been out together in a hurricane.

Perhaps she'd slept—for an instant? an hour?—or perhaps she'd simply been wandering in the new country whose citizen she'd become, the republic of love and pleasure. In any case, when she heard the hoarse whisper of his voice, she couldn't tell if it came from far off or very near indeed.

"I was nervous, you know. About competing with Monsieur X."

His arm tightened around her, and his thigh wrapped around both of hers. She nestled into him, the side of her face happily burning from the growth of new beard on his cheek. The country she'd been exploring—she realized now that it was his body, its paths and byways, curves and arches and moist, voluptuous gardens. She found his hand, squeezed it, kissed the knuckles. She turned her head a little, so she could see his eyes, his slightly anxious smile.

"After all," he continued, "he's an awfully impressive gentleman in bed. I've been worrying all day that I might disappoint you, being just of flesh and blood as I am."

Just of flesh and blood.

"You're quite impressive enough for me the way you are," she assured him. "But there's so much you'll have to teach me."

He rose on his elbow, his face glowing, his mouth solemn, his eyes like warm, velvet night.

"I would be honored and grateful, Marie-Laure," he said, "if there were anything at all that I could teach you."

Chapter 13

Of course he was very much more experienced than she was. But it seemed to Marie-Laure that he and she taught each other, as every night their fingers and lips described the lines and arcs of each other's bodies—curve of belly, articulation of wrist or collarbone, small of back swooping to slope of buttock.

They became explorers, discoverers of landmarks and natural wonders, collectors, connoisseurs of oddities and curios. The wound in Joseph's thigh that Gilles had sewn up: Marie-Laure traced it in wonderment. It was almost all healed now, and "a much neater job than the one on my side—yes, there—the work of a butcher of an army surgeon." She shuddered, not wishing to think what would have happened if the bullet had been an inch higher and to the right.

The burns on Marie-Laure's fingers, from oven and hearth: Joseph brushed his lips against them with the lightness of cobwebs. "I dreamed," he whispered one night, "that my kisses turned them back to ink stains."

The twin deep dimples above the curve of Marie-Laure's derriere: "You don't know that you have them?" he exclaimed. "Come to the mirror, I'll show you." She'd never had a three-sided mirror. What an astonishment, she thought, to see her small, freckled, rosy self together with him, long-limbed, olive-skinned, tautly muscled and proudly erect. She peered within the triple frame at an infinity, a lifetime of Josephs and Marie-Laures—surrounded by the shifting rainbow edge of beveled mirror—from virtually every angle.

They posed, giggling, as though for a series of engravings of the sort that he had once smuggled into France. They made up titles for the tableaux they struck:

"The Importunate Master."

"The Bawdy Serving Maid."

"The Sultan," he announced, wrapping his cravat around his head like a turban, "and his Odalisque." She stared nervously, wondering about the sudden keen look he'd given her.

And so her life was transformed. Quietly and invisibly, everything had changed forever. She was grateful for the invisibility, glad she'd endured everybody's teasing at a time when there hadn't been anything to tease her about.

Whereas now—when all the pretense had come true—no one cared a fig about what she and Joseph might be doing during their night meetings. During these anxious days after the old Duc's death, the servants were far too preoccupied with their own uncertain fates. They worried continually: the most trivial of rumors would be seized upon and plumbed for every possible shred of meaning, only to be rejected in favor of the next equally baseless speculation.

And when the firings actually did happen, they weren't the ones anyone had expected. Everyone was surprised, for example, that the old Duc's valet Jacques had been kept on. Pierre, the quiet, circumspect fellow who'd looked after Monsieur Hubert since his boyhood, had been given the sack and Jacques had taken his place.

"I smell a rat," Monsieur Colet confided to Nicolas, Robert, and Marie-Laure. "He's a sneaky piece of work, that one. Who knows what he promised to do for the family in return for them keeping him here?"

Marie-Laure took his meaning. Planting a spy among her servants was exactly the sort of thing the Gorgon might try, and

Jacques was certainly scoundrel enough. She and everybody else would be wise to hold their tongues in his presence.

And indeed, for a week everybody exercised prodigious restraint when Jacques was around. But for a week only—because nobody liked being rude or stingy with household gossip. And anyway, however Jacques had managed it, the fact was that he'd kept his job; everyone hoped his good fortune would somehow rub off on them.

Besides, he was a good entertainer. Unlike his loyal, boring predecessor, Jacques was willing to share the funniest, nastiest stories about the new Duc and Duchesse. Everyone enjoyed his descriptions of their grim, tooth-gritting efforts at conceiving an heir.

"He'd drink himself into a stupor if I allowed him to," Jacques confided. "I have to be careful not to let him have too much, the nights he visits her. Just enough, you know, to—to take the edge off the encounter. But not enough so he'll wilt completely."

Marie-Laure laughed and hooted along with the rest of them. But every now and again she'd also feel a surprising twinge of pity for the new Duchesse. How sad, she'd think, to have to make love to someone you weren't in the least bit attracted to and who didn't want you either.

How dreadful to have to wait, night after night, for an inebriated, unwilling partner—instead of someone madly eager to sweep you into bed and cover you with kisses.

And how embarrassing it must be when the gentleman—but what had Jacques called it?—when the gentleman *wilted.* What did one *say* in those circumstances anyway? Not that there was any chance, she thought proudly, that *Joseph* would ever have such a problem.

It all seemed unspeakably sad; perhaps it even explained the Gorgon's meanness.

Of course, these flashes of pity would only last until the new Duchesse hurled the next insult or inflicted the next bruise upon someone—for the smallest clumsiness, or for no reason at all. Upon hearing the latest outrage Marie-Laure would happily join her colleagues in heaping curses upon Madame Amélie, all the while secretly glorying in her own superior situation.

Too bad for you, Madame, she'd think, that *you* won't have somebody wonderful waiting for you tonight. Somebody who'll hold you tightly when you throw yourself into his arms. Whose eyes will shine and whose grin will betray the lascivious thoughts he's been having. And who—after a few long kisses—will whisper the naughtiest, most mischievous ideas in your ear, overwhelming you with all the new and fascinating things he wants to try tonight.

At which point in her thoughts Marie-Laure would shrug her shoulders, forget about the Gorgon, and turn her mind toward more interesting matters. . . .

. . . like exactly *which* new thing she and Joseph might be trying tonight.

Of course, practically everything was new to her—new and absolutely fascinating.

So many positions, she marveled. So many angles of entry, points of contact, thrilling secret explorations along the nerves' pathways. So many moods and modes: flamboyant, triumphant, shy, and everything in-between. So many languages, so many geometries, so many nuances and shades of meaning, depending upon whether you were horizontal or vertical, above or below, facing one another or turned away . . . last night he'd lifted her in his arms while she wrapped her legs around his waist. She'd levered herself into place and shaped herself tightly around him as he moved into her. She'd thought he'd carry her to bed, but he didn't, until he had to climax. For as long as he'd been able, he'd fucked her right there, standing in the center of the room while she howled and thrashed about in his arms, catching occasional glimpses of their dual reflection in the mirror across the room.

How strangely and well we fit together, she'd thought; *what a fierce, beautiful beast-with-two-backs we make.*

They played and laughed, coaxed and teased, whispers and giggles shading to half-voiced entreaty, "yes, there, more, *mon Dieu*, don't stop"—entreaty shading to imperious command. They pleaded, insisted, demanded and exacted tribute—"yes, again, just like that."

Was there a line of poetry more beautiful, Marie-Laure wondered, than a lover's summons? Any pair of syllables more glorious than "I want"? Their shouts crashed like ocean waves, breaking into a thousand crystal droplets at passion's crest, and ebbing and subsiding to groans and growls and giggles—it was comical that two such word-struck people could communicate with such lusty, simpleminded crudeness.

She smiled, remembering that first morning in the barn, when she'd anxiously and fearfully asked whether people really did such scandalous things. Right now she was a great deal wiser, knowing with the certainty of a fortnight's experience that people did just about everything, earthy or lyrical, with an infinity of miraculous results.

The results—ah yes, the results. The sense of satisfaction, of satiation, of absolute harmony and completeness—to be followed, surely as the night follows the day, by the next slow, delicious gathering of desire. Delicious and unbearable at the same time: well, it *would* be unbearable, she thought, if she didn't have tonight's visit to look forward to.

She discovered that she might experience these new feelings at any time at all. Sporadically, unpredictably—and quite brilliantly, she congratulated herself—her body could reconstruct the most complex and ephemeral sensations. She marveled at how a memory (only a memory!) of a caress could set her trembling.

Standing at the kitchen washbasin, she'd be taken unaware by an errant sensation, a stray resonance in her tightly strung sensorium. Suddenly she'd be transported back to the first time he'd laid his tongue in the hollow of her throat, or when his fingers had touched her (merely touched her!) in the fold where her buttocks met her legs.

She'd vibrate like a tuning fork—her insides wet and burning, and her imagination as deeply in thrall to memory as her body had been to touch. Useless to resist: it was all she could do to maintain her center of gravity while the feelings roiled through her. She'd plant her feet firmly, stretch her neck, curl her toes, and purr with the delight of simply inhabiting her own body.

For a moment she would feel absolutely, purely, and perfectly whole. But only for a moment. Immediately afterward, she'd begin to want him so badly—*him* and not a memory of him, him right *now* and not tonight—that her muscles would clench and her eyes would smart with tears.

Enough, she'd scold herself. *Enough, there's work to be done.* She'd shrug off her feelings, and force herself to get the pots washed and dried before Nicolas passed by on his rounds through the kitchen. Carefully, she'd dry a fine porcelain plate and pile it on top of its fellows. Desperately, she'd drag her thoughts back to the conscious, workaday world—the steamy, noisy, greasy kitchen, where her head ached and her chapped hands smarted and the tired muscles in her shoulders grew hard as rocks.

It wasn't easy to come back. It was a constant struggle not to give way to the demands of her overwrought nerves and lascivious imagination. But to lose control would be to court disaster.

Her most insistent fear was that she'd break some horribly expensive piece of china. She could only hope that it would be something the family owned a lot of, like cups or saucers. Nicolas wouldn't be able to hide it if she dropped a teapot. The Gorgon would have to be told; the crime would demand a suitable punishment.

Not an immediate punishment, of course—Marie-Laure knew that whatever penalty she'd incur would have to wait until Joseph was safely married and the dowry signed over in its entirety. Until then, the Gorgon wouldn't risk angering him by mistreating the girl he'd chosen to amuse himself with. Marie-Laure's whipping or her dismissal—or perhaps both—could wait until after he left. . . .

She drew a sharp, whistling breath, suddenly noticing a nasty bit of burned-on grease that had been entirely invisible the moment before. It seemed to taunt her, to grimace at her. Furiously, she tried to rub it away. The spot became her mortal enemy and there was nothing more important than making it disappear.

But it hadn't been the fear of punishment that had disrupted her reverie, or even the possibility of being thrown out without her twenty livres.

She'd been jolted back to present reality by the horrid phrase that had crept into her thoughts.

After he left.

Yes, *that* was enough to shake her free of her fantasies and leave her with the bare facts of her situation: an aching back, a pile of unwashed pots, and a crust of grease that refused to be loosened by any amount of scrubbing.

He'd be leaving for Paris a week before the Feast of All Saints. The date was immutable, signed and sealed within the provisions of the betrothal contract. It would happen whether she broke a teapot or not.

Well, if she couldn't change it, she simply wouldn't think about it. Wouldn't count the nights remaining to her—there were too few of them anyway. She'd live in the present, finish the pot (the grease spot had finally yielded to her efforts), and concentrate on whatever way she could affect her circumstances. If she couldn't have him forever, she'd have him as completely as she could in the time left to her.

She knew that physically he wouldn't hold anything back from her. But she wanted more. She wanted to know him: his moods and secrets, not to speak of those mysterious papers on his desk—the ones he would take a final hurried scribble at and then sweep under the blotter when she entered the room.

Looking up from whatever he'd been concentrating on so passionately, his eyes would need a moment to focus upon her. She was sure he was writing something fictional: he had the bemused look of someone returning from a distant place in his fancies. He'd gaze at her as though surprised that she was there in front of him instead of in whatever fabulous principality he'd dreamed up. He'd peer at her curiously and she could tell he was considering whether he'd gotten it right.

Gotten what *right?*

And then he'd smile—a wildly provocative smile that seemed to bridge the realms of the fantastic and the physical. His smile would turn to a delighted laugh; he'd leap up, reach out for her, and draw her to him.

I'm quite mad, she thought. He could be writing about anything at all.

It's only a reader's fancy, she told herself. The fancy of a reader in love.

Madness or fancy—she was nonetheless certain of it. Whatever he was writing had something to do with her. It was *about* her.

She'd demand to know what it was.

Ridiculous! Joseph told himself. He *never* blushed. But right now he could feel the blood rising to his face.

And there was no way to hide it, for Marie-Laure was looking straight at him, sitting up alert against the pillows, her eyes shining and her breasts still heaving from the last hour's lovemaking.

"So you still want to talk about writing," he murmured, "even in our current situation."

"Of course I do." She laughed. "But you don't *have* to tell me. If you think it's too . . . ah, *racy* for me, too scandalous for my innocent ears . . ."

He took a quick nip at her left earlobe. "I adore your innocent ears."

"Then tell me," she said. "What are you writing?"

Why not? He'd read it aloud to Madame de Rambuteau. He'd even pretended it was about her. But it was different, somehow, when a story really *was* about someone. When someone had seized your imagination and taken you to new—and yet hauntingly familiar—places. . . .

"It's a fable," he said. "An oriental fable. They're popular at Versailles, you know."

She nodded. "We sold a lot of *The Arabian Nights* in Monsieur Galland's translation. People liked the genies and the dervishes, and . . . and the harem scenes, too."

"This one has harem scenes," he said.

It was about a sultan, he told her. A young, very rich and powerful sultan, who possessed everything he might desire and a thousand wives and concubines—so many that he hadn't even had them all yet. Some of them had been gifts from political allies, others the spoils of war. Or he might buy one, on a whim, while passing through a slave bazaar, have her sent home to the palace, and forget about her for months.

Like the young woman, naked up there on the block, who'd stared boldly at him, with piercing gray eyes.

"Gray eyes?" Marie-Laure asked.

"Gray eyes, with not a trace of blue in them. So you see, it's completely a fiction. Of course, the girl in the story is rather petite in stature, with round little breasts. . . ." He dropped a kiss on each of hers.

"And when she's angry—for she does become angry at him, though she's forbidden to show it—she stands with her back very straight and her chin very high. She has a will of iron, you see."

He looked away. And when he spoke again his voice was very soft.

"He puts her through some rather extreme ordeals. I'm not sure why. To prove that he can, I suppose. But in the end, he's as much her slave as she is his."

She'd crept into his arms and was planting tiny kisses on his chest. Her tongue flicked against one of his nipples.

He tightened his arms' hold and rolled over so that he was lying on top of her. She was kissing his throat now. He sighed and felt himself tighten between his legs. Between *her* legs now, for she'd opened herself to him. She'd arched her back; he could feel her reaching for him.

"I . . . *will* read it to you," he managed to say. "A-another time." But his words were swallowed up in a kiss and for that night, at least, it seemed that they were done with literary conversation.

He read it to her a few nights later, when they'd summoned up enough self-control to allow them to get through it. After several unsuccessful attempts, they'd decided that both of them needed to get out of bed and decorously put on their dressing gowns.

For she had a dressing gown now—shell pink velvet with a bit of Venetian lace at the sleeves. He'd posted an order to a dressmaker in Aix and sent Baptiste in a donkey cart to pick it up a few days later. She'd protested—"I don't want anything from you but . . . you." But he'd insisted—"It's for me, not for you. It's so I don't have to unlace you and then lace you up again every night." So now when she visited him she came to him in the most beautiful thing she'd ever worn. And if Louise wondered why Marie-Laure was making her nightly visits in such gorgeous semi-undress, she never said a word about it.

Smiling shyly, he sat down in his armchair, manuscript in hand, and cleared his throat.

She took her old place in the window seat, tucking her bare feet under her as she listened with parted lips to his story. It *was* salacious: the sultan *did* put the harem girl through some cruel and fascinating ordeals. And then, just when Marie-Laure had begun to wonder what he could possibly do next, the story took a marvelous reversal: the sultan's kingdom was besieged; the ruling family overthrown; the harem girl rescued and restored to her rightful position (for she was, in fact, an English lady of quality), and . . .

"Well, it's not finished yet," he murmured. "But what's going to happen is that he stows away on a ship, comes to England, and gets the humblest of jobs in her service. . . ."

"And is she cruel to him?"

"Yes, rather, for a while. . . ."

"Does she demand that he take off his dressing gown and come to her on his knees?"

"I'd rather thought of that, though I don't know if he has a dressing gown. . . ."

"She buys him one."

"Yes, of course."

"After all," she told him, "she wants him to look his best when he comes to her. Because she so, *so* loves to look at him."

She leaned back on the pillows, watching intently as he rose to his feet and dropped his robe to the floor. And this time she could match the easy delight and frank carnal appreciation with which he'd gazed at her, their first night.

She could even pretend to be the heroine of his story—the "English lady of quality" who had the deposed sultan completely at her service.

Well, she could *try* to pretend. Though she wasn't very good at being anyone but herself.

Perhaps for a moment, though. It was just a matter of playacting after all. Surely she could do that.

Timidly, she attempted a curt, proprietary nod in his direction.

He sank to his knees immediately. The rush of power was thrilling; she tried not to show how much she'd enjoyed it.

She nodded again, this time a bit more boldly, and he shuffled forward to her, still on his knees. His eyes were meek, his lips slightly parted. She untied the sash of her robe, feeling his warm breath in the space between her breasts.

She opened her mouth to give the next command. . . .

Oh dear. This business of giving orders wasn't as easy as one might think. At least when one wasn't used to it.

A smile hovered at the corners of his mouth. "And if my lady will allow me . . ."

He dipped his dark head between her thighs. She reached down to touch his neck, his shoulders, his silky hair, while he nibbled at her, nuzzled at her, and then quickly parted her with his tongue.

He's as much her slave, Joseph had said of his sultan, *as she is his.*

How like him, she thought, to turn complicated desire into provocative conundrum.

But she'd puzzle it out some other time.

Because right now she could barely think at all. Right now there were no more words, no more stories—nothing but the ragged fabric of her breath and the slow, insistent, movement of his mouth.

She closed her eyes.

His tongue was light, delicate—almost not there at all and yet inescapable, a tiny torch flickering in the darkness, a glowing brand, a white-hot iron.

His hands had crept up to her hips; he held her firmly, gently, while she writhed, shuddered, screamed for release and prayed that it would never end. *How long,* she wondered, *can I bear these feelings?*

But there was no time, no duration, only a shimmering, everchanging *now.*

Now, while her center exploded into a million tiny lights, like the night sky over Provence, and she tumbled from a great height through crystalline darkness.

Now. If she couldn't have forever, at least she had *now.*

He raised his head, kissing his way upward—her belly, her

breasts, her throat, and then her lips. She could taste herself in his mouth.

She leaned back in his arms as he carried her back to bed. They held each other tightly; stretching her body against his, she tried to touch him with every inch of her skin.

As though their bodies were the world and the present moment the entirety of history. As though *now* was the only word in the language.

Well, *now* was all she had, anyway.

Now would have to be enough for her. And—for the rest of that evening, anyway—it almost was.

Chapter 14

She really didn't know, Joseph thought a few days later, just how astonishing these past weeks had been.

And as she had nothing to compare them to, it was quite reasonable that she'd think lovemaking was always so wonderful.

Well, he wouldn't enlighten her on the subject. She'd find out the truth for herself one day, when the man who deserved her finally made his appearance. No doubt he'd be a hardworking, high-minded sort of fellow; in truth, Joseph felt a bit intimidated by the exemplary personage he'd dreamed up. Marie-Laure's future husband would be worthy of her in every way, with not a hint of petty spite or shallow self-regard in his fine, upstanding character. Still, Joseph consoled himself, this paragon of virtue would quite likely be rather a bore in bed.

But no more tormenting himself, he decided. Far more pleasant to devote his imaginings to her—as she'd looked last night, her hair like flame against the purple velvet bed curtains, skin glowing pink beneath the freckles . . .

Merde, his thoughts *would* take that turn just at the moment when Baptiste was trying to button his new breeches for him. The valet gave a low whistle.

"That's enough," Joseph said.

Baptiste assumed an air of exaggerated respect while his eyes shone wickedly. Holding out his arms for the sleeves of his new coat, Joseph scrutinized his reflection in the mirror.

The suit *was* rather becoming, he concluded. The black brocade had violet threads subtly woven through the background of the pattern: rich, yet suitable for mourning. He moved slightly to the right and the left as Baptiste tugged it here and there, smoothing it down over his flanks until it followed his torso like a second skin.

A distant echo of Marie-Laure's voice wafted through his memory.

. . . *she so* so *loves to look at him.*

The little phrase had been hovering at the margins of his thoughts for three days now, light as a hummingbird, piquant as a whiff of lavender.

He loved the way she looked at him. So hungrily and yet so trustingly. There had only been one other woman who'd ever looked at him that way. . . .

He shuddered.

Well, in any case, he thought hastily, Marie-Laure would see him this morning. She'd be in the courtyard for the ceremony, along with the rest of the household, captive audience to Hubert's public ascension to his title.

The formal name of the thing was "Homage to the New Lord." Hubert and Amélie had decided to do it in a tedious style that no one used anymore. It would probably take hours.

No matter. He could spend hours simply thinking of her. And if anybody happened to notice that the front of his breeches wasn't as smoothly decorous as it might be, it was no concern of his.

"It's in the worst of taste," Nicolas had told the group in the dessert kitchen. "They're intending to stage the ceremony in a way that's been obsolete for almost a century."

"Nowadays," he continued, "when a nobleman comes into his estates, he just goes down and signs a notarized document. Actually, it's good enough simply to send a proxy."

But not good enough for this Duc and Duchesse.

The October weather had turned cold, too.

So for several chilly, boring hours, Marie-Laure had stood shivering with the rest of the servants in the château's courtyard. Clutching her shawl about her, she gazed at the unprepossessing figure of the new Duc de Carency Auvers-Raimond, seated in a large, thronelike, ceremonial armchair while a priest blessed him and little armies of village children presented him with bouquets of late-blooming flowers.

Dressed in a velvet suit, mink-lined cloak, and tricorne hat trimmed with marten, the Duc Hubert accepted each new expression of fealty with a befuddled look. He was too small for the chair; his feet had dangled like a child's until someone had been sent for a footstool. When he'd sneezed, upon being handed a particularly large bouquet, the Duchesse had scowled at the few giggles that broke out in the crowd. Marie-Laure felt unaccountably mortified for her, depressed by the spectacle, and grateful to have Joseph to look at instead.

He stood at easy attention behind his brother, in a lovely black suit, with a blank, distant expression on his face. As though, Marie-Laure thought, in his mind he wasn't here at all, but (perhaps) back in his bedchamber, where . . .

. . . *he'd drawn the purple bed curtains closed around them like an oriental tent. And then he'd nodded. The nod had been almost imperceptible, but somehow—for it seemed that they'd begun to share a secret language of command and consent—she'd known exactly what he'd wanted. Somehow he'd made it absolutely clear that she should position herself at the center of the bed on hands and knees.*

A loud sigh escaped her lips. Vainly, belatedly, she tried to turn it into a cough, shrugging her apologies when Monsieur Colet turned to her with a questioning look. Pardon, Monsieur. No, nothing wrong. Nothing at all.

Nothing except the sudden throb between her legs, the poignancy of her body's memory . . .

. . . *of what it had felt like to be so open, so docile—vulnerable as an animal that allows itself to be taken from behind.*

She'd thought that Joseph would enter her immediately. But he'd simply let her wait.

Untouched.

For a minute, perhaps?

It had felt like an eternity.

And then he'd stroked and squeezed and played with her breasts until she'd thought she'd go mad with wanting him inside her. . . .

Ah, there she was, Joseph thought, half hidden behind the man in the chef's toque.

But how visible, how utterly available and present she'd been last night. His to do what he liked with . . .

For now he knew the meaning of his oriental fable. It was about the intricate pleasures of power and submission, the joys of mastery and the willingness to be enslaved by your own desire. He'd conceived the story in an unreasoning haze of frustrated yearning, at a time when he'd thought he'd never see her again. But it was only in the past few weeks that he'd begun to understand what he'd been trying to say.

Ironic, he thought, that he'd called Monsieur X's book *A Libertine Education.* His real education had begun with Marie-Laure.

She'd said that he needed to teach her about lovemaking and he'd responded that he'd be honored to do so. But they'd both been wrong: the truth was that each of them needed the other's help—to understand what was happening, to give shape to the passions that threatened to engulf them. They were still discovering things, still teaching each other the pleasures of offering and giving—and of demanding and taking.

He hadn't been surprised that he'd needed to learn to give; for him the big revelation was that taking wasn't so simple either. There was something shamelessly intimate about it, something deliciously humbling about revealing exactly what you wanted. Even—or especially—when you wanted something as subtle, as ephemeral as an inch of elastic flesh.

He'd wanted her breasts to swing freely under his hands. And he'd realized that they would only do so if she were on her hands and knees.

He'd been right. Oh yes, exactly what he'd wanted—that little bit of womanly pendulousness her breasts had taken on in that position. He'd slapped them lightly, catching at them as though they were fruit on a tree, squeezing as though to calculate their ripeness. He'd caressed her belly, teased and flicked at the knot of hardening flesh at the apex of the triangle between her legs. She'd whimpered and shuddered. And then she'd begun to moan. He'd kept control of himself as long as he'd been able, savoring his anticipation, glorying in his (rapidly diminishing) self-discipline.

The Duc Hubert blinked, perhaps drunkenly, as each of the local mayors and deputies knelt before him, head bared. He must have rehearsed for this ceremony, Marie-Laure thought, but he seemed as astonished as everyone else as he acknowledged each man in turn as his vassal, with a kiss.

With a kiss. *How she'd ached for a kiss last night, during those endless moments she'd spent waiting—her nipples stiffening, her vulva's lips swelling and moistening, with every maddening, teasing caress.*

"Don't speak," he'd whispered.

Her face had been turned away from him; kneeling as she was, she'd already been deprived of the use of her hands. And now, to be forbidden to speak! It meant that she had only the most primitive ways to signal her impatience: arching her back, spreading her legs, (yes, even) wriggling her derriere at him and all the while making pleading sounds in her throat. She felt herself blushing, her cheeks warm against the chilly air in the courtyard, as she remembered opening, displaying herself so vulgarly.

She hadn't been able to see him, but she'd felt his body's heat, heard his calm breathing at her back. Finally (thank heaven) she'd heard his muffled groan—reassuring her that the extravagant slowness of his caresses had taken a bit of self-control on his part too.

But when he finally entered her, he did it quickly, confidently.

The new Duc's "vassals"—bluff, reasonable-looking officials from the surrounding villages—recited hastily memorized pledges, cribbed by their lawyers from musty medieval books that no one had opened for generations. They were clearly impatient to be done with this nonsense, Joseph thought.

As far as he was concerned, it could go on forever.

As long as he had those mental images of her to sustain him.

Not to speak of those delicious sensory impressions that had been stamped, it seemed, upon every nerve and muscle of his body. . . .

"Now," he'd whispered, rising upright on his knees, pulling her up along with him. She'd leaned back against his chest, buttocks pressed against his groin, his thighs. He'd lifted her hair, buried his lips in the nape of her neck, moved his hands up and down her front. Closer, tighter, she'd squeezed him within her, bearing down upon him. . . .

One could hardly make out what the bored-looking gentlemen were mumbling, Marie-Laure thought. Good thing Nicolas had explained it beforehand, that each of them was swearing to be "a good, loyal and faithful vassal of my lord Duc and his heirs . . ."

His heirs. A snicker came from somewhere in the courtyard. The Duchesse cast a defiant look at the crowd. Bertrande nudged Nicolas and shrugged.

Horrible old verses. And yet Marie-Laure felt herself responding to those phrases she could make out.

For there had been something lordly about the way he'd held her against himself, something of the conqueror in his hands' insolent, proprietary slowness, even while he continued driving deeper into her.

She'd grasped back at him with all the force at her body's center, she'd ground herself against him until she could feel the tiny muscles at the root of his sex, the wiry hairs at the bottom of his belly. But still he'd moved within her, thrusting upward, driving toward the mouth of her womb.

Her womb.

Dear God how much she'd wanted him to empty himself within her.

She caught her breath. Until this moment she hadn't admitted to herself how desperately she'd wanted to feel that.

But she *couldn't* want it. It was insane to want it. Yes, yes, of course she wanted every bit of him . . . but not so that her life could be ruined or ended. No. *That* was simply impossible, even if not having it was impossibly frustrating. She should feel glad, she should be grateful that he'd been so careful. But she wasn't.

She forced herself to relax her clenched jaw, to breathe and collect herself. And right now, she thought, she should also be grateful for the sharp twinge of frustration that had brought her back to the present.

The endless ceremony was finally drawing to a close. There would be a big dinner for the participants. It was almost time to get back to work.

They seemed to be finishing their oaths, Joseph thought. The tedious reciting droned to a close.

". . . to keep his secrets, to refrain from doing him harm, to seek his honest profit with all my power, and not to renounce or flee his jurisdiction."

Not to renounce or flee . . .

And *to keep his secrets . . .*

"And at least to get a good meal out of it," Robert whispered to Marie-Laure. She giggled, while Monsieur Colet hissed at both of them to be quiet.

"Well, a good meal is all they're going to get," Nicolas concluded that evening, as the plates were returned to the scullery for washing. "I've already heard grumbling in the village about how cheap this new Duc is. He hasn't even granted his peasants and villagers the reduction in dues that traditionally goes along with a gentleman's assuming his title."

Well, that was the way of it with aristocrats, Marie-Laure thought. Always cheating you out of something they owed you.

"No," he told her that night. "Absolutely not."

She wasn't surprised. It was really quite wonderful how much care he'd taken during these past weeks. And equally absurd how intent she was on taking this crazy risk.

"Just once?" she pleaded. "Just once to have your skin next to mine inside of me? Wouldn't that be nice?"

He looked away. "Yes, of course it would be *nice.* It would be more than nice."

His voice was harsh. "You haven't any idea how very very nice it would be."

"Well then show me. I know how good and decent you are. But just this once . . . my brother told me about it . . . you could, um, pull yourself out before . . ." Though in fact, what Gilles had told her was never to agree to such a thing if a man were to propose it.

He'd been in the midst of putting the sheath around himself. She reached to pull it off. To discover—*mon Dieu*—to discover that during the course of their little argument he'd quite fully, and quite uncharacteristically *wilted.*

He looked as astonished as she felt.

"I take it," she said softly, "that this doesn't happen to you very often."

His mouth curved downward. "I believe that that's approximately what I'm supposed to say at this moment. But it's true, as it happens. There's not a lot in this world that I depend upon myself for—certainly not any sort of goodness or decency—but . . .

"You don't have to stay," he added quickly. "In fact, perhaps it would be better this evening if you were to go. And I'm sure that tomorrow night . . ."

"I'm sure of it too," she said. "I'm sure that by tomorrow night you'll have contrived a way not to think about whatever made it happen. You'll bury it deep with those other secrets I don't know. And then I'll never know them."

She'd almost forgotten how cold his eyes could become.

"Always wanting to read what's not on the page," he muttered.

"It *was* on the page," she said, "just not in so many words. And now it's written on your face. I knew it then and I know it now."

He'd wrapped his dressing gown around himself and was pacing the room.

"And if you found Monsieur X's secrets? If you found out he . . . I was a murderer?"

"You're not a murderer. I would feel it if you were. You were a soldier, of course . . ."

He'd collapsed into his armchair. "Well, not exactly a murderer, I suppose. But I'm not talking about death in battle. I'm talking about the death of an innocent . . . and very dear . . . person. And I caused it."

She caught her breath, unable to quite believe that he *was* going to tell her. For a moment she considered taking her place in the window seat.

But it wasn't that sort of story.

"Come here," he said. "I don't know if I can tell it if I'm looking at your face. But if I'm holding you . . . well, that might help a little."

The story came out haltingly, without any of his usual facility or elegance of phrasing. Sometimes he'd speak in a monotone, sometimes in a breathless rush. Sometimes there were long silences when he wasn't able to say anything at all.

It started at school, before his fourteenth birthday. All his friends had already had their first sexual encounters, most of them with their mothers' seamstresses or chambermaids.

Curled up in his lap, her head against his throat, she could feel his choked breathing and the vibrations of his voice.

"But I was the youngest of the group, and hadn't yet. Of course I was mad to try it, after hearing their stories all spring. And so, when it was time to go home for a summer visit, I knew I was ready. I'd just celebrated my fourteenth birthday; I'd become a head taller in the past year. Suddenly I didn't look like a little boy anymore."

His voice slowed, stumbled.

"Her name was Claire. She helped my mother with her hair, or ribbons . . . or something, I don't really know what. All I know is that she was remarkably affectionate and patient with me.

"She seemed very old at the time—I remember her telling me that she was twenty-six—and she wasn't terribly pretty. She had a broad, flat, rather stolid-looking face, and large, capable hands. And a wonderful touch—I know that now, though at the time anybody's touch would have been wonderful. But the important thing was that she enjoyed our lovemaking. *That* was the miracle for me. She was such a passionate lover that even a clumsy fourteen-year-old boy could move her to ecstasy."

He'd spent the summer in a sort of dream; the only reality had been her visits to his bed. And then he'd gone back to school and rather forgotten about her. Except, of course, to boast to the other boys about his new status as a man of the world.

"But when the Easter holidays came, I found myself overwhelmingly excited to be going home. I made hasty greetings to my parents and ran up the back stairs to where the servants slept."

"But she's gone, Monsieur Joseph," Bertrande had said. "Monsieur le Duc let her go, you know, as he always does when a girl becomes pregnant." Her voice had been choked with helpless rage. But he'd only understood that later, after he'd thought about it. Right then his only thought had been to find Claire.

Where? He'd demanded. Where did she go?

She'd shrugged. "Home to her village. Where else could she go?"

He took the best horse they had, packed all his money and his most cherished possession, and galloped furiously through lonely mountain country.

"It wasn't difficult to find out what had happened. It was a small, mean village; everybody knew everybody else's business and seemed to take spiteful pleasure in it. The baby had come early, two weeks before I'd arrived. It had been a painful, bloody stillbirth, and when it was over, Claire was dead too.

" 'Well, can I at least give her family some money?' I asked the innkeeper who'd told me the story. 'I have a rather good telescope with me that I think will fetch a reasonable price.' But the innkeeper said that Claire had no living family.

" 'What did she do?' I asked him. 'Who helped her?'

" 'She came here, to my place,' he replied. 'She had the last of her wages but she was saving that for the child, so I let her wait on tables when we had an overflow crowd, and clean the privies, and she slept by the fire and I gave her the food scraps, so she got by. And when the baby started to come, I only charged her a sou for a room to have it in. Half price.' Looking very pleased with himself for his charity, too."

Marie-Laure shivered. *He's never forgotten a minute of that day,* she thought.

He must have felt her shiver. "Quite astonishingly stupid, wasn't it," he asked, "to tell him about the telescope?"

"That's not what I was thinking about," she said.

"Well, it's what somebody at the inn was thinking about," he said. "Because the next thing I remember is waking up in the courtyard with a nasty bump on my head and the telescope and money gone. The horse too."

"So I walked home. Well, halfway home, until I met up with

Baptiste, who was out looking for me. We passed a monastery on the way and I had a fleeting fantasy of confessing my sins, pleading for asylum, and giving up women forever. But of course," he laughed abruptly, "I didn't say anything and we didn't stop.

"Instead I demanded that Baptiste take me to the inn in Carency. I'd remembered comments my father had made about the girl who worked there. And he was right—with talents like hers she should have gone to Paris and made something of herself. I went there every day for the rest of my school holiday, befuddling my senses and acting as depraved as I felt the world to be.

"Which didn't stop me from informing my father, the day I was to go back to school, that he was a tyrant, a murderer, and the scourge of everything innocent and good. And I never came home again. Until this visit.

"I didn't tell anyone at school what had happened to Claire. In fact, I've never been such a consummate playactor as when I regaled my friends with salacious tales of what she'd allowed me to do during *this* vacation (drawing upon what I'd learned from the girl at the inn), until I wasn't sure what was true and what wasn't."

He paused. "I haven't told anyone the whole story until . . . until now. Baptiste knows, of course; I tend to mumble about it when I'm drunk. I think it's always with me, though, making me guilty and angry and . . . confused. Terribly confused, Marie-Laure."

"I know," she whispered.

"Yes," he said, "I suppose you do know."

But should she say something else? Should she comfort him, reassure him that she loved him as much as ever?

Perhaps she might tell him that he needn't feel guilty.

"You were young," she could say. "You were only a boy; you wanted to do the decent thing; it's not your fault that nobody had taught you how."

Or perhaps: "It's in the past. You can't spend your life blaming yourself for it."

She could tell him that "it does no good, you know, to pretend to be a nasty, shallow person, just because you're frightened that you might actually *be* that sort of person. Because you're *not,* even if you're not sure exactly who you really are."

Worse and worse. Facile and preachy.

And so she said nothing at all. And did nothing except hold him tightly and mourn with him, until the sky had gone from black to blue and it was time to kiss each other good night.

Chapter 15

They didn't speak of it again, at least not in so many words. In fact, the next night they hardly spoke at all, so eager were they to taste and touch, to kiss and stroke and fuck and fondle and hold each other—to make up, in every way they could, for an evening's lost lovemaking.

Of course, after hearing the story of Claire, Marie-Laure knew that there could be no possibility of unprotected lovemaking. Although, as Joseph suggested quietly a few nights later, if she wanted to feel him discharge within her she could always learn to take him in her mouth.

"You want me to," she said, "don't you?"

He lay on his back, naked, loose limbed, open and unguarded, with one arm lightly about her shoulders. He laughed as he prodded her to sit up beside him.

"Well, yes," he replied. "I rather do want you to."

She reached to touch him, but the expression on her face was a bit dubious.

"I don't know," she said. "It seems to me that you're too big to fit in my mouth. Even . . . now."

His penis was soft, spent, still moist with his semen of an hour ago. She cupped his scrotum, stroking the shaft with the fingers of her other hand, giggling with anxious pleasure as it rose and stiffened at her touch. "You were too big a moment ago, Monsieur. And *now* . . ."

I'm teasing him, she thought, *I'm teasing him just as I'm teasing myself.*

For the truth was that she'd wanted to try it for some time—if she could only get herself beyond a certain lingering shyness.

He sat up slightly against the pillows, reaching to touch her face.

"Gently, gently, *doucement.* Don't fret, *chérie.* We'll simply see how far we get."

Bending his knees and widening his legs so she could kneel between them, he continued to croon encouragement as he stroked her eyelids, her cheeks and jaw. His fingertips traced the outlines of her lips, swollen with his kisses. He grasped her head and guided it downward.

"Breathe," he told her.

And so she did. She breathed him past her lips and against her tongue, past the soft liquid insides of her cheeks and down into her arching, widening, opening throat. It was a new sort of opening and relaxing, she thought, another way of dropping the barriers between yourself and someone you loved. She gagged a little; he'd continued to grow since he'd entered her mouth.

"Breathe." His voice trembled and commanded at the same time.

Yes, she definitely needed to breathe.

But how?

With your nose, *idiot.*

The draughts of air she took in were freighted with precious private smells. No wonder she'd felt shy about it, she thought: the intimacy and audacity of the act were dizzying, overwhelming. As was—she realized a moment later—her growing sense of her power over him.

She sucked and pulled. Teasingly, she flicked at him with her tongue as she loved him to do at her breast.

He groaned. She moved her mouth, her lips, her tongue over him more confidently. Quickly at first, and then as slowly as she was able. And then quickly again—rhythmically, she could feel her breasts bouncing—until he began to buck his hips and to cry out. He'd taken hold of her hair to guide the movement of her head, but there was nothing he could do, she thought, to control her wanton, arrogant tongue.

Scenes from his harem story flashed through her mind. Was she leader or follower, imperious lady or humblest concubine kneeling abject on aching knees? She couldn't tell. Perhaps it simply didn't matter. Or perhaps—in certain circumstances—it was possible to be both at once.

His cries became louder, harsh now. She gasped and shuddered, her body locked between his thighs, his sex buried deep at the back of her mouth. She hugged his waist and widened her throat just the slightest bit more—to receive, to swallow the hot salty fluid that exploded from him.

She collapsed on his belly.

"Oh Marie-Laure," he sighed, reaching down for her, drawing her beside him on the pillows, and cradling her in his arms. *"Oh* Marie-Laure."

"A letter for you, Joseph," Hubert announced at tea a few afternoons later, "with a very impressive seal on it. And nothing"—he barely looked at his wife—"for you, Madame."

Nodding curtly, he took the letters from the silver tray the tall, silent footman held out to him. "That will be all. You needn't stand here gawking."

"The one addressed to me looks official," he added with a frown, "and will probably oblige me to do something tedious."

Joseph recognized the familiar handwriting on the letter his brother handed him.

"It's from Jeanne," he said.

"The Marquise de Machery," he added a moment later when it had become clear that his brother and sister-in-law had forgotten the Christian name of the woman they'd betrothed him to.

"Ah." The Duchesse's saccharine smile did little to mask her disquiet. Joseph knew she wouldn't sleep easily until he'd been delivered to his fate, reciting his marriage vows at the large ceremony in a Paris cathedral, with some of the highest members of the King's court in attendance.

"How congenial," she said, "a letter from the bride. I remember how nervous I was, after the contract had been signed, sending my first little scented note to my intended husband . . ."

Her anxiety made her voluble. The wedding would mark her debut in Parisian society; she was having elaborate gowns prepared, and new suits for Hubert as well.

Joseph thought she'd probably make a success of it. Although still a harridan at home, nowadays she was quite presentable in public, having picked up some social graces from her friends—or allies—among the local gentry. Whatever her private struggles with Hubert, it was clear that she'd gained in confidence and social stature since becoming Duchesse. Hubert had been right about her will and energy. No doubt she'd exploit every social opportunity this Paris wedding provided; perhaps she'd even manage an invitation to Versailles.

He nodded politely while Hubert grimaced at the memory of the "little scented note."

Of course, Jeanne's letter wouldn't be a shy missive from a terrified girl being bartered into marriage. It would be an easy, erudite communication from an old friend.

He broke the seal and unfolded the heavy paper.

The letter was written in a large, clear, schoolgirlish handwriting, with ornate, imperiously drawn capitals.

Mon cher ami,

I miss you and so does all of Paris. How delightful that you'll be among us again so soon. . . .

He smiled. Her writing style was unmistakable: hyperbolic, magisterial, and always entertaining. An astute political observer and a waspish gossip, she always knew what the leading intellectual lights of the city were talking about. And she liked to pepper her news with bits picked up from her actor friends at the Comédie-Française.

. . . no one knows whether the company will be permitted to perform this marvelous play. The King changes his mind every day, it seems. Some mornings he wakes up emboldened to allow an entertainment that dares to make the same jokes everybody makes (only, of course, with a great deal more flash and brio). And sometimes he's sure that a simple comedy will bring the walls of the Bastille crashing down. And so he renews his censorship of The Marriage of Figaro *yet again. . . .*

Ah yes, he thought. It would be amusing to be in Paris again.

Oh no, he thought next. He winced. No. He didn't want to go. Not now, anyway.

He'd expected to be ready to leave by now. After all, it had been four weeks (four weeks and a day!) since that delicious morning in the barn.

Absurd—four weeks was a lifetime in a libertine's career, even a libertine who'd broken the rule against revealing his inner thoughts to the woman he was bedding. Four weeks with the same woman was a disgrace; certainly by now the inevitable slaking of desire ought to have set in.

For the last night or two he'd been examining himself for signals; like an imaginary invalid obsessed with bad humors, he'd been sure the decline was imminent. Pacing the floor or leaning back among the disheveled bedclothes, he'd scanned his emotions for the familiar signs: a creeping sense of tedium, a deadening of affect, a nagging feeling that he would have been better entertained spending the evening with a good book. In short, the complex of symptoms that Monsieur X had described as "the metallic taste of a stale affair."

But he hadn't found any of that (and anyway, if he were to read a good book, he'd surely want to know Marie-Laure's opinion of it). His mouth didn't taste anything like metal—it tasted like young red wine. His desire hadn't weakened. If anything, he wanted her more than he had before.

None of which made the least bit of sense to him; the storms of emotion he weathered these past weeks had left him stranded, marooned without a compass on the shoals of his desire. He ought to take a leaf from Monsieur X's book, he thought. *Cut off the entanglement—and while you're at it, Joseph, trim that awful metaphor about shipwrecks and compasses.* Of course, the entanglement would end soon enough in any case. Shrugging away his confusion, he turned back to Jeanne's letter.

> *. . . the prospect of our marriage has made my life a great deal easier; Uncle still frets about the reputation I've earned, but even he has become convinced that we've contrived a way to silence the gossips—or at least divert them to more acceptable slanders. It's humiliating to have one's affairs dictated in this way, but I confess that I'm in your debt,* mon vieux, *and will do whatever I can to make your life as agreeable as possible. We shall have to find someone for you to amuse yourself with, of course. Or is a series of someones still more your style? Well, even if it is now, it won't be so forever.*

Could it be true, he wondered, that he no longer wanted "a series of someones"?

> *And naturally* (the letter continued) *I look forward with keen anticipation to the moment when Monsieur X stops being the proverbial bad boy and succumbs, like the ordinary run of frail humanity, to love's exigencies. . . .*

Damn Jeanne anyway. He was happy that things were working out so well for her, but even so, it didn't give her license to tease him.

Even if she'd meant it fondly.

And expressed it with such infuriating precision.

He looked up from the letter and stared into the fire.

"Nothing wrong, I hope?" His sister-in-law had been watching him while he read. He pretended not to hear her. Let her worry, he thought, at least for a few moments more. Let her fret that her scheme might be encountering some resistance.

"Well, there's a great deal wrong with the communication *I've* received," Hubert burst in. "This damn police inspector has come all the way from Montpellier and insists upon seeing me early tomorrow morning—can you believe that the incompetent ninnies still haven't found the Baron Roque's killer? At the height of grouse-hunting season, too: the weather will be perfect."

His voice had risen to a high whine. "What's the use of being Duc," he demanded, "if I can't hunt when I want to?"

The Duchesse swiveled her head toward her husband. "I'll receive the inspector, Monsieur. By all means, do go kill a few more little creatures tomorrow morning. But about your fiancée, Joseph." She turned to him again. "I do trust that she's well.

"You needn't be troubled," she continued, "if she seems a bit hesitant. A little nervousness, you know, even a hint of vaporishness, is quite normal for a girl in her situation."

Amusing to try to imagine Jeanne with a fit of the vapors.

"She's quite well, Madame," he murmured. "In fact, she's in excellent form—at least in her letter."

"Whereas, when it comes to her *real* physical form," Hubert crowed, "we know she's somewhat *less* than excellent."

Delighted that nothing would interfere with his grouse hunting, he tried to extend his witticism. "Or *more* than excellent, I suppose one could say. Well, she's *fat* anyway." His braying laugh was loud enough to compensate for his companions' embarrassed silence.

"Give me the inspector's letter," his wife said, "so I can see what he wants of us. You say he's investigating a murder? Well, it might be a diversion at least."

> . . . *but I must go, dear Joseph.* (It was the final page of the Marquise's letter.) *My garden needs hoeing and this evening Madame Helvétius has planned a gathering in Ambassador Franklin's honor. A charming man, one is tempted to call him "Papa" as his intimates do. . . .*

His eye slid down the page of last-minute exclamations and well-wishes. And then back up to her observations about Monsieur X and "love's exigencies."

He stood up, bowing to his brother and sister-in-law. "A thousand pardons, Monsieur and Madame," he murmured, "but I must leave you to each other's charming devices. I need to . . ."

He didn't know what he needed to do. Walk, ride—or plunge into the river and swim until the cold water calmed his blood. For he'd just had an idea that was either completely wonderful or entirely crazy. He wasn't sure which, but he knew he wouldn't be able to puzzle it out among the present dreary company.

As though drunk on his thoughts, he stumbled out of the room, after waiting what felt like a week for an uncharacteristically slow Arsène to open the door for him.

The impending journey—just three days hence now—meant an enormous amount of packing for the servants, not to speak of washing, ironing, and mending. Madame Amélie's wardrobe would fill seven trunks. Small items like jewelry needed to be inventoried and packed carefully. The necklace the old Duchesse had promised for the bride would be carried in Monsieur Joseph's pocket during the nine-day coach ride to Paris. Lisette, the old Duchesse's chambermaid, had invited Louise and Bertrande for a glance at it that morning while her mistress was at her prayers—for she'd be returning to the convent the next morning.

"The colors, the sparkles," Louise marveled later in the dessert kitchen, "it's like bits of a cathedral window I once saw in Aix. Those blue stones are like wearing a piece of paradise against your throat."

Even Bertrande was awestruck. "I should think that if you sold it you'd get enough to feed all of France."

"It's too beautiful to sell," Louise said dreamily. "It's something for a man to give to someone he loves."

"Instead of to a fat old thing he's been forced to marry," Bertrande snapped.

"Shhhhh!" It sounded rather harsh in Louise's mouth, but the other two women knew what it meant. And sympathetic silence reigned as a pale, exhausted-looking Marie-Laure came in from the scullery, for a cup of reheated coffee to help her through the workday.

Poor thing, thought Louise, *I wish she'd confide in me, but she thinks*

I'm too pious to bear hearing the truth of these past weeks. And perhaps she doesn't know how she weeps in her sleep, the hours before daylight.

She'll get over him, thought Lisette, and all the better for her, too. *And next time she'll be wiser and get more than a few scraps of lace and velvet out of Monsieur Whoever-It-Is.*

As long as she's been careful, thought Bertrande, letting herself remember, just for an instant, the child she'd left, one gray early morning long ago, on the steps of an orphanage. But the memory was too sharp to be endured for more than an instant, so she stood and quit the room, dragging Louise with her, and scolding her soundly for the poor state of the carpets in the château's north wing.

It's ending. Perhaps it's already over.

The flat words seemed to accompany every breath Marie-Laure took, lodged like something hard in her chest. Was it her imagination, she thought, or had he seemed abstracted during her last visit, as though he had something difficult to tell her?

Perhaps, she thought, *he doesn't want to see me anymore—perhaps, in his mind, he's already living with his new wife in Paris.*

Well, she could hardly disapprove of that. He should be thinking of her and not of me, she told herself; even a loveless, arranged marriage deserves some respect.

Not that he hadn't been ardent or energetic last night. On the contrary: he'd plowed her until she was raw. Which was exactly the trouble. Whatever else was inspiring him, his lovemaking didn't have the *esprit* she'd become accustomed to, the sweet attentiveness or sly wit.

He's not thinking about me anymore, she thought. *Perhaps I shouldn't visit him tonight.*

But she knew that she would. For at this point in time—only two more nights before his departure—she'd settle for whatever she could get.

The interview with the police inspector had been as diverting as the Duchesse had hoped: diverting and even—in a louche sort of way—rather exhilarating. "Yes, Monsieur Lebrun," she'd murmured, "of course my husband and I knew the Baron Roque. A very old family you know. It was a great shock."

She'd allowed her shoulders to slump, as though weighed down by the magnitude of the crime. It was difficult, she told him, for a person of sensibility to hear such sordid things, from someone so close to the official investigation.

And was it true about the blood in the crème brûlée?

The inspector nodded gravely. *Mais oui* Madame, in *that* respect it had been just as the scandal sheets had reported. But in other ways it was even more interesting. . . .

Basking in her attention, he'd painted a vivid picture of the crime, pausing only for sips of coffee and bites of excellent pastry. Horrible, the Duchesse agreed, to think of the Baron gagged and bound to his chair as he slowly bled to death from a hideous stump of a wrist; his murderer had severed the hand from his right arm.

She nodded. The Baron had been the vilest of old-guard snobs, with a corrosive sense of humor. His jokes about her own less-than-aristocratic forebears had been repeated in high circles, and everyone (though not a common police inspector, she suspected) knew that he'd sworn never to call upon her.

"Didn't he have a bodyguard?"

"Yes, and a huge hulking professional of a fellow too. Who'd suddenly been taken ill that day. They'd even had the doctors—the bodyguard had been vomiting horribly."

"And the hand was never found?"

"No, Madame la Duchesse. Which may provide a clue, for he always wore a brilliant ruby ring on that hand—we're expecting the ring to turn up at a fence sooner or later. We suspect a crime of passion, given the Baron's record of amours, but we're not ruling out simple theft. It's a most valuable ring."

"But how does one cut off a hand?"

"Slowly and most painfully in this case, Madame. With a knife, it seems, though the weapon has never been found. All we know is that a tall, dark man was seen fleeing the Baron's Montpellier townhouse soon after the murder."

The truth was that the police had made no progress at all. The case, which had dragged on now for more than half a year, had become a severe embarrassment.

It didn't help matters that the Baron had been hated by his servants and peasants. The murderer must have had some help from the household staff; at the very least, the police surmised, his servants had looked the other way. Nobody had been very forthcoming under interrogation, but they'd all worked up convincing alibis nonetheless.

The Baron had no close family. And his distant relatives, all of them squabbling to lay claim to his property, could all prove they'd been many leagues away from Montpellier the day of the murder. A chambermaid had died a week or so before, but that had proved to be a suicide, not a murder, and didn't seem to have any bearing on the case. So there were virtually no clues to what looked embarrassingly like a miniature revolution.

"Which is why, Madame la Duchesse, we've been investigating common people who might have a grudge against the Baron. And given our suspicions of complicity by his household staff, we're particularly interested in servants.

"Of course," he added apologetically, "we hadn't thought we'd have to take the investigation to this side of the Rhône, but . . ."

Unfortunately she'd had no information for him. No, all her servants had been accounted for, the day of the murder. Well, surely she'd know, Monsieur, if any of them had been off to visit family members or anything like that. And the only newcomer to her household was an insignificant girl in the scullery—quite common enough, but certainly not the tall dark man he was looking for. But she'd certainly keep a sharp eye out—and yes, it would be quite permissible to interrogate the household staff. He might even search their quarters and their possessions. She, and of course her husband, were leaving for Paris, quite soon—a wedding, very charming, yes, another very old family—but she'd tell her general manager to cooperate in any way he could.

He'd nodded gratefully. "Yes, thank you, Madame la Duchesse, I'd hoped to get your husband's permission—or yours, of course. Always need the cooperation of the ruling nobility when one is out of one's local jurisdiction." But that, he hastened to assure her, was as it should be—Inspector Lebrun had only the most profound respect for local authority.

The Duchesse could hardly restrain herself, that night at dinner, from repeating the inspector's story. She'd already explained it all to Nicolas, but the horrific details only got more interesting the more one dwelt on them. Being at table, she was forced to elide the goriest parts; her enthusiasm, however, more than made up for her lack of specificity.

"They think it was a tall, dark man." She helped herself to the hothouse asparagus Arsène held out for her, put down the serving implements, and turned to Joseph with a smirk.

"I hope *you* have a suitable alibi, Monsieur le Viscomte."

What was that? He looked up, startled to be dragged away from his thoughts—of the dimples below the small of Marie-Laure's back, and of burying his tongue in one of them after slowly kissing his way along the bumps in her spine.

He'd teased himself with images of her all through dinner, distracting himself from the decision that faced him, and paying barely a whit of attention to the conversation at table.

Where were we? Oh yes, the unspeakable Baron Roque.

Hubert turned to him. "Actually, you were in Montpellier just around the time of the murder, weren't you? I seem to remember Madame de Rambuteau saying something like that in one of her letters."

Joseph shrugged. "I was delivering smuggled books, as every bookseller in Montpellier can attest. No thank you Arsène, no more asparagus for me."

His father might have liked the idea of smuggling forbidden literature; a pity he'd never told him. Amélie pretended to be scandalized, but Hubert tried for a thoughtful expression.

"I don't approve of it. Not for the general run of people, anyway. Subversive literature erodes their respect for authority.

"Nor," he continued, "does it sound like the best of alibis. For if you actually ever were accused of the murder, you'd have to get those booksellers to testify for you in court. And why should they let on that they were buying illegal books?"

Mon Dieu, it was all so boring. Still, he supposed Hubert was right.

"Well, that would rather compromise my alibi, wouldn't it? My only other defense, Monsieur and Madame, is that I'd had enough of the Baron years before, having once bested him quite decisively in a duel. He was a tiresome gentleman, really; I pity anyone who'd have to endure his company for the length of time it would take to dispatch him."

A chorus of laughter greeted this sally.

"Then you're clearly not the murderer." Hubert nodded. "And your secret is safe with us."

Should have denied I was there, Joseph thought. *My secret's probably only safe as long as I bring in that dowry*. Still, he was going to bring in the dowry, so in the end it didn't really matter. "Thank you, Monsieur, I trust that it is."

And rather more politely, over his shoulder, "Yes, I'm quite finished, thank you, Arsène."

His participation in the conversation no longer required, he retreated back into his meditations while Arsène served the fish course and Amélie complained about the state of the château's carpets.

The dimples above the swell of her buttocks. The swooping curve of her nape below her waves of hair. The weight of her legs slung over his shoulders as she lifted herself to receive him. Her eyes. Her lips.

He moved his hand over the cut-crystal goblet. No, no more wine. *And get your mind off those dimples as well, Joseph*. He'd need a clear head if he were to make this all-important decision.

His thoughts occupied him through the rest of dinner, and later as well, as he made his way back to his bedchamber through a precarious, half-demolished corridor, the walls swathed in scaffolding and drop cloths, the silvery stone soon to be hidden from sight by the Duchesse's mirrors and molded plaster.

Chapter 16

What a relief, he thought an hour later, finally to have made up his mind.

And now that he had, he was astonished that it had taken him so long to do so. Absurd even to consider doing otherwise, and foolish to dither about it until the last minute. Well, almost the last minute: he, Hubert, and Amélie would be departing the day after tomorrow.

Still, better late than never. What was important was the decision he'd made. He grinned, imagining himself telling Marie-Laure about it. But perhaps, he thought at the next moment, she wouldn't be as surprised as all that. She knew him so well, after all; she was probably wondering why he hadn't announced it already.

He had Baptiste lay out the new dressing gown: satin, and of a brilliant blue the tailor had told him was called "Queen's Eyes." It was the sort of thing a gentleman might wear on his wedding night, to do his duty by a blushing, innocent bride. But perhaps you could consider tonight a sort of wedding night. The start of a new life for the two of them.

We shall have to find someone for you to amuse yourself with, Jeanne had written. Of course. A gentleman needed a mistress every bit as much as he needed a valet, a tailor, an excellent glovemaker. . . .

He'd always imagined an actress, perhaps because Jeanne knew so many of them. Or a dancer, perhaps—a performer of some sort, anyway: a high-priced courtesan who'd perform privately for him in bed and publicly when he paraded her about the city; someone who'd be recognized, and whom people would envy him for possessing.

He'd imagined someone tall. Perhaps so that she'd be more visible on his arm, promenading at the Palais Royale. He certainly hadn't imagined a small, bookish girl (no matter how pretty) that no one would recognize.

But why not? He was going to be able to afford anything he wanted. Why couldn't *he have the only woman he'd ever cared about?*

He ran his hand along his jaw. Rough. Damn, he should have had Baptiste shave him. It would have been a nice, celebratory touch. She said she liked him a little bristly, but he wanted to give her all the smoothness her recent life had lacked.

Well, she'd have it soon enough. He smiled to think of all the things he'd buy her—all the ways he'd spoil her, pamper her—as soon as he had the money to do so.

Lace-trimmed stockings and dainty, pink velvet shoes with high, curving heels and silver buckles. Tiny diamond earrings. She'd wait for him on silken pillows, dressed in nothing but those stockings, shoes, and earrings.

His groin tightened as the fantasy grew more detailed.

She'd wait in a room decorated after an oriental theme. Purples, paisleys, heavy gold fringe. Tall vases for exotic flowers; squat, tooled-leather ottomans for exotic postures and positions.

In his mind, he arranged her among pillows and draperies. He parted her legs a little and caught his breath at the picture his inner eye had painted.

He'd send flowers every morning. Jasmine and tuberoses, gardenias and frangipani, to fill the vases and flood the house with heavy fragrance before his arrival.

Rosemary and lavender were all very well, he told himself, but it was time to move on to something richer.

He heard Baptiste's key in the keyhole. And then there she was: pink dressing gown, shy smile, bare feet. Amazing how familiar, how indispensable she'd become; impossible that things could ever be any different than they'd been this last lovely month. Too bad it couldn't be like this forever. For a moment he felt a stab of regret.

But just for a moment. Desire chased away the regret—desire and a restless compulsion to get on with things. He peeled the dressing gown from her shoulders, picked her up and deposited her onto the bed.

Who could blame him, he thought, if he paced things a bit precipitously tonight? He had so much to tell, so much to give. He only wanted to make her happy.

And anyway (he happily reassured himself), it seemed that she was quite ready for him.

But—he wondered this sometime later—which emotion, what pained thoughts, had darkened her eyes like that?

He told himself that he must be mistaken to suppose that he saw confusion, disappointment, even suspicion in her gaze. But that would be absurd, considering how flushed and breathless she still was, and how hot and moist and yielding she'd been just a moment before.

Still, there was no denying that her eyes were clouded. She seemed puzzled, a bit impatient—rather as though he'd just told a riddle she'd found tiresome.

He scanned her expression as he lifted himself off her. Ridiculous suddenly to feel so timid, after what he'd been feeling (what they'd *both* been feeling) just minutes before. She was only inches away and yet he couldn't help feeling that she was scrutinizing him—critically, and from a distance.

Not—he hastened to assure himself—that she hadn't arched and shuddered and cried out, more than once and from a nice array of positions, too. But—*oh, admit it, Joseph*—the truth was that there *had* been something lacking. He hadn't been able to make love to her in a way that was as special, as ceremonial as the occasion warranted.

He frowned as he leaned back onto the pillows. *She's awfully quiet,* he thought. *Perhaps she's just tired, though.*

He rolled over onto his front, lifting himself on his elbows to peer down at her.

"So you're not asleep," he said, gently stroking her eyelid with a finger.

She smiled and shook her head.

He took courage from her smile.

"I'm sorry," he said, "that I have not been quite myself this evening. But I've been doing a lot of thinking."

In another minute, she thought, *he's going to bid me farewell. And then he'll say he doesn't want me to visit tomorrow night.*

Well, she wouldn't be able to come tomorrow anyway. Nicolas had announced that the entire household would be pressed into service for last-minute laundry, mending, and packing. Perhaps she'd be ironing his drawers, or hemming a new cravat for him.

But if he was intending to say good-bye, she thought, he was going about it rather oddly, first with all that frenzied mechanical fucking and now by a flurry of nervous, nostalgic chatter.

"Do you remember the day we met?" he asked.

Only as well as I remember my own name, she almost said.

But then he grinned and for a bereft, panic-stricken moment she could only wonder how she'd possibly get through the rest of her life without seeing that grin anymore. Her confusion and suspicions fell away. Wordlessly, helplessly, she felt herself smiling back at him.

"I'd dealt with quite a menagerie of booksellers that day," he said, "old ones, young ones, fat and thin, dimwits and subtle fellows like Rigaud, and I was feeling tired and ill, and wanting to get back to the inn where I'd put up, on the outskirts of Montpellier. But the most difficult bookseller of all was the last one.

"Of course I hadn't expected a girl bookseller, a quite wonderfully pretty, if sharp-tongued, girl bookseller. What do you think I noticed about you first, while you were endeavoring to demonstrate that I didn't frighten you?"

She wasn't in the mood for a guessing game. Still, he looked so sweet and eager. . . .

"That's easy. My freckles."

"Wrong."

"Oh, well then—the ink stains on my fingers."

"Guess again."

"My 'determined mouth'?" This with a grimace.

He shook his head, smiling. He kissed her mouth until the grimace disappeared and then he dipped his head to gently kiss each breast, before adding, "And no, not even these."

"Well, then *what?*" This could take forever. Which wouldn't be so bad, she supposed, if he exacted a kiss for every wrong guess. Kisses or not—what *was* he trying to tell her?

"What I noticed first was your eyes. You looked boldly up at me, to take my measure, and I looked back into your eyes, all the restless, shifting blues and grays of them . . . the gray tones shade just a bit to violet near the center, didn't anybody ever tell you about the violet, *mon amour?* And I thought, that girl has the skies of Paris in her eyes."

"I've never seen Paris," she whispered.

"It's the center of the world," he said softly, drawing her into his arms. "Oh, parts of it are cruel and noisy and filthy. There are half a million people living there; the smells in some of the streets are indescribable. The King hates the city. He fears it, I think, and buries himself at court in Versailles, a half day's journey away.

"But Versailles isn't the true capital of France. Paris is, beautiful, foulmouthed Paris, with its cafes full of scribblers and its salons full of philosophers, all that energy, art, wit, and clamorous talk. You'll adore it, Marie-Laure. There's possibility in the air, immense, thrilling possibility."

Suddenly she knew what he was going to say.

Of course she knew. How could she *not* know? She'd wished for it, dreamed of it in fevered predawn reveries. She wanted it more than anything in the world, ridiculous and impossible as it was. She tried to imagine herself as a nobleman's pampered mistress and had to suppress a most inappropriate urge to laugh. It was all wrong; she'd be dreadful at it. She'd quickly grow bored with nothing to do all day except dress—dress and *undress,* she supposed. And he'd become testy, defensive.

Of course, there'd be all that lovemaking. And lots of time to read, too.

Still, it wouldn't work and it wouldn't last.

And yet, if it were the only way not to lose him?

Could she really find the strength to refuse?

He plunged on, oblivious to the sudden tension in her body. "And the air, Marie-Laure, the light in the air is blue. They say the east wind causes it—the light is blue and so beautiful some days that it breaks your heart.

"I want you there with me. I'll rent a beautiful little house. And I'll come to see you every day, buy you anything you want, everything you've ever dreamed of."

She opened her mouth to speak, and realized that she had no idea what to say.

How sweet, he thought, that she was so grateful, so deeply touched. He'd never set up a woman before. He'd never had the money to do it properly; his lovers had come to him for pleasure while their rich, official protectors paid the bills. But how exciting to plan an entire establishment, even a modest one, and to have it all on his own terms.

"I'll look for a house around the rue Mouffetard. You'll like it there, it's an old, hilly quarter, with air and light, and not too far from the universities: there will be scholars and students and bookshops nearby. I'll engage a chambermaid, but if you don't like her you can dismiss her. And a cook—of course you'll need a cook."

"No."

"All right, you can hire the cook yourself. Anyway, it's sad, isn't it," he tightened one hand around her waist and moved the other to her breast, "that we've never made love in the afternoon. I'll find a place where the rooms get a lot of light—several exposures, so the quality, the colors, the mood of it will change with the angle of the sun and the whim of the clouds. . . ."

"Please, no."

". . . so that whatever time I come, there you'll be, naked in the shifting lights and shadows of Paris."

"*No*. No, not like that. I won't be your mistress, Joseph."

Later, he would wonder how many times she'd had to say it before he'd finally stopped his prattling. And how much more time had gone by before he'd freed himself from the quivering fury that had possessed him.

It was as though he'd been taken prisoner by his worst self.

No? Had she really said "no?"

But that was impossible. Because after all (his worst self told him) it was one thing for a Madame de Rambuteau to dismiss him in favor of a pretty boy who played the clavichord. But it was quite another for this common chit of a bookseller's daughter—a bookseller's daughter, mind you, who didn't even sell books anymore, a bookseller's daughter who washed the plates he ate from—to inform the Viscomte d'Auvers-Raimond that she'd rather not be his mistress.

No?

And didn't she owe it to him, for shielding her from his father and brother's predations?

NO?

She wouldn't—couldn't—refuse like this. It was an outrage, an insult. . . .

Forget about the insult. His better self had finally managed to break into the prison house of his thoughts. *It's worse than an insult. It's a rejection from someone I love more than my life.*

"But . . . why?" he asked quietly. "Don't you love me as much as I love you?"

She'd been sitting up straight against the pillows, slow tears sliding down her cheeks. The air was cold tonight. She sniffled, hugging the coverlet to herself against the autumn air.

But it wasn't the air that made her shiver. The expression on his face was what had chilled her. The sneer of an offended aristocrat was a lot like the bared fangs of a feral cat, she thought, or the snarl of a street urchin battling that cat for food.

And yet he'd managed to put the sneer aside; he'd risen above the spite and selfishness that he'd inherited along with his title. *Perhaps,* she thought, *there* was *a way . . .*

He waved a bewildered hand at the sheets and pillows and covers tangled and strewn everywhere. "You've allowed me everything," he whispered, "and we've been so happy. Why won't you come with me to Paris?"

. . . but first, she had to make certain things absolutely clear.

She wiped away the last tears and sat up straighter.

He looked at her curiously. *Good,* she thought.

"I've allowed you no more than I've allowed myself," she said. "I've allowed myself to have everything of you that I could possibly have in the little time I had. You will have to understand this. And you *do* understand it, I know you do. After all, it's the idea behind your story, the idea of giving and taking between"—*astonishing how difficult it was to actually say it*—"between equals."

He frowned, the thoughtful frown of someone puzzling out a difficult conundrum.

"I won't be your mistress," she told him, "because I don't want to be a sort of superior . . . servant, or . . . or a possession. I don't believe a woman should be treated that way."

"Nor do I," he protested. "But after all, many wives are treated just as badly, if not worse. And you know that I'd never use you that way, no matter *what* you were called. Anyway, 'mistress' is just a word, a convenient way of expressing . . ."

She shook her head. "We're creatures of the words we use. 'Life, liberty, and the pursuit of happiness' aren't just words, they're ideas."

He shrugged, not quite ready to admit she'd scored a point. "And so you'd deprive us both of so much, just for the sake of—ideas?"

She hated it when her feelings got ahead of her ability to express them.

"I *will* come to Paris," she told him.

"Ah . . ."

She held up a hand. "But *not* as your mistress, Joseph. As . . . as your lover, I guess one would say. As an independent person. I'll work. I'll see if Monsieur Colet can find me a job as a cook. If I stay here until the end of the year I'll have my twenty livres after all, and I'll . . . I'll sell this dressing gown to buy the coach fare to get to Paris. Well, I need to work out the figures, of course, but . . ."

"But that's silly, waiting here for such a tiny sum when I'll be able to help you so abundantly. Don't tell me you won't accept any help from me."

"A loan, perhaps. Later, when I'm ready to buy a bookstall . . .

you know, it would be very helpful if you could make inquiries about what it actually costs to set up such a thing. . . ."

She would have the most splendid bookstall in Paris, he thought. And surely—as the realities of life in an expensive city became more evident to her—she'd relax some of her stiff-necked notions about accepting help.

But how charming she was, asserting her independence so insistently. He nodded, his mobile features suddenly becoming meek and solicitous.

"Of course, you'll be dreadfully busy," he said. "Too busy to see me, I expect."

She smiled. "I shall be busy," she agreed. "But not too busy to see you."

He wasn't convinced that any of this made sense. But he was too happy to care.

"I'll inquire about the bookstalls as soon as I get to Paris," he said. "As it happens, I know some people who make their livings that way, on the quays along the Seine. I'd be honored to be your agent in this matter." His mouth twisted a bit.

"What is it?" she asked.

"Oh nothing, it's just that—well, I'd wanted to give you Paris when the fact is that you're quite capable of taking it for yourself. So tell me, Mademoiselle Bookseller, what *can* I give you? Besides my promise to love you forever."

She let the coverlet slip down her breasts. "Do you think, Monsieur le Viscomte, that you could give me yourself one more time tonight?"

The sky outside his window was no longer black. No matter, he thought. He'd make love to her as though the night would last forever. Sitting facing her on the bed, he wrapped his legs around her, drew her close, and shuddered as the hard points of her nipples grazed his chest.

He kissed her mouth and cheeks, nose and eyelids, while she slid her tongue along the sinews of his neck. Her hands moved up and down his flanks. Her legs parted a bit; he felt her vulva swelling, the lips moistening, to allow him entrance.

He grasped her buttocks, lifting her an inch or so before he entered her. She growled, and then she laughed, and then she began to moan as he moved her up and down.

Slowly. Sweetly. Strongly and inexorably. Like the rhythm of the tides, the weathering of rock. Like a lullaby, crooned almost silently, after a child has fallen asleep at its mother's breast.

Forever, Joseph heard—or imagined he heard; he didn't know which it was and didn't care. Whichever it was, the syllables rang, resonated and receded just as his blood began to pound too loudly for him to hear anything at all.

Forever, Marie-Laure had whispered the word so deeply in her throat that she wasn't sure if she'd actually given voice to it, or whether she'd moaned it or screamed it or simply breathed and believed it.

To love you forever, she thought later, as they clung together, wordless in the gray early morning light, next to the door that neither of them could bear to open. She peered over his shoulder and saw their reflection—pale pink velvet and bright blue satin—in the three-part mirror across the room. An infinite procession of reflections. Forever.

Their final words came haltingly.

"I'll write to you," he whispered, "and you must write to me, too. The address is on the paper I've given you. Two months—*mon Dieu*, it seems such a long time."

"It's not a long time," she said. "You'll be busy. And productive, too, though I know you won't want to admit that. You'll have to adjust to a new life, after all. And a new . . . home, too."

She'd almost said *a new wife.* But she hated to think about that part of it.

"You know . . ." he began.

"Yes, what, Joseph?"

"Oh nothing, it's just that you needn't worry . . . about the Marquise, I mean. She's . . . well, it's difficult to express it tactfully, but she's not what you'd expect."

She shrugged, not wanting to hear about the woman he was going to marry. He looked relieved, as though he'd been uncomfortable with whatever he'd been trying to say.

"Oh well, you'll see what I mean when you get there," he said quickly. "What's important right now is that you'll be safe here."

There were times, she thought, when he'd be better off expressing himself less delicately. But in this case she understood what he was getting at. *Safe from my brother,* he meant, though it clearly embarrassed him to think about it. Well anyway it wasn't a problem. For the Duc *wouldn't* be bothering her, as he and his wife would be spending November and December in Paris.

"She's promised to pay our end-of-year wages as soon as she returns," Marie-Laure said. "And I'll leave directly after that."

"Yes, but if she doesn't—if she cheats you or if she or . . . or anyone else—tries to mistreat you, you must leave without the money. Promise me that," he said.

"I'm not afraid of being mistreated." She smiled, raising her fist. "But yes, all right, as soon as you're gone I'll sell the robe and hide the money. That way I'll always have coach fare in case I need to leave quickly."

She kissed him for the last time, opened the door, and gently shook Baptiste until he groaned and began to rub his eyes.

"I won't worry about anything, Joseph," she said. "And I shall love you forever too."

Forever, God willing, he whispered to himself as he stood at his room's threshold and watched her hurry down the dim corridor. And even some minutes after she'd disappeared around a corner, he stood motionless, his eye directed upon the empty space where she'd been. As though he could discern the path she'd traced through the air. As though he could keep her safe.

The hunched figure watching him from beneath the carpenters' scaffolding, hidden behind the folds of a drop cloth, silently cursed the man standing in the doorway. Bad enough, Jacques thought, that he had to endure this nightly reminder of Marie-Laure's rejection of his own advances. And even worse that he was obliged to scrunch himself up every night and listen to all that fucking without being able to see anything. There was a clear chink in the stone wall—good for listening, but placed at a frustrating visual angle—all he got was a shadow once in a while, or even worse, a pair of shadows; he'd had to use his imagination to supply the imagery.

Which had been entertaining in its own way, but ultimately uncomfortable and frustrating. As uncomfortable as his right leg, which tended to fall asleep during these vigils. And the itch on his rump. Not to speak of a bursting bladder.

Would the young mooncalf never go back into his room so that Jacques could scratch his arse and hop about a bit? Still, he thought, he'd certainly gotten the goods tonight. If he told the story skillfully enough, they might even pay him a bonus.

The door closed and Jacques sighed ecstatically. Revenge on the standoffish little bitch would be its own reward. But right now, all he wanted was a good scratch, a good piss, and the prospect of a few more livres clinking in his pocket.

Interlude:

MASTERS AND SERVANTS, PARIS AND PROVENCE

November–December, 1783

Mon cher *Joseph,*

How good and how strange it feels to write to you. The post is expensive, you know, and so I shall have to write very small and in the margins. Which is fitting, as I have only small things, and of marginal importance, to write about. But I'll try to tell you everything, because it makes me feel that you are nearer. . . .

"You've received the letter you've been waiting for." The Marquise de Machery's low, even voice was as smooth as the breakfast chocolate she poured from a silver pot.

She handed a cup across the table to her husband of two weeks. "And you're dumbstruck with happiness. I'm so glad, *mon ami*—but I must stop addressing you that way." Her face was grave, but her brown eyes glittered above wide pink cheeks. "It sounds too sympathetic. People will find it indecent and I'll be an object of scandal again."

Joseph laughed. "We shall have to practice ignoring one another—except for the occasional insult in company. We have an excellent model in Hubert and Amélie; we can study their manners tonight at supper."

He downed his chocolate in one long swallow. "But you're wrong about one thing—I'm not in the least dumbstruck. Be forewarned, you're going to hear everything. More than everything. I shall amplify, exemplify, explicate and pontificate—assault your ears with Marie-Laure this and Marie-Laure that until you beg for mercy. I'm awfully relieved to hear from her, Jeanne. I didn't tell you I was worried about her, but I was. I know how ridiculous that sounds."

"Of course it's ridiculous. But of course you worried. And of course I knew."

"Anyway, she's safe and well," he said, "except for missing me terribly, though she confesses to enjoying her full nights of sleep. She took some books from the château's library—there was no one to stop her—she found the Shakespeare and she says that when she gets a spare moment she reads the romantic comedies. And then she says . . . hmmm . . . where is it? Ah yes, squeezed in at the bottom: *'The only thing I want to read more is a letter from you.'* Well, by now she must have received one—or more than one, I hope.

"Unfortunately, it seems that she doesn't get a great many spare moments, because they're busy making jams and jellies, preserving fruit and vegetables for the winter. . . ." He shrugged. "Peeling, blanching, pickling . . . I'm not sure what she's actually talking about in this paragraph."

The Marquise laughed. "I am. We used to have to help in the kitchen at convent school, though I could sometimes contrive to work in the orchard instead.

"But it's delightful," she continued as they rose from the table, "to see a gentleman puzzling over the mysteries of pickles and preserves. And since you're showing such an interest in life's homelier details, Joseph, do you think you could assist me in the garden this morning?"

"Of course. There's a meeting of the Anti-Slavery Society today at La Grange—Lafayette has been very genial, welcoming me back into his circle and introducing me around; Marie-Laure was right, it's been good for me to get settled into a productive life here. But I have a few hours before I have to go. I'd be delighted to help."

She led him into the house's inner courtyard, where a gardener who'd been trimming a large, conical yew stepped down from his ladder to help her into a smock like his own.

"Thank you, Gaspard," she said. "And we'll need another smock for Monsieur le Viscomte."

Her daily routine didn't admit of alteration. Mornings—in all but the most inclement weather—were devoted to planting and weeding, raking and hoeing, pruning the trees and tying up the vines in the formal garden behind the hôtel Mélicourt, her family's vast Paris townhouse. She'd then take a plate of fruit, a glass of eau-de-vie, a bath, and a siesta, before settling down for an afternoon with Homer or Herodotus, her progress carefully recorded in her journal. After which it would be time for an evening at the salons or the theater, followed by an intimate supper with a companion or two. It was a civilized gentleman's life, she'd explained to Joseph, and she was happy to share it with him.

"We'll be spreading mulch over these flowerbeds," she told him now. "Here's a trowel and a cushion for you to kneel on. You can continue to chatter about your Marie-Laure, but only so long as you make yourself useful."

He shrugged, pretending to grimace at the prospect of getting his hands dirty. And then he buttoned his smock, hoisted up his breeches at the knees, and gracefully lowered himself to the cushion. He took a deep breath; there was a bracing chill in the air and the dead leaves and peat moss had a pleasant, earthy smell.

"It was a very sweet letter." He dug his trowel into the leaf and peat moss mixture and began spreading it over the flowerbeds where she'd planted next year's hyacinths. "Cheerful, newsy, and on the whole very decent and schoolgirlish. She's obviously never written to a lover. But when she receives *my* letters—well, she must have begun to receive them by now—she'll learn how it's done."

What luxury it was to prattle on, he thought, after months of pretending to his family that Marie-Laure didn't matter in the slightest. Jeanne was a good audience, sympathetic yet critical, with a sharp ear for self-deception—the sort of listener who made one want to get all the details right.

"It was stupid of me, though, not to give her money for postage," he continued. "She says she won't be able to afford to write to me every day, because of her confounded habit of saving every sou. Such a little bit of money, you know. I could have slipped some coins into the pocket of her dressing gown."

He stopped. "No, no, of course I couldn't have done that. She would have felt degraded by it."

The Marquise sniffed. "She felt degraded, it seems, by the prospect of being *my* husband's mistress. I don't know if I can approve of such stiff-necked pride from a scullery maid—even one who aspires to be a bookseller."

Joseph held up his trowel in protest. "You're a snob, Jeanne. Bookselling is an honorable trade and honorable tradespeople cherish their independence. I admire and rather envy her for it, as I envy anyone who hasn't been forced into a marriage, no matter"—he nodded politely—"how necessary it was for the both of us, and how pleasant it's turned out to be."

She returned his nod, but he could tell that she wasn't persuaded.

He spoke more forcefully. "And anyway, it's clear as day why she won't take anything from me. It's to prove that she doesn't care what I can give her, and that she'd love me no matter what. I think it's rather beautiful. . . ."

The Marquise shrugged and he gave up trying to convince her. Because—although of course he wouldn't tell Jeanne this—he also wished Marie-Laure were not so stubbornly self-sufficient. Still, there was nothing to be done about it. And anyway, the waiting would soon be over; before he knew it she'd be with him in Paris.

Better to turn to more agreeable matters. He drew a deep breath, paused, and allowed the next phrases to tumble from his lips in a boyish rush.

"But she has the most extraordinary, changeable eyes, Jeanne—sometimes blue, sometimes gray, they even shade to violet if you know how to look for it, and they're enormous . . . and did I tell you about her freckles?"

The Marquise laughed from deep within her generous chest and belly. "Only about eighty times, Joseph. But I don't mind; it's a most agreeable way for me to get a good laugh for today. How marvelous to watch the fastidious Monsieur X grubbing around in the dirt, besotted by a pretty, bookish scullery maid with wide eyes and freckles on her cheeks. It restores one's faith in the unpredictability of human nature.

"And you've done a lovely job with the flowerbeds, *cher ami;* all that's left to do is make sure the pyracantha by the west wall are tied securely to their trellis, and to check for spider mites. We doused them last week with a soap solution, but sometimes one has to repeat the treatment."

She rose to her feet and waved to the gardener, who scrambled down his ladder again, this time to pack away her tools.

"I'll be pruning with you tomorrow, Gaspard," she called, "so be sure to bring another ladder."

The pyracantha vines were quite secure, and the Marquise's careful investigations revealed no mites among their stems, leaves, or orange berries.

"In a month," she said, "the berries of this firethorn will turn a brilliant, seductive red. The sparrows will eat them and become drunk on the fermented juices. They'll be as giddy as you are, Joseph, and some of them will fly directly into the wall and smash themselves against it. It's a pity, really, but I've never known how to stop it."

He bowed over the hand she held out to him. "I'm not going to smash anything. Except perhaps Hubert if he spills his soup at supper.

"Until tonight, then, Jeanne. And I look forward to seeing Ariane as well."

She watched him stride down the gravel path to the house.

"Until then, *mon vieux,*" she called.

But it was evident that he hadn't heard her, for he'd taken the letter from his pocket and was rereading it, head bent and steps slowing in rapt contemplation of its decent, cheerful phrases.

The hôtel Mélicourt had fine bright lamps and splendid mirrors in its guest wing. Perhaps a bit too splendid, the Duchesse de Carency Auvers-Raimond found herself thinking that evening; there were times when one preferred one's image rather more obscure. She scowled at the reflection of her chambermaid, struggling with the hooks at the back of her gown.

There was no escaping it: the truth confronted her as though illuminated by the clear light of reason. The satin around her torso simply would not sit smoothly; the new gown, which had fit perfectly a month ago, was clearly too tight around the waist. She waved the maid away. No time now to let out the seams—she'd simply have to go down to supper with the violet fabric wrinkled and bunched.

She nodded thoughtfully at her reflection. Embarrassing to appear at supper this way: she'd been raised to always look her best in company. But then (she assured herself), tonight's supper could hardly count as company. Besides herself and Hubert, there would only be Joseph, his dreadful new wife, a doddering uncle, and that actress, Mademoiselle Beauvoisin from the Comédie-Française. And in truth, the actress was so beautiful that it wouldn't matter what anyone was wearing. Ariane Beauvoisin had a way of absorbing all the candlelight in a room, leaving everyone else in shadow.

An odd friend for that dowdy bluestocking of a Marquise, the Duchesse thought. But perhaps it hadn't been the Marquise who'd invited the actress to supper; perhaps it had been Joseph. Interesting, she'd have to keep an eye out for developments in that quarter.

She turned her attention back to the mirror. The badly fitting gown wasn't absolute proof, but taken together with other signs it constituted definite encouragement.

Of course, she hastened to remind herself, she and Hubert had been eating and drinking at some marvelous tables since their arrival in Paris a month ago. Her new sister-in-law's chef was as good as Monsieur Colet, and the dinners they'd attended at Versailles had been superb. Perhaps she was simply getting fat, like the overbearing, autocratic woman she and Hubert had saddled Joseph with.

No.

It was all very well to be cautious, the Duchesse told herself, but current circumstances allowed for more optimism. One missed menstrual period wasn't enough to go on—but two, and it almost *was* two by now, could be taken more seriously. And there had been other changes—subtle, but consistent ones that she'd been observing since Hubert had ascended to his title. Perhaps becoming Duc had helped him overcome his deficiencies. Or perhaps it was the reports she'd had his valet pass along to him, of what he'd overheard during his late-night spying.

But what had most likely done the trick for Hubert, the Duchesse decided, was the bargain she and he had struck. It had been her idea, of course; Hubert didn't have ideas, but he could recognize a good one when he saw it. *Do your duty, Monsieur,* she'd told him, *and I'll make sure you get what you so evidently covet.*

He hadn't asked her how she'd manage it, and in truth she didn't know herself. But she was confident of finding a way to do her part, if he could only get on with it and free her from the vile nightly necessity of trying to conceive. She'd be free for almost a year, anyway. Or—if she was lucky enough to produce a boy on her first try—she'd be free of him forever.

Oddly, she was sure that it *would* be a boy, as sure as she was of her ability to secure Hubert the prize he wanted so badly. Luck was on her side, the sort of luck that came to people who worked for what they wanted, and who weren't afraid to exploit every opportunity that came their way.

Her plans weren't fixed yet; it would still be necessary to improvise. But she'd manage it somehow. Setting Jacques to spying had been a good first step. The next steps would follow, in a carefully plotted sequence, immediately after she and Hubert returned to Provence.

Provence. She frowned, thinking how deadly it would seem after this glittering month in Paris—the lazy, spoiled servants with no respect for authority, the tedious family dinners, the trifling society of inconsequential local gentry. Amazing how intimidating she'd once found it.

But those days were over. After a few false starts she'd easily picked up the old aristocracy's gestures and language. It wasn't as difficult as she'd been led to believe: just witness her success this past month in Paris, and—she smiled triumphantly—at Versailles.

It had been glorious. She wanted to stay here forever. More realistically, she hoped to return next year, *without* Hubert. Was there a way to manage *that?*

There must be a way. There was always a way for intelligent, energetic people—just think how far her father had come, on the backs of the poor unlucky devils who harvested the sugar on his plantations. It wasn't as easy for a woman, of course. And yet, the Duchesse reflected, a woman had the advantage of being consistently underestimated. There would always be opportunities for a woman with money, strength of will, and unlimited resentment for the slights she'd suffered, especially from her husband's lazy, overbred family.

Finishing her slow turn in front of the mirror, she was startled to see a familiar plump figure in the doorway—almost, she thought, as though she'd conjured poor Hubert's presence by force of her meditations.

He appeared equally surprised to see her. His clothes were rumbled, his face drawn, his posture uncertain. Leaning on the doorframe to steady himself, he focused his red-rimmed eyes with evident difficulty. No doubt he'd been wandering muddleheaded through the corridors, aimlessly walking off the effects of alcohol and the aggressive ministrations of the girls at the Palais Royale this afternoon. After a hearty supper at the Marquise's table he'd be useless.

Controlling an urge to scowl at him, she turned for a final scrutiny of her reflection in the mirror. Yes. The evidence was convincing—and not simply because she wished it so heartily.

In which case, she concluded, it didn't matter how useless Hubert was.

I don't need him anymore.

She motioned for her maid to fasten the amethyst necklace she'd bought yesterday, on the rue de Rivoli.

"Good evening, Monsieur," she said.

He mumbled an apology for disturbing her.

Cordially, she assured him that she wasn't the least bit disturbed. Of course, they did have a few minutes before going down to supper. But perhaps he'd like to take a sip of brandy with her.

His eyes brightened above his livid cheeks and slack mouth.

"For I have some good news to report, Monsieur. And some interesting new thoughts about the bargain we made."

Mon Amour,

There are thousands of places to be alone in Jeanne's immense house. But I'm never alone now that I have your letter. I carry it everywhere and kiss it—and I kiss you, too—constantly, tenderly, passionately . . .

Marie-Laure smoothed the letter and tucked it under her pillow with the others. It was already a bit stained with grease, as she'd been carrying it in her apron pocket. But he'd used good, heavy paper and so the pages hadn't torn, though she'd been folding them and unfolding them all day—reading and rereading between her chores, each time adding a few new words or a provocative phrase to the increasing store she kept in her memory.

He'd sent a whole portfolio of letters this past week, far too many to keep with her at any one time. She'd decided to keep the most recent one with her, the last three under her pillow, and the rest of them in the hiding place she'd created for the sixty-three livres she'd received for the pink dressing gown, when Nicolas had taken the peignoir to market and sold it for her. "No, Marie-Laure," he'd said, "I don't want a commission—a pretty smile from you is as good as a commission." She'd hugged him and he'd laughed and said that now he'd been overpaid.

She'd never held so much money in her hand; coach fare to Paris only cost fifty-six.

And so, late one night when she was alone in the kitchen, she'd loosened a brick from the hearth. She'd wrapped the money, the letters, and Papa's spectacles in an old stocking, scraped out some loose mortar, and placed the stocking in the hollow she'd created, carefully replacing the brick. Except for when it was time to add one of Joseph's letters to the pile, she tried not to visit her treasures too often.

In my mind I kiss your eyelids, the little blue veins in your temples, the tip of your nose, and the quick pulse in your throat.

My tongue, my lips, wander happily over the sweet geography of your flesh—the gentle hills of your breasts, the serene flat plain of your belly between your hipbones, the flaming curls on the plump mound below. I linger here for a moment, at the entryway, and you gasp, arch your back . . . but no, not yet.

I shall be back, mignon, *after first turning you over and kissing my way down, down, until I reach the delicate skin at the back of your knees, being most careful not to miss a freckle anywhere on my way.*

Perhaps she wouldn't hide this particular letter away so soon, at least not until it had lost its power to make her tremble. Or until she'd figured out how to pen an equally erotic response.

But so far her efforts in that direction had come to nothing.

It wasn't that she'd stopped thinking of him that way. Quite the contrary. But it was quite a different thing actually to put her thoughts down on paper. She'd already wasted a precious sheet, trying to tell him what it felt like to have him inside her. But somehow it had come out all wrong—she'd wound up telling him that she'd felt "filled up" and "stuffed" and that he'd been "big as a baguette." Which was true enough, but hardly created the effect she'd hoped for.

And so she'd finally had to apologize to him (humorously, she hoped) for being unable to express what she felt, and to promise to make it up to him in person when she saw him in a month.

Well, perhaps a month.

It was only two weeks more before the Duc and Duchesse were scheduled to return. And even assuming that they took their time paying her wages, she ought to have her twenty livres in hand by the start of the new year.

Louise had explained to her how wages were paid here. The Gorgon liked to make a little ceremony of it: every six months, from when you'd been hired (or whenever the Duchesse decreed she had hired you), you'd be summoned to a small room in the Duchesse's wing of the château. The Duchesse would be seated in front of a a big ledger ("as though on the day of judgment"), ready to deliver a little speech about all the ways you'd been inadequate during the last few months. ("She's got sharp eyes, Marie-

Laure; you'd be surprised what she knows. And a sharp tongue, too.") It was only after bowing your head and humbly promising to do better that you'd receive your money.

Fine. She'd bow her head, promise to do better, and then—money firmly in hand—she'd announce that she was leaving, and that the Duchesse could go hang herself.

Yes, certainly in a month, probably even sooner.

Monsieur Colet had given her a list of likely employers in Paris, along with a letter of introduction. She had only to pack her belongings, take her eighty-three livres, pay fifty-six of them for a coach seat to Paris, post the letter she'd already written to Gilles, and voilà, she'd be on her way.

It *sounded* like such a happy, exciting plan.

So why wasn't she happy or excited?

Why (except in the buoyant letters she wrote to Joseph) was she so tense and irritable, anxious and fearful—and absolutely certain that something was going to go terribly wrong?

She, who was usually so patient and optimistic: hadn't it been she, after all, who'd assured Joseph that two months wasn't really such a long time to wait? But he'd been right and she'd been wrong; the time since he'd left had seemed endless and she'd begun to feel like an oppressive, sullen presence among the rest of the servants, who were all enjoying their masters' absence.

"While the cat's away, the mice dance," Bertrande had crowed six weeks ago, as she, Louise, and Marie-Laure watched the family coach rattle over the drawbridge and down the hill.

Hugs, smiles, and bawdy jokes were exchanged; Nicolas and Monsieur Colet huddled in consultation, and Nicolas produced some serious calculations in the matter of how many bottles of wine the servants could reasonably consume from the Duc's cellar, to be accounted for in his ledger under the category headings of "spoilage" and "breakage."

His double-accounting schemes extended even to the footmen, Marie-Laure surmised from a conversation she'd overheard a week or so later, one night when she'd come downstairs to squirrel away another love letter. Arsène was whispering confidentially to Nicolas that something had been "completely taken care of."

Neither of them had noticed her at the doorway; she'd shrugged and tiptoed away back upstairs. The men who supervised France's finances were probably a lot like Nicolas, she thought: subtle, good at details—only not so kind as Nicolas, nor as willing to share the spoils of their cleverness.

Of course, there was still work to be done, even during this little saturnalia. Nicolas was generous, but he wasn't about to let anyone shirk his or her chores. The Gorgon had left strict orders about what she expected to see accomplished upon her return.

Things did seem to get done, too; it was wonderful what people could accomplish, working at a pleasant, reasonable pace. People relaxed as they ate their meals, joked and flirted and sometimes even danced in the evenings, like Bertrande's proverbial mice. They made nice fires in the kitchen hearth and enjoyed each other's company, keeping snug and warm against the autumn rains that had swept down over Provence, and the mistral howling in the hills.

While Marie-Laure tried to keep her bad temper to herself and not to dampen anyone's spirits.

Probably it was nothing more than exhaustion, she thought. She trudged through her workdays, yawning, rubbing her eyes, swaying on her feet at the washbasin, and one day almost toppling into a pot of bubbling jelly. Guiltily, she accepted Robert's help with some of her chores, all the while shrugging off Bertrande's worried inquiries.

"But I'm fine, Bertrande. Really I am. Why wouldn't I be?"

Of course I'm tired, she'd told herself. Making passionate love until dawn every night for a month would make anybody tired.

As soon as I get caught up on my sleep, she decided, I'll be good as new. Or at least not so depressed by Joseph's absence, and not so fearfully envious of his wife. She wished now that she'd encouraged him to say more of whatever he'd been trying to tell her their last night together. Perhaps he would have argued her out of her worries.

Or perhaps not.

For suppose the Marquise turned out to be prettier than she was reputed to be? Or had starved herself into a more fashionable figure?

Not that her looks really mattered. She was still his wife, and still an aristocrat. Aristocrats had to have children; Joseph would be duty bound to oblige in the matter. Anyway, Marie-Laure thought, what woman *wouldn't* want a child who stood fair to inherit Joseph's gifts? Of course, only an aristocrat could afford to give such a child the advantages it would deserve.

She squeezed her eyes shut to block out unpleasant images, pressed her fists in front of her eyes to push away unpleasant thoughts.

The pressure made her lightheaded. And the giddiness, when it had passed, left her drained and rather terrified.

Louise was down in the kitchen tonight, dancing jigs with Martin and the others. Marie-Laure had been looking forward to reading snugly under the quilt.

She pushed the book away and blew out her candle. For words—even Shakespeare's words—seemed to hold no magic for her tonight.

"Sweet are the uses of adversity," the character in the play had proclaimed.

Oh really?

And she knew another wrongheaded example, too, from another popular writer. It was somewhere in the back of her head, or perhaps on the tip of her tongue. But she was too tired to remember it now . . . her limbs felt like lead, and . . .

What *was* that horrible sound, waking her from a deep, almost drugged sleep? It sounded like an enormous voice from the heaven she didn't quite believe in or the haunted forest the other servants liked to tell stories about. And it seemed to cry *Nooooooooooooooooooo*, as though it were talking to her alone, spitefully informing her that all her hopes would come to nothing.

It was pitch-black outside. She didn't care. Shuddering, she threw herself at Louise, rudely jostling her out of her own slumbers and drenching her with tears.

"But Marie-Laure, it's just the mistral . . . oh don't cry, Marie-Laure, of course he still loves you."

"No, no, he can't, Louise. Not as I am—angry and exhausted all the time, with my hair all stringy and my belly not flat anymore, and with . . . a baby coming." She gulped back her tears and peered anxiously at Louise. This was the first time she'd admitted it to anyone, even herself.

But Louise hadn't looked the least bit shocked or surprised. "We wondered how long you'd pretend it wasn't so," she whispered, "like Arsène's . . ." She clapped her hand over her mouth, eyes very large for a moment. And then, smiling her sweet, misshapen smile, she kissed Marie-Laure gently and stroked the strange new convexity to her belly.

"Monsieur Joseph will love you all the more as you grow," she said. "You'll look like a beautiful ripe winter pear."

And didn't Marie-Laure know, Louise added soothingly, that men loved babies?

"They pretend they don't, of course. Well, they don't like the crying and the messes, but they're so proud of having made a whole new person. I could see it in my father's face every time one arrived, though he was never sure how we'd manage to feed it. Don't worry, Marie-Laure, you'll see, he'll be happy and proud. And it's not such a long time to wait, is it, until you go to join him in Paris?"

Marie-Laure had shaken her head, sniffing back her tears, smiling despite herself, allowing herself to be convinced. It wasn't such a long time to wait. The Duc and Duchesse would be back in almost two weeks.

One week.

Two days.

PART TWO

Chapter 17

Provence
Late December 1783

Bertrande had a less cheerful proverb to offer, the day the Duc and Duchesse's carriage rattled back over the drawbridge and into the courtyard. "He who laughs on Friday will cry on Sunday."

Saturnalia was over. The Duchesse summoned Nicolas that very afternoon.

He spent an hour with her, and the next few hours pacing and making notes, trying to parcel her orders into new tasks and responsibilities.

He had new chores to assign, he announced at supper in the dessert kitchen. His shoulders sagged. It wasn't going to be easy for anyone, he added.

"All right," Bertrande replied, "but first let us listen to some of Jacques's stories of Paris, for we'll need some diversion in our heads, when our backs begin to ache. Tell us about the wedding, Jacques."

"It was in a cathedral," Jacques began, "with stained glass windows painting us all with wonderful colors, and . . ."

He continued on, describing the hubbub of the Paris streets, the wealth and splendor of the hôtel Mélicourt, the amazing abilities of the girls at the Palais Royale (where, it seemed, the Duc had spent much of his visit—and had even, Jacques added with a leer, shared the goods with his valet once or twice).

And what, someone asked after the envious laughter had subsided, of the Viscomte's new wife? Terribly plain, Jacques replied, impossible to imagine a gentleman taking her to bed. (Marie-Laure couldn't help breathing a bit more easily.)

Still, he continued, the Marquise was a good employer; her servants were loyal: you could barely pry any gossip out of them, that's how well they were paid. She set a good table, too, though she didn't receive many guests. But those she did receive, he added, were quite interesting, like her actress friend Mademoiselle Beauvoisin (he shot a keen glance down the table at Marie-Laure)—"*O-là-là,*" he said, "I've never seen such a beauty."

He paused for effect. Well, *nobody* had ever seen such a beauty. And she had a reputation, that one . . .

"All right, all right, that's enough for now, Jacques. We must all wait until tomorrow to hear more." Nicolas's interruption was greeted by groans and catcalls. Jacques smirked and turned back to his supper, while everyone else quieted down to hear the onerous list of announcements.

There would be a banquet and a ball in two weeks, Nicolas said, to celebrate the New Year. So the ballroom must have a thorough cleaning. (He nodded grimly. "And yes, that means every crystal of every chandelier.")

Menus from the kitchen would have to be reconsidered, he continued, because the Duchesse was finally, miraculously, pregnant. (A few more catcalls accompanied this announcement, accompanied by a few stares at Marie-Laure. "Quiet," Nicolas snapped.) Anyway, the pregnant Gorgon had informed Nicolas that her appetite was most delicate these days. (Monsieur Colet stalked away in high dudgeon, offended that anything his kitchen produced could be considered difficult to digest.)

The carpenters would be back directly after the holidays, he told them now, to build some sort of new hunting lodge for the Duc, as well as a suite of rooms for the new member of the family.

("That means scaffolds and drop cloths again." Bertrande groaned. "And plaster dust everywhere.")

And of course, Nicolas concluded, the Duchesse's wardrobe would need extensive renovation, in light of her condition. Her chambermaid wanted help (he nodded to Louise) unpacking the eleven trunks they'd brought back from Paris. Not to speak of miscellaneous boxes of ribbons, stockings, hats, and gloves.

"Oh, and Marie-Laure . . ."

Thank heaven. At least she'd be getting her money.

". . . Madame wants you to serve tea this afternoon, in the library."

Her face fell.

"And no," he added, "she didn't say when she'd be paying you." Marie-Laure could discern the tinge of guilt shading his voice. Nicolas wouldn't say so, but he'd clearly forgotten his promise to ask the Duchesse about her twenty livres, no doubt because he'd been so addled by all the demands that had been made upon him.

She nodded, swallowing her disappointment. No point creating more difficulties for Nicolas, and anyway, she wasn't awfully surprised. Louise had explained that wages were almost always paid late, "so they can collect a few sous more interest on it."

"Wear a clean apron," Nicolas told her, "and don't rattle the teacups."

It had been good advice about the teacups. For she'd been seized by an unaccountable wave of anxiety upon entering the library, and it had lasted the whole uncomfortable hour she'd spent with the Duc and Duchesse.

Not that either of them had acted so strangely. The Duchesse was no more peremptory than usual and the Duc only mildly inebriated. He'd peered down her bosom, of course, when she'd leaned over to give him his tea, but he would have done so at any time. His gaze had been calmly proprietary rather than guiltily lustful.

He and his wife said little to each other, and they hardly addressed a word to her.

But it seemed to Marie-Laure that their eyes followed her about the room, flickering with a sort of cold self-congratulation. The Duchesse (now quite knowledgeable about these matters, no doubt) had directed a keen stare at her newly swollen breasts and slightly thickened waist. For a moment Marie-Laure had expected to be fired right then and there, so obvious was the evidence of her "lewd behavior."

But the Duchesse had only nodded, rather thoughtfully, before demanding that "Marianne" bring the Duc some more cake.

Carrying the tea things down to the kitchen later, she allowed herself some slow shudders to dissipate the afternoon's queasiness. It had been a nasty business, all that bending and curtsying in menacing silence, and feeling all the while as though she were being assessed and appraised, like a piece of property. Nasty, intimidating, and rather disgusting, but now that it was over, it all seemed pretty meaningless. And certainly harmless, which was the important thing. Marie-Laure was sure that if Monsieur Hubert were planning a late night visit to her room he would have looked guilty about it, especially in front of his wife.

If they try to mistreat you, Joseph had said, *you must leave without the money. Promise me that.*

But they hadn't mistreated her, and it didn't look like they were going to. They'd merely humiliated her.

And it would be considerably more humiliating to leave without the money she'd earned. Especially now, with the baby coming. She hadn't written to tell Joseph about it yet. Of course, she reminded herself, he *might* be as proud and happy as Louise had predicted, but (she thought briefly of that actress, his wife's beautiful dinner guest) it would be best to have a little extra money in her pocket, just in case.

She hadn't received a letter from him today. Too bad; she could have used one, both to take the bad taste of the past hour out of her mouth, and to give her courage to announce the baby. She'd wait, she thought, until she heard from him next—surely it would be tomorrow—and then she'd write and tell him.

* * *

"You can't imagine it, Marie-Laure, all the beautiful things the Duchesse has brought back with her from Paris."

Of course, Louise had added, the Duchesse's snooty chambermaid had gotten to unpack all the best items—small, fascinating articles like ribbons and stockings, linens, laces, and of course jewels; Louise had been set to lugging around heavy rolls of silk and satin, velvet and brocade. She sighed; they'd be seeing a lot more of those fabrics. The Duchesse's dressmakers had already begun to cut and drape the stuff, but with her typical thrift, the Duchesse had decreed that her house servants would do most of the stitching.

"She intends to have an entirely new wardrobe," Louise said. "With seams wide enough to be let out in the months to come and then we'll have to take it all in later."

"And such colors," she continued. The Duchesse had made a study, it seemed, not only of the latest Paris fashions, but of the fashionable vocabulary as well. She'd brought back a pile of ladies' journals, and her maid had proudly told Louise that new ones would be arriving regularly, by post.

"You'd think that words like gold or blue or brown or white would serve, but now she calls them things like 'Queen's Hair,' 'King's Eyes,' 'Paris Mud,' or 'Goose Shit.' "

She frowned, and reached into the big basket she'd brought upstairs with her.

"I'm sorry, Marie-Laure. I know I promised to help you let out your dress, but it looks like both of us are going to be up late tonight hemming this 'goose shit' satin."

They'd have to wear their cloaks as they did so, and wrap their feet in shawls as well. For an especially cold and querulous mistral had arrived in the wake of the Duc and Duchesse's return.

The wind's howls woke Marie-Laure briefly in the middle of the night; the air in the room felt like ice, and she had to snuggle up to Louise in order to fall back asleep. And she was entirely unprepared, the next morning, for what the mistral had brought with it from the north.

"Marie-Laure, come see how beautiful." Louise pulled off the covers and hustled her out of bed.

"But what is it?" Marie-Laure asked in amazement, staring out of the small window at a world that seemed covered in whipped cream and silvery spun sugar.

"It's snow, silly. Don't tell me you've never seen snow. Really? It doesn't snow in Montpellier?"

Marie-Laure shook her head. She'd heard about snow, of course, and read about it, but she hadn't expected it to glitter so enticingly in the sunshine. It weighed down the pine boughs. Even the cypress trees wore quaint little white caps on their lofty tops. She peered at the vines whose tendrils crept onto the outside of the window. Each twig and stalk and leaf was encased in its own perfect little covering of ice.

Her breath clouded the small windowpane. And when she put out a hand to wipe away the steam, she was surprised by how cold the glass was.

"Come on." Louise tugged at her nightgown. "Get dressed. We'll have a few minutes to play in it before breakfast if we hurry. See?" She pointed to a few figures stomping and sliding about in the white expanse. "There's Martin," she said, quickly pulling on three layers of stockings, and multiple layers of everything else, ending with a heavy wool cloak.

Marie-Laure tried to dress as Louise was doing. But even one layer of clothes was a clumsy fit nowadays, and her own cloak wasn't very heavy at all. She followed Louise down the steps. But by the time she'd reached the door to the courtyard, Louise had already run outside.

Still, it was lovely to enter the quiet, crystalline world the snow had brought, even if the beautiful stuff did make your feet terribly wet. Marie-Laure walked in footprints other people had already tramped down, to the archway between the château's courtyard and the hillside that sloped down to the river. Martin had brought some feed sacks, and she watched him and Louise lie down on the sacks, belly first, and fly down the hill.

And here was Robert, trudging back up the hill, his nose, and especially his ears, bright red.

"Time for breakfast, Marie-Laure," he grinned. "Come on back inside; it doesn't look like you're dressed for this weather."

They walked back across the courtyard and into the château.

"I've never seen snow before," she said. "We didn't have it in Montpellier," she added, "or in any part of Languedoc. In school we learned to be proud of our 'gentle and felicitous Mediterranean climate.' "

"Well," he answered, "in Provence the snow sometimes surprises us up in the mountains here. It's the only good thing the mistral brings us.

"Along with icy, dangerous roads—no post today, of course—and winter chills and coughs and sniffles," he added. "So be careful."

No post today. No, of course there wouldn't be one.

And by evening both Marie-Laure and Louise had itchy red eyes and runny noses. And yards of ivory satin still to gather into ruffles.

"We should take a rest, go down to the kitchen and brew a pot of tea," Marie-Laure suggested. "Otherwise we're likely to sneeze all over the Gorgon's new finery."

Louise clapped her hand to her forehead. "But what an idiot I am. She gave me some herbs today, in case the chill in the air had made you and me sick. In fact, she expressly told me they were for you—because of your condition, I guess."

Still chattering, she handed a carefully folded sheet of printed paper to Marie-Laure. "I thought it was unusually kind of her, though perhaps it contains something to keep us awake so we can finish these infernal ruffles. But . . . what *is* it, Marie-Laure?"

For Marie-Laure had suddenly turned pale, and her eyes had darkened. She dropped the open sheet of paper onto the ivory satin in her lap, scattering dried peppermint and elderberry leaves over the shimmering fabric.

"Be careful," Louise exclaimed, "the ink from the print could smudge the cloth." And then, hearing what she'd just said, she peered sharply at Marie-Laure. "The print—the marks, the . . . the *letters* I suppose they are—Marie-Laure, do they say *Joseph?*"

Marie-Laure smiled bitterly. "I'll read it to you."

"It's about an actress," she added, "in Paris. And it tells its readers that 'the sublime comedienne, Mademoiselle Beauvoisin, fresh from her triumph on stage in *The Prodigal Son,* seems to have scored an offstage triumph as well, for she is seen everywhere with her new protector, the handsome Viscomte Joseph d'Auvers-Raimond. Sharp-eyed observers have spied her slipping from a covered carriage into the Viscomte's grand home at midnight. And all of Paris is whispering that she has taken up recent residence in a certain small house on the rue Mouffetard . . .'

"I won't read you the part about the beading and appliqué work on her new gown," Marie-Laure said, "though this journal describes it for two paragraphs, and concludes that it's a good thing Mademoiselle Beauvoisin's patron has such a rich wife. It's from one of those Paris fashion magazines."

I'll buy the most expensive mistress in Paris. . . .

But he hadn't really meant it, she told herself.

The mistral growled, somewhere in the distant hills. It sounded angry, and impatient with her stupidity.

She emended her thoughts. Well, he might have meant it at the *time . . .*

The mistral gathered strength, like Gilles clearing his throat for a pompous, older-brother lecture.

She hastened to defend herself. (To whom, she wondered. To Gilles? To the mistral? Or to her angry, frightened self?)

All right. He probably *had* meant it. But he'd changed. She knew he had. He'd said that vicious thing *before . . .*

Before what? the mistral asked in its vilest, most querulous tone. *Before he came under* your *wholesome influence, Marie-Laure? Or before you gave him the chance to get you into the mess you're in?*

Do you think a damn aristocrat ever really changes? Remember his dear, dead, distant cousin, King Louis XV, who used to have his own whorehouse?

But Joseph isn't like that. He believes in liberty and equality and . . .

Ah yes, Marie-Laure? And have you also forgotten the Comte de Charolais, who used to amuse himself by shooting commoners from his rooftop and was pardoned for it, more than once, by that same old King Louis?

No, she told the mistral (or Gilles, or herself, or whomever she was arguing with). No, I haven't forgotten.

She balled up the paper in her hand and threw it across the room, suddenly aware that Louise had been watching her for what must have been an awfully long time.

She smiled—a rather ugly, wolfish smile, she supposed—and shrugged carelessly.

"Well, it didn't take him long, did it?" Too bad she couldn't keep her voice steadier, she thought.

"Oh, Marie-Laure . . ."

"And yes, it *was* 'unusually kind' of the Duchesse to send me this. No, Louise, I didn't mean that—yes I know I said it, but sometimes, you see, a person can say something and mean the opposite . . ."

She and Joseph had had a wonderful, complicated discussion of irony once. It seemed a very long time ago. She felt very alone.

"But, Marie-Laure . . ."

"Yes, I suppose it is confusing. Do you think you could go make some tea and bring me a cup—no, not this stuff, something that doesn't stink of peppermint, all right?

"While I finish stitching this damn goose shit satin."

She felt calmer the next day, at least while the mistral was quiet. Calmer, more reasonable, and readier to give him the benefit of the doubt; after all, the piece about him and the actress could just have been slanderous gossip.

The roads were bad and there was still no post. And there was a lot of work to do. Moreover, it seemed that she'd developed a nagging chronic backache that lasted through the next two snow storms—and made her terribly uncomfortable while she scrawled her brief letter telling him about the baby.

But even when the snow had melted and the post had been restored, she still didn't receive a letter. The fashion magazines still came, though, and Jacques could be depended upon to pass around the clipped items about the Viscomte and his gorgeous mistress. The New Year came and went.

The Duchesse handed Marie-Laure a small sack, with twenty livres in it. She sat behind her big ledger, just as Louise had described. But Louise had been wrong about one thing: the Duchesse hadn't accompanied the payment with a lecture. Just a murmur of "Thank you, Marianne, for your faithful service to the Duc and all his family." Accompanied by a lewd, level glance at the little belly Marie-Laure had developed.

And except for a soft "Thank you, Madame la Duchesse," accompanied by a curtsy, Marie-Laure didn't say anything either.

Chapter 18

The servants at the hôtel Mélicourt each received a gold louis for the turn of the year, as well as personal well-wishes from their mistress and her husband. It had been a busy holiday season; there had been holiday balls and parties, sumptuous banquets and amusing theatricals.

January was crisp and cold, Paris uncharacteristically quiet and serene under a mantle of snow.

The Marquise's pyracantha had turned flaming scarlet, and every day she swept up a pile of tiny corpses, looking up from her broom to the window where her husband sat writing.

He'd finished a story, he told her. Perhaps he'd read it to her someday, but first he was going to send the manuscript to Marie-Laure, to see what she thought of it.

She'd asked if he was planning any more fiction. He didn't know. Not right now. These days most of his writing was devoted to the antislavery campaign. Well, and letters of course, he added quietly, he was still writing letters.

Poor boy, she thought, it had been weeks since he'd received a response. It would soon be February. What could the silly, stiff-necked girl be thinking?

* * *

"Perhaps she took a little holiday," the Marquise suggested at breakfast. "Went home to visit her brother for the Noël, you know, and stayed through the New Year. Time rather slips past one, during this season."

He grimaced.

"I've considered that."

"And?"

"I've also considered that perhaps, upon seeing her again, her old sweetheart decided hang the dowry, he wanted her even without it. And that his uncle agreed to it this time. And that she . . ."

"You think that *she* also . . ."

"Well, in some ways she's very conventional. I know she respects the institution of marriage. And that she never really liked the idle life I lead. She thinks a man should leave the world a better place than he found it, you see."

"As you have been trying to do."

"In a small way, perhaps."

"But you think she's jilted you." Her gaze was keen, though her voice was quiet.

He paused, forcing himself to maintain an impassive expression. Only a spark or two, somewhere behind his dark eyes, betrayed evidence of inner struggle.

"No," he said. "No, when all is said and done I still think she loves me. Something's wrong, Jeanne. I'm going to Provence, and if I don't find her at the chateau at Carency I'll go on to Montpellier. I'm worried that she needs my help. I should have gone already."

"It would have been difficult, with the roads so bad. And there was Uncle's illness, and the Anti-Slavery Society—not to speak of all that business with Ariane. You've been very good, Joseph, and I shall miss you. But of course you have to go, *mon ami.*"

"I've ordered the coach for tomorrow. Baptiste is packing my things."

"But you'll come to the rehearsal tonight, won't you? We promised to take the actors to supper, you know. And you'll love the play."

"You forget, I've already seen a private performance of *The*

Marriage of Figaro, at Versailles. But yes, I admire it immensely; of course, I'll come. I can sleep all day in the coach tomorrow."

The gossips, scandal-sheet writers, and Mademoiselle Beauvoisin's claque of faithful admirers weren't the only ones keeping close watch on the hôtel Mélicourt.

"He's ordered the traveling coach, Inspector Marais. He intends to leave Paris tomorrow. If you're planning to arrest him, you will have to do it tonight."

"Gently, gently, Pierre." The Chief of the Capital Crimes Division of the Paris Police glared at his enthusiastic assistant, from across a vast, cluttered writing table.

"Remember, if you can, that I am not *planning* to arrest him, merely to search his possessions. I can't arrest him unless we find some palpable proof. And even so . . . searching an aristocrat is a touchy business. Are the warrants in order?"

Proudly, the younger man produced a large pasteboard portfolio.

"Put it down. Yes, there, on top of that pile of paper."

Marais opened the cover and gave a low whistle. "*Mon Dieu*, enough red wax on those documents to light a candelabrum. Very official. My compliments, Pierre."

"They're demanding an arrest, Sir. Some of these papers come from Versailles."

"And the other papers?"

"I thought you'd want to review the dossier we've been keeping, on the Viscomte. No, not that file, Monsieur *l'Inspecteur*—that one's from several years ago."

"Hmmm, it's got my handwriting on it. But I don't remember . . . no, wait a minute, I do remember. Auvers-Raimond . . . we arrested him, I believe, for a duel, with . . . merde, with the same Baron Roque. I'd forgotten that part. The Baron tried to get us to lock him away but the charges didn't stick."

Rather a blunder to have forgotten, the inspector thought; it would be awkward for him if the higher-ups got wind of his omission. He looked at his assistant with keener attention, and some gratitude as well.

Loyally, Pierre pretended not to notice the gratitude. "And then there are those rumors about his wife, Sir."

"The wife's not our department, Pierre. Still, I suppose it does contribute a certain irregularity. And that folder?"

"The reports from Inspector Lebrun in Montpellier. Well, some of them—you've read all the early stuff, all those months when he couldn't find anything. These later reports are more interesting, especially the testimony he took from a servant in Provence. The Viscomte had been in Montpellier, it seems—the servant overheard it while giving him his dinner one night—Auvers-Raimond was in Montpellier the same day as the murder. Smuggling books."

"Rough work for a gentleman, book smuggling."

"So is murder, Sir."

The inspector grunted.

"And did anyone actually see him in Montpellier?

"Not," he added, "that I'd expect much corroborating testimony there. After all, if you were a bookseller, with the censors always sniffing after you, would *you* admit to trafficking in smuggled goods?"

Pierre smiled in agreement.

"You're right about that one, Sir. There wasn't a bookseller in Montpellier who would admit to having so much as laid eyes on a smuggler. But Lebrun found someone who had. Well, he's not really a bookseller; he's a medical student.

"His late father was the bookseller. Good thinking of Lebrun to question everyone whose family was in business *last* year, instead of just the ones selling books now. It's a rather cutthroat profession, evidently; in Montpellier one ambitious fellow keeps buying up his competition.

"Anyhow, this Vernet reports that his father got a visit from someone of the Viscomte's description about a year ago—and rather worse for wear, too. And this is the interesting part: the gentleman was wounded. Lebrun speculates that perhaps the murderer was wounded during the commission of the crime itself."

"No evidence of that, you know, Pierre. And I take it that this Vernet didn't find the Baron's ruby ring."

"No, Monsieur *l'Inspecteur*—he only mentions an onyx signet ring. You're right; the pieces don't quite fit together. But Lebrun was overjoyed nonetheless. It was the only break he'd gotten on the case and it's been more than a year now. And so he asked us to apply for a warrant to search an aristocrat's home for evidence of a capital crime."

Chief Inspector Marais nodded. "Hence all the red wax."

He leafed through the pages. "Allows me to search the gentleman's home and personal possessions, though not his aristocratic person itself. Versailles wants action, even if it turns out to be one of their own. Of course," he added, "if I don't find anything, it'll be my skin."

Pierre laughed, as though to dismiss that possibility. Ambitious young puppy, Marais thought, overconfident, and with a better understanding of paperwork than of people. Still, he'd done an impressive job of preparation.

"Well, it'll be *our* skin then, Pierre. For you'll accompany me tonight. Good experience for you, I think."

The Viscomte and his wife, the Marquise de Machery, arrived home around eleven, in a small covered carriage. They were in great spirits. The rehearsal had been lively, if unpolished. Well, it was just a first reading, to allow the actors to get a feel for their roles. Nonetheless, they'd thrown themselves into it with gusto, encouraged by news that *this* time the King might actually allow a public performance.

Joseph recited some phrases that had stuck in his mind:

"*Because you are a great lord you think yourself a great genius . . . nobility, wealth, rank, office! all this makes you so high and mighty! . . . for the rest you're an ordinary person while I, damn it, lost in the anonymous crowd, have had to use all my science and craft just to survive.*"

His wife applauded.

"Bravo, Joseph. Well delivered."

"They're strong phrases," he replied. "They speak themselves. And they'll speak to the audience."

"I wonder," the Marquise said, "what will happen when all of Paris is repeating these phrases."

The coachman had leaped from his seat to help her down the carriage steps. He hurried to care for the horses now, leaving the carriage discreetly parked in the courtyard. It would remain there for an hour, while he took a quick supper. But just before midnight, he'd drive back out through the mansion's porte cochere, into dark streets, past a slumbering Notre-Dame, across the Seine and up a steep hill, to fetch a visitor from the rue Mouffetard.

The couple crossed the chilly moonlit courtyard, both of them laughing as they tried to reconstruct other speeches, especially the self-serving ones the playwright had written for Figaro's master, the lecherous Comte Almaviva.

"You know, Joseph," the Marquise said, "you have a bit of both protagonists in you—Almaviva the privilege-loving aristocrat and Figaro the wily democrat. A composite character would be an interesting hero for a comedy."

He managed a tight smile as the mansion's double doors swung open. "Always caught between two worlds, two points of view. But I don't think such a hero would do for the stage, Jeanne. Perhaps in a novel. *But what's this?*"

The chief footman was in a state of great agitation.

"I beg your pardon, Madame la Marquise, but there are two policemen in the green sitting room. Got here two hours ago. With, with . . . a warrant, Madame. They showed it to me, Madame.

"They said they'd be happy to wait for you, Madame. Well, for Monsieur le Viscomte actually."

All in all, Inspector Marais thought later, the handsome Viscomte and his fat, plain wife had acted quite decently.

Both of them had seemed utterly astonished at first. They spoke so sincerely and seemed to have so little to hide that he'd been sure the affair would prove an embarrassment for himself and his superiors. Both of them carefully read the warrant and agreed that they had no choice but to allow a search. And both of them were intelligent enough not to say anything that might worsen the situation.

They'd had the footman bring a pot of tea. But of course he and Pierre had refused. They'd wanted to get started as soon as possible, and to avoid any irregularities. The inspector had supervised every detail of the search, watching closely as Pierre and a uniformed gendarme sifted through the trunks and boxes packed for tomorrow's journey. Not finding anything there, they started in on the paneled armoires and inlaid commodes, the chests and dressers and wardrobes of all sorts.

The gentleman dressed well, Marais thought, in sober colors for the most part, but richly, elegantly. And what an array of toiletries and accessories. So many clever, beautiful little items, jeweled, enameled, or bound in good, expensive leather. The Inspector didn't even know what most of them were, while Pierre seemed almost in a dream, as though he'd stumbled into Ali Baba's cave.

But no ruby ring.

They'd tried not to make too much of a mess. Putting everything back would be a lot of work for the gentleman's valet, anxiously watching from outside the doorway.

The Inspector had begun preparing his apologies to the Viscomte and his wife when he'd noticed the dressing gown, crushed and wrinkled in a back corner of an armoire. It seemed to have been rolled up in a ball and sloppily tossed there, quite unlike any of the rest of the gentleman's well cared-for possessions. Bright blue. Very luxurious.

Odd.

"Let's have a look, Pierre."

The valet said that he'd packed it this morning, but his master had tossed it aside.

"He told me that if his trip proved a failure I was to give it to a used clothing dealer; for he'd never want to see it again."

Which would, the Inspector thought, have been rather a windfall for the used clothing dealer. Because sewn into the lining of this dressing gown was a fabulous ruby ring.

"I don't know, Jeanne. I simply don't," was all the Viscomte had said when the Inspector had formally arrested him for the murder of the Baron Roque.

"Well, then it's nothing but a mix-up," his wife had answered briskly, "and we'll all be laughing about it soon enough."

"Take a warm cloak," she told him. "It's going to be cold tonight. And I'll be sending you food and more warm clothes tomorrow at . . . at?" She turned questioning eyes to the Inspector.

"At the Bastille, Madame."

"Ah." The Viscomte smiled. "Not like the trivial prison where they put me the last time. You know, Jeanne, I'd be awfully put out if they didn't think I was important enough for the Bastille. Along with the truly subversive writers."

"I'll be speaking to my lawyer first thing in the morning," she told him. "Don't worry, we'll get you right out."

"But I am sorry for the trouble I'm causing you, Jeanne."

Odd embrace the two of them had exchanged, the Inspector thought. Warm and even passionate in a way, but the sort of passion shared by comrades in arms rather than an intimate married couple. Well, they were an odd pair; he rather liked them. Not that he was surprised at that. Unlike Pierre, Chief Inspector Marais was past being surprised at his own personal response to a suspect.

"You've been kind, Monsieur *l'Inspecteur,*" the Viscomte said, "to let me bid farewell to my wife in a civilized fashion. But can we go now? This is hard on her.

"No, wait a minute, just one thing more." He turned to Pierre.

"You see, I've already paid for my next regular Friday visit to The Pearl in the Rose. Of course *you* remember it, Monsieur . . ." Pierre turned bright scarlet. ". . . that sober-looking establishment near the quay on the Left Bank. You'd followed me there a few weeks ago, though at the time, I'd thought you were fascinated by the place itself. Of course it *is* awfully expensive—available only to those who've inherited or married great fortunes. I'd considered inviting you in, as my guest.

"Well, it would be a pity, don't you think, to leave the girls unattended this Friday? So why don't you go in my stead? Explain the situation, Monsieur, and give Madame Alyse my apologies and best regards."

An odd speech for a man to deliver in front of his wife, the Inspector thought. Pierre stammered his incoherent thanks, while the Marquise seemed torn between rueful laughter and barely suppressed tears.

"I'll miss you while you're away, Joseph," she said, "but I'm sure this silly affair will be settled quickly."

"And now you'd really better go, Inspector," she said.

Marais had led his little procession out of the place as quickly as he could, to give the lady a chance to let her tears out in peace and privacy.

Instead of crying, though, she helped a distraught Baptiste put Joseph's rooms in order. And then she went to her study and penned two lists. First she recorded every word that she, Joseph, and the policemen had uttered, to give to her lawyer. And second, she enumerated an extravagant array of things to send to the Bastille.

Lists were comforting things, she thought. Unlike letters to worthless, stupid people.

Still, the letter had to be written, and the sooner the better. And so she penned a letter to the Duc and Duchesse de Carency Auvers-Raimond, outlining the state of affairs and asking for any assistance they could offer. Not that she really expected their help. But it was only decent to inform them of Joseph's situation rather than let them read about it in the scandal sheets.

And only when a side door opened and quick familiar footsteps clicked on the marble floors did she relax her composure and allow herself to weep in a pair of loving, sympathetic arms.

Chapter 19

"That will be all, Marianne," the Duchesse said. "And be sure to close the door behind you. I'll ring for a footman if Monsieur le Duc or I need anything else."

Marie-Laure curtsied, picked up the tea things, and quit the room, shutting the door behind her by nudging it with her hip and elbow. The Duc and Duchesse listened to the receding sound of her footsteps on the corridor's parquet floor.

"She's looking well," the Duchesse remarked to her husband. "And Jacques reports that she doesn't complain of any maladies to the other servants. But it's wise to check on her from time to time, I think, just in case."

He nodded distractedly, his eyes on the door, where Marie-Laure had pressed her hip against it.

The Duchesse cleared her throat. "And as for this news about your brother . . ."

Wresting his attention from the doorway, he turned to face her. "Did *you* have anything to do with that?" he demanded.

She gazed back at him with flat green eyes. "Not a thing. Of course, it's rather a stroke of luck for us. But no, it never occurred to me—either to betray him, if he's the murderer, or to plot against him if he isn't."

She spoke softly, as though to show him she wasn't affected by the skeptical look on his face. "I'm flattered, Monsieur, that you suppose I have the wit for such a thing. I know that you haven't, no matter how much you might wish to."

"*I?* But I'd *never* . . . I mean, he's my *brother*, damn it, Amélie." The Duc didn't seem able to finish his thought.

He stopped, shrugged. "Do you think he did it?" he asked.

"Does it matter if he did?" she replied. "Does it matter *who* did it? Or who informed on him, for that matter?"

He thought for a moment. "No, I don't suppose it does," he said slowly.

She nodded, watching his expression change while he considered what she'd just suggested to him. He was hardly a logician, she thought, but he'd work it out. Best, though, to offer a little assistance.

Her voice became warmer, more confiding. "After all," she said, "he's gotten so much attention all these years, so much of everything that should have been yours. What difference will it make if he spends a little time in prison, while events here take their natural course? Nothing serious will befall him; he'll slide by, as he always has. It will probably be resolved quite easily, without any assistance from you or me. Someday soon I'll answer Fat Jeanne's letter though; some sympathetic, sisterly clucking, just to be polite.

"But what's important," she added, "is to be sure that no news of this comes into the house."

The fashion magazines and scandal sheets had stopped arriving by post, much to Marie-Laure's relief. At least, she thought, there wouldn't be any more of those items about Joseph's mistress.

Nor, it seemed, would there be any more letters from him.

Not that she expected to receive one. She'd stopped hoping to hear from him some weeks ago.

No, she corrected herself, she'd *thought* she'd stopped hoping, but her heart had leaped when Nicolas had handed her a letter this morning.

But it had only been from Gilles. It was thicker than his usual communications, though—and uncharacteristically lively and voluble, she thought.

Well, he'd been working so terribly hard, she reminded herself; it was nice to see him enjoy a moment of self-congratulation now that his prosperous, productive future was finally coming into view. The school term would be over in a few months. He was studying hard for his examinations, but confident of passing them; he was already planning his medical practice. He and Sylvie would be married at the end of June. The dowry would help him rent an office, as well as a place for all of them to live.

And then (he'd written) you'll be able to come home, Marie-Laure. (She could construe his satisfaction from his even handwriting, with its sturdy capitals.) It was a shame, he continued, that she'd had to spend a year at the beck and call of some damn aristocrats. But she shouldn't lose heart, things would soon be comfortable and well ordered again.

She smiled wryly, imagining herself bringing an aristocrat's bastard into Gilles' well-ordered world.

Not that he'd turn her away: Gilles was incapable of family disloyalty; he'd care for her and the baby both, and defend her stoutly to anyone who might hazard a disapproving glance. But he'd be saddened and humiliated, and during his first month of marriage and his new professional life, too—for it was in June that she expected the baby to arrive.

She had no way of fixing the date exactly, but Marie-Laure suspected that she'd conceived almost immediately. Such a shame, she thought: all that maddening, frustrating care Joseph had insisted upon—and for all the difference those damn sheathes had made, they could have made blissful, unprotected love every night.

She figured that she was about four and a half months' pregnant—well, she was the right size for that, Louise had told her, with the authority of the oldest child of a brood of ten. And her exhaustion and queasiness had disappeared completely right after the New Year, which was what was supposed to happen, according to Bertrande, at the end of the first three months.

Not only had she stopped feeling dull and depressed; the absurd truth was that—physically at least—she felt wonderful: strong as an ox and hungry as a bear. She could tell that she looked wonderful, too, with all that energy coursing through her veins. In fact, she rather wished she didn't look so vibrant, at least during those unpleasant and mysterious sessions, every few weeks, when she was summoned to serve the Duc and Duchesse their tea. But she'd usually forget the couple's humiliating stares as soon as she closed the library door behind her, because her optimism and determination had returned as well. Which, she told herself, was certainly a good thing in her present difficult circumstances—not to speak of the endlessly detailed demands the Duchesse had been making on the entire household.

"Never," as Nicholas summed it up, "in all the history of the French nobility, has there been a more pampered and cosseted expectant mother."

Louise and Marie-Laure were still stitching their yards of satin into an endless array of loose, comfortable gowns and peignoirs. And Monsieur Colet found his ingenuity sorely taxed by requests for menus that were mild and sustaining "yet elegant and varied too, to tempt a delicate appetite." His mouth twisted sardonically as he repeated the Duchesse's words.

"Do you think she's really pregnant?" Robert asked. "Maybe she's stuffing pillows under her gown and plotting something."

"What, to steal a baby from somewhere?" Nicolas laughed and Marie-Laure's stomach lurched. "Don't be ridiculous, Robert."

"She's not pretending," Louise told the group. "I peeked into her chamber one day when she was having her bath. She does have a big belly—I saw it, all shiny and soapy."

"She's clever," Monsieur Colet said. "She probably figured out a way to bribe our little Monsieur Hubert to do his job.

"Which means," he added, "that I now may do *mine.*" He winked at Marie-Laure. "And feed an expectant mother as best I can."

So Marie-Laure had enjoyed delicate, delicious, and wonderfully digestible meals these past months, along with lots of support and advice from the rest of the servants. Except for spiteful Jacques and prudish Arsène, most of them had been as nice as possible. And a few of them had taken her and the baby on as a joint project.

Monsieur Colet supervised her plans for future employment. He was keeping an eye on the market for cooks in small households in the region. She'd have no trouble finding a new job, he assured her, with his recommendation.

And as February drew to a close, and she was about to enter her fifth month of pregnancy, Bertrande helped her find lodgings with cousins in the village of Carency. For a deposit of five livres, the cousins had promised to hold the room until Marie-Laure needed it. She hoped to be able to work another three months before she had to start living on the remainder of her money.

If things went as planned, she'd spend two months in the village—one before the baby's birth and one after—before going to her new job and boarding the child with a wet nurse.

She hated the idea of her baby taking nourishment at someone else's breast. She'd always despised the custom of putting a baby out to nurse, entrusting its care to an indigent, overworked woman who was only doing it for pay. And she knew the dangers: children—rich and poor alike—often died as a result of the indifferent care they received.

In fact, she could recite by heart a passage from one of Rousseau's novels, about certain mothers who, "having got rid of their babies, devote themselves gaily to the pleasures of the town." Ruefully, she remembered her indignant adolescent response when she'd first read those words. How passionate, how ready she'd been to ignore the plight of mothers who had no choice in the matter. Like the great philosopher himself, Marie-Laure had not given a moment's thought to what it would feel like to send your baby away and hope for the best.

Just another example, she shrugged, of life teaching you what books did not. She'd have to be vigilant in her choice of a wet nurse. Surely some of them must be more generous, less harried, than others. With luck, she'd also find a job that afforded her some occasional free time; she'd accept lower wages in exchange for the chance to visit her child now and then. And during the month before she returned to work, she'd simply have to give the baby so much love (and so much milk of her own) that little Sophie or Alexandre (for she didn't care whether it was a boy or a girl) would be sustained through the separations to come.

The bookstall, of course, was postponed indefinitely. What

counted was maintaining herself and the child, staying independent, and never (she only let herself think of this for moments at a time, when she woke up in the middle of the night) being reduced to cleaning some horrible innkeeper's privy for room and board.

Time passed surprisingly pleasantly. She seemed to have locked away all her sadness and disillusionment with Joseph into some dark, inaccessible place. She'd misjudged him, she told herself; well, all right, that was that. Oddly, she was quite sure she still loved him—perhaps because of a private notion that it would be better for the baby if she felt that way. She didn't suppose medical science would agree, but Marie-Laure was sure that a baby would be happier and healthier if it spent its nine months of gestation curled up close to a loving heart. What was important was that the baby never felt a lack of love. She and the baby, she told herself, were lucky to be safe and well cared for. Even the weather had agreed to be gentle; it was March now, and Provence was enjoying a mild, wet early spring.

The almond trees had just begun to blossom. Robert showed Marie-Laure a knobby black branch he'd broken off, with a few blooms forcing themselves through the hard buds.

"Let's put it in the chipped pitcher on the windowsill," she suggested, looking up from the young green beans she was snapping. "It'll be nice to watch it come into flower, a little more every day."

They smiled at each other over their work, in honor of spring and new life.

Robert was making madeleines for tea today. Carefully, he measured out flour, sugar, salt. The little tea cakes shaped like seashells were easy, especially compared to puff pastry, but Robert was a perfectionist. He beat three large fresh eggs into the batter and began blending in half a pound of melted butter. Merde, he muttered, skinning a knuckle as he grated the lemon rind.

"Have you decided about middle names yet?" he asked as he poured the mixture into the aspic molds that gave the cakes their shape.

"For a boy I have," she told him. "If it's a boy it'll be Alexandre

Joseph," she added. "The *Alexandre* is for my Papa, and the *Joseph,*" her voice became careful, controlled, "well, you know who that's for."

Robert shrugged and went to put away the butter. Someone brought in a pile of greasy pots and Marie-Laure hauled some fresh hot water from the hearth. Jacques passed by, made a lewd gesture at Marie-Laure's belly, and laughed harshly as Robert chased him away.

"And for a girl?" Robert asked sometime later.

"What? Oh, a middle name, you mean. No, if it's a girl, it'll be Sophie, for Mamma. But I don't have a middle name for her yet."

"You'll find one," he said.

He held up a newly baked madeleine. "Have a bite."

"Mmmmmm." The bite of cake dissolved slowly against her tongue, light and rich at the same time, with just a breath of lemon to keep it from being insipid.

"It's wonderful, Robert," she said. "It's perfect, you're going to be an artist like Monsieur Colet."

He blushed. "Oh no, Marie-Laure."

"And you're a good friend too," she added.

A teasing light appeared in her eyes. "In fact, if the baby is a girl, I'm going to name her after you, to remember you at just this moment."

"Sophie Roberte?" It didn't sound very mellifluous to him.

"Sophie Madeleine." She smiled triumphantly. "Isn't that pretty?"

He agreed that it was pretty, and Marie-Laure dove into the rest of her chores with a sense that she'd accomplished something, if only in her mind. *Sophie Madeleine or Alexandre Joseph,* she thought, *you will be a lucky child, for you are sure to inherit some of your Papa's gifts. While from your Mamma—well, my gift to you will be a certain tenacity. And the capacity for an abiding love.*

Chapter 20

April arrived in a gorgeous flurry of cherry blossoms, loud choruses of calling birds, brilliant days and warm starry nights. And no letters for Marie-Laure, except a brief, embarrassed-sounding note from Gilles, announcing that Augustin Rigaud had married his cousin Suzanne from Nîmes.

After Easter the Duc and Duchesse demanded a series of elaborate feasts to make up for their Lenten privations. And suddenly Marie-Laure found it difficult to keep up. She felt swollen, enormous, weighed down by her increasing bulk.

Her clothes barely fit, even with the ugly new panels she and Louise had sewn into them. Even her shoes and stockings felt too tight. And her back hurt devilishly.

She took it day by hard, slow day. Soon she would quit, she told herself. Any day now. She woke slowly in the mornings, struggled into her clothes and thrust her bare feet into wooden clogs someone in the house had lent her. The only thing within her control seemed to be her hair, which she tried to keep pretty and shining.

She murmured encouragements to herself and to the baby. "We'll get along without him," she repeated patiently. "We don't need him. We'll take care of ourselves. We have our own money."

She tried not to count her stash of coins too often. But sometimes the seventy-eight livres in their little sack were the only thing that comforted her. And one bright April morning she couldn't resist the temptation.

No one was about, though she could hear Robert and Monsieur Colet bustling around the storeroom. Just a quick little peek before they returned. She wiggled out the loose brick to find—nothing.

She blinked. No, nothing at all except some loose straw. *All right,* she told herself, *willing herself to be patient in the face of rising panic, don't worry, it's the wrong brick, that's all.* She tried another. And another still. She tried every brick on the left side of the hearth and then for good measure every brick on the right. None of them even budged.

But what was that, almost covered with cinders in the front corner of the large fireplace? It sparkled—well, there were actually two kinds of sparkles—the glitter of broken glass and the gleam of thin gold wire . . .

She knew what she'd find, even before she dug Papa's ruined spectacles out of the ashes.

Her finger was bleeding. She must have cut it on a sliver of glass, but she couldn't feel any pain. She felt, instead, a sort of movement within herself. As though something solid had given way: all her months of plotting and planning, of looking on the bright side and keeping up her hopes and optimism, seemed to crumble into dust and ashes. She curled up on the hearthside and wept.

"It's the Duchesse. It's Jacques. I know it is," she wailed to Robert and Monsieur Colet when they found her there.

Feebly, Monsieur Colet tried to reason with her. There was no point making accusations with no proof to back them up, he told her. She glared at him as though he were an enemy.

"And what *do* you suggest I do?" she asked. The disrespectful tone she heard in her voice shocked her. And the fact that he didn't seem offended alarmed her. If he were allowing her to speak so rudely, she thought, her predicament must be every bit as awful as it seemed.

He shrugged, poured himself a glass of wine and offered her one as well. She shook her head. The silence in the room felt hollow, hopeless.

"Well," Robert offered timidly, "you might still hear from Monsieur Joseph."

Her eyes blazed. "Thank you, Robert."

Her mouth twisted into a cruel smile. "Indeed, he might appear this very morning carrying a glass slipper. Having somehow dispatched his wife and mistress both. And having found the only pair of glass slippers in all of France to fit my swollen feet. Quite the modern fairy tale, don't you think?"

"That's enough, Marie-Laure. Don't taunt Robert." The wine had restored some authority to Monsieur Colet's voice.

She nodded. "I'm sorry, Robert. And please pardon my disrespect, Monsieur Colet." She rose unsteadily to her feet.

"But I can't just sit here weeping and wondering," she continued. "And so I'm going to have to go demand my money back from that bitch. . . ."

"Marie-*Laure!*" Monsieur Colet's voice rose.

". . . that Gorgon, that *hyena* of a boss-lady."

"Marie-Laure," he repeated, "this is *not* a good idea."

It probably wasn't, she thought as she mounted the stairs. But she didn't have any other ideas and neither did her friends in the kitchen.

She needed to do something definite. Something audacious. She didn't actually suppose she'd get her money back, but perhaps she might finally find out what these awful people had wanted of her, and why they'd insisted she'd spend all those humiliating hours giving them their tea.

There were a lot of stairs between the kitchen and the Duc and Duchesse's wing of the chateau. Panting as she climbed the last of them, she nonetheless kept up a brisk march through the plastered and gilded hallways. She grimaced at her repeated reflections in the hallways' large mirrors, and blinked in the sunlight flooding through recently enlarged windows and dancing on delicate chairs and inlaid tables.

Purposefully as she could, she strode through the Duchesse's antechamber and tapestried bedchamber.

Her clogs made a racket on parquet floors and sank into thick rugs. She hurried through splendidly decorated spaces, afraid she'd lose her courage if she slowed down.

Until finally, pausing at the doorway of the Duchesse's *cabinet*, she took a few deep breaths, knocked, didn't wait for an answer, and threw open the door.

To be greeted by a low laugh that chilled her flushed cheeks and made her wish she'd stayed downstairs in the kitchen.

She knew I'd come. She planned this.

The Duchesse was drinking tea behind a long low table, in an armchair upholstered in apple green silk. There was a low fire in the grate, its warm air currents wafting the steam from the Duchesse's teapot across the room to Marie-Laure's nostrils. Peppermint and elderberry leaf. It should have been a soothing smell, but it wrenched her stomach.

She stared at the elegant clutter on the table: the gay Sèvres tea service, a half-eaten meringue, a leather folder thick with correspondence. A silver tray held a tooled ebony box and a perfect white rose in a tall crystal vase. The Duchesse's soft white hands emerged gracefully from the flounced sleeves of her ivory satin robe. Ivory—or goose shit satin, if you preferred.

The robe fell in stately pleats from the Duchesse's shoulders and draped subtly past her belly. Marie-Laure thought of how she'd tugged at her own dress to get it to fit around her this morning. *What will I do,* she wondered, *when it ceases to fit me at all?* The Duchesse was carrying her pregnancy splendidly. *Well she has the height for it,* Marie-Laure thought. *And the clothes, thanks to Louise and me.*

Hortense, the maid who'd been with Madame Amélie since before her marriage, looked up sourly from the lace christening gown she held. For a moment it seemed as though she were going to chase Marie-Laure away from her mistress's private sanctum, but she remained silent at a nod from her mistress.

As she slowly raised her eyes to the Duchesse's calm, attentive face, Marie-Laure felt all her boldness drain away, like sand in an egg timer.

She's not the Gorgon any longer, she thought. *She's finally at ease with her privilege and power and doesn't need to scowl at her hirelings. She's playing with me; she's enjoying this. Like a cat. No, like a snake, coiled around a field mouse before it sinks its fangs into the little creature's neck.*

And I look ridiculous. Like a clumsy, swollen, tongue-tied idiot.

She curtsied awkwardly and winced at the noise her clogs made on the parquet floor. She cleared her throat.

The Duchesse smiled and nodded pleasantly, as though it were the most natural thing in the world to entertain a stained, perspiring, and extremely pregnant scullery maid in one's boudoir of a morning. She took a tiny bite of the meringue and another sip of tea. She put down her teacup, wiped her mouth slowly with a lace-trimmed napkin, and bent her head to sniff the rose, closing her eyes as though communing with its essence.

When she opened her eyes, they were flat, green, and opaque, and her voice was venom laced with honey.

"Good morning, Marianne."

Quickly then, feigning embarrassment, "Oh, but I believe it's Marie-Laure, isn't it? Forgive me, yes, of course, it's Marie-Laure, from the scullery."

"Yes, Madame la Duchesse."

"Well, you look very well, my dear. Especially in your—well, in *our* condition." The cold smile affected a sisterly complicity. "And how far along do you suppose you are? Or don't you know?"

"Uh, twenty-eight weeks, Madame la Duchesse. Almost seven months. At least I think so."

"Good, good, twenty-eight weeks. And still busy down there with all that scrubbing and scalding and peeling and chopping?"

"Yes, Madame la Duchesse."

The Duchesse wrinkled her nose slightly at the soot on Marie-Laure's skirt and apron. "Yes, well, I can see that you are. Good, good, we couldn't afford to keep a scullery maid who wasn't doing her work, you know.

"But of course," the Duchesse murmured, "that's the lifeblood of our French nation, the wonderful strength and endurance of our common people."

She gave a self-deprecatory little laugh. "I don't suppose *I'd* last an hour in a scullery."

"No, Madame la Duchesse."

Another sip of tea.

"So refreshing, this mint tisane, and so comforting to a delicate digestion, don't you find?"

And when Marie-Laure hesitated, "But Louise *did* give you the herbs I sent, didn't she? Though I'm such a scatterbrain that I can never find a bit of stationery when I need one. So I fear it came to you wrapped up in silly Paris gossip. But surely you're too sensible a girl to pay any attention to any of that."

"Oh yes, Madame la Duchesse. Oh no, no attention at all. Oh yes, thank you, it was very refreshing."

"Well, I'm glad you liked it. It's dear of you to come all this way from the kitchen just to thank me for it. A bit belated perhaps, but I know how marvelously busy and efficient all of you are down there and how much you have to do. . . ."

The perfect hostess at a loss for how to get rid of a tiresome guest, she turned her gaze back toward the white rose. "And so, Marie-Laure, perhaps you had better get back to . . ."

Marie-Laure took a deep breath.

"Madame la Duchesse, someone stole some money from me. And I think—I think it was Jacques."

The Duchesse raised her eyebrows.

"Really? How very strange. Because do you know, Marie-Laure, I've had some money taken from me as well. Seventy-eight livres, to be exact. It was returned to me just this morning, by a faithful servant.

"Of course," she continued, "I don't like to use the word *stolen.* I hadn't thought I'd bother the magistrate about it. So unpleasant, all of that. The penalty in such a case, I believe, is branding."

She opened the ebony box, picked up Marie-Laure's sack of coins, and weighed it in her hand.

"Public, ceremonial branding in the village square. On the cheek, so that the thief may be instantly identified and henceforth avoided by all decent people."

"But—but that's my money," Marie-Laure stammered.

"We seem to disagree on this point," the Duchesse replied.

"Still," she added, "that's what our courts of law are for. I'm sure the magistrate will be open to your claim. He seemed quite fair and unprejudiced, the day he swore fealty to my husband as his lord."

A snake. Powerful and poisonous too.

She opened her mouth to protest. And then she closed it, curtsied and began to back away.

No use. I should never have come.

"I beg your pardon, Madame la Duchesse. I must have been mistaken. And yes, I have a lot to do downstairs, so if you'll excuse me . . ." Her clogs seemed to thunder beneath her.

"Oh, will you hush," the Duchesse interrupted her.

"And stop shuffling your feet in those dreadful clogs, you're giving me a headache. Just take them off. That's right, you can stand there in your bare feet while you listen carefully to what I have to say to you."

It was actually rather pleasant to stand barefoot on the cool, smoothly varnished parquet, but it made her feel like a beggar or a criminal making a public confession. Which, she supposed, was more or less what the Duchesse had intended.

"Stand straight. And look at me. Show a little respect when I speak to you. Yes, that's better. Well, I'm glad to get a look at you this morning anyway. My husband's been too busy lately for our afternoon teas and I'd rather lost track of your condition.

"It's clear as day that you'll soon be useless down there in the kitchen. In fact I wouldn't be surprised if in a week or two you'll hardly be able to stand on those swollen ankles of yours."

It doesn't matter how much she insults me, Marie-Laure thought. *But is she right about my ankles?* For they *had* swollen quite a bit in the last few days.

"But luckily, Marie-Laure," the Duchesse's voice became more honeyed and more venomous too, and a gleeful light appeared in her sharp green eyes, "luckily, Providence has a way of working things out for the best. And has given you an opportunity to redeem yourself and your bad behavior.

"Because you see, my husband the Duc and I have need of a girl like you. We want someone strong and healthy to play a very important role in the future of this family.

"For you must know how difficult it is to find a clean, healthy, devoted wet nurse for a child. And not just any child, but," she paused, frowning slightly, "the future Duc de Carency Auvers-Raimond. But just think—how blessed we are, how rewarded for all our charity, to find just such a person in our own home. And someone, moreover, who is just a few weeks further along than I am. So you'll have time to practice on your own brat, perfecting your nursing technique and in all ways becoming a docile, dependable little dairy cow by the time my child is ready for your services.

"You'll get plenty of rest—no more exhausting kitchen work. And you'll have lots of time and solitude to meditate on how badly you've behaved, and resolve to do better. Do you like this gown?"

Marie-Laure nodded, dumbfounded.

"You can have it. Shorten it. And loosen the neckline so that you'll always be ready when our little heir is hungry."

"There's a charming cottage," the Duchesse continued, "near the river, that we've set the carpenters to renovating. It's very comfortable. Quite isolated and picturesque. Very Rousseauesque, I'm told, if you like that sort of thing. You've read this Jean-Jacques Rousseau, Marie-Laure?"

"Yes, Madame la Duchesse."

"Well then you're familiar with his tiresome preaching, mothers nursing their own children and so forth. It's getting to be quite the fashion at court, it's a novelty, a diversion for ladies who've already had their breasts immortalized by the court painters and don't mind having them ruined by all that nasty suckling.

"Ah well, fashions come and go, but we all have our duties, don't we, Marie-Laure? And my duty, sadly, must entail a separation from my family, for I'll be going to Paris, with only Arsène and Hortense for support. Well, to Versailles, actually, at the invitation of some dear friends I met last winter, to represent this family at the King's court.

"But never fear, my husband will be staying behind to supervise the château, and to look after his heir's welfare. And, of course, to look after *you*, Marie-Laure."

So this is where it all leads.

"He's been unusually diligent, too, setting up the cottage to his own specifications, so snug and private and convenient to hunting and fishing. I know that you'll put your best efforts into your new duties. Well, what choice do you have after all?

"Gather your things. We'll move you into the cottage this afternoon, and I'll send my doctor to have a look at you."

The Duchesse's voice became softer and more conspiratorial, even as her neck seemed to lengthen and her eyes took on a reptilian glassiness.

"Poor Hubert," she said. "I find, now that it's almost over, that I'll miss him now and again. He might have developed into something more than he is, you know, if he hadn't always shown to such disadvantage, compared to his precious little brother. Well, it's too late to worry about any of that, I suppose. It's all spilled milk, as the proverb says—so aptly in this case, don't you agree? And as for the brother . . ."

Madame Amélie's eyes strayed to the letter case on the table. "At least *he* won't be bothering us any more . . ."

Had something happened to Joseph?

The Duchesse waved Marie-Laure's questioning face away. "The news is being discussed at length in the scandal sheets. I'll be sure to send you all the best accounts."

She opened the letter case, glancing dismissively at a sheet of heavy, crested stationery covered with incisive handwriting. She pulled out a pile of flimsier, more familiar sheets of paper, crumpled them, and tossed them into the fire.

"You might have been a bit more poetical, when you told him about the child," she said. "Or a bit more respectful in your remarks about myself and the Duc. But it hardly matters now.

"Of course I'm no literary critic," the Duchesse continued, as Marie-Laure stared at the cinders her letters had become, "but one could say you've rather a talent for comedy—at least for genre scenes among the lower classes. A sense of humor is a wonderful gift, Marie-Laure, and I'm sure it will be a comfort to you in times ahead."

She brought forth a thicker sheaf of papers. "Whereas the Viscomte . . . *mon Dieu*, what *could* he have been thinking, sending pornographic tracts to a servant in a decent house?"

She rolled up Joseph's letters and sent them to the same fiery death as Marie-Laure's letters to him.

She picked up another set of papers.

"And to send such a scandalous story as well, about a sultan and his perverted, unspeakable . . . Well, it was amusing enough for someone in *my* position, but I can only thank heaven that the common people of France are protected by the King's wise censors. And that I was here to do the same service for you, Marie-Laure, and protect you from such filth."

The sultan and the English lady of quality. Equals in passion and desire. Both reduced to ashes.

Marie-Laure thought she might scream. Or, perhaps, she thought for just a moment, she could pull the Duchesse out of her chair and knock her to the ground. Kick her. Pour mint and elderberry tea over her head and break the teapot.

Marie-Laure, that is not *a good idea.*

Nor was it a good idea, she thought, to be saying what it seemed she was saying.

"It's only filth to you because you don't understand about love and desire. And because no one ever wanted you that way, even though you wanted Joseph. I know you did. And I know that you envy me."

The Duchesse almost winced, but at the last moment merely nodded.

"Under the present circumstances," she replied, "I think that 'envy' is taking it a bit far. Still, I have pondered our relative fortunes, yours and mine; well, the comparison calls out to be made, does it not?

"It's a bit of a fairy tale, isn't it? About two young women, neither of them highborn, both of them entangled in the same rotten branch of the old aristocracy. Two alert, intelligent young women who know how to keep their eyes open. Until one of them becomes blinded—by passion, I suppose you might say. Or by pleasures the other one hasn't yet come to know.

"But I will, Marie-Laure. The difference between us is that your pleasures are behind you, while mine are still to come. How interesting—how poetical, in a sense—that it's you who'll free me to live the life I deserve."

It *was* an interesting construction, Marie-Laure thought. She opened her mouth to speak and then she closed it again. She could probably manage a saucy enough reply. But an additional insult would be superfluous.

Because clever as the Duchesse's rejoinder had been, it didn't obscure the truth, which was that she did envy Marie-Laure and always would. Rejected for a scullery maid, the Duchesse had already corrupted herself with hateful, envious brooding.

So Marie-Laure stood quite still on her bare feet and remained quiet. She was trembling, of course. And her vision was tinged with red, as though she were seeing the Duchesse and her white rose through a haze of blood. But part of her mind, some cold, critical intelligence, remained crystal clear and even fascinated.

Best to hear it out. For it was clear that the Duchesse had prepared her last speech very carefully.

Because we must always be at our best for those we envy.

How very strange it was, Marie-Laure thought.

Strange or not, a lifelong reader knows how to recognize and appreciate heightened literary effect. And Marie-Laure found that she was eager to hear how the Duchesse would frame her final lines.

She widened her eyes attentively while the lady in the green armchair took another sip of tea.

"There now, where were we? Ah yes. Well, I think you'll find, all in all, that Hubert has simple needs. He'll make them clear to you in due time; never fear, I'm sure a girl like you will manage splendidly. Of course you needn't worry about him getting you pregnant again. *That* end of things has never been his forte.

"He has very few wants, really," the Duchesse continued. "He'll be quite happy so long as he's killing little birds and animals, and has his hunting dogs and his brother's little slut to play with. And he'll enjoy watching his child thrive at your breast, you know, especially . . ."

And here's the eloquent touch, Marie-Laure thought. The pause, the ellipsis, the words deleted in order to exaggerate the effect of the words already said.

Especially.

Slowly, lovingly, the Duchesse drew out the long *ssss* sound, showing her teeth as she did so. And then she stopped abruptly, leaving the unfinished sentence half-coiled, like a hissing serpent poised to strike. She knew that Marie-Laure had grasped her meaning, and would parse the rest of the sentence with perfect accuracy in her own mind. *He'll enjoy watching his child thrive at your breast, especially because it will mean less milk, less care, and less attention for his brother's child.*

Brava, Madame.

But in the end it seemed that the Duchesse wasn't up to the standard of rhetorical subtlety she'd set herself. For she couldn't resist tacking on a far less artful and really rather banal finale.

"Now go," she hissed. "You're boring me."

Chapter 21

Marie-Laure stumbled out of the *cabinet* and through the bedchamber. Her senses were clouded, her steps so disjointed that she nearly knocked the Duc over when she bumped into him at the threshold of the Duchesse's rooms. She had enough of her wits about her, though, to regret that she hadn't sent him tumbling onto his bottom.

He'd been hunting. There was a gamy, bloody smell about him; a couple of whining, panting hounds, with loud bells at their collars, trotted along after his muddy boots. She murmured excuses for her clumsiness and gave a shallow curtsy, enduring his small blue eyes and alcohol-laced breath on her breasts, her mouth, and the pulse at her throat.

For a moment he seemed fractious, like a child who'd done his sullen best to behave, but wasn't sure he was going to be given the reward that had been promised. Then, realizing that she must have just completed an interview with his wife, he smiled with sudden wolfish delight.

"So it's all settled," he said. His open mouth and red lips shone with drool.

He reached to grab her, but she swooped into a deeper curtsy, bending her head over his hand to kiss it. The gesture seemed to puzzle and please him. It would be nice, she could see him thinking, to get a little respect once in a while.

One of the hounds had poked an inquisitive wet nose under her skirt. She wished with all her heart that she could kick the filthy beast across the room. But she forced herself to ignore the sniffing and nuzzling, while she continued to press her mouth against the Duc's puffy, beringed little hand; it was like a fat white maggot, the starched lace cuffs not quite hiding the dirt beneath his fingernails.

Stifling the urge to retch, Marie-Laure peered up at him. He was giggling with pleasure at the sight of her swollen breasts, pushed up and almost out of her too-tight dress. In another moment, she thought, he'd dribble saliva on her.

One of the dogs whined jealously. She felt a tightness at her throat, as though someone had buckled a leather collar around it. Which was, she thought, really quite appropriate to her situation, since the Duc clearly had no intention of treating her as someone with a will or intelligence of her own. He was happiest with dumb animals, anyway. What had the Duchesse called her? Ah yes, a docile little dairy cow, at his beck and call like the dogs.

She thought she might choke. But she found, as she raised her head, that she could speak calmly enough.

"You must excuse me, Monsieur le Duc, for I fear I'm a bit faint, with . . . with pleasure, and with . . . with the honor of my new position, and I must . . ."

She prattled on about how, in her condition, she was often seized by the urge to vomit, particularly when overtaken with such intense sensations as she was feeling at this moment.

Mercifully, he recoiled and let her step away while he stammered a witticism about how she must take good care of herself, for in the future he'd be seeing a great deal more of her, oh yes (his eyes shining), a great deal more indeed.

As she hurried out of the room and down the corridor, she considered for a moment that she didn't exactly loathe him. She pitied him rather, this lumpish, sad, unlovable boy in his stocky adult body. *It's not really your fault, Monsieur le Duc,* she thought, trying to wipe the feeling of his puffy hand from her lips. *But if you believe for one instant that I'm going to sacrifice either my child or myself to make up for slights you suffered twenty years ago . . . well, dream on, Monsieur le Duc. Dream, or do whatever it is you do with a mind you've pickled in alcohol.*

She regretted that there wouldn't be time to say good-bye to Louise. Or Robert, Monsieur Colet, or any of the others who'd tried to help her.

But she had to leave *now.* Even if she didn't have a sou. Perhaps, she thought vaguely, she could get her deposit back from Bertrande's cousins in the village. Or perhaps not.

She didn't know where she'd go or what she'd do. But she did know that no one was going to imprison her in a cottage with Monsieur Hubert and his simple needs.

So she stepped through the tall, arched doorway, crossed the courtyard and drawbridge, and walked away from the château. Away from all her carefully laid plans and hopes.

How easy it was, she thought. How simple just to *go* when you had no idea where you were going. There was a certain exhilarating sense of freedom when you were desperate, a purity of action when no action made sense.

When you were acting from your most elemental instincts for self-preservation. And when the only way to go was *away.*

She wanted to look back just one last time. Absurdly, as she hurried down the steep winding road, she found herself wondering if she'd be able to tell which of the windows belonged to Joseph's bedchamber. No. She wouldn't turn her head or even her thoughts in that direction.

Anyway, merely keeping going was difficult enough. The morning sun was rapidly climbing in the sky and her feet wobbled in her clogs above the road's uneven stones and gravel. The day would only get hotter. Her back hurt and she was already thirsty.

Perhaps, she thought, she should walk a bit more slowly, to conserve energy for the long trek down to the village. But she was afraid to do so—any minute, now, she thought, someone would realize she was gone and come after her.

Oof. She slipped on a gnarled root and gave her ankle a turn. She waited, panting in the still, bright air, hoping that the pain would subside. Mercifully, it did. But she'd have to be more careful, and keep a sharper eye on the road's treacherous, uneven surface. And she'd also have to keep a sharp ear out for sounds on the road behind her, sounds of someone—probably Jacques—in pursuit. *If I hear him,* she told herself, *I'll get off the road and hide in the thorny bushes at its edges.*

"I won't go back," she repeated to herself. "*We* won't go back," she corrected herself, "will we, Sophie-or-Alexandre? We'll continue on until we find a safe place for you to be born, you can trust me on that absolutely."

She rounded a turn in the road, and the view of a hillside unfolded before her eyes: a field of lavender, a vineyard, and off in the distance, a small flock of sheep. Words from an ancient and familiar lullaby drifted into her mind, "Sleep, baby, sleep . . . there's no reason to cry . . . the lamb doesn't bleat in his meadow, his eyes are gay, filled with happiness . . ." Her own eyes stung for a moment, with bitterness and fear, before she hurried on.

But it wasn't only bitterness and fear that had brought tears to her eyes. It was dust. And it seemed to come from everywhere.

She could hear Jacques now, running thunderously after her from the château. But the breeze also seemed to be picking up a little dust from a mule cart that she could hear somewhere down the hill. If, she thought, she could fight Jacques off until the mule cart traveled up to where she was standing, perhaps she could get some help. And in any case her struggle wouldn't go unwitnessed.

He was advancing on her. She looked around for a bush to hide behind, but she was on a terrible stretch of road here, with only steep hillside on either side of her. She could hear his breath now; she could almost feel a bony hand grasping after her. She pivoted, barely avoiding a ditch, and crossed her arms.

"All right," he said. "Now, why don't you come quietly and save me the trouble of dragging you all the way up the hill?"

Her mouth was full of dust. She spat it out at him.

"Stay away from me," she said. "Stay away unless you want me to set you howling again. Like I did last time you tried to lay a hand on me."

In truth, she didn't think she could execute that move anymore. Nor did she have surprise on her side this time. But the memory of the pain she'd caused him made him cautious.

Damn, where was that mule cart she'd thought she'd heard?

He grasped her shoulders, and she tried to position herself to knee him in the groin. But it was an entirely different thing with a big belly in front of her. He laughed, and then yowled as she raked her fingernails across his cheek. And even if she couldn't get him where it really counted, a wooden clog aimed hard at the shin does at least a little damage.

"Bitch," he muttered, finally able to immobilize her arms by bending them behind her back, "aristocrat's whore, and shameless about it too. Well, at least I'll get to keep the seventy-eight livres after I get you up the hill."

There was nothing to do but scream. Which she did with some creativity, bellowing out epithets she wasn't even aware she knew. She screamed her hatred for the vicious people who were using her so spitefully; her rage at having her arms painfully bent behind her back; and her fury at being pushed back up the hill, toward the château she never wanted to see again.

She screamed so loudly that she quite drowned out the squeaks and rattles of the mule cart as it pulled to a stop behind Jacques. And she was so intent on resisting Jacques's shoving that for a moment she didn't hear the droll, familiar voice protesting at his back.

"Hey, let her alone, Jacques, you're hurting her."

She turned her head in midscream, letting the sound dissolve in her open, astonished mouth.

"Baptiste?"

It was most definitely Baptiste, accompanied by a thin, soberly dressed gentleman with deeply rutted cheeks and small, piercing eyes. The thin gentleman was holding up a sheet of heavy white paper, as though it had some sort of magic power.

"Jean-Marie du Plessix, my good fellow"—he bowed coldly to an astonished Jacques—"lawyer in the employ of the Marquise Jeanne de Machery and her husband, the Viscomte d'Auvers-Raimond."

"Monsieur du Plessix and I were just investigating..."

Baptiste had begun to say something, but Monsieur du Plessix interrupted him.

". . . some of the Marquise's financial holdings in this region," he said, "and some legal matters in addition. But we were also searching for this young woman, who, with my help, may want to initiate a lawsuit against certain parties, for abduction, by the look of it."

"I've taken the liberty, Mademoiselle," he said to Marie-Laure, "of drawing up some preliminary papers, if you'd like to take a glance at them."

Jacques still had Marie-Laure's hands pinned behind her back, but his grip had loosened, and Marie-Laure jerked herself free, walking over to Monsieur du Plessix to scan the papers he held out to her.

"Thank you, Monsieur," she murmured, though what she was reading was merely an accounting of the food and wine the lawyer and valet had consumed between Paris and Provence. "Thank you, I'll review the details with you at my leisure, while we're . . ."

"While we're on our way to Paris," Baptiste sang out, guiding the mules carefully through a turnaround at the widest part of the road.

He and Monsieur du Plessix helped Marie-Laure into the cart, climbed in after her, and began their rolling, jolting trip down the hill, leaving a gaping Jacques behind them in the dust.

Chapter 22

Except for a certain dankness in the air, Joseph had found his couple of months in the Bastille exceedingly tolerable. Even comfortable—well, it was comfortable, he thought, if you had a large cell with a window that faced the ever-changing city streets. And a rich wife to supply you with every conceivable amenity, from rugs, furniture, and tapestries for the stone walls, to books, warm clothing, and cartloads of nourishing and delicate foodstuffs.

He regretted the lack of exercise. A daily walk in the prison yard wasn't nearly enough to keep his muscles in tone, so he practiced fencing for an hour every morning and afternoon. Of course, he wasn't allowed a weapon, but he amused himself by holding a quill pen in the hand that thrust and parried. Wasn't that what writers did, after all? And if he had no opponent except himself? Well, he'd probably always been his own worst enemy anyway.

Of course he felt stifled by the lack of society, the unvarying company of a few guards and fellow prisoners instead of the wide, brilliant circle of acquaintances he'd enjoyed as Jeanne's husband. And naturally he hated not being able to come and go as he wished.

But with all that duly noted, it astonished him how little changed he felt his life to be. The hôtel Mélicourt had been rich in creature comfort and convenient to every diversion Paris could offer. But in truth he'd felt imprisoned within it, since the turn of the year especially, without any mail from Marie-Laure to remind him what his life might really be about.

Accommodating to the Bastille had been a challenge and a novelty. Discomforts could be overlooked or circumvented; solitude engendered meditation. It was interesting to observe the system of guards and security, too: there were some inconsistencies, he noted, some gaps in security that might allow a clever prisoner—one who was quick on his feet and good at disguise—to engineer an escape attempt. Someone a bit more desperate than he was. Someone as desperate as he might become, if there wasn't a break in the case soon.

Jeanne visited every week: he laughed at her stories and gossip, nodded at her piercing commentary on the political scene. He wished he could tell her that she needn't be quite so unfailingly optimistic about his prospects. Luckily, Monsieur du Plessix had been more straightforward.

Joseph liked the quick-witted lawyer. Dutifully, in response to questions, he'd recounted every detail he could remember about the day of the murder. He found that he could easily reconstruct the list of booksellers he'd visited and even the approximate times of each visit. If the Baron had really been dispatched during a late midday luncheon, it was probably while Joseph had been delivering books to a plump, scatterbrained fellow called Bluet, who specialized in pious literature but liked to keep a few atheist philosophers in stock as well.

After Bluet, he'd been jostled by passersby as he made his way to the back door of Rigaud's grand establishment. He remembered vaguely that his leg had begun to hurt just about then. And then things had gotten hazy—no wonder Rigaud had been able to wheedle those extra books out of him. He'd gone to the Vernets' last because their shop was too small to have a separate delivery entrance and was therefore more safely visited under cover of dusk.

"Ironic, isn't it," he commented to Monsieur du Plessix, "that it was only the Vernets—well Dr. Vernet, anyway—who told Inspector

Lebrun that I was in Montpellier? Just enough evidence to establish that I was in the city. And none to prove that I wasn't at the Baron's."

Du Plessix nodded and jotted down the most important points.

"We must get Bluet or Rigaud to confirm your alibi," he said. "We're lucky that the King has recently eased up on the censorship laws," he added, "because it'll be easier to get you off on any possible book-smuggling charges."

"And what are the chances," Joseph had asked, "of any bookseller admitting to having dealt in forbidden books? Even when interviewed by as meticulous and engaging an investigator as yourself, *cher* Monsieur?"

Du Plessix had sighed. *Eh bien,* he'd admitted, none whatsoever. Still, he and Baptiste would be taking a coach to Montpellier that very evening to see what they could turn up. They'd been gone now for several weeks, since Easter. Well, at least it gave Baptiste something to do, Joseph thought. As for the efficacy of the trip—he shrugged. One must hope for the best, of course, but he had his doubts.

He stared idly out the window at a troop of street urchins begging a sou from a well-dressed passerby. The passerby shrugged, dug into the pocket of his alpaca cloak, tossed some coins into the gutter, and hurried on. A handsome light cloak, Joseph thought, the weather must have turned mild. Yes, now that he was paying attention he could feel a spring breeze. And the children's feet were naked as well. Last January, when he'd begun watching them, they'd run and skipped through patches of dirty snow with layers of rags wrapped from toe to ankle.

Most touching, Monsieur, your concern for the common people.

He winced at the sound of a familiar, sneering voice. Solitude could be restful, even a sort of discipline. But when one was feeling—well, oddly agitated, as he seemed to be today, the solitude might engender unpleasant phantom encounters, with alternative selves one had been trying to avoid.

Like a certain sneering, highly strung aristocrat, quick to anger, absurdly sensitive to slights. The same Viscomte d'Auvers-Raimond who was determined to convince him that Marie-Laure had married her old sweetheart. *She's deserted you,* mon vieux. *Forget about her.*

Luckily, he knew another phantom gentleman—call him Joseph Raimond—who found it easier to keep faith. *She promised to love you forever. She does love you. She needs your help.* Monsieur Raimond visited him a bit less frequently than the cynical Viscomte did. But today—it must be the unsettling effect of the spring breeze, the disappearance of the last snow from the cobblestones—today it seemed that both phantom selves had chosen to visit him simultaneously.

And suddenly *she* was with him in his cell as well—warm and alive, flushed and smiling. She held out her hand; he could see ink stains on her fingers. He felt himself go hot and cold. It had been a long time since he'd let himself imagine her. He had to stop. But he didn't. It might be painful, it might even be madness, but he felt freer than he'd felt in months.

His chest was tight; how long, he wondered, since he'd taken a decent breath? He thrust his nose between the bars at the window and inhaled a deep draught of warm, stinking Paris air. It was foul. It was thrilling. It stirred something within him.

He heard a rattle at the barred door of his cell. A key turned in the lock. He'd forgotten it was Thursday, the day of Jeanne's visit. His little crowd of phantom guests evaporated, scared off by her footsteps and her reassuring corporeality.

He turned to embrace her, waiting until she dropped her parcels on a table. A burly footman put his heavier load of boxes and baskets next to hers, bowed, and stood at attention next to the warden, who took a stool by the cell door.

Visits couldn't be private, but Jeanne treated the prison officials like servants anyway. "You *will* see that he gets some fresh water every day for these hyacinths I've brought," she murmured to the warden as she settled into her seat.

And to Joseph, "Perhaps you would have preferred daffodils. They're running riot over the garden this week. But I thought the hyacinths, because of their scent . . .

"But you're looking unusually well, *chéri,*" she interrupted herself.

He smiled. "It's the spring, perhaps. I can't help but feel stirred up by it."

"Well, sit back in your chair then," she said, "and brace yourself. Because you're about to hear some extremely stirring news. You see, I've received a letter from Monsieur du Plessix today, from Provence . . ."

Monsieur du Plessix had quickly penned the letter at the inn in Carency, a few minutes before they'd boarded the coach for Paris.

"They'll be delighted, Marie-Laure, to learn that you're coming back with us," he'd assured her. "And I want them to know it as soon as possible. So they can prepare for your arrival."

She'd frowned. "Delighted? When I'm in this condition?"

"The Marquise is an unusual woman," the lawyer said. "She and the Viscomte have a very liberal relationship."

Whatever *that* might mean. She supposed she'd just have to wait and see.

Baptiste assured her that Joseph had been devastated not to hear from her. He'd be overjoyed to hear that she was coming. And *especially*—the valet put an affectionate hand on her belly—about the baby.

Well, maybe he would be and maybe he wouldn't. At least now she knew that he'd sent more letters. But there was something suspicious about Monsieur du Plessix's bland good humor; he and Baptiste were clearly hiding *something.* Perhaps Joseph truly was in love with the sublime Mademoiselle Beauvoisin. Perhaps he would have stopped writing to her in any case. She thought of his letters, reduced to ashes in the Duchesse's fireplace; it was maddening not to know what he'd written.

Still, what mattered was that he'd treat her and the baby decently—and this she refused to doubt. She would simply ignore her fears, she told herself, while she endured the rigors of the nine-day journey: the bumping and jolting of the coach, the all-too-infrequent rest stops, the dubious quality of the food and beds at the inns where they stopped.

Discomfitted by the idea of a young woman in an advanced stage of pregnancy undertaking such a trip, her fellow passengers stared disapprovingly at her. On the second day of the journey, Marie-Laure awoke from a nap to hear Monsieur du Plessix "explaining" her situation to their coach mates. Pretending to doze, she listened in astonishment as he spun out the story's details. Deftly, effortlessly, like a fortune-teller in a carnival booth, he conjured up a husband away on important military maneuvers, a contested inheritance, and a family tendency toward difficult births.

"And so you see, Messieurs and Mesdames," he concluded, "how absolutely necessary it is that the young lady be confined in proximity to a certain eminent Paris physician, under the patronage and protection of the gracious and generous Madame la Marquise de Machery, a distant relative who has interested herself in the case."

Absurd, she thought, that anybody would believe this fatuous concoction when she was so evidently a seduced and abandoned kitchen maid in clogs and a stained apron. But her fellow travelers seemed quite satisfied with Monsieur du Plessix's version of the facts, and began to treat her with increased sympathy and affection.

"Travelers enjoy sentimental stories," the lawyer told Marie-Laure and Baptiste over a dreadful mutton stew that evening. "Would you begrudge them their entertainment?"

"I've ordered a freshly killed and roasted capon for tomorrow from the market stand down the road," he continued, "so we won't have to depend on what we get from the next inn.

"Happily, the beds at this place are not as bad as the food. Well, *your* bed is all right anyway, Marie-Laure. But what's the matter, *petite?*" he asked, for she'd suddenly turned pale.

"Just a headache." She gasped, surprised by its intensity. "I think I'd better go to bed. Could you help me up the stairs, Monsieur?"

He was already at her elbow. Smiling as they mounted the stairs, he assured her that there was nothing to worry about: his wife had had just such headaches with their third, a vigorous eight-pound boy. His volubility and matter-of-factness were so comforting that by the time they'd reached her room she'd decided that the headache must not be so bad after all. And it was only after a miserable, sleepless hour that she remembered he'd told his lies in the coach that afternoon with the same cheerful certainty.

Her head felt a little better the next morning, but the ache never entirely disappeared. Her vision was sometimes blurred, and the coach's jolting made her dizzy and fretful. She tried to ignore it, sleeping fitfully as the pastures and vineyards of Burgundy rolled by. As they drove through the majestic forest of Fontainebleau the next day, she couldn't remember ever having been free of the insidious pain flickering behind her eyes. Still, she was determined to stay awake. For they were approaching the city gates of Paris.

Joseph felt as though he'd never sleep again.

Pregnant with his child! He paced the cell, trying to absorb the wonder, the enormity of it. The baby would look like her, of course—though if it were a boy, he supposed a little of his height might be a good thing. He tried to imagine its face, its limbs. And failed utterly. How big were babies anyway? Could they smile? He'd seen very few of them in his life; the women of his acquaintance bundled off their offspring to wet nurses as soon as possible, returning to society a week after the birth as though nothing had happened.

Well that wouldn't be the case with this baby. And even if he were still locked up when it arrived, he knew that mother and child would be safe with Jeanne.

Safe. His eyes grew hard. According to Jeanne, du Plessix said very little about why Marie-Laure had been running away from the château. Well, he could guess readily enough what must have happened.

I should never have allowed her to stay with those monsters, Joseph thought. *When I get out of this place, I'll . . .*

But would he ever get out of this place? He resolved that he would. No more cynicism about his chances. With Marie-Laure and the baby on their way to Paris, he couldn't afford the luxury of cynicism.

The stewed partridge on the table in front of him had grown cold an hour ago. The candle sputtered out. He shrugged. He'd been living in a sort of semidarkness anyway: his success in maintaining faith had been intermittent at best.

He lit a new candle. Perhaps it was time to learn to live secure in the light of someone's love.

Paris began even before its city walls. Marie-Laure stared at the outcroppings of small, temporary-looking dwellings: shanties for the poor souls who'd come to escape their misfortunes in the countryside. She supposed she should feel saddened, but instead she was energized by the city's force, attracted to its center like a bit of iron leaping to a magnet.

The customs officials at the gates were rude, canny, and quick to make personal remarks. She didn't mind in the slightest. They were city people, their attitudes laced with the ironic intimacy engendered by urban crowding and anonymity. She returned a wink with a haughty nod. And then a grin.

An open carriage—it belonged to the Marquise, Monsieur du Plessix told her—awaited them at the city gate. Low and elegant, upholstered in plush velvet, its outside was painted gaily in blues and violets and trimmed with gold. A fairy coach, she thought wryly, to bring a sooty, pregnant Cinderella to her prince—if he could spare a moment from his mistress. But she wouldn't worry about that just yet. She turned her attention to the city: the tall, narrow buildings that sometimes blocked the sky, the noise and the crowds, carriages, peddlers, beggars, dogs, children. She wanted to know these streets.

"Look," she cried excitedly, "there's a bookshop! And oh, what a beautiful church. Is it Notre-Dame? No, it can't be, for that's on an island, isn't it? And oh my goodness, look at the cakes in that shop window, the bonnets in that one."

They drove close by a coffee-seller, a tall man dispensing steaming cups from a tank on his back. It smelled delicious. She wished they could stop and buy some; maybe it would help her headache.

They were approaching the river now, the Seine. She peered at the boats and barges, at the people unloading crates of fruits and vegetables, rabbits and chickens; she gaped at the marvel of Notre-Dame, its lacy towers and the soaring buttresses supporting it.

The river disappeared as they crossed over a bridge densely lined with buildings. She couldn't see it anymore but she could still smell it. A blind person could probably navigate Paris quite well, she thought, with only his nose to guide him—his nose, and a sharp ear for approaching carriages.

Their own carriage jerked to a halt, and Baptiste jumped from his perch on the back to argue with the servant from a similar equipage. Somebody would have to back up and move aside. She enjoyed the volley of insult and invective; Baptiste was the more creative combatant, in her opinion.

And indeed, the other carriage finally allowed them to pass. They zigzagged through a warren of narrow streets, past more crowds of people, including some bearded men in wide fur hats ("Jews," Monsieur du Plessix explained). They drove through a large, symmetrical square, with graceful redbrick buildings ranged around the green, manicured lawns at its center.

"We're almost here," Monsieur du Plessix announced. "The hôtel Mélicourt is just around the corner."

The coach turned and stopped in front of an enormous stone facade. It took Marie-Laure a moment to grasp that it was a single building, its yellow-gray stone decorated with sculpted bas-reliefs, and going on for hundreds of feet on either side of imposing wooden doors large enough for the carriage to drive through.

Her excitement dissolved. And her headache felt very bad indeed.

"*This* is her house?"

Her voice sounded small and thin, even to herself.

"But do you really think she wants me here? I appreciate her assistance, but perhaps it would be more tactful to take me to an inn where I can speak to Joseph alone. Don't you think so, Monsieur du Plessix?"

The lawyer cleared his throat and fixed his eyes on her.

"You will be meeting the Marquise today, Marie-Laure," he

said. "And she'll be very kind to you and give you everything you need. But I'm afraid that the Viscomte can't be here to receive you at this time."

For the first time since she'd made his acquaintance his voice sounded neither glib nor confident.

"Because, Marie-Laure," he continued, "I'm terribly sorry to have to tell you that Joseph is in prison. He's been in the Bastille for the past ten weeks, falsely charged with the murder of the Baron Roque."

She thought—for a moment she hoped—that she might faint. But when the vertigo passed she found that she was painfully alert, if strangely chilly. It was as if a heavy curtain had descended over her emotions, isolating them from her sharpened senses and disjointed perceptions. The sun shone just as brightly as it had a moment ago, but it was a cold glare, reducing everything to abstract form, lifeless diagram.

She gazed numbly in front of her as the doors opened and the carriage clattered into a cobbled courtyard, the huge house spreading out beyond it. Stately, symmetrical, the house kept its own silent counsel behind banks of damask-shrouded windows; sphinx-like, it reached its two arms forward to the facade, enclosing the courtyard within a geometry of columns and pediments, balconies and bas-relief.

Servants ran toward the carriage to care for the horses and lift down the baggage. They looked like the miniature figure drawings a mapmaker or architect adds to an illustration to indicate the scale of things. Monsieur du Plessix took her limp hand and tried to squeeze some warmth into it.

"Courage, Marie-Laure," he said. "We're doing everything we can to prepare his defense in court, and meanwhile, to keep him hopeful and comfortable. But what he most needs is to know that you're safe and healthy.

"And now," he added, picking up his tricorne hat from the carriage seat at his side, "it's time to meet the Marquise."

Ah yes, she thought, Joseph's wife. Odd how frightened she'd been of meeting her just a moment ago.

The house was magnificent, she supposed. They climbed shallow steps to large front doors that opened silently, as though of their own accord. As they entered, she could see the footmen, in lemon yellow velvet, at each door. Such a pale yellow—her thrifty mind tried to register the cost of keeping those coats and breeches clean. The doors had swung open in such measured, simultaneous arcs that the footmen might have been automatons. Puppets.

Another yellow puppet led her and her companions through a vast, echoing foyer. High-ceilinged, marble-tiled, it was almost empty, perhaps with the intent of directing a visitor's eyes to the huge staircase at the right. The iron balustrade, painted black and decorated with gold, was wrought and hammered into the most extraordinarily sinuous curves.

Her vision blurred, shimmered, regained its focus. The balustrade was like a branching forest fern. It made you imagine branches too tiny for your eyes to see, spiraling into infinity, like the wondrous seashell Mamma and Papa had once given Gilles for his birthday. She lost herself for a moment in the swooping, asymmetrical curves, nature's dizzying fecundity cast in iron.

"Marie-Laure!" Baptiste hissed.

She ran to catch up with him and Monsieur du Plessix.

The next room was of black-and-white marble, with just a few frighteningly delicate chairs set among a clutter of bronze and marble statuary and huge, lush houseplants.

Doors opened into a room that at least seemed to have furniture to sit on, the better to survey the painted scenes from mythology that covered the walls and ceiling. Her eyes swept upward over Theseus escaping the labyrinth, Atalanta outrunning her suitors.

A dining room now, paneled in painted leather.

And finally an overfurnished but relatively intimate salon, thickly carpeted and hung with old tapestries.

Two women sat near a marble fireplace, and a few spaniels and a hideous pug dozed on the hearth.

Baptiste and Monsieur du Plessix bowed, while Marie-Laure managed a clumsy curtsy, peering at the women as though they were further instances of the mansion's fantastic decor.

And indeed, the younger woman might have stepped out of one

of the mythological paintings. Her gown, of pale, silvery green, was like the sea at sunset, foaming with creamy lace and twinkling with pearls and diamonds. Her smile was so lovely it penetrated Marie-Laure's baffled emotions and made her heart ache.

Oh dear, wasn't the Marquise supposed to be stout and plain? This sea nymph of painted rosebud lips, of dimpled cheeks and tumbling golden curls and sparkling eyes of aquamarine, was the most beautiful woman Marie-Laure had ever seen.

"*I'm* the Marquise." An amused, throaty voice issued from the other side of the fireplace. "And *this* is Mademoiselle Beauvoisin. You'd better sit down, *chérie*, you look exhausted."

She sank gratefully into a chair. *But what was Joseph's mistress doing here?*

"Marie-Laure's rather in shock, I'm afraid, Madame," Monsieur du Plessix explained, "for I've just now told her about your husband's arrest."

The Marquise nodded. "We're happy to have you here with us, Marie-Laure. We feel we know you a little, after all that Joseph has told us."

"Thank you, Madame la Marquise." Confused by her own response, she nonetheless found herself liking this woman.

She was stout and plain after all. Or perhaps, upon second glance, not exactly plain. She was a comfortable presence, almost handsome, if a woman could be handsome; squarish and thick-waisted in a wide, dark, satin dress. Was she in mourning? Marie-Laure couldn't tell. The dress was subdued; wildly expensive, of course, but also oddly functional, like a riding habit. It was as though the Marquise had no patience with style and had simply ordered herself a suit of acceptable noblewoman-livery. Marie-Laure smiled into knowing brown eyes, before stealing another awestruck, jealous glance at Mademoiselle Beauvoisin.

"I was sorry to hear about your uncle's death, Madame," Monsieur du Plessix was saying.

The lady nodded. "Well, we had our differences, but at the end we managed a certain rapport. It was he who forced me to marry, you know."

"Jeanne *chérie.*" Marie-Laure wondered how Mademoiselle

Beauvoisin's low, melodious voice could carry through the galleries of a theater. "It's a blessing that you married Joseph, because no other wife in Paris would have put as much effort into getting him freed as you have."

"Well, I owe him a great deal." The Marquise sounded embarrassed.

The other woman smiled. "*We* owe him everything."

Marie-Laure could only stare and wonder about the smile and the words, while a few faint gleams of comprehension shimmered at the edges of her vision.

No, she scolded herself, it couldn't be. It was too scandalous even to consider.

But somehow she felt warmer and happier, the happiness bringing her closer to her fears for Joseph but also to her love for him. For it seemed that there was love in this world of unspeakable wealth and overwrought decoration. She could feel love's presence, alive and well in this room.

The Marquise laughed. "There aren't many wives in Paris who are as rich as I am, especially now that my uncle's dead. But have we made any progress on our case, Monsieur du Plessix?"

"Not as much progress as I'd hoped, Madame," he answered. "Every bookseller has denied having forbidden books delivered the morning the Baron was murdered. In fact, they each, to a man, denied ever in their lives having bought or sold an illegal book."

So that's what he and Baptiste had been doing before they'd come to find her. Silly of me, Marie-Laure thought, *not to ask.*

"Monsieur Vernet agreed to testify about the visit to his father's shop."

Monsieur Vernet? But he must mean Gilles.

"But he couldn't in honesty swear the wounds might not have been caused by a fight with the Baron."

No, she supposed Gilles couldn't in honesty swear to anything he didn't know was true.

"Still," he continued, "he *was* willing to swear that the Viscomte hadn't had the ruby ring on him when he and his sister here undressed him and put him to bed. An onyx ring, but definitely not the ruby."

"Someone must have smuggled the Baron's ring into Joseph's possession later." Mademoiselle Beauvoisin sounded weary, as though this point had already been discussed many times. "But how to find out . . ."

"Meanwhile, I've dispatched an assistant to inquire about the Baron's chambermaid who killed herself," Monsieur du Plessix added. "We've found out her name—Manon—and the name of her village—Sazarat, in the Lubéron. It turns out she was pregnant."

"What about the papers Joseph had to sign at each bookseller's, in order to certify that he'd delivered the books? He signed *ours* with an *X*, but that was just a private joke to me. But perhaps he signed Monsieur Rigaud's with his real name or at least a verifiable signature. . . ."

Everyone seemed surprised to hear the words tumbling out of Marie-Laure's mouth, but the Marquise nodded vigorously.

"Well, Monsieur du Plessix, what of those papers? How can we get hold of them?"

While Monsieur du Plessix contemplated and considered, Marie-Laure felt Mademoiselle Beauvoisin's bright eyes sweeping over her. She blushed, suddenly very aware of her stained, smelly, too-tight dress and the wooden clogs she'd worn since they'd left Carency.

"Do you have a headache, Marie-Laure?" Mademoiselle Beauvoisin asked.

Marie-Laure nodded, surprised that someone could tell. In a flash of diamonds and a rustle of silk, the woman in pale green was at her side, her sparkling eyes keen and concentrated. The pug had risen from the hearth and was watching attentively.

"Give me your hand, I want to take your pulse. Yes, it's too fast. And you've been dizzy as well these past few days, *non?* Blurred vision sometimes too? I thought so. Well, come along. Jeanne, I'm putting Marie-Laure to bed. That's all right, you stay with Monsieur du Plessix.

"Georges," she called to a footman, "go get Doctor Raspail, and tell him Madame la Marquise's houseguest may have toxemia."

"Yes, that's tox-eem-i-a." She shaped the syllables with great elegance, as though they were a pretty speech by Marivaux, and Marie-Laure began to understand how the shadings and tonalities of that voice might fill, and captivate, a theater. She took Marie-Laure's elbow, to help her out of her chair. But what was this toxemia? Was the baby in danger?

"I'll give you a little pull to help you onto your feet, good, that's it. You'll be much more comfortable in bed. That's it, come this way." She chuckled as Marie-Laure directed a hesitant farewell curtsy in the Marquise's direction.

"Don't trip on Figaro here," she added, for it seemed the pug was coming with them. "And don't worry so much about propriety. Jeanne is a snob, but an inconsistent one. She won't mind if you miss a curtsy now and then.

"My mother's a retired midwife. I helped her with hundreds of births when I was a girl," she told Marie-Laure as she helped her off with her clothes in the spacious blue and white bedroom. The walls were covered in fine, shiny cotton, printed in robin's egg blue with harlequins, columbines, and girls kicking up their petticoats in garlanded garden swings. The rugs were a deeper blue, with designs of lilies around their borders, and the armchairs and chaise longue were pale blue satin damask. Even the tin bathtub by the hearth was enameled in slate blue. "It's still warm enough," Mademoiselle murmured, dipping her fingers into the water, "from the fire."

It felt good to get out of the clothes. And even better to feel Mademoiselle Beauvoisin's small but surprisingly strong hands gently scrubbing her back and belly and then drying her with towels that had also been heated by the fire.

"But you've gotten your lovely gown all wet."

Mademoiselle Beauvoisin shrugged. "I have others. Come on, we don't want you catching a chill."

There was a nightgown spread out on the bedcover, a simple, voluminous garment of fine muslin, with rows of intricate smocking at the top.

"It's Jeanne's," Mademoiselle Beauvoisin explained as she

pulled it over Marie-Laure's head. "She does the smocking herself. Learned to do it at school and still does it to relax; don't let on that I told you.

"Of course it's vastly too large, but I thought it would be comfortable, since there's no lace or ribbon or much in the way of detail. Now slide under the covers. Are you warm enough? I'll put another log on the fire. And I want you to lie on your left side, with your feet on these pillows, *oui, comme ça*—it will help your baby breathe more easily."

She leaned over to stroke Figaro, who'd installed himself on the bed, curling into a tight little ball at the small of Marie-Laure's back as though to remind her to continue lying on her side.

Her face grew serious.

"But you're frightened, aren't you? And here I've been chattering like a magpie."

She sat in a small chair over to the side of the bed and took Marie-Laure's hand.

"No one knows what causes toxemia," she said, "or really how to stop it. But according to Mamma—and her experience is prodigious—mothers who are lucky enough to be able to spend the remainders of their pregnancies in bed are likely to do perfectly well. So please try not to worry."

Marie-Laure nodded. She'd try. She felt warm and comfortable. And she'd never in her life lain between such smooth, finely woven sheets.

"But Joseph," she asked, suddenly tormented by the image of him lying on a pile of straw in a musty dungeon, "is he cold and hungry in the Bastille?"

Peals of silvery laughter greeted her question.

"Oh, I'm so sorry, I'm being awfully tactless, aren't I? But if you'd only seen the little procession of wagons that Jeanne dispatched to the Bastille the day after they took him away. Rugs, chairs, tapestries, even a painting or two . . . And the baskets of food her footman drags in every week when she visits him—the cheeses and pâtés and roasts and casseroles, not to mention the wines and pastries, and bread still warm from the baker. I tease her that she'll make him fat, but most of the food gets gobbled up by a prisoner he often dines with, one Marquis de Sade, he's also a Provençal nobleman, oddly enough. Very depraved, Joseph says, and also very witty and learned.

"He's quite comfortable, Marie-Laure, you needn't concern yourself about that. But I'll be honest: he's in serious danger of being convicted."

Marie-Laure nodded, resolving to be equally honest, even if it meant finding out something she didn't want to know. Focusing her wavering vision on Mademoiselle Beauvoisin's eyes and smile, she grasped the little hand that held her own so comfortingly.

"But how . . . why . . . is his mistress being so kind to me?"

For a moment, her question drew only an uncomprehending aquamarine stare, followed by a dazzling gleam of understanding, as though the sun had suddenly turned the sea to diamonds.

"You read one of the fashion magazines, didn't you? But how did you get hold of that trash, tucked so far away in Provence as you were?"

"The Duchesse, his sister-in-law, receives them every week by post. She . . . she cut out the pages for me."

"Ah, the sister-in-law." The rosebud lips curled in delicate distaste, as though sipping chocolate made from milk that had gone sour.

"Marie-Laure, you must believe me that those stories were all lies, categorical untruths told by journalists who wrote what they were paid to write. No, *chérie*, I promise you. I have never been Joseph's mistress."

Mademoiselle Beauvoisin turned her head, at the sound of a step in the doorway.

"She's read *The Ladies' Journal*, Jeanne," she called. "Or perhaps it was *Paris à la Mode*. That bitch of a *belle-soeur* did her the service of sharing the little fictions we concocted."

"Merde, the sister-in-law." The Marquise deposited a pile of beautifully bound books on the bedside table. "I thought you might learn a bit about your new city from Rétif's *Paris Nights*. But if you don't care for it, there's always Richardson. In English."

Joseph must have told her I know English, Marie-Laure thought. *How good of her to remember. And what lovely, welcoming words: "your new city."*

But she'd think about all that later. She turned her attention back to the two women.

"So she doesn't know?" the actress was saying.

"No, not yet. A pity Joseph didn't tell her, but he worried that she might be a bit too conventional to understand; he thought it would be better to wait until she arrived."

"Doesn't know *what?*" Marie-Laure blushed at how peremptory her voice sounded.

The Marquise laughed.

"Well, it did seem like a perfect cover story. All of Paris was delighted to laugh at the ridiculous Marquise—fat, foolish, a bluestocking, and too rich by half—who introduced her handsome husband to a siren of an actress. Give people a chance to sneer at you and they'll believe anything."

"Though the truth is that Joseph introduced us to each other years ago." Mademoiselle Beauvoisin smiled. "And very prettily too."

"Which was exactly the sort of thing that my uncle was frantic that we cover up," the Marquise added. "For people were beginning to talk, prejudices are becoming stronger these days, and we needed a decent scandal to cover up the indecent one we're always in danger of creating."

She stood behind Mademoiselle Beauvoisin's chair, her wide, square hands on the damask upholstery, a beringed index finger carelessly coming to rest in the rounded hollow of a naked, delicate shoulder. As the finger made small, practiced circles, gently smoothing a tiny tense muscle, Mademoiselle Beauvoisin's eyes became softer; her dimples just a bit deeper.

"I love Joseph as a brother," she said. "Jeanne and I both do. But," and Marie-Laure knew that this soft, warm, exquisitely shaded voice could have soared, as on angel wings, up to the highest seats in the largest theater in Paris, "*he* is not my lover, Marie-Laure."

"Thank you," Marie-Laure whispered to the two women at her bedside.

She felt strangely honored by the understanding they'd conferred on her, though just an hour ago she'd dismissed the very possibility as too vile to consider. Joseph had been right: there were ways in which she was very conventional. But she trusted her instinct—the inner compass that told her a passionate, caring, and deeply shared love could never be vile or wrong.

"Thank you," she spoke up more clearly this time. "Thank you both for everything. And especially for trusting me."

Chapter 23

Mon Amour,

If you receive this, it's because I'll have succeeded in performing a bit of sleight of hand, befuddling the guard's eye as I substitute it at the last minute for a list of foods I'll demand that Jeanne bring me on her next visit.

And even if it doesn't work, and for punishment they take away my exercise walks in the courtyard for a week or two, it will have been worth it, just for the pleasure of writing again and telling you again how much I love you. Je t'aime je t'aime je t'aime je t'aime.

I'm sure Jeanne has told you about my daily routines here. It's comfortable enough, especially for someone who spent his childhood in a drafty château. I'm undoubtedly more at ease than you were in your garret, so please don't worry.

Sade is a witty companion, though he chides me mercilessly—and enviously—about my "harem" back at the hôtel Mélicourt. Of course he understands the true facts of the situation; Jeanne and Ariane's liaison could hardly shock him. But he prefers to reshape things after his own fancies. Well, he's been in prison for years now [a thick line of ink obscured whatever he'd written here]

In truth, I think my unusual marriage has changed me for the better. Living in fraternal harmony with two women for whom I was entirely superfluous (at least in one critical way) was a most enlight-

ening experience. It's one I recommend to all Frenchmen, noble or not, who may have too high an opinion of themselves.

And now that you're with these dear friends who've taken such good care of me you must let them take care of you as well.

I marvel that you're less than a league away—so terribly, wonderfully close that I feel I can touch you through these walls. And so I do. I use my hands, my lips—all my senses and my imagination too—to learn and try to understand the mysteries of what's happening inside you.

But the cruel truth is that I am entirely dependent upon my imagination.

And so you must help me. You must write to me and describe how you look these days. Tell me what it would be like to touch you all over, experience all the new shapes and tastes and textures of you.

I understand the profundity of what I'm asking, chérie. *I know that finding the right words for very physical things isn't easily done. I can see your lip curling sardonically even as you read this. Well, you think, now this lubricious, decadent libertine has gone too far!*

I plead guilty—to that, at any rate. I throw myself on your mercy, be generous to me in my excess of desire.

And in return, I'll help you.

We shall begin very simply. Just follow my finger—no, not even my finger, merely my fingertip. It traces the curve of your lip, caresses the line of your jaw and—very slowly now, very lightly—it has moved to the hollow of your neck.

You love that. You arch your back when I touch certain places on your neck.

And I *love* that. *Well, of course I do, because when you arch and bend like that I know you want me to play with your breasts.*

I touch a nipple. I draw a little circle around it with that same fingertip, watching the flesh darken, pucker, stiffen.

I want to do a great deal more. I want to tongue your flesh, suck it, squeeze it—no, not just the little bit of you that I'm touching, but your whole breast now, both breasts, I want to put my face between them. But for the sake of this fiction, I do none of these things.

I simply touch the tip of your breast and marvel at it.

And you must tell me what I see.

You must introduce me to your body as it is at this moment. You must help me to see it, tell me how to touch it. To touch you.

Tell me, Marie-Laure. Touch me, mon amour.

With all my heart,
Joseph

Mon cher *Joseph,*

I have to lie on my side, you know, to help the baby breathe. What extraordinary luxury. Just to lie in this big, beautiful bedchamber and do—nothing. Of course, I can read if I want to. Or write to you, resting the paper on a little oak box that serves as a bed-desk.

I can toss a ball for Figaro to chase or eat the lovely meals that are brought to me.

Or I can worry—for example, that something will go wrong and you won't receive this letter, wrapped around an apple tart in Madame la Marquise's latest food package to you.

Or better, to try not *to worry about such things. And instead to fret about more immediate matters, like:* however shall I manage to write the things you've asked of me?

Well, if I make a botch of it, I can throw this letter into the fire, and begin a fresh new sheet (another astonishing luxury), from the stack of paper the Marquise has given me.

All right. I shall try. Don't laugh at me.

[She'd paused here, but you couldn't see the pause on the paper. In fact, her handwriting had continued firmer, more resolute than before.]

When you trace the shape of my mouth with your finger, you make me smile. A little smile at first, but then a wider one, and soon I find that I must part my lips and kiss your fingertip—touch the tip of my tongue to it, or even bite it, very lightly of course, and catch my breath, rubbing my jaw against the back of your hand like a lazy, spoiled cat in front of a fire.

Do you hear me purring? It's not very loud, but you're stroking the slope of my throat now, and I know you can feel the happy vibrations.

Do I always arch my back when you touch my neck like that? (Yes, I know just the places you mean.) Do I always throw back my head and offer you my breasts?

I didn't know. Well, how could I know, when you so confound me with pleasure that I can't know what I'm doing?

Ah yes, please, bury your face between my breasts—and you truly can bury it; they're quite formidable these days, you'd be astonished.

They're heavy. The neck of this nightdress is too loose, I can reach inside it. I can hold a breast in my hand. Yes, there's a definite heft to it. And the veins are more prominent and bluer.

Is it my finger or yours now, that makes such small, precise circles around the dark spot surrounding the nipple? But that's not so small either nowadays. It's darker and wider, a kind of purplish brown, and the nipple is thicker, less girlish . . . would you think it pretty, I wonder?

I'm blushing now, scandalized by what I've written. If I don't stop I shall probably throw this sheet of paper into the fire.

But in fact I must stop, for I hear Dr. Raspail. It's time for his regular visit. He doesn't esteem me very highly; he's a bit offended to be treating a body that doesn't have a title attached to it, though he couldn't refuse the Marquise's guest.

But though I lack a title, I still maintain certain standards. And chief among them is that I don't want anyone examining me while I'm still at the mercy of your very dear, gentle, and oh-so-provocative fingertip.

So I must compose myself. Breathe, Marie-Laure, as Madame Rachel never fails to insist. She's Mademoiselle Beauvoisin's mother, you know, and very wise and reassuring. Breathe slowly and deeply, she says.

And so, in and out, with every steady heartbeat, I breathe you. Adieu, Joseph. Be well. I love you.

Adieu. Be well. I love you.

Marie-Laure

Confirming upon his first examination that she suffered from toxemia, Dr. Raspail had consigned her to total bed rest for the remainder of her pregnancy.

"Keep a footman at her door," he'd instructed the Marquise, "in case convulsions develop."

He'd considered bleeding her as well. "But let's start with medication and bed rest," he decided, to Marie-Laure's great relief. To relax her, he prescribed a draught of medicine, to be taken every morning and evening. It had opium in it, he said.

"And as for her keeping to her left side," he added peevishly, "well, I don't see what good it could do, but I suppose it couldn't hurt."

"It offends him to defer to Mamma's experience," Mademoiselle Beauvoisin had explained, "but he's prudent enough to take her advice into account, for he knows there isn't a scientific explanation for your condition."

In any case—and for whatever reason—the headaches and blurred vision had eased, and even sometimes disappeared for hours at a time.

Joseph replied the next week.

I was charmed and delighted by your letter, mon amour, *but you must have more confidence in me. Yes, of course, I find that thicker, less girlish nipple pretty—pretty! I'm quite beside myself, I held it in my hand all night. Kissed it, fondled it, flicked my tongue over it while you moaned and gasped. I flatter myself that you screamed with pleasure, and that together we made an absolute chaos of the bedclothes.*

But then I realized I didn't know how to envision our two bodies among that rat's nest of sheets and pillows. For I'd imagined myself on top of you, and perhaps that isn't comfortable for you any longer.

Yes, the more I think of it the surer I am. You must sit astride me, while I lie back and gaze at the belly that overwhelms me with pride and desire. And which you must describe to me.

If you're able to, of course.

No, you must. I insist.

It's not so bad, you know, for me to insist on things from time to time. For I was absolutely wrong last autumn not to insist that you come to Paris earlier. I love your independence and your stiff-necked shopkeeper's pride, but you should have accepted assistance, Marie-Laure.

So now, I shall insist upon your describing yourself to me. . . .

She nodded slowly.

Perhaps she *should* have accepted assistance. She'd have to work all that out later.

Right now, though, she had something very important to write.

It's as big as a pumpkin, Joseph.

All right, [she added] *I suppose even a nobleman knows that pumpkins come in all sizes. So I must be more precise.*

A fifteen-pound pumpkin, then. Or a melon. A lovely big round prize winter squash with a sort of squash blossom poking out where my perfectly ordinary-looking navel used to be. Reminding me that the baby is similarly connected.

And reminding me of what I can't do right now: move too much, or get too excited.

You, of course, should continue to imagine making me scream amidst a chaos of bedsheets.

But my imaginings must be quieter.

I'm still on my side; I lie curved around this astonishing belly. Come to bed, Joseph. Lie on your side facing me.

Here's my hand. I'm stroking your cheek. And now your mouth. Yes, you know what I'm doing. That's right. Lick the palm of my hand. Get it very wet, ah yes just like that, so that when I touch you, when I wrap my hand around you, my hand will slide up and down the length of you.

Up.

Down.

And again, so many "agains."

You're harder now, so beautifully bowed and taut, and I'm moving my hand more quickly now, watching your jaw loosen, your eyes widen. What do you see at that moment, just before? I hope you see me, smiling proudly, laughing perhaps. . . .

I have a very sticky hand now—no, I don't know how to be more poetic here and even this is probably a bit too exciting for me and so once again I must only breathe you in and out. . . .

Ah good. My supper is coming on a tray, and the distraction will probably help to calm me. I've become friends with the maid who brings it. Claudine is a very worldly Parisienne and thinks that I must be very good in bed to have attracted such a rich and handsome gentleman. I was shocked when she first told me that, but now I find it very amusing. . . .

Arranging the dinner tray at Marie-Laure's side, Claudine poured some fresh water with the tiniest bit of wine mixed in to sweeten it, and then gave an expectant little *ahem.*

For it was a Wednesday, and Claudine always spent her free Wednesday afternoons shopping.

"But what wonderful stockings, Claudine," Marie-Laure exclaimed.

Claudine nodded modestly. "And what about this fichu?" she asked. "Look, the linen and stitching are almost as fine as what you'll find on the rue Saint-Honoré. Well, it's the details that matter, don't you think?"

And Marie-Laure, thinking of the letter she'd written that afternoon, had to agree. It was always the details that mattered.

Ma belle *Cinderella with her pumpkin,*

Less poetry is always better. I loved reading about your sticky hand, and spent some delightful minutes imagining you licking me off your sticky fingers.

Jeanne tells me that Madame Rachel has been rubbing almond oil into your skin where it's been stretched by your growing belly, so that the marks will fade after the baby comes out. I wish I could do that. I'd warm my hands over a candle flame, and rub it in so slowly and carefully that you'd never want anyone else to do it. I'd measure your waist with my hands every morning; I'd discern the tiniest changes . . . and I'd lie quietly behind you, my lips pressed against the nape of your neck, my front curved around your back while you curve around this astonishing belly of yours.

And so you see what peaceable fancies I can have—while still (late at night) having the wildest, most wanton visions of you and me. For there are a few things we haven't yet tried, you know. But I'll save them. For the future. For our future . . .

But Joseph, [she wrote back] *I've never told you that the baby kicks! I forgot, until Mademoiselle Beauvoisin reminded me, that you probably haven't seen very many pregnant women, or very many babies, for that matter.*

Anyway, if you put your hand on my belly you can often feel it. It's a dancer, it's an acrobat, a fencer—it will be as graceful and light-footed as its papa.

Mon amour,

Can someone have erotic fancies when he's trying his best to imagine being called "Papa"?

And can someone imagine being called "Papa" when he's spent his life being a scamp, a scapegrace, an enfant terrible?

Well, he can try. And I am, I am.

But since I once chastised you for your excess of responsibility, I can hardly, in fairness, not confess to my own sins. And not just of impulsiveness, or hypersensitivity, or all the absurdities of my libertine life. But of something else I don't quite understand.

I feel that somehow I brought this imprisonment on myself. Yes, I know it's absurd, but I can't lose the feeling. And not because of anything I did to the Baron Roque, for I had nothing whatsoever to do with his death.

Perhaps it's just my fears—or my guilt for leaving you at the château. But I don't think so. I truly believe that there's something I should be remembering. Or dreaming, perhaps. Something that will tell me what I need to know.

I shall try to dream then. I shall go to bed and bring your letters with me. And I shall bring you too. You that first day in the barn, with rays of sunlight slanting onto your hair and your little pink tongue darting out of your mouth—I was breathless, thrilled, and almost mortally astonished that anyone could be so brave and so shy at the same moment. And you as you are now—formidable breasts and luscious belly—but, I dare to imagine, still the same bright hair and pink tongue and ah, the same determined mouth.

Lie down on your side—there, you needn't strain. I've covered your breasts and belly with kisses and now I'm putting my arms around you. Holding you, rocking you, our lips opening and tongues meeting. . . .

But you must imagine what you want to imagine. I won't share what I'm thinking this time; take whatever you need of me, Marie-Laure, be it pleasure or comfort or simply—whatever else happens—my undying love.

Joseph

Whatever else happens.

She read the letter so many times in the next few days that it was beginning to fray along the folds.

It wasn't quite coherent. But how could it be? The truth was that he and she—each in a different way—were in mortal danger. And yet they'd shared earnest hopes, pretty thoughts, and overwhelming desire. Nothing made a whole lot of sense in such a situation; she wasn't surprised that he was plagued with muddled, nonsensical fancies about there being something he needed to remember. She folded the letter and put it back under her pillow, rearranged herself carefully on her left side, and fell into a troubled sleep.

She dozed fitfully, plagued by dreams. She was running along the path by the river, but a tangle of vines—or were they serpents?—threatened to bar her way. She had to keep going, though, because a pack of baying hounds were trying to get at her—horrid dogs, with Monsieur Hubert among them. She could feel her pursuers' hot breath; the hounds were tearing at her clothes with dripping fangs. She was helpless, naked now, and someone was leading her—where?

She forced herself back to sweaty, gasping consciousness. Her head still ached; she was weak and shaky. But when she lit the candle at her bedside she was surprised that her vision was clear. In fact, everything was preternaturally clear and distinct, the colors deeply saturated.

She could pull the bell cord at the side of her bed and bring the footman running. But she really felt more strange than bad. So she lay quietly on her side for the next few hours, forcing herself to breathe slowly and evenly, until daylight stole under the bottoms of the heavy curtains and Claudine appeared with her breakfast.

She wasn't hungry, but the coffee smelled good. Pulling herself to a more upright position, she suddenly felt . . . wet.

"Please," she whispered, "please, I think you'd better call somebody. I feel . . . well, I feel very odd."

She paused.

"I think . . ." she began. And then she smiled. "No, I'm *sure* that was a contraction, and that the baby's coming."

The contractions were weak, but the baby was undeniably on its way.

Dr. Raspail looked solemn: a six-week-early baby might not be entirely prepared to eat and breathe on its own. But there was no stopping the inevitable, and nothing he could do until her labor was more advanced. He'd return, he said, in a few hours, after visiting a dropsical prince in the Faubourg Saint-Germain.

"It might be a blessing," Mademoiselle Beauvoisin suggested. "Perhaps the baby is wise to leave before the toxemia gets any worse."

Marie-Laure sat flanked by the actress and her mother. Madame Rachel was a small, silent, faded woman with endless knowledge of the mysterious processes underway.

The day progressed slowly, the women taking turns holding Marie-Laure's hand and helping her accept the gradually deepening contractions—to breathe through them, they'd insist.

"Good, good," they'd murmur from time to time.

Good? By early evening she couldn't decide whether she wanted to hug them for their patience or strangle them. Strangle them, she decided; she wanted to strangle anybody and everybody who wasn't feeling their middles squeezed in an iron vise. Cursing softly, she turned back to the business of breathing, when she heard heavy steps on the marble stairway.

It must be Doctor Raspail, she thought. But those didn't sound like Doctor Raspail's measured steps. What they did sound like were . . .

But that was impossible. Still, the footsteps sounded (for hadn't she heard him clomping up the staircase to his bedroom every day of her life until she'd left Montpellier?)—they sounded exactly like . . .

Gilles?

With the Marquise bringing up the rear.

"But . . . but . . ." She forgot to breathe, and the *but* transmuted into a howl of pain.

"Breathe!" the command issued in unintended unison from Gilles and Mademoiselle Beauvoisin, the simultaneity surprising each of them and Marie-Laure as well.

"Breathe, *chérie!*"

"Breathe dammit, Marie-Laure!"

The two of them stared at one another. Mademoiselle Beauvoisin was clearly relieved to see Gilles. And Gilles was just as clearly determined to trust no one in this vile den of aristocrats—even a disarmingly beautiful woman who seemed to know something about obstetrics.

"Here, Jeanne." Mademoiselle Beauvoisin prodded the Marquise toward Marie-Laure's bedside. "Take my place for just a moment, while I speak to Monsieur . . ."

"*Doctor* Vernet."

So he'd passed his final examinations. How wonderful, Marie-Laure almost had time to think, before she howled again against the massive force of the next contraction.

"Um, breathe please, Marie-Laure," the Marquise offered timidly.

Marie-Laure tried to obey, but the Marquise's entreaties—and even Madame Rachel's confident touch—weren't enough to distract her from what Mademoiselle Beauvoisin was whispering to Gilles.

"Second stage . . . difficult transition . . . effaced . . ."

And then, "Toxemia, seems to be controlled with . . . but we're not sure . . . pulsebeat . . ."

"*Bien,*" Gilles took off his coat. Rolling up his sleeves, he strode to the pitcher of warm water on an inlaid commode. Marie-Laure expected him to stare disdainfully at the commode's elaborate gold trim, but he seemed to have slipped off his edgy class-consciousness with his coat, and become entirely a very intent and very capable physician.

"Thank you, Jeanne." Mademoiselle Beauvoisin had rejoined the pale, perspiring Marquise. "And now, we're going to prop up Marie-Laure's legs on these pillows and bolsters, that's right, *ma chère,* just pile them there . . ."

"And *you,*" Gilles announced to Marie-Laure, "are going to push the baby out." He stood between her raised legs, looking down at her as though he were preparing another lesson in how to fight like a boy.

"But how . . ." She wanted to ask him how he'd known to come and who had told him where to find her, but the questions evaporated somewhere between her mind and her mouth. Suddenly she didn't care how he'd gotten here, she cared about nothing except a sudden overwhelming urge to push. And it seemed that she knew how to do it. Of course, it would be more like pushing an immense pumpkin than a baby—*well, perhaps* (ma belle *Cinderella*), *perhaps it* was *a pumpkin after all. What else* could *it be? For surely a baby couldn't be so enormous.*

Well, whatever it was, she knew what to do. *Yes, Gilles, I know exactly. And it* is *a kind of fighting,* she thought, between pushes, gasps, groans, bellows, and curses. *Fighting like a woman.*

How strange that the pain should cease so abruptly—exactly as Gilles had given a satisfied little grunt, the one that always signaled an experiment had been a success. *The baby isn't inside me anymore,* she thought. *Gilles must have it in his hands.*

The grunt had sounded reassuring. But suddenly she was alone and everybody was terribly busy somewhere else. She heard someone mutter, "Blue, stressed." Finally, eons later, she heard a lusty, outraged, energetic scream, and a relieved collective sigh.

"*Look* at you," she whispered to the tiny, waxy, purplish creature Gilles put down on her naked belly.

"Breathing all right, thank God," she heard someone say.

"Just *look* at you," she half crooned and half sobbed, as Madame

Rachel helped her gather the baby into her arms. The child was wrapped in a heavy blanket ("These little, early ones do better if they're kept warm," Madame Rachel said), so all she could see was a tiny, thin face: the little features were scrunched up, exhausted by a long, hard journey. But there was no mistaking them. They were Joseph's features, stamped as clearly on the new-made flesh as the King's on a gold coin.

Church bells rang somewhere.

"It's just after midnight," the Marquise said in a dazed voice. "It's Thursday, the day I visit Joseph."

"And you will tell him," Mademoiselle Beauvoisin said softly, "that another beautiful, *healthy* young lady has come to stay with us, and that she is as eager as the rest of us for his release."

Chapter 24

Gilles was at her bedside when she woke the next morning. "The Marquise wrote to me," he told her, "probably the very day you arrived here. It was good of her to alert me about your condition.

"Toxemia's mysterious," he added, pouring her a cup of coffee from the silver pot on the table, "and it can be extremely dangerous. You were lucky. They took good care of you—that actress especially." He turned his eyes away.

She wished she could calm his offended sensibilities. *Yes, Gilles, it is what you suspect. But it's not vile or scandalous—it's really quite natural, once you get used to the idea.*

No, better not to embarrass him. She concentrated on her coffee, the still-warm bread wrapped in a linen napkin, the little crock of sweet butter beside it on the tray.

"I checked up on the baby," he said. "She's doing very well, sleeping soundly. Madame Rachel has her in the next room."

"She's little and scrawny, of course," he added, "but you can see that she's one of the tough ones."

He looked away again, obviously at a loss for what to say next.

She supposed it was up to her to begin. "This must come as something of a shock to you."

He rolled his eyes. *Well, yes, that's* one *way to put it.*

His face fell into familiar lines: a responsible older sibling's exasperation with a flighty younger one.

"Come home with me," he demanded. "You can't just let them keep you and the baby like house pets." He grimaced at Figaro, curled up on the bed at her feet.

"I can't come," she answered. "I have to wait for Joseph. Sophie and I need to be here, for when he . . . in case of . . ."

"You're really naming her Sophie?" He allowed himself a quick smile of pleasure before continuing. "Your . . . your . . ." Considering possible ways he might refer to Joseph and rejecting them all, he shrugged his shoulders and continued. "His prospects don't look good, you know.

"Everybody at home talks about his case, Marie-Laure. They say it's about time a damn aristocrat was prosecuted for something—though they admit it's nice that he knocked off one of his own instead of taking it out on commoners. If public opinion counts for anything—and sometimes it does, even under our ridiculous Bourbon monarchy—he'll never get out of the Bastille."

He seemed determined to be brutal. Or maybe the facts simply *were* brutal.

"But the truth ought to count for *something,*" she retorted. "And the truth—as you very well know—is that Joseph didn't do it. He was making deliveries to booksellers all day. His signature is probably filed away all over the city in offices like Rigaud's."

Damn Gilles for goading her into arguing the point. She crossed her arms, leaned back against the pillows, and glared at him.

"He didn't do it and that's final. Joseph's not a murderer, Gilles."

He glared back at her. "Still, he took advantage of *you,* didn't he? Don't you understand that I'll never forgive myself for allowing you to work there? It was my duty to protect you from libertine scum like him. I would have killed him rather than let him touch you. In fact I should never have . . ."

She stared while his voice turned uncertain, the irony of what he'd just said becoming clear to him. And while he stammered, she could feel her own mouth shaping a small and not very tactful smile—at the memory of her determined self, maneuvering Joseph toward that pile of hay in the barn.

Quite a contrast, she thought, with whatever lurid seduction scene Gilles must imagine.

But before Gilles's personal honesty forced him to concede that he understood the meaning of her smile, they heard the sounds of a baby's whimpering.

"Ah," he said quickly. "Ah good, she's going to wake up. Sometimes you have to shake these little early ones awake to get them to eat enough.

"I'm going to book a place on a coach back home tonight." He took her pulse as he spoke, nodding at the results. "You're bouncing back remarkably well.

"I've put a deposit on some space," he added proudly, "to rent for an office."

Oh dear, was he really going so soon? Wasn't he going to help her learn to take care of the mysterious creature in the next room? Just how did you hold a baby when you nursed it, anyway? How did you know when it had eaten enough? Did it hurt when they sucked, she wondered suddenly. Suppose she didn't have enough milk in her breasts, or even worse, suppose the baby didn't like the way it tasted? But she couldn't ask Gilles to stay and disrupt his life more than he already had.

He took some gold coins from his pocket and laid them on the table.

"Buy yourself something new to wear," he said. "You shouldn't have to depend on the Marquise for *everything*.

"I've been tutoring some rich, dim-witted first-year students," he explained. "Don't want them killing their future patients, after all."

Briskly, he turned to the next order of business.

"And while I'm in Paris, I have to buy some stockings for Sylvie. Maybe some perfume as well, and something for Madame Bellocq, and for Augustin and Suzanne too. But I don't know . . ."

Marie-Laure laughed. "You don't know which shops you can afford, which ones won't cheat you, and which ones won't be too snooty. Neither would I, even if I were strong enough to accompany you today. But as it happens, there is, in this household, a most expert and accomplished Parisienne shopper."

The shopper had just appeared in the doorway to get the breakfast tray. And yes, Claudine was quite sure that the Marquise would allow her to guide Doctor Vernet through the perils and pitfalls of the capital's shopping districts.

I hope, Marie-Laure thought after the two of them had left her alone, *she doesn't congratulate Doctor Vernet on his sister's snaring a rich protector like the Viscomte.*

Doctor Vernet. How fine it sounded, and how wonderful that he'd soon have his own office. Her moment of satisfaction, however, gave way almost immediately to simple panic, as Sophie let out a furious and hungry yell.

Madame Rachel quickly assumed command, showing Marie-Laure how to pump her milk into a clean bowl and feed the fussy, immature little mouth from an eyedropper. Sophie was too little to take the breast the first week; it was slow, exacting, anxious work to make sure that she was eating enough. And as Gilles had said she might, she sometimes drifted off to sleep before she'd finished, needing to be coaxed awake again.

Marie-Laure learned to burp her, and to clean and diaper her. And when there was nothing to do, she simply gazed at her limbs and toes and fingers, talking and singing softly to her. A funny new chair was installed in the blue bedchamber: it had curved wooden parts at the bottom, so you could rock back and forth in it. The motion was comforting; the Marquise said the American ambassador, Monsieur Franklin, had recommended it. Marie-Laure spent hours rocking with Sophie in her arms, tracing Joseph's features in the baby's little face, wondering if *he'd* ever get to do so, and reading and rereading his latest letter.

. . . and as for our daughter—our daughter!—I can only stare at the words in wonder and wish with all my heart that I could see her.

I received a communication this week, by the way, from Amélie, telling me that the Prince de Condé is to be godfather to the new little Comte de Carency Auvers-Raimond when he makes his appearance.

Of course she assumes it will be a Comte and not a Comtesse. Poor child—they'll probably never even look at its face. Just a quick peek under its gown and then Amélie will pack it off to a wet nurse she'll hire on the cheap.

This is the first letter I've received from either her or Hubert, its sole purpose being to gloat about an impressive new social connection. No desire, it seems, to help me. Well, why should they? Evidently my imprisonment hasn't hindered Amélie's rise through the social ranks.

[A word was crossed out here—probably "if," Marie-Laure thought.] *When I get out of here, you'll have to explain why you were leaving so precipitously that day. I'm so sorry for whatever happened,* mon amour.

But enough unpleasantness. I don't know why I've written at such length about them, except that I seem to think more about family now that I'm a father. (I'm *a* father!)

Sophie Madeleine is a lovely name, my only sadness being that you and I weren't able to choose it together. Jeanne says she looks like me. I can't imagine it. I never imagined a child to love and protect, to care for and even to try to set a good example for.

But then, I never expected to find someone to love as I love you. So [a few more words were crossed out here] *life has really been surprisingly kind to me.*

[A catalog of kisses followed, in a hurried, less elegant handwriting.] *I bury my face in your breasts, my hands in your hair, I lower you to the bed, gaze at you against the pillows. I hold back—for a delightful instant, for an excruciating eternity, for just as long as I dare—before I enter you . . . like . . . ah, but whereas Monsieur X had metaphors for what comes next, I find that I do not. It simply is what it is, and I think I would happily die to have it, to have* you, *just once more. Au revoir. Keep happy and safe and tell Sophie I love her.*

Joseph

She wept, for the first time since she'd arrived in Paris.

"*Eh bien,*" Madame Rachel told her, "the tears often come when the milk does."

Perhaps. Her body and emotions, it seemed, were still not her own, and wouldn't be until her nerves had learned to bond themselves to the baby's demands. She heard Sophie's cry in the wind, in the calls of birds and vendors outside her window, even in the plumbing of the water closet. It took a week or so until the cry became part of her, utterly unmistakable and unlike any other sound in the world.

The Marquise suggested hiring a wet nurse but Marie-Laure wouldn't consider it. It took another two weeks, some close supervision from Madame Rachel, still more tears, and not a little frustration, to sort out the mechanics of breast-feeding and to get Sophie settled down to a regular eating and sleeping schedule.

"You're doing much better than the Queen did with the Dauphin," Madame Rachel told her—for she was well connected in her profession and had the story on good authority.

"But," Mademoiselle Beauvoisin asked, "isn't it true, Mamma, that the Queen gave it up after a pretty short time anyway?"

"Oh yes, after a while she just sent for Madame Poitrine, as the lady was called, and dumped the baby on her."

Marie-Laure tried to look modest. "Well, what's important is how nicely Sophie is growing. And she's so alert, don't you think?"

The Marquise sniffed. "*She* may be alert, but you'll continue to doze through supper while you keep this up. In my opinion there's absolutely nothing natural about this business—even if the great Rousseau thought so."

"Natural" or not, nursing had absorbed a shocking amount of Marie-Laure's attention. Still, Sophie had stopped looking like a half-starved monkey and Marie-Laure had quickly lost some of the weight of pregnancy; no doubt, Marie-Laure thought, the Queen had liked *that* aspect of it. While as for the other, less felicitous aspects—scrubbing a stain that evening from the front of a pretty muslin dress that had once belonged to Mademoiselle Beauvoisin, Marie-Laure wondered if the Queen had given up breast-feeding after a royal baby had spit up over one of her gowns.

She'd have to ask Claudine to take her shopping.

I must be feeling more like myself, she thought. But who *was* that self? she wondered. It felt like ages since she'd actually cared—or even exactly known—what she looked like.

Sophie wouldn't wake for a few hours. There was a huge three-sided mirror in the corner of the room. Slowly and carefully, she undid hooks and eyes, untied a satin sash, laid objects of clothing on a nearby chair, and (not without some trepidation) surveyed her reflection.

Pas mal. No, not bad at all.

She grinned with delight at her ankles, which were trim and neat again, shook her head at a little bit of belly that simply would not disappear, and examined her swollen—quite impressively swollen—breasts with something like awe.

The fire had burned down. It was a bit chilly this evening. She threw the huge smocked nightgown over her head; nowadays it felt like a tent. But she didn't button the top buttons.

Barely breathing, she took his letter from under her pillow. *I bury my face in your breasts, my hands in your hair . . . before I enter you.*

He'd written it as though he knew—in the mysterious way he always knew such things—what she was ready to think about again.

She fell into a deep sleep with a smile on her flushed face and the letter clutched in her hand.

And woke up an hour later in a panic. Someone was screaming, but it wasn't Sophie. According to the clock on the mantel, Sophie wouldn't wake for another hour and a half.

The screams were those of a naked girl pursued by drooling hounds through a nightmare forest.

You'll have to explain why you were leaving, he'd written.

But she'd never be able to tell anyone about that last hour in the château. She'd lock it away in her dreams and bear it all by herself. Pacing the pretty blue room as though it were a prison cell, she waited for Sophie to wake.

Chapter 25

"Please, Madame la Marquise, I want to see Joseph," she announced two weeks later.

Rehearsing the request in her blue bedchamber, she'd decided that a direct approach would be the most effective, but evidently, she thought, she'd mistaken *heavy-handed* for *direct.*

Mademoiselle Beauvoisin winced from across the supper table.

"What Marie-Laure *means* to say, Jeanne *chérie,* is that she and I thought it might be possible for her to accompany you to the Bastille . . ."

"Impossible. She's not on the approved list of visitors."

". . . dressed as your footman."

"Well, as a page, anyway, Madame la Marquise."

"A very small page, Jeanne. A boy in training to be a page, perhaps."

"I see. You two thought it *might* be possible. And did you also think it *might* be possible to find a pair of breeches that would fit her?"

"Georges says there's just enough yellow velvet in the storeroom. . . ."

"Hmmm."

"And Frédéric needs a new coat anyway; have you noticed how

worn his is in the back? He says Monsieur de Cordon's footman poked fun at him the other day, and I assured him you'd save him from any further such embarrassment. So we'll use his old coat and alter it to fit Marie-Laure."

"Hmmm."

"Of course, we'll have to bind her breasts in order to turn her into a convincing boy. It'll probably hurt, but in Mamma's opinion . . ."

"Is there anyone whose opinion you have *not* consulted on this matter? Except mine, of course."

So on a bright, humid June afternoon, dressed in velvet coat and breeches and with her hair tied back in a queue, she jumped onto the back of the Marquise's carriage and held on tightly as the horses clattered through the courtyard's doors.

Paris streamed by on either side of her.

It was a wonderful view: close to the streets but high enough to see over the heads of tall pedestrians. She was beginning to know some quarters of the city now. Claudine had taken her on a shopping tour—from fabulous boutiques in the rue Saint-Honoré to ateliers in the faubourg Saint-Antoine where you could get something almost as good for a tenth of the price.

And she'd made some discoveries of her own as well, like Monsieur Moreaux's bookshop in a modest quarter on the Left Bank. She'd bought a few books, and they'd exchanged anecdotes about the book trade. He reminded her of Papa in some ways, though more practical, less visionary. His selection was excellent, if a bit too directed toward a male clientele; Marie-Laure had persuaded him to try more fiction. And she'd also made friends with the proprietors of the bookstalls along the Seine.

She'd sipped lemonade while she nursed Sophie at an outdoor table at the Palais Royale, listening to fiery political oratory and watching shoppers, pleasure-seekers, and prostitutes stroll through the arcades that lined the huge enclosed square.

But what she'd loved best was exploring the streets, tramping over cobblestones and leaping out of the way of carriages. She'd marveled at the endless crowds—the elaborate costumes of the finest ladies and gentlemen, the energy and variety of the tradespeople, the unbelievable decrepitude of the beggars. She'd wept to see abandoned babies transported by threes in the backpacks of porters. And laughed at dozens of small human comedies, laced with invectives as pungent as the smells rising from the gutters.

Out in the streets, she always felt as though she were on stage in the midst of a drama—thousands of dramas, as many overlapping, intersecting tragicomical spectacles as Paris had inhabitants.

In stuffy, provincial Montpellier, she reflected, you always knew who everybody was: merchant or magistrate, servant, shopgirl, or laborer. You knew by their dress, but also by their bearing. Somehow, you'd intuit a person's place in the scheme of things as soon as you saw him or her on the street.

Whereas in Paris, decoding the identities of the mass of people rushing past her was like trying to read the patchwork tapestry of posters, playbills, and announcements pasted on the walls. New ones half covered old ones, bits were torn off or worn beyond recognition; you couldn't get a fix on any single reality. In this city of actors and strivers and seekers—of *shoppers*—everyone was busy patching or replacing the roles life had handed them. Or trying to piece together something new, striking, and original, at the best possible price.

The King fears Paris, Joseph had said. And well he might, Marie-Laure concluded. For how could one dull, timid, and entirely conventional gentleman rule a city that was constantly remaking itself?

The carriage turned a sharp corner and stopped in front of a hideous fortress of filthy yellow-gray stone. She clung to the railing for a moment, frozen in fear and anticipation, staring at barred windows and armed sentries.

"But what are you dreaming about, Laurent?" the Marquise called. "Fetch Monsieur Joseph's packages immediately."

Laurent? Oh yes, her boy's name, adopted for the afternoon. She jumped from the back steps of the blue and violet carriage, hoisted up her breeches and retied the velvet ribbon around her queue of hair. She scrambled to fetch the boxes and baskets and pile them into her arms. And staggering under the unsteady load—which perhaps was fortunate, since the top basket hid her face from the guard at the gate—she followed the Marquise into the Bastille.

He'd been nervous and testy all morning. The infuriating letter from his sister-in-law had been bad enough, but the news Monsieur du Plessix had brought him was far worse. They'd lost a legal motion to compel the Montpellier booksellers to produce their bills of sale from the day of the Baron's murder. So all that priceless evidence—those pieces of paper with *Joseph Dupin* written in his unmistakable hand—would languish unseen in the booksellers' files forever.

There'd also been some confusing rubbish about the girl who'd committed suicide—an odd coincidence, her brother working as Amélie's footman, but nothing, as far as du Plessix could see, that would help their case.

Du Plessix hadn't yet had a chance to tell any of this to Jeanne and Joseph wasn't looking forward to doing it himself.

Stupidly, he supposed, he'd let himself hope a little since the baby's birth. Perhaps they all had, inspired by how brilliantly Sophie had beaten the odds and survived. He'd been more or less resigned to losing this case before Marie-Laure's arrival; perhaps he'd better try to get some of that resignation back. It would hurt less, he thought, when he was declared guilty.

The trial was scheduled for a month from now. And given how slight a case Monsieur du Plessix had been able to build, it would be quick. In nearly no time at all, he thought, it would be official: a convicted murderer, he'd be locked in here forever, never to see Sophie, never to touch Marie-Laure again.

He heard the sounds of keys turning in locks, of doors opening in distant corridors. He composed his face into the mask he assumed for Jeanne's visits: bland, alert, optimistic.

The key rattled, his door opened. He rose as Jeanne swept in, followed by the usual lackey carrying the usual superfluous baskets and boxes. Whatever had she thought to bring him *this* time?

His cell was actually becoming a bit cluttered, but he didn't have the heart to tell her that nothing could make a difference.

They exchanged affectionate kisses. Her face was warm, her upper lip a bit moist. Normally at this time of year she'd be preparing to visit her farm in Normandy. He'd persuade her to go as soon as the trial was over. She'd done quite enough for him already; it was time she and Ariane got on with their lives.

The footman piled all his useless stuff on the table and backed away, standing a bit farther from the warden than he usually did. And he's a bit clumsy today as well, Joseph thought absentmindedly.

Jeanne pulled a fan out of her reticule.

Joseph cleared his throat, in preparation for an awkward visit. "I spoke to du Plessix yesterday."

But hold on. The clumsy footman—now that Joseph looked at him more closely—seemed to have shrunk a few feet since last week.

Stupid. It wasn't the same fellow at all. No, this time she'd brought a boy, more a page than a footman really, and a very pretty boy too—look at his delicate ankles in their white stockings.

Merde, he'd been in here too long if he'd begun to ogle the ankles of page boys.

He cleared his throat again, turned back to Jeanne.

"Yes, well about what du Plessix said . . ."

His throat was dry. He hadn't noticed how warm it was in here. As he poured himself a glass of water from the pitcher on the table, he felt his eyes stray back to the boy's ankles.

Upward a bit now. To his legs.

His pretty yellow velvet thighs and neat waist.

The boy parted his legs a bit. Joseph felt a disturbing response between his own legs. He calmed himself by noting that the youth was somewhat oddly built above the waist. A bit bulky, a bit puffy in the chest—as though he were trying to hide or smuggle something under his coat. . . .

Fanning herself slowly, Jeanne had begun to chatter in a low, comforting voice. Something about having taken tea with a distant cousin last Friday.

"A surprisingly cultivated woman, well read in the classics. I confess I'd expected rather less from her, with those hordes of children she's raising. Which goes to show that one should never depend upon one's preconceptions . . ."

Marie-Laure stared at the floor in front of her. It was stone, covered with overlapping Oriental rugs the Marquise must have sent him. Perhaps he should roll up some of the rugs to make the cell cooler.

She raised her eyes an inch or two to the table, to his hands folded upon it.

Her stomach tightened, trembled; her skin tingled as though he were touching her with those deft magician's hands. But the only way he was touching her was with his eyes. She hadn't dared look at his face, but there was no mistaking the force of his casual, interrogatory gaze at her thighs. Almost involuntarily, she parted her legs (just the tiniest bit) wider. And yes, she could feel his response—a glinting, glancing warmth, a quickening pulse—his gaze making its curious, delighted way between her legs, up along her belly, around her waist. Suddenly befuddled, his eyes flickered for a moment, his perceptions rendered uncertain by the clumsy shape of her bound breasts.

Think, Joseph. Remember what I wrote. And how you answered. "I held it in my hand all night. Kissed it, fondled it, flicked my tongue over it . . ."

I imagine your tongue there now. And in another moment I shall scream, I think—I'll bellow with frustrated desire, to be so visible and yet so hidden away from you like this.

She sighed a tiny inner sigh and lifted her chin. *Help me, Joseph. Raise your eyes. Please. I want—I need—to feel your eyes on my neck, my throat.*

The Marquise had begun a long story—Joseph couldn't follow its logic but it seemed to have something to do with the Persian Wars. The warden raised his head: prisoners and their visitors weren't supposed to discuss politics.

"Those wars were fought a long time ago, Warden." Jeanne smiled gently. "In Greece, more than two millennia ago."

The warden shrugged suspiciously, but seemed reassured by names like "Aristotle" and "Thucydides." He tried to keep a stern eye on the Marquise, but her voice was monotonous, the motion of her fan hypnotic, the air in the room still and humid.

The boy had tied his cravat around his graceful throat with great elegance, Joseph thought. How smooth his freckled cheeks were, how flushed and downy.

His freckled cheeks indeed.

Look at me, mon amour. *Raise your eyes. Part your lips.*

He'd have to wait. Her eyes—slower, more persistent than his—had only reached his chest. His shoulders now. Measuring their span. Remembering, tracing the lines of muscle and tendon stretched across them. Caressing him. Patiently, languorously, possessively.

He moved his chair a few inches, to the end of the table, to allow her a better view. For the smallest of instants, he leaned back, miming a yawn, stretching his legs and hips under her gaze. Silly, he supposed, but how delightful to be so silly—like a peacock spreading his tail for his mate. *You see,* mon amour, *how profoundly, how painfully, how massively and spectacularly I want you.*

Her lashes flickered, her mouth curved around a tiny dimple at its corner. Her cheeks grew pinker; she was sharing his giddy delight as though it were a kiss. Her pelvis, in its lemon yellow velvet, tilted forward an inch or so. To meet him, to welcome him.

He moved back behind the table. Enough. He couldn't risk any more of this.

The Marquise had begun a secondary narrative. A few decades of ancient history had passed, it seemed, and now the Greek states were fighting each other in what came to be called the Peloponnesian Wars. On and on she droned, about Athens and Sparta and the treacherous Persian Empire. One could be lulled to sleep by it, Marie-Laure thought, if one didn't have something wonderful to concentrate on. Like the little notch at Joseph's upper lip. So like Sophie's and so unlike anything else in the world. Or the lines at the corners of his mouth, the planes of his cheekbones, the black silk of his hair as it swept behind his ears.

Her eyes widened. There were a few silver strands—just a very few—where before there had only been black.

It wasn't that they were unattractive. On the contrary, they were devastating; they made him look more elegant, less boyish. But she hadn't expected them, hadn't supposed that time could change him in any way.

He shrugged, unsure of what she'd made of his altered appearance. He locked his eyes on hers and stared full out.

She could drown in those black depths, she thought.

He could fly, he thought, through the transparent skies of her eyes.

I love you.

He'd shaped the words inaudibly with his lips, but for Marie-Laure it was as though he'd shouted them from the rooftop. She sighed a tiny rapturous sigh, which would have been just loud enough for the warden to hear if he hadn't just that moment woken himself from a sound sleep with his own snoring.

"No matter, Warden," the Marquise assured him with breezy condescension, as though he'd dribbled his wine at a formal dinner party. "Perhaps it's really too hot a day for ancient history. Still, it remains a joy for some of us, and perhaps I'll be able to interest you in it on another visit."

She glanced at her pocket watch. "My word, it's been more than an hour. How good of you, Monsieur, to allow me the extra time with my husband today.

"But I won't presume on your hospitality. And *so* . . ." She rose and kissed an exhausted-looking Joseph on the cheek.

"*Au revoir, chéri.* No, don't get up. I'm sorry to have interrupted your account of Monsieur du Plessix's visit, but he'll be coming to dinner tomorrow evening in any case, and of course I'll see you next week.

"Do try the cherries and triple-*crème* cheese in the little basket, they're delicious. And all my best to Monsieur le Marquis de Sade. Come, Laurent."

Graciously, she allowed the blinking warden to lead her and a dazed Marie-Laure through the Bastille's dark corridors and out into the humid, filthy, and never more glorious streets of Paris.

Chapter 26

Her elation ended abruptly when she, along with the Marquise and Madame Beauvoisin, heard Monsieur du Plessix's somber news at supper the following night.

For not only had the judge rejected their petition to subpoena the booksellers' records, he'd forbidden any appeals. So they had no evidence to corroborate Joseph's account of his whereabouts at the time of the murder—and no possibility of obtaining any.

"It's a serious blow to our case," the Marquise said faintly.

"I can't deny it, Madame."

"And the only stone left unturned," Mademoiselle Beauvoisin added, "was the girl who committed suicide."

"But in the end all we could find out," Monsieur du Plessix said, "was that she had a brother in service at Carency. Which at first had seemed hopeful . . ."

". . . but came to nothing, since Inspector Lebrun had already established that no one had been away from the château on the date of the murder." The Marquise preferred to finish Monsieur du Plessix's sentences when it seemed likely he'd draw them out past usefulness.

A gloomy silence descended upon the table.

The only other news—which no one really cared about—was a

letter from the Duc and Duchesse de Carency Auvers-Raimond, smugly announcing the birth of a son, Alphonse Louis Charles François, Comte de Carency Auvers-Raimond, and adding that the Duchesse, who was relocating to new apartments at Versailles, would be enchanted to receive the Marquise there, after the tenth of the month.

So she managed that part of her plan even without me, Marie-Laure thought. She shrugged. It wasn't important. Except as they figured in her nightmares, the Duc and Duchesse didn't matter anymore.

"Not a word about Joseph," the Marquise looked up from the letter with a sour face. "But just listen to her going on about her 'duty,' as she puts it, 'to represent her family at the King's court.' "

Marie-Laure's stomach suddenly turned queasy, as though hit by an unexpected whiff of peppermint. But there was no peppermint on the table, only a smooth, splendid, ginger-flavored *pot de crème* and a pot of excellent Chinese tea.

Anyway, she thought, it was clear that her sudden disorientation was intellectual rather than visceral. Some phrase or self-serving tonality in the Duchesse's letter had set it off. Some stray word had sparked a memory, like electricity trying to jump between two bits of metal.

But what word, what hint, what clue?

I truly believe, Joseph had written in one of his letters, *that there's something I should be remembering.* At the time she'd dismissed this as mere anxious muddleheadedness, rather lovable in its way and brought on by the exigencies of their situations. He'd been right, though. And there was something she needed to remember as well.

Because when she did, everything else would make sense.

"I think," she announced, "that if you all will excuse me I'll go see to Sophie."

The Marquise's eyes were gentle. "Of course, *chérie.*"

She walked slowly up the stairs, her fingers trailing over the iron balustrade's intricate convolutions. Twists and turns. Reflections and repetitions.

A clever reader could tease out a story's subtlest meanings, distinguish figure from ground, discern an urgent message from frivolous chatter.

She hoped so, anyway. Her head began to ache with trying to sort it out; so many people had said so many things since she'd ventured outside the walls of Montpellier.

Mustering as much calm as she could, she forced herself to listen to the clamor of voices in her memory. To hear it dispassionately, and to try to catch the pattern.

I should have killed him, someone had said.

While someone else had reported having taken care—*completely taken care*—of what? Whatever it had been, Nicolas had entered it into his meticulous double-accounting system.

Follow Nicolas's example, she told herself. Read events as Nicolas recorded them—with a double meaning, a true one for yourself and a sham one for the enemy. Without a double set of meanings, there was nothing but endless, fathomless repetition.

She grimaced, passing through a mirror-lined corridor.

But if one could grasp the pattern . . .

If one could find the thin thread to lead oneself out of the maze . . .

Louise had said something.

No.

Louise had almost *said something. And then she'd clapped her hand over her mouth to stop herself from telling Marie-Laure what Marie-Laure wasn't supposed to hear.*

In the blue bedchamber, Claudine had been listening for Sophie's cry. She helped Marie-Laure unfasten her dress and stays.

"Thank you," Marie-Laure said, pulling on one of Mademoiselle Beauvoisin's hand-me-down silk peignoirs, "And you can go now, Claudine. Sophie and I will be fine."

Last winter, she hadn't cared what Louise had almost said. She'd only wanted to be reassured that Joseph would still want her.

It was a relief to be out of her stays. Her breasts were uncomfortably hard and taut; the baby would be waking soon. She allowed herself to be lulled by familiar natural sensations—those mysterious compounds of instinct, desire, and practice that people liked to call "natural." She corrected herself: nature was a matter of instinct, desire, practice, *and luck;* other scullery maids mightn't be lucky enough to keep their babies.

Which made it all the more infuriating that the Duchesse had chosen to desert poor little Comte Alphonse Louis whatever-it-was. And that she'd had the gall to announce that "duty" compelled her *to go to Paris, with only Arsène and Hortense for support. . . .*

With only . . .

Sophie began to cry.

"Yes, yes," Marie-Laure called to her.

"Absolutely, *chérie,*" she cooed as she lifted her from the white basketwork cradle where she slept, "just as soon as we let a little air into this stuffy room."

Opening the doors that led out to the balcony, she caught a vague glimpse of something stirring in the shadows.

Some leaves, perhaps. The Marquise had said the wisteria needed trimming. The vines had become almost tropical in this hot weather; someone could climb the walls by holding onto their woody stems.

And someone had.

A tall, dark-haired man stepped in from the balcony.

For a dazed moment she thought it must be Joseph. But of course it wasn't Joseph. It was—ah, a tall dark man. Of course. The Baron's murderer.

And what Louise had been going to say was: "We wondered how long you'd pretend it wasn't so, *like Arsène's sister.*"

Arsène's sister Manon.

All the servants at the château must have known about Manon, she thought. All of them except for the literate girl from the city, the one who wasn't party to their secrets—and who had been too absorbed in her own romance to notice what was going on.

If I'd been wiser, Marie-Laure thought guiltily, *I might have been able to help Joseph.*

* * *

Arsène looked dreadful. She could hardly recognize the handsome, circumspect footman from the château. His skin was livid, cheeks sunken, teeth bared. A knife blade glinted at his hand.

Clearly, his revenge on the Baron hadn't satisfied him. Holding the baby close, she wondered what he saw when he looked at her. Nothing good, she decided.

His eyes seemed to soften for a moment, though, when they fell on Sophie. Thank heaven, she thought. Somehow she was sure he wouldn't harm Sophie.

"The baby's hungry, Arsène." She tried to keep her voice casual, offhand. "Let me feed her."

He nodded.

"But don't try screaming for help." He locked the door to the hallway.

She shook her head, sat in her rocking chair, loosened her dressing gown, and lifted Sophie to her breast.

Too restless to sit, he planted himself a few feet in front of her, a dark looming presence, his knife and eyes glinting unsteadily, like the light of a guttering candle.

"And so you're installed at Versailles with the Duchesse?"

Absurd, she thought, to be making polite conversation. Still, perhaps he needed to talk. The trouble was that she'd never really spoken to him before. Among the clatter and hum of the dessert kitchen, he'd been a silent, circumspect, and rather straitlaced presence.

"Versailles must be quite a change for you," she added. "A change from the château at Carency, I mean."

He shrugged. "No change. Just a deeper circle of hell."

He cast a contemptuous glance over her pretty dressing gown. "But *you've* done rather well for yourself, haven't you?"

"The Marquise is very generous." She stroked Sophie's flower petal cheek with a fingertip.

"*Her.*" He sneered. "I've heard the gossip about *her.* Her and the other one, too. What sorts of filthy things did you have to do with them to get them to be so generous?

"But perhaps you enjoyed it," he continued. "Perhaps you were as shameless with them as you were with your precious Viscomte."

She supposed she had been shameless with Joseph. Well, love *was* shameless, wasn't it?

"My sister wasn't like that," he told her.

He stopped, his eyes betraying the awful fear that perhaps his sister *had* been like that—perhaps she'd been worse—with the Baron Roque. Marie-Laure kept her eyes on his face, waiting until he could speak again.

"But at least," he continued, "Manon had the . . . the decency . . . the modesty . . . the respect for a brother who loved her more than anything in the world . . ."

He seemed to have lost the ability to speak.

"To kill herself." Marie-Laure finished his sentence when it became clear that he couldn't.

"To kill herself rather than tell you that the Baron Roque had gotten her pregnant." She said it as gently as she could, allowing herself to feel something of the grief beneath his hatred.

For a moment he looked almost grateful that she'd said it. And then a shudder of unspeakable rage contorted his features.

"She wasn't a whore like you," he said, "flaunting your happiness for everyone to see and then—even after he deserted you—still so proud of carrying his bastard."

"He *didn't* desert me. He would have come to help me. If . . . if *you* hadn't planted the ring on him." She felt rather foolish, having taken so much time to figure that part out.

He chuckled. "When the inspector came to search us, Nicolas told me to hide it in the forest. All right, I said, all right, it's all taken care of. He'd be furious—all those silly fools would be furious to know what I really did with it."

Ah. Somehow it mattered to her, that only Arsène was responsible for Joseph being in the Bastille. Not Nicolas, Bertrande, Louise . . .

He snorted; her relief must have been obvious. "Oh yes, they all wanted to help you. They'd sit around the dessert kitchen, jabbering about you and your Viscomte like it was a fairy story with a happy-ever-after ending. I kept trying to make them understand that anybody who consorts with aristocrats is a fool or a traitor."

"My brother," she heard herself saying pleasantly, "is in complete agreement with you.

"But Nicolas supported you, in any case," she added. "At least enough to lie about where you'd been at the time of the murder."

He nodded. "He wrote down in his records that I was sick that week. Other fellows did my work for me. They're good, I'm not saying they're not, but they're weak. They understood my business with the Baron Roque, but they were soft on their own precious Viscomte. I couldn't make them understand that it's all the same thing."

For a moment there was just the sound of her chair rocking back and forth, while she shifted Sophie to the other breast.

"And so you think I should suffer as deeply as your sister did," she said.

"You'll *never* suffer as she did," he told her. "You'll die quickly. I don't have time for anything else."

She tried to concentrate upon the chair's comforting rhythms, and on keeping her breathing slow and even. Sophie continued to suck, her big trusting eyes trained steadily on Marie-Laure's face.

Oddly, even Arsène calmed down a bit.

"She was a bit feebleminded, you know, though by and large people didn't notice it." His voice became confiding, conversational.

"They only saw how beautiful she was. Statuesque, I guess you'd say. I was proud of her, of course, but I was scared too. I didn't want her to work for the Baron; I tried to get the Gorgon to hire her, but of course she wouldn't, and of course the Baron wasn't going to hire me—he wouldn't want anybody to look out for her . . . I learned later," he said flatly, "that the Baron used to joke about her with his cronies. Said he'd found the perfect woman—no mind at all to interfere with his pleasures."

She must have made some sort of outraged sound. He paused, stone-faced.

"But when her pregnancy began to show more than he found attractive"—his voice became harsher—"he gave her a gold louis and threw her out. She used the money to buy arsenic."

She stopped rocking and stared at him, ignoring Sophie's restless whimpers.

"The baby's had enough," he told her then. "Burp her and put her in her cradle."

She looked down at the baby in surprise. He was right; Sophie *had* had enough.

"I learned all about babies," he told her, "when I was eight. I fed Manon with a bottle of goat's milk after our mother died. She wouldn't have survived without me—not that our father would have cared, or even noticed." He shrugged. "And not, I suppose, that it mattered in the long run."

Absurdly, he handed her a towel to protect the shoulder of her robe. "I've been a servant for too long," he said with a grimace, "but I'm finished with all that now."

Hearing his story had drained her of energy. But it seemed that her only hope was to keep him talking.

"And then what will you do?" she asked. "Besides be a servant, I mean."

He didn't answer. Instead, he reached out a powerful hand. She shrank back and held the baby tightly, while he methodically stroked an index finger along Sophie's little spine, bringing a string of bubbles up and out of the baby's mouth.

"Now put her into her basket and kiss her good night," he said.

His voice was cold, final, and quiet.

Good night.

Slowly crossing the room to Sophie's basket, she breathed the clean, innocent baby smell, all milk and lilies of the valley. Good night, Sophie Madeleine, little cookie, cabbage, angel—funny, all the names you gave a baby when you cuddled and cooed to it. She knelt to kiss the little face, already half asleep; to stroke, one last time, the tiny eyebrow with its precise flaring arch. She felt his eyes on her from across the room. She heard his shallow, excited breathing—his eagerness to destroy the girl who'd gotten away with what his sister had died for.

Good night, Sophie.

All over Paris, bells tolled eleven. Sophie stirred, whimpered a bit, and then closed her eyes and drifted off to sleep.

Marie-Laure raised her head from the basket and turned back to face Arsène. Was she imagining it, or was there a shadow on the balcony behind him?

She had to keep his attention fixed on her.

She spoke more loudly. "The misery won't go away after you kill me, you know. You won't bring her back."

Yes, there was definitely someone out there. A man had climbed up while the bells had been ringing. Clever of him, she thought wildly; no one had heard him over the sounds of the bells. *But how-ever had he managed to escape?* No matter. She was sure. The shadow that was rapidly becoming flesh and creeping silently behind Arsène, raising his knife (*but how had he managed to get a knife?*) was clearly . . .

Don't kill him, Joseph!

It must have been me who screamed that, she thought.

For a tiny slice of time, she could see a spark of surprise in Joseph's eyes—before Arsène whirled around, all a blur, to lunge for him. Joseph leaped back. They circled each other warily, thrusting with their knives, knocking over furniture as they went. Sophie began to scream, and Marie-Laure ran to the basket, push-ing it into a corner and shielding it behind her.

Advance and repel. Thrust and parry. Joseph fought coldly, ele-gantly, his moves like dance figures, while Arsène lumbered about, single-minded, outraged. Their styles were so ill-matched that she couldn't tell which of them had the advantage.

She heard cries and pounding at the door Arsène had locked. The Marquise, Mademoiselle Beauvoisin. And every servant in the house.

She inched away from her corner, carefully drawing Sophie's basket with her. But it was a slow business, because the two men were moving closer to her now and she needed to keep herself be-tween them and the screaming baby.

A surprisingly quick move from Arsène; a thin red slash ap-peared on Joseph's cheek.

Was it deep? Was Arsène gaining ground?

Joseph's expression was impassive. The pounding at the door had stopped. Perhaps—she hoped—they'd gone to get the police.

The two men were on the floor now, wrestling, grunting, both of them smeared with blood, their knives terrible at such proximity. There must be a way to help Joseph, she thought: perhaps a well-placed vase to Arsène's head, as in a comedy. No, this wasn't comedy. She saw Joseph's hand squeezing Arsène's wrist, trying to get him to drop his knife. Was he strong enough?

An angry grunt from Arsène now—Joseph must know something about dirty fighting, she thought—and the knife clattered to the floor, with a bloody, panting Joseph pinning Arsène beneath him and clearly possessing the advantage.

The relief that flooded through her was oddly shaded with resentment. *Of course he has the advantage,* she thought, *he was* born *with the advantage.*

She picked up Sophie and opened the door. Not a moment too soon: a police inspector was aiming his pistol at the lock. The Marquise had a poker in her hand, while Madame Beauvoisin had armed herself with a curling iron. There were a few more policemen, Monsieur du Plessix cowering behind them.

"Arsène has confessed to killing the Baron Roque," she told the police inspector quietly. She opened her mouth again, to say something else, she supposed, but there were no more words. Just tears—for Manon and the brother who had loved her so much.

The other policemen were leading him away now. He stopped in front of Marie-Laure for a moment.

"She was afraid to tell me that she was pregnant." His eyes, in his crumpled face, were dark and half-dead with awful guilt. "But I wouldn't have minded," he said. "I would have forgiven her, I would have cared for her and the baby too. You know that, don't you?"

"Yes Arsène," she answered. "I know that absolutely."

He turned and allowed them to lead him down the corridor.

Flanked by the Marquise and Mademoiselle Beauvoisin, Joseph stood with the inspector in the center of the room. It seemed that he'd figured out the story for himself, in the Bastille, after Jeanne's last visit with (he glanced at the inspector), with her new footman.

"I have to arrest you again, of course," the inspector told him, "for escaping. Cleverly done, by the way—they'll have to do something about the inadequacy of their procedures.

"And you're damn lucky you didn't kill that fellow, Monsieur le Viscomte, because his confession will quickly get you off."

"I was frantic when I realized my sister-in-law was bringing him to Versailles," Joseph said. "My plan was to come and warn you, Jeanne, so you could keep Marie-Laure safe. But then I saw the vines, growing up the wall to Marie-Laure's room and . . ." He grinned. "She and I have rather a tradition of late-night visits, you see.

"I'd have killed him for sure," the grin half disappeared into the handkerchief Joseph held against his bloody cheek, "if Marie-Laure hadn't screamed not to."

"But you'll have to excuse me for a moment, Inspector," he said now, "while I'm properly introduced to my daughter."

He peered down at Sophie, but she'd fallen back to sleep, and he had to content himself with a few shy kisses on the top of her head, gently wrapping his arms around mother and baby both.

The solidity of his body was overwhelming. She pressed against him, almost horrified by the thrill of arousal that shot through her belly and thighs even as she wept.

The Marquise seemed to have ushered everyone else out of the room.

"Shhh, shhh, *mon amour,*" Joseph murmured, "it's over, it's all over."

But it wasn't over.

Don't kill him! Everyone would think how clearheaded she'd been to warn Joseph not to kill the man whose confession would prove his innocence. Only she would know that at that moment she'd had no thought except to protect poor Arsène.

It goes deep, she thought, this solidarity with common people like yourself—and this resentment of aristocratic privilege.

Could it go deeper than love?

She stood alone with Sophie in her arms, long after the tears had dried and the inspector had taken Joseph away.

Chapter 27

"Stop fidgeting, Marie-Laure," Mademoiselle Beauvoisin scolded her. "Just hold your arms out, to get them out of the way, *oui, comme ça*, while Claudine reties the bows down the front of your gown."

She spread her arms obediently, wondering whether she could raise them higher than shoulder level and finding that she couldn't. The stays Claudine had laced her into were too constricting, compressing her waist and shoulders while they lifted her breasts like cream cakes on a tray.

She surveyed herself in one of the blue bedroom's tall mirrors. At least one lifelong wish had been granted her. Her freckles had quite disappeared; the layers of powder and rouge had transformed her face into the cool, pleasant countenance of a doll.

A more interesting wish was soon to come true as well. She was going to meet Ambassador Benjamin Franklin. Well, if he really showed up at the reception the Marquise was giving this afternoon. He'd promised to try his best to attend, if his gouty leg and the stone in his bladder were not too painful.

The party was for Joseph, who was due to be released from the Bastille today. The state had withdrawn its case against him, but he'd still had to go through a small trial and acquittal for having escaped. The Marquise thought he'd be home by early evening, to join the celebration.

"We're going to invite everybody," she'd proclaimed, "who is anybody. And everybody we like as well. We'll begin in the late afternoon, we'll have a good, light supper, and then fireworks in the garden."

But Ambassador Franklin would outshine even the fireworks—or *Doctor* Franklin, as people liked to call him in Paris, in deference to his scientific achievements. The flirtatious ladies who surrounded him wherever he went also liked to call him Papa. Marie-Laure thought of her own papa. How thrilled he'd have been to meet the great man, she thought. And how amazed by the gown she was wearing. If you could really say she was wearing it; perhaps the complicated construction was wearing *her.*

Mademoiselle Beauvoisin had announced a few days ago that she was dissatisfied with the light silk ensemble she'd ordered.

"The apricot color does strange things to me." But perhaps Marie-Laure would like to try it. Marie-Laure supposed this was as tactful a way as any to supply her with clothes for the reception. Or perhaps simply to keep her busy, so she wouldn't expire of the fidgets while awaiting Joseph's release.

She'd already spent two hours under the hands of the hairdresser, part of the time with Sophie at her breast, while he gushed over the Rousseau-esque charm of coifing a nursing mother.

"And your *hair,* Mademoiselle . . ."

He'd have given anything, he told her, to arrange it in one of the grand high styles of a few years ago, when he'd used a portable ladder to get to the top of the soaring edifices he'd erected upon women's heads. Ah, the accessories, such a shame that they were no longer *à la mode*—the plumes, the flags, the clipper ships riding high atop towering waves of hair; he remembered with particular pride a lady who'd carried an entire village at the crest of her mountainous coiffure.

He swept some of Marie-Laure's hair up—not too high, he assured her, merely a little tease, a hint of nostalgia, *une bagatelle, une petite plaisanterie*—in order to set off the long curls around her neck and shoulders. Very *jeune fille*, girlish and ingenue, he declared. A veritable milkmaid's coiffure: the Queen herself was wearing just such simple styles these days. "So fresh, so naive, so . . ." he hesitated, pondered, gave a final, expert twist to one last flirtatious spiral of hair and brought his fluttering hands down to rest at his sides.

And as he'd clearly exhausted his store of adjectives, he concluded by repeating the very first one he'd used. "Voilà, Mademoiselle, it's so, so very . . . Rousseauesque, *n'est-ce pas?*"

Mademoiselle Beauvoisin had pronounced the "milkmaid's coiffure" a great success. And perfectly in keeping with a gown that might seem monstrously elaborate to Marie-Laure but was actually quite a bit simpler and more girlish than last year's styles.

At any rate, the modiste had endeavored to create that impression. The apricot silk opened below the waist to reveal cascades of dazzling white ruffled underskirt, with only a whisper of embroidery at the bottom to echo the blue of the big floppy bows that closed the bodice.

"Just what every milkmaid in France tosses on in the morning," Marie-Laure murmured, "when she sallies forth to bid the cows *bonjour.*"

She turned carefully in front of the mirror. The blue satin slippers pinched just a little—hardly enough to distract her from the iron constriction at her waist and belly—but she adored their high spool-shaped heels and delicate buckles.

"I *do* look nice," she marveled, "and not so dwarfish as usual. But what a lot of work it took."

"Too much work," the Marquise appeared in the doorway, rather grim-faced under her own layers of rouge and corseting, but imposing in deep green silk with a faint pink Oriental print woven through it.

"I've got to attend to the food," she said, "which is much more rewarding than all this tiresome primping, but I wanted to see how pretty you looked before I went down to the kitchen."

"And I'm going to be late," Mademoiselle Beauvoisin interjected, "unless I simply toss on my own gown. Come help me, Claudine. No, don't feel guilty, Marie-Laure," she called over her shoulder, "An actress can always dress quickly."

Marie-Laure smiled shyly at the Marquise, who was studying the details of her attire with unusual interest.

"Very nice indeed. But you need something bright at your neck."

Something winked and sparkled between her fingers. "Try this. It was a gift from Joseph's mother."

Marie-Laure stared at the finely wrought chain and its graceful pendants of starry diamonds, cloudy opals, and sapphires like the sky an hour before dawn. "Oh no, Madame," she whispered, "I couldn't.

"I mean," she added, trying to turn her confusion into a joke, "do you think it accords with the simple *jeune fille* effect I'm supposed to be creating?"

"*That*, I couldn't possibly tell you. But I think it accords extremely well with the depth and resolve of your character. So you will please oblige me by wearing it."

"Of course, Madame," she turned, bending her head so the Marquise could fasten the clasp. "Thank you, Madame."

"It's yours, Marie-Laure, in exchange for what you've taught me about love."

Of course she couldn't really keep it. Still, it was a thrill even to borrow such a necklace.

Alone in front of the mirror, she took a last, long, appraising look at herself. How lovely to be slender around the middle again. Her waist rose from the profusion of silk skirts and petticoats like the stem of a flower. It seemed almost too narrow, too delicate to support the swell of her all-but-bare breasts, the jewels blazing coldly at her throat, the copper curls spilling down her naked shoulders to her ruched and ruffled sleeves.

Cinderella dressed for the ball. She shrugged her shoulders (the tightly laced stays allowed one to do *that*, at any rate) and grimaced at her fanciful idea. She might imagine herself a Cinderella, but she'd never marry her prince.

Because life wasn't a fairy tale—nor were wishes granted in threes. She'd been given a day without freckles and a chance to meet the ambassador, but as for happily ever after *(don't kill him,*

Joseph!)—well, the truth (Gilles's truth, Arsène's truth) was achingly clear.

And the truth was that it wasn't enough simply to love someone. Not when so much hatred and injustice stood like the walls of the Bastille between the two of you.

She smiled sadly into the mirror. Tomorrow was going to be difficult. But she'd think about tomorrow . . . tomorrow.

"Monsieur de Calonne. Madame Helvétius. The Abbé Morellet and the Marquis and Marquise de Lafayette. Monsieur Caron de Beaumarchais. Monsieur and Madame Lavoisier . . . May I present my houseguest, Mademoiselle Vernet."

The introductions rolled on; amazing that the famous names had actual faces and bodies attached to them. It was fun to smile, to murmur modest replies to compliments, even to flirt a little.

She helped the Marquise usher people into the grand salon with its murals painted from mythology. Chairs had been set up in conversational groups; footmen served glasses of champagne and cups of tea, in deference to Doctor Franklin's preference. But neither the ambassador nor Joseph had arrived yet.

An argument about taxation broke out among bankers, statesmen, and economists. The Marquise stepped in to smooth things over, suppressing an all-too-evident desire to fan the disagreement into raging controversy.

"Come over here, Marie-Laure," Mademoiselle Beauvoisin called from the midst of a different group: handsome, rather overdressed people whose mobile faces and extravagant gestures seemed to demand adulation. Actors, some of whom were appearing in the wildly successful *Marriage of Figaro.*

"And so," Mademoiselle Beauvoisin concluded her story with a flourish, "she faced the Baron Roque's murderer alone, in this very house." The actors applauded, but the sound of their clapping was drowned out by a sudden hubbub at the door.

Papa!

L'ambassadeur! Doctor Franklin!

One mostly heard the delighted squeals of young ladies. But

formidable older ones glided quickly across the room as well. The Marquise hurried to greet him.

The American ambassador would have disappeared completely in a sea of lace and silk and kisses if he were not so tall. Surprisingly upright for a man of seventy-eight, he wore an unadorned dark red coat, his sparse gray hair falling to his shoulders, his famous spectacles worn low on his nose. You wouldn't suspect that he had gout, Marie-Laure thought, if it weren't for the attentive young man at his arm—his grandson and secretary, one of the actors said.

"Would you like to be introduced to him?" the playwright Caron de Beaumarchais turned to her.

"Oh yes," she breathed. "Oh, please, Monsieur."

As the whole room seemed to be moving in Franklin's direction, they made slow progress. The playwright took Marie-Laure's arm and drew her into line with the others waiting to greet the ambassador.

"Aristocrats," he murmured, casting his eye over the crowd that surrounded them, "are a bunch of big children in search of ceaseless amusement. I created Figaro's lecherous master, so you can take my word for it. But *I* am an adult: I purchased the *de* in my name and I know the value of a livre—and of a woman. So when your Viscomte tires of you, please consider paying me a visit."

She forced herself to maintain a cool, bland expression. This, she told herself, was what it would be like to be Joseph's official and paid-for mistress.

"Ah, it's Beaumarchais," a friendly voice interrupted her reflections, "one of the authors of our revolution."

The two men embraced while the ladies surrounding them chirped and twittered like birds pecking at a fruit tree.

"But what do you mean, Papa?" an ethereal blonde in pale blue satin demanded. "How could Monsieur Caron de Beaumarchais be the author of a revolution? A revolution isn't a play."

A chorus of voices broke in, each endeavoring to capture Franklin's attention.

"Ladies, ladies," the ambassador protested, "you may kiss me all at once, but my French is too weak to allow me to understand when you all speak at the same time.

"And as for our dear Beaumarchais . . ." he started to say, when suddenly he caught sight of Marie-Laure's face.

"Ah. I believe that *this* new Mademoiselle knows what I meant."

Beaumarchais hastened to introduce her.

"And my little remark, Mademoiselle Vernet?" the ambassador asked.

"It was as clear as it was witty, Monsieur Franklin. Monsieur Caron de Beaumarchais procured weapons and supplies for the American colonies back in 1776, when this was a dangerous and unpopular thing to do. And as this effort constituted one of his finest moments (and perhaps his most gentlemanly), it entitles him to be called an author—in the sense of a progenitor—of your country's revolution."

Beaumarchais winked at her. A bit apologetically.

"How did you learn so much about us, Mademoiselle?" Monsieur Franklin asked.

"My father taught me—he was a bookseller," she added. One or two of the young ladies moved a few steps away from her. "And," she concluded in English, "a fervent believer in 'certain unalienable rights.' "

"A bookseller's daughter?" The old man grinned at her, also speaking in English now. "Well, this is an unexpected pleasure. And I thought all I'd meet tonight were the daughters of Ducs and so forth."

The chirps and twitters grew louder, as the ladies demanded to know what the exchange in English had been about.

"Nothing, nothing at all," Temple Franklin, the grandson, assured them. "It's simply that my grandfather needs to take a chair for ten minutes to rest his leg." He guided Marie-Laure and the ambassador to a pair of seats in a corner. "And a taste of the English language to refresh his prodigious brain."

"He's careful, you see," she heard Temple Franklin whisper to Beaumarchais, "never to express his antiaristocratic prejudices in French. It's part of the secret of his success in this country."

"And you ladies," Beaumarchais announced loudly, "will have

to make do with Monsieur Temple Franklin and myself. But only for the tiniest, most miniscule, of instants. Ten minutes, I promise you, and then your *cher* papa will be back to collect all the kisses you owe him. With interest."

The ambassador sipped his tea.

"I did need to sit down. But more than that, I needed a moment away from the crowd. For you French do like to speak all at once. A little conversation in English with a pretty young lady will set me up for the rest of the evening and allow me to be a diplomat once more. So you see, you owe these moments to me, as your private contribution to the fortunes of the American republic."

For a moment she didn't think she'd be able to say anything at all. But he drew her out with questions, and with anecdotes about his own businesses—stationary, printing, bookselling. He was as interested as she was in paper and typeface, and of course in the development of literacy.

There hadn't been any bookshops in Philadelphia when he'd settled there fifty years ago, and so he'd begun America's first subscription library. Of course there were booksellers there now—the city had grown amazingly—but to his mind they could use even more of them. And he liked knowing that he had helped to make reading a fashionable pursuit in the new nation's leading city. He'd even published an edition of Richardson's *Pamela*—though, to be honest, he'd been left with an overstock. American readers weren't the world's most sophisticated.

"I think the less sophisticated readers were my favorite customers in some ways," Marie-Laure told him. "But I enjoyed helping everybody. I felt rich and happy doing it, and privileged to be part of the world of letters."

"My wife Debbie took care of the shop in front, while I worked with the printing presses in back. She sold stationary and printed matter, and very ably too, when she was alive."

Marie-Laure couldn't tell whether his sigh was one of grief or of remorse, for having left his wife behind while he'd been in Europe so many years. She gazed curiously at him, but he was too shrewd to reveal any more of himself.

"I do hate the idea of aristocracy, you know," he said now. "It offends me, not so much politically—your country has a right to its traditions—but from a scientific point of view. I once wrote in *Poor Richard* that any nobleman who traces his lineage back to the Norman Conquest is actually descended from more than a million persons who were living then. He ought to acknowledge all of them—great, small, and middling—as his ancestors."

She laughed delightedly. "Joseph's father claimed that he could trace their family's ancestry back to Charlemagne—and Aeneas."

The ambassador laughed too. "Tonight I must work out the mathematics of descent from Charlemagne. But I'm afraid it wouldn't be possible to compute the ancestry of a descendent of Aeneas.

"Who is Joseph?" he asked after a brief pause.

She felt her rouged cheeks grow warm. "I mean the Viscomte d'Auvers-Raimond, the gentleman whose release we're celebrating."

"Ah," he said.

But here was Temple Franklin, come to deliver his grandfather back to the twittering ladies. The ambassador climbed slowly to his feet.

"Good evening, Marie-Laure. It has been a pleasure to know you a little." Benjamin Franklin smiled as he steadied himself against his grandson's arm. She stood on tiptoe to kiss his cheek.

"Au revoir, Monsieur Franklin," she whispered. "And thank you."

For what, she wasn't exactly sure. A modicum of self-confidence, perhaps. A reassuring glimpse of herself and the convictions she intended to live by.

Joseph still hadn't arrived by suppertime, but even without him the party had been an enormous success. "What's important," the Marquise told Marie-Laure, "is that all of Paris has assembled to celebrate his innocence and acquittal. But the only person he's really going to care about seeing is you."

Marie-Laure smiled. *All of Paris* was hardly here tonight, she thought, as images from the raucous streets superimposed themselves upon the well-dressed and distinguished crowd in the grand salon. The Marquise's Paris was very small.

"I'm going upstairs to see to Sophie," she said. "I'll be back in a little while."

In truth, Sophie wouldn't be waking so soon. But Marie-Laure had had enough of the party. Meeting anyone else would be an anticlimax after the American ambassador.

I should call Claudine to help me take off this gown, she thought, wandering distractedly around the blue bedroom as she checked, for the thousandth time, the preparations she'd made for tomorrow.

It was stupid to wait up here dressed like this. The wide skirts of her dress wouldn't fit in the rocking chair and it would be ridiculous to nurse Sophie in all this finery, like an elaborately attired Marie Antoinette posing with her children for a domestic portrait in oils. But there was something too final about taking it apart. She knew that the elegantly gowned and bejeweled woman in the mirror wasn't really herself, but she couldn't help it; she wanted to look this way just a little longer. Just until Joseph came home.

It was almost an hour later, and growing dark outside, when Sophie woke up. Marie-Laure lit a lamp. Carefully, gingerly, she swathed herself in towels, lowered herself and her wide dress onto the side of the chaise longue, and brought the hungry baby to her breast. "Yes it is pretty, isn't it, *chérie?*" she whispered, as Sophie fixed her fascinated eyes upon the sapphire necklace, batting her fist at it as she sucked.

A small sound across the room made her start and look up. How long had Joseph been leaning against the doorway with his arms crossed? He was going to have a scar on his cheek, she thought.

"Excuse me for spying, but I rather lost myself, watching the two of you.

"I've been down at the reception," he added. "I had to speak to people. Jeanne, of course, and Monsieur Franklin."

"Of course," she said. If she stayed with him, she'd always be waiting while he spoke to "people." But she wouldn't think about that now.

"Come over here," she said, "so you can see Sophie."

He stood behind her and peered down at the baby. "Her eyes are blue," he whispered.

"We thought at first that it was that false blue that infants all have," she replied. "Everybody thought she'd have black eyes because she's so like you. But she surprised us."

"*Your* eyes." His voice trembled. "She's like you and like me at the same time. How astonishing."

"She's going to smile any day now," she told him. "She was born so early that she's more like a six-week-old than a ten-week-old. At least that's what Madame Rachel tells me. But she eats very well."

As though to demonstrate her skill, Sophie narrowed her eyes and sucked all the harder. Marie-Laure winced.

"Ah," she crooned, "gently, darling. *Doucement, doucement, chérie.*"

"Does it hurt?" the veteran of duels and military engagements asked anxiously.

"Sometimes," she said. "Yes, a bit. But it's not a bad kind of hurt."

She smiled up at him as she put Sophie to her shoulder. He became silent, entranced and rather intimidated by the mysterious arts she'd mastered—burping, cleaning, diapering.

"We can put her back to sleep now," she told him. She almost asked if he'd like to hold the baby but she held back at the last moment, quietly watching him bend over the lace-hung wicker basket to kiss his daughter good night.

They stood a few feet apart in the center of the blue bedroom, shy and deliberate as on their first night. Marie-Laure removed the towels she'd swathed herself in.

"I've been afraid to disarrange it," she murmured. "It took so much work, you know."

He breathed shallowly, taking the last few steps toward her. "It's beautiful. You're beautiful." He pulled at a ribbon at her bodice, "Let me disarrange it."

The clothes came off slowly: silk, ribbon, and lace drifting to the dark carpet like flower petals in a breeze. She became a bit afraid, when the stays and panniers and petticoats came off, of how he would respond to the rounded belly she hadn't quite gotten rid of, but he smiled delightedly and bent to kiss it. Straightening up, he squeezed her heavy breasts in his hands and kissed them too.

"Stand still," she said hoarsely, quickly unknotting his cravat, "it's my turn to undress you now."

Coat, waistcoat, shoes, stockings, shirt. She brushed her lips briefly over his neck, his chest and belly, feeling the muscles tremble at her mouth's touch.

"You *are* good at this," he said, as she bent to unbutton his breeches. "I mean," he laughed, "at the unbuttoning part."

But of course he hadn't only meant that. They stared at each other for a moment before she pulled the breeches down over his thighs.

"No," he said now. "I mean you're good at the whole thing—just like that maid said you were. You wrote to me about it. Do you remember?"

Good in bed, as Claudine had inelegantly expressed it. Well, perhaps she was. She shivered, disturbed and yet a bit aroused to have her measure taken so coldly.

And then she lost herself in the sight of him. Lithe and beautiful, taut and erect, he preened beneath her gaze, his swollen, purplish member rising from the black tangle of hair below his flat belly. So lovely, she thought—elegant as a sultan's curved scimitar, the tracery of veins so clearly, so intricately, molded in the dark flesh. She remained on her knees, bold and humble at the same time, and breathed him into her mouth.

He lengthened under the strokes of her tongue, thickened within the ring of her painted lips. She sucked, pulled at him, played with him, voracious as Sophie had been.

She slowed down, caressed him more fully, more carefully; she let him take the lead now, to explore her mouth, probe at her throat. She breathed his smells, her mouth happily remembering, busily relearning, his shape, his taste. *Mon Dieu,* it had been a long time.

He took her head into his hands, moving it back and forward, quickly and then slowly and then quickly again. He sighed triumphantly as the hairpins tumbled out, the carefully arranged coiffure giving way to luxuriant anarchy. His sighs grew darker, deeper, shading to moans, growls, shuddering roars from deep within his belly. She hugged him to her, pulling him closer, crushing her breasts against his thighs. Closer, she thought, as tremors began to cascade from his center, she wanted him closer, she wanted to drown in him. She clung to his legs as though she were lashed to a ship's mast in a storm; she drank the tides and torrents that spilled into her mouth, live and salty as the sea.

She swallowed, breathed deeply, like a swimmer coming to the surface. He pulled her to her feet, nuzzled and nibbled at her mouth.

"Is it terribly egotistical to enjoy the taste of myself?" he murmured. Bodies entwined, they were taking tiny, clumsy steps toward the bed.

"Probably it is," he laughed as they collapsed together onto the satin coverlet. "But now I'm ready for something sweeter."

He hadn't changed. He was still selfish and insistent, hungry and deliberate, and demanding equally robust appetites from his partner. Slowly, patiently, with teasing, maddening self-confidence, he moved his hands, his lips, over her, his eyes wide and bright, amused, delighted as always by the spectacle of her desire.

He disappeared from view. She arched her back, throwing her arms over her head to steady herself against the bed's carved headboard. Slowly, adoringly, he kissed her belly, licked at the mound of her sex; his warm breath on her skin was as provocative as his lips and tongue. Phrases from his letters drifted through her mind. *My tongue, my lips, wander happily . . .*

Ah yes.

I linger for a moment . . . and you gasp, arch your back . . . but no, not yet . . .

Not quite yet. Her ragged breathing quickened to deep, shuddering gasps and hoarse groans. His hands cradled her buttocks, lifting her, immobilizing her. And still he waited—sly, teasing, infuriating—taunting her with hundreds of little kisses on her thighs.

It was a challenge, a humiliation almost, not to insist that he hurry; it was a duel she'd always lose in the end, when he'd bring her to the limits of her "stiff-necked shopkeeper's pride" and strip every bit of shame and rectitude from her.

"Now," she almost screamed, "right *now.*" Obediently, he parted her with his tongue. Slowly, precisely, drawing an ecstatic shudder from her, he licked at the aching, swollen knot of flesh at her center. She wasn't going to last; she'd dissolve immediately. No matter. She'd lost the battle but she'd won the war.

Oddly, there did seem to be a war outside her window. Dull thuds like distant thunder, multicolored flashes of light. She must be imagining it, she thought. He'd excited her so profoundly that the entire world appeared to be aflame, exploding into sparks just as she was.

He raised his head, overcome by laughter.

"The fireworks," he managed to gasp. "Jeanne's precious fireworks." He took a long breath—unbearable, excruciating, her body protested—and quickly dipped his head back down, to tend to the fireworks of his own making.

For she hadn't dissolved completely. *More,* her body seemed to cry, *I want more, I want enough to last all my life.* Until at last he exhausted her and she screamed and tightened and finally relaxed into throaty laughter at the wondrous absurdity of it all.

"Fireworks," she giggled, as he pulled himself up beside her and gathered her into his arms, "oh dear, *fireworks.*"

He grinned, raising an eyebrow. "Rather de trop, wouldn't you say?" he murmured. The murmur became a purr as she gently licked the skin below his throat.

"Ummm," she whispered, "rather."

"They're winding down out there, I believe," he said. "Do you want to go to the window and see the end of it?"

She didn't ever want to move again. "I've seen quite enough fireworks. At least for a while."

He held her more tightly. "At least for a while."

The night continued, soft, warm, blurred by passion and exhaustion. They'd doze, and then they'd wake to find that they wanted each other again.

"*Again?*" one or the other would whisper in mock consternation.

"Again." The other would smile—fiercely, proudly.

"Again," they'd both sigh afterward, sinking heavily back onto the pillows and curling into each other, neither of them sure anymore which intertwined limb belonged to whom.

"You're different than before," she seemed to hear him whisper sometime during the night. "You've grown up . . . and I have too."

Had he really said that?

She couldn't remember what she'd replied, or even if he seemed to think that their growing up was a good or bad thing. For sometime after midnight she fell into a deep and blissful sleep, a sleep too deep, mercifully, even for dreams.

Chapter 28

She woke in the wildly disordered bed, to the sound of Sophie's predawn whimpers. Not quite consciously, she reached for Joseph. But there was no one beside her on the pillows.

She rubbed her eyes open. Just as well; if he'd been there she couldn't have pulled herself away. Without him, though, she might actually muster the will to carry out the plans she'd made so carefully.

It was a pity not to get one last hot soak in the blue bathtub. But she couldn't heat the water and fill the tub by herself, and she wouldn't be ringing for help this morning. The hôtel Mélicourt was still and silent; the Marquise had given everyone leave to linger in their beds today. Shivering in the early morning air, she scrubbed away last night's sweat and smells with tepid water from the basin.

A weary face stared at her from the mirror: eyes with shadows like bruises beneath them, mouth soft and yielding, cheeks reddened by the bristles of new beard on Joseph's cheeks. The milkmaid coiffure was a nest of Medusa tangles; it took some work to brush it out and tie it back with the ribbon that she'd bought earlier in the week especially for today.

She fed Sophie, dressed and diapered her, and quickly pulled on a dress she'd bought with Gilles's money. She'd be leaving behind the Marquise and Mademoiselle Beauvoisin's gifts and hand-me-downs, most particularly—and most imposingly—the necklace that still lay cold below her throat. She struggled with the clasp, cursing her clumsy fingers. When she finally got the thing undone, she laid it on the writing desk, on top of three folded letters she took from the drawer.

The ones addressed to the Marquise and to Mademoiselle Beauvoisin had been easy: she'd thanked them from the bottom of her heart for everything, and wished them every happiness. She'd also asked the Marquise to give Claudine the clothes she was leaving behind, and to see if Monsieur du Plessix could do something to defend Arsène.

But writing to Joseph had been a challenge. Her sentences were awkward, knotted. Of course he knew a lot of it already. Long ago in the château, she'd told him about the sort of life she'd wanted: a shopkeeper's life, decent, busy, and dull. And independent. No matter what the risks, she needed to be independent.

She hadn't changed her mind since then. But her convictions had deepened. Paris, it seemed, had taught her a few things about herself.

> *I have to live my life among ordinary people, Joseph,* she'd written. *The mass of people who crowd the streets and curse when a nobleman's coachman (your coachman, perhaps) shouts to get out of the way.*

She needed to live her life at street level.

For she *was* a common, ordinary, street-level person, with a common, ordinary person's loyalties and resentments. A common person and a conventional person—with very little patience for elegance, or games of power, seduction, and egotism.

> *And so, Joseph* (she'd concluded), *although I'll love you for the rest of my days, I can't love the life you were born into.*

And until she could think her way through this muddle, it would be best not to see him—for a little while or a very long one, she wasn't sure yet. She knew what she wanted; it was a whole new world really. What she didn't know was what she'd finally settle for, in the world she actually lived in.

No wonder her sentences had become so tortured. But she'd straightened them out as well as she could and made a clean copy, blotting it meticulously with sand that seemed to have gotten into her throat and eyes.

No tears though. There'd be plenty of time for crying after she was settled into the tiny apartment down the street from Monsieur Moreaux's bookshop. The rooms were quite decent and just big enough for her and the baby. Of course there were no tin bathtubs or thick carpeting. But it was cheap; she'd be able to afford it on the wages Monsieur Moreaux had offered to pay her.

He'd made the offer a week ago, after assuring her that he didn't want to pry. And he wished her only the best if—he'd stammered here—if the Viscomte would be keeping her from now on.

But, he'd continued, if she was in need of a position—well, might he suggest a way of earning her living that might be congenial to herself? And to him as well, he'd added, for she was a gifted and hardworking bookseller and would be a tremendous help to him in his work.

She'd been touched by his delicacy.

Yes, she'd replied, she might well be in need of a position. But she was afraid to definitely accept his offer, for fear that she'd change her mind at the last minute and leave him and the landlady in a bad situation. Could they wait three days? she asked. Just until Thursday. If she hadn't shown up by nine Thursday morning, she told him, it meant that she hadn't found the courage to accept this kindest and most generous of offers.

The clock on the mantle struck six. She straightened out the bed and picked up last night's finery from where it lay on the carpet. Still too early. Monsieur Moreaux wouldn't be at the shop until eight. But she was packed and ready to go, with Sophie in her arms and a few clothes, diapers, and books packed in a cloth bag that dangled from her shoulder.

Better to leave now and get it over with.

She slipped down the stairs, turning quickly at the corridor that led to the mansion's side door, the one that tradespeople used. Fitting, she thought.

It would be a warm, beautiful day. The Paris streets were never empty, but there was a lull at this hour: the bakers who'd been up all night had gone home and the gardeners weren't yet marching to work with rakes slung over their shoulders like muskets. She yawned as the sun climbed over a row of buildings.

A cup of coffee would be nice, but she'd wait until she'd gotten a little farther. Fifteen minutes later she stopped in front of Notre-Dame, where the coffee vendor, a brawny woman who carried the tank easily on her back, admired Sophie while Marie-Laure sipped the strong brew from a tin cup.

"She looks like her papa," Marie-Laure told the woman. Stunned by the pain it cost her to say these words, she quickly handed the cup back and hurried on.

She lingered on the bank of the Seine, watching men and women unload the crates that would feed the city today. "Look, Sophie, look at the ducks and chickens, the sweet little rabbits." How sad that someday she'd have to explain that the "chicken" that had clucked and pecked and scratched in the morning was the same "chicken" they'd eaten for dinner at noon. But at least that sadness lay in the future. Sophie waved her hands happily at the sunlight dancing on the water.

"You're open early this morning, Madame Mouffe," she greeted the round-faced, wrinkled proprietress of a bookstall a little farther on.

A toothache, the old woman told her with a grimace. Might as well get to work if you can't sleep. Marie-Laure nodded. She told Madame Mouffe about her new job, and enlivened by the thought of money coming in, the old woman invited her to scan the bookshelves. If she wanted anything, it could be held for her until she got her first week's pay from Monsieur Moreaux.

Not now, Marie-Laure told her, reaching into her bag.

"But perhaps you'd like to buy this from me." *A Libertine Education,* Monsieur X's memoirs—she'd bought the book on impulse the first day she'd wandered into Monsieur Moreaux's shop.

No point keeping it; she knew it by heart and right now she needed the money.

Toothache or not, Madame Mouffe drove a hard bargain. Still, Marie-Laure thought, even the little bit she'd gotten would help furnish the new apartment.

She traced the narrow streets to the bookshop. It was still early but she'd wait out in front until Monsieur Moreaux arrived for work. She didn't mind: Sophie had dozed off and there were people to watch and the sounds of the city to listen to.

Shop clerks passed by on their way to work. Street vendors sang out odes to the quality and cheapness of their wares.

Herrings—buy my sweet herrings!

Beets—a sou for the pound!

Lettuce, sorrel, purslane, peas!

Marie-Laure! Marie-Laure!

It wasn't easy to pick out all the different vendors' calls from the cacophony in the streets; people said that only a native Parisian could get every word. Clearly, Marie-Laure reflected, she still had a way to go. She could hear *herring* and *beets,* but one of the calls had utterly befuddled her provincial ear. Because it sounded for all the world as though the peddler were shouting *Marie-Laure.*

It wasn't a peddler.

She could see as well as hear him now, running down the street, disheveled in last night's coat and breeches, inelegantly yelling her name. The silver streaks in his hair caught the sunlight. And he had a book in his hand.

He drew nearer. The book was *A Libertine Education.*

Damn Madame Mouffe and her toothache anyway.

His eyes were huge and frightened, their rims darkly shadowed in a face flushed from running. He hadn't shaved this morning and he looked as though he'd gotten even less sleep than she had.

"Thank God," he panted. "Marie-Laure, thank God I found you. The coffee-vendor . . . said a woman . . . a baby that must be mine . . . crossed . . . to the Left Bank."

It wasn't fair. It would be much more difficult this way. He had to go away.

"I didn't want you to find me," she said. "Please. Didn't you read my letter?"

He'd almost regained his breath. "I'm sorry. I can imagine how this must look to you. But please, just let me tell you one thing. No, two things. Two, that's all, I promise. Please. And then I swear I'll go away if you want me to."

"What time is it?" she asked.

"Almost eight."

"All right," she said. "Let's go for a walk. But I have to be back here by nine."

She waved away the hand he held out to her. "Let's just . . . walk."

As though by mutual agreement, they headed toward the Seine.

He swallowed a few times before he began. "I didn't want to leave you alone in the middle of the night like that. But I promised Jeanne I'd come for some sort of midnight supper she'd planned. Very mysterious; I didn't know why it couldn't wait until today, but she insisted."

Her insides clenched. Perhaps the Marquise had decided it was time to find out what men were all about.

He looked down at her and smiled. "No, it wasn't that. Not that at all. On the contrary," he paused, "she wants me to marry *you.*"

She hated it when he spoke in riddles. "Don't joke about something like that," she said.

"That's what I said to Jeanne. But it's no joke, Marie-Laure. She means an annulment. She's been discussing it with priests—well, the very liberal Abbé Morellet, anyway, who's written articles for Diderot's *Encyclopedia.* And Morellet thinks it can be done. After all, she and I never did go to bed together. And she's prepared to make a fairly staggering donation toward rebuilding some cathedral tower, I forget which now—well, it was late when she told me."

She stared at him dumbly.

"I know, it's a lot to take in at once. But as she put it, 'I couldn't buy you out of the Bastille, but it seems I can buy you out of this marriage.' "

"But why would she want to? Aren't she and Mademoiselle Beauvoisin better off—safer—this way?"

"They are, but when I asked her about that she said she'd learned that love wasn't about safety. Love was about committing yourself any way you could and this was her commitment."

"My God."

"They want to go away," he said, "to travel together—Venice, Berlin, even Russia—they want to see the world. Ariane has some invitations to perform. But the main reason, according to Jeanne, is that they don't think France is going to become a better place for women like them. They think that whatever other changes occur—even good ones—the country's going to become more straitlaced and puritanical, and they don't want to be here when that happens."

The ground seemed to be moving under her feet.

"And . . . and . . . you'd marry me then?"

"Are you proposing to me?" he laughed.

"I'm asking you if you're proposing to me."

"Of course. Or I will, in a few minutes. But wait. Because you won't know which *me* I'm asking you to marry until I tell you the other thing."

"I hope," she murmured, "that Sophie doesn't inherit your taste for conundrum."

"Just be patient," he told her.

"You see," he continued, "I had another very important conversation yesterday as well. With Doctor Franklin. I suppose I should have told you about it last night, but you kept me pretty well occupied."

They had reached the quay now, and he nodded a familiar hello to each bookseller, in his or her stall, as they passed. Madame Mouffe waved.

"I should have realized you'd know them," Marie-Laure said.

"I paid Madame Mouffe double," he said, "after she told me where you were headed. I hope she uses the money for a dentist, but she'll probably dose the tooth with brandy.

"But as for Doctor Franklin," he continued. "We got on very

well last night, and he offered me"—he tried to say it casually—"a means of employment."

She had to smile; his aristocratic mouth was having some difficulty shaping the word *employment.*

"As an assistant to the French consul for Philadelphia. Well, actually, the position's not his to offer, but he promises to recommend me for it. If I want it.

"If you want me to take it, Marie-Laure. Or, as he put it, 'if that intelligent, industrious, and wonderfully pretty young woman wants you to.' "

"If I *want* you to!"

"I think they'd look kindly on me," he continued. "After all, I did fight in America, and Monsieur Franklin's recommendation is worth a lot. Then, of course, I can write, and I get on with people when I want to. And there's no question, Monsieur Franklin said, of my bravery or daring.

"I'd have to organize an office though. And I'm not very patient or good at details."

He's nervous, she thought. *He's frightened of taking it on.*

"My father tried to be a diplomat once," he said, "and failed miserably."

His voice faded for a moment. He forced himself to continue. "But I wouldn't *have* to fail, you know. I think if I applied myself I could develop a little patience and *become* good at details." His eyes pleaded for confirmation.

"I know you could." She looked at him levelly.

"Because after all," she added, "you are *not* your father."

He laughed with surprise and confusion. "No," he said, "I'm not, am I?

"I'm glad," he continued, "that you don't think this is a ridiculous idea. Because I wouldn't want to renounce my title and move us to Philadelphia and then discover that I wasn't any good at work I'd committed to do."

In truth, she thought, he could become a wonderful diplomat. It was a perfect opportunity for him to use his charm, his cleverness, and the passion for liberty and equality that he'd never known what to do with. As well as his newfound seriousness.

And then the import of what he'd said sank in.

"Move us to Philadelphia!"

"Doctor Franklin said that *you* were halfway toward being an American already, so the change wouldn't be too much of a strain on you. Whereas for me—he thinks I'll probably live out my days somewhere between the old culture and the new. But he thinks this could be a good thing—for I'd understand both sides of a negotiation."

Doctor Franklin was very wise.

"But I'm still not sure." He gestured at the river, the jostling crowds, the spires of Notre-Dame. "What do you think, Marie-Laure? Paris is a lot to give up."

She was too overcome to speak. But Sophie, who'd been watching him wave his hands about, suddenly bestowed upon him a wide, glorious, toothless, and just slightly crooked smile. An absolutely genuine, bona fide smile—no possibility of it being gas or fleeting accident—that demanded matching smiles from both her parents.

"She's a miracle," Joseph whispered.

Marie-Laure nodded. "And she's given you *her* answer."

"Yes, but what's *your* answer, Marie-Laure? Do you want to be . . . *Meessus* Raimond?"

"*Missus* Raimond," she corrected him, partly out of the delight of saying it.

"I'll have to help you with your pronunciation," she murmured. "Yes, yes I do, of course I want to be Missus Raimond, but . . ."

Without warning, it welled up within her: the nightmare fear and horror she'd vowed never to reveal, choking her with sudden bitter tears.

"Here," she sobbed, "take the baby while I try to compose myself. It's . . . it's not going to be easy to tell you this."

He held Sophie carefully, cradling her head as though he'd been doing it all his life.

The story emerged slowly, in fragments, as they walked along the Seine. His brother's desire for her. His sister-in-law's vindictiveness. Their plans to use her for their own indecent ends. She watched a tiny muscle tremble in his jaw.

"I'll kill him," he said, looking straight ahead. "I'll kill both of them."

"You'll do no such thing," she said. "Hasn't Arsène taught us anything?"

He nodded soberly. "You're right, but I'm glad I'd already resolved to give up my title."

"And after all," she concluded, "not much actually happened to me. Except that I felt so guilty, you know, and so frightened and powerless, and not like a human person entitled to . . ."

". . . the pursuit of happiness," he concluded.

She smiled a wobbly smile and dried her eyes. The world looked newly washed; the spires of Notre-Dame glittered.

Joseph had once called Paris the center of the world. He'd told her she'd adore it. She did adore it; it *was* a lot to give up. But she'd happily give it up for a world that wasn't divided into nobles and commoners. All of Paris wasn't too much to exchange for a chance at the pursuit of happiness.

And while she was thinking of exchanges, while she was thinking of business . . .

"The necklace," she asked. "Is it really mine?"

"Of course. Here it is." He nodded and patted his coat pocket. He stood still, his eyes clouding.

"Here, take Sophie for a moment." He frowned, shrugged, fumbled in each pocket in turn.

"Oh dear, was your pocket picked?"

He winked, producing the necklace from somewhere behind her left ear.

Well, every love affair could use some magic. And in a moment she'd see if theirs was magical enough to survive what she was going to tell him.

"I'm going to sell this necklace," she announced. "It should bring enough, don't you think, to finance a little business in Philadelphia?"

He grinned. "A bookshop. Doctor Franklin wondered how you'd decide to finance it. He offered to help, though, if you'd rather keep the necklace."

"I'd rather pay my own way."

She turned to embrace him. The busy crowds along the quay would simply have to make their way around their entwined figures, she thought.

But instead she yawned and so did he. Enormous, gaping, ungraceful yawns that released an eternity of tension, fear, and suspicion in their wakes. She laughed.

Neither of them had gotten much sleep last night. How nice though—and what a rare new pleasure—simply to be tired together, to want to lie down together just to get some rest. Well, maybe not *just* to rest . . .

"I wish," he said, "that I could say, 'let's go home,' but we don't have a home yet."

It was true. A home still lay in the future and beyond a wide ocean.

"But we could take a rest, and a bath. The two of us, I mean." She peered up at him from beneath her eyelashes. "Well, the bathtubs in the hôtel Mélicourt are rather large, you know, and . . ."

He laughed. "Ah *oui*, the hôtel Mélicourt in all its splendor. Well, I suppose it will have to do for now."

And so they walked back together, slowly, across the Seine, and through the busy Paris streets, taking turns carrying the book and the baby.

Epilogue

Philadelphia
1789

The autumn days were still warm, but it grew dark early. Too dark, Marie-Laure thought, to let the children play outside after supper. But she shouldn't have brought them down to the bookshop at dusk if she'd truly expected to get any work done.

Or perhaps she should only have brought Sophie, who was quietly teaching her dolls to read. The glamorous Venetian, the flaxen-haired German, and the Russian—a newcomer in her fur coat and boots—smiled politely as Sophie explained about putting a *T* before an *H* and getting an entirely different sound, as in "Thank you." Sophie had begun a letter just this morning thanking her aunts Jeanne and Ariane for the Russian doll; she was extremely proud of having constructed that fascinating *Th* combination.

But the dolls were a bit too polite to hold Sophie's attention, especially when she was missing an exciting sword fight between her brother Benjamin and cousin Alphonse. Any minute now, Marie-Laure thought, Sophie would grab her own sword and leap into the fray. And with all three of them darting about, it was only a matter of time before one of them knocked over the new display.

Marie-Laure had worked hard to assemble it: the few available children's books that addressed young readers as reasoning, imagining beings and not vessels for moral instruction.

"*En garde,* Alphonse." The graceful arc of Sophie's arm was an unconscious miniature of her father's.

Deftly, her cousin parried in turn. They were well matched. The green-eyed boy had inherited his height and bearing from his mother. He'd grown so tall this year that it was hard to connect him with the tiny terrified child Joseph had brought back, wrapped in his cloak, from France three years ago.

"It's the little Duc de Carency Auvers-Raimond," Joseph had whispered. He'd found him half-starved in a wet nurse's shabby cottage after he'd attended Hubert's funeral. A hunting accident, near Versailles. People suspected the Duchesse's lover, a foppish courtier, but the King had refused to investigate.

"We don't have Ducs in America." Sophie had had sharp ears, even at two and a half.

"Sophie's right," Marie-Laure had said. Softly, she'd told the little boy that they wouldn't be calling him "Monsieur le Duc." But, she'd added, they were very happy to have him with them; perhaps he'd like to come down to the kitchen with her and Uncle Joseph (he was clinging to Joseph desperately) and choose what he wanted to eat for dinner. And so she'd wound up caring for the Duchesse's son after all, while the Duchesse flitted about the gardens of Versailles, a rising favorite of the Queen herself.

Three-year-old Benjamin had flung away his sword and was shouting encouragement to Alphonse from midway up the bookshop ladder.

"Not any higher, Ben. If you climb any higher I'll lift you down entirely, do you hear me?"

Normally she would have left the children with Tabitha, who'd been helping with the housework since Joseph, Marie-Laure, and baby Sophie had arrived on this continent. But Tabby had gone, at Marie-Laure's urging, to apprentice to a local midwife. Even if it meant losing cherished household help, Marie-Laure was determined that Tabby, the intelligent and hardworking daughter of former slaves, become an independent woman with as much of a profession as she was allowed to have. Her little sister Sarah would be taking her place in Marie-Laure's house, starting tomorrow.

She comforted herself that the shop wasn't really in bad shape. Business was steady and growing; she hoped she would soon be able to hire an assistant to help her catch up on her inventory. And to rearrange the shelves: she didn't like the way the pious books were creeping into the Shakespeare collection.

But she'd have to find time to write to the supplier who'd sent the hopelessly garbled order she'd received yesterday. Amazing, she thought, how many details there were to a business most people thought was a simple matter of sitting magisterially behind the counter among neat rows of books.

She'd wanted to get a head start on at least one of her chores before Joseph returned from France. His impending arrival was the real source of the children's wild exuberance. And perhaps why she was finding it difficult to keep her mind on her work as well.

He'd be bringing important news. For in July the common people of Paris had taken history into their own hands and stormed the Bastille, freeing the few prisoners still locked up in the hated fortress. In some ways the act was only symbolic, but its audacity and ferocity had made it clear that France would never be the same.

And one of the newly freed prisoners was Arsène.

Monsieur du Plessix had used an ancient legal ploy in his defense. Even though he was a commoner, Arsène had escaped hanging for the Baron's murder because Monsieur du Plessix convinced the judges that he'd been "maddened by the mistral." But Marie-Laure suspected that Arsène's own simple testimony of his sister's sufferings had swayed the judges as well. Joseph had visited him several times in prison; it hadn't been easy, but they'd managed to forge a wary relationship over the last few years.

Of course, Joseph would have a lot to say about the current political scene in Paris. Marie-Laure had read everything she could in the newspapers: everyone agreed that change was inevitable, but nobody agreed on the form change would take. As an intimate of the present American ambassador, Mr. Jefferson, Joseph would know as much as anybody could about the situation.

He'd been successful in his work at the consulate. He'd brought his native impetuosity to the position, approaching it with the pent-up enthusiasm of a talented late starter. Just as he'd promised himself that morning on the bank of the Seine, he'd "*become* good at details." He'd become such a meticulous administrator that Mr. Jefferson had come to rely on him, demanding that he work with him in France from time to time. Marie-Laure wasn't fond of these periodic absences, but she'd never forgotten Doctor Franklin's appraisal of her husband: he thrived in the clash of old and new worlds, negotiating their differences and trying to help each side understand the other.

He was a good enough diplomat even to have made friends with Gilles. Marie-Laure was looking forward to his latest reports of Gilles, Sylvie, and their household full of tiny children as much as to the news of the political situation in Paris.

And so she'd reconciled herself to the separations. When your happiness spanned two continents and encompassed three clamorous, demanding, and highly individual children (but were there any other kind?) you learned to make the best of life's imperfections.

She'd come to terms with other imperfections as well—like the differences between her and Joseph that simply wouldn't go away. Try as she might, Marie-Laure would inevitably become befuddled by Joseph's accounts of the diplomatic intrigues that so captivated him.

"But why do grown men act so foolishly?" she'd ask. "Can't they just compromise and make peace, as I insist the children do?"

While for his part, Joseph would yawn discreetly when Marie-Laure launched into a disquisition on typefaces and bindings—the relative virtues of morocco leather and tooled calf; the inferior new thread some of the bookbinders were using lately.

It was the price you paid, she thought, for loving someone so different from yourself. But a small price: when each of you woke up in the morning eager to get to the work you loved—and when only the other's touch was enough reason to stay in bed . . .

But if she thought too hard about *that* she wouldn't get any work done at all. She smiled to think of how often her mind had strayed in that direction this week. At least as often as she'd thought of Gilles or Sylvie or the street riots in Paris.

The crash had finally come. She turned back to the miniature riot raging round her feet.

"Sophie, Alphonse, pick up those books immediately! Yes, I can see they're not creased, but you knocked the stand over, didn't you? And Benjamin—*Benjamin Alexandre Joseph*—didn't I tell you . . ."

The shop suddenly grew dark. Someone standing in the doorway had blown out the candles. Perhaps he'd done it on purpose, as a reminder of how far they'd come since Montpellier. Or perhaps he'd simply blown them out by his hearty laughter at the domestic disorder that meant *home.*

"Joseph!"

"Papa, Papa!"

"Hooray, it's Uncle Joseph!"

He swept Benjamin off his ladder as Sophie and Alphonse flung themselves at him. His skin was deep olive from his weeks on board ship, and he looked just a little more French than when he'd gone away, for he'd visited his tailor in the rue Saint-Honoré.

His hair had a few more streaks of silver. But his grin was as crooked and infectious as ever. He looked worldly, substantial, competent. And as lithe and mischievous as the night he'd pounded on the door of her attic room in the château.

He'd grown up. He hadn't changed in the slightest.

"Papa, I can read now!"

"I have a new kite, Uncle Joseph. Will you fly it with me?"

And inevitably, "What did you bring me?"

She lit the lamp while he untangled himself from the laughing, chattering knot of children. He stroked Benjamin's red hair as he set him onto the floor.

She gazed at him, for the moment or the heartbeat or the eternity before his eyes met hers. Before he was beside her, gathering her into his arms and pressing his mouth to hers.

And the news, and the children—even America and France—would all have to wait. Now that Joseph was home and Marie-Laure was at the center of the world.

AFTERWORD AND ACKNOWLEDGMENTS

I like to include real historical personages in my romances. In *The Bookseller's Daughter*, you met notable figures like Benjamin Franklin and heard about notorious ones like Joseph's prison dinner partner, the Marquis de Sade. But the book's central historical figure is one you probably took for my own invention: the predatory bookseller Monsieur Rigaud of Montpellier, who slyly remains off stage but who had a good deal to do with this book's creation.

The actual historical Isaac-Pierre Rigaud made a good living selling books (smuggled and not) during the second half of the eighteenth century. His business correspondence survives in the archives of his Swiss suppliers, and these archives constitute the core of Robert Darnton's wonderful historical study, *The Forbidden Bestsellers of Pre-Revolutionary France.*

Darnton tells us that in the decades preceding the French Revolution, a remarkable selection of literature was smuggled over the French borders and past the censors—to be sold "under the cloak" by booksellers bold and shrewd enough to do so. Rousseau's *Confessions* made its way into France this way, among other famous titles we credit with creating the intellectual ferment of the time. But so did many lesser, smuttier works, especially erotic (or "libertine") fiction. Eighteenth-century French booksellers didn't distinguish between different orders of subversive literature: they called them all "philosophical books."

Darnton doesn't draw easy conclusions about the political effects of reading. His arguments and speculations are subtler, and I recommend his book to anyone interested in how history works and ideas change, day by day and on the ground. I especially recommend his explanations of the mechanics of book smuggling—since I'll confess (with some embarrassment) that my own account is tailored to the requirements of my plot and highly simplified.

I'm not embarrassed, however, by my simple emotional response to *The Forbidden Best-Sellers*, which my husband and I both read when it came out in 1994. My husband's interest was as an independent bookseller, mine as an erotic writer. But I'd spent some time in the book trade myself, and the early 90s were a time of energetic and baleful concentration in our industry, as large chains began forcing smaller independents out of business.

As I followed Rigaud's cutthroat strategies and watched him buy up his competitors, I started to resent him—and to imagine another competitor, someone poor but honest, with a fetching bookish daughter. And once I'd caught an imaginary glimpse of Marie-Laure's ink-stained fingers, it was easy to see Joseph's crooked grin.

And what (I asked myself) if the smuggler with that captivating grin were actually a libertine writer himself? What if he were the son (the second son, *naturellement*) of the meanest duke in the Provence? And so *what-if*'ed myself into *The Bookseller's Daughter*. I'm sure I wouldn't have bothered if I hadn't been so personally ticked off at Rigaud—so you can thank or blame him as you please while I do my own thanking and blaming.

Well, not a real blame, but I do have one long-cherished comment: to an early reader (and contest judge) who thought Marie-Laure made an undue fuss when Joseph shorted her order: Honey, you should hang out with some booksellers when *they* get short-shipped.

There, I feel better now.

Otherwise I have only my most grateful thanks. To my best and toughest critics, Ellie Ely and Michael Rosenthal, for forcing me to fix gaffes and problems I would have preferred to ignore. To my agent, Helen Breitwieser, for never losing her resolve that we'd see an ISBN on this thing someday. To the folks who insisted on this book's virtues: Ellen Jacobson, Robin Levine-Ritterman, Jesse Rosenthal, and Jeff Weinstein. To my brothers, Doctors Jeff and Ricky Ritterman, for their respective advice about wounds and preeclampsia.

Special thanks to Kensington's gifted art director, Kristine V. Mills-Noble, for the amazingly lovely covers she's given me. The quill pens and rococo flourishes on this one are absolutely in the spirit I tried to convey. And to Howard Mittelmark, whose deft copyediting brought order to some anarchic sentences.

Thanks also to the whole, supportive Ritterman-Bard-Krasner clan. And to the San Francisco Bay Area Chapter of Romance Writers of America; the Unreadables (thanks especially to William de Soria); my colleagues at the San Francisco Fed who came to my booksigning and bought up every copy of my book; my fellow Welloids; Michael's colleagues in the San Francisco independent bookselling community who buzzed *Almost a Gentleman* so enthusiastically; and my talented web designer, Emily Cotler at Waxcreative. Come visit me at www.pamrosenthal.com and see Emily's gorgeous handiwork.

And—most importantly—to a reading community every bit as avid as Rigaud's: thanks and thanks again to the romance readers who said such great things online and the ones who took the time to write to me (pam@pamrosenthal.com). I can't tell you how much I value you.

In case you missed Pam's first book with Brava,
please enjoy an excerpt of

ALMOST A GENTLEMAN

by Pam Rosenthal.

Available now in bookstores.

He lowered his eyes, trying to compose himself. But there was no help for it now that she'd guessed the truth: that while she'd turned away he'd been staring at the curve of her derriere and thighs.

My *thighs*. Phoebe's. *He's been looking at my legs, which he can see quite perfectly in these closely fitting trousers. And he wants* me.

She held herself at rigid attention. Three years of masculine masquerade was nothing, she thought, compared to the control it took not to betray the melting softness invading her body's center at the present moment.

Caught looking, dammit. But upon brief reflection, David decided that being caught might not be such a bad thing after all. She'd quickly regained her self-control, but he knew what he'd seen: the momentary pleasure she'd taken in his eyes' caress. David was an experienced enough fighter to press his advantage when he'd suddenly—even if accidentally—gained the upper hand.

He raised his eyes, grinned, and quickly swept his eyes over her legs.

Her mouth parted into an *O* of surprise. He could see a velvety pink tongue peeping between her white teeth.

Eyes lowered again, he sipped his tea as though nothing had happened. He'd won a small battle, but there was a whole war ahead of him. He was glad; she was too spectacular a prize to be taken easily. He leaned back in his armchair, watching appreciatively as she paced the length of the small room with her graceful, mannish stride.

She stopped now, seized by a sudden insight that lit the gold flecks in her eyes.

"You say, Lord Linseley, that your concern was my safety. And yet you clearly admit that you allowed this Stokes to pursue me into the Lake District."

"Only after I'd clearly seen that you and the other lady were headed in the opposite direction."

You and the other lady. As soon as he said it, he realized that she'd led him into a trap. *There's no going back now: I've just admitted that I know she's a woman.*

It had been clever of her, he thought, to turn the argument so deftly. But of course she was clever: from the very beginning he'd been charmed by the lively intelligence that animated her gestures and expressions.

"And how could you have known *that*, my lord?"

Caught like a clumsy bear with his leg in a trap. It was humiliating. It was delightful. And there was nothing to do but concede defeat.

"Because I saw you depart in the carriage. Southwestward. Toward Devonshire, perhaps."

Devonshire must have been a good guess, he thought, watching her eyes narrow slightly.

His grin widened, crinkling the corners of his dark blue eyes. "You were very beautiful in pink, Mr. Marston."

"And you're surprisingly insolent, Lord Linseley. Not to speak of inconsistent. You did say, after all, that it wasn't your intent to infringe upon my privacy."

"I lied. I want to know everything about you."

"But why? Not for gain, surely? Though I imagine there are those who'd pay for the information."

"I don't want that sort of money."

"For influence, then? To exchange for votes during the next session of Parliament? To sacrifice me and my petty secrets on behalf of England's deserving yeomen?"

"You're cleverer than I, Mr. Marston. I assure you I never considered such a thing. But must I continue to call you Mr. Marston?"

She laughed. "For the time being."

He'd never heard her laugh before. The sound was rich, languorous, like the murmur of springwater spilling over mossy rocks. He wanted to bathe, to luxuriate in that sound. He wanted it to last forever.

Please turn the page for an excerpt
from a contemporary sensual treat

DRIVE ME CRAZY

by Nancy Warren.

Coming from Brava in February 2004.

Duncan Forbes knew he was going to like Swiftcurrent, Oregon when he discovered the town librarian looked like the town hooker. Not a streetwalker who hustles tricks on the corner, but a high class 'escort' who looks like a million bucks and costs at least that much, ending up with her own Park Avenue co-op.

He loved that kind of woman.

He saw her feet first when she strode into view while he was crouched on the gray-blue industrial carpeting of Swiftcurrent's library scanning the bottom shelf of reference books for a local business directory. He was about to give up in defeat when those long sexy feet appeared, the toes painted crimson, perched on do-me-baby stilettos.

Naturally, the sight of those feet encouraged his gaze to travel north, and he wasn't disappointed.

Her legs were curvy but sleek, her red and black skirt gratifyingly short. The academic in him might register that those shoes were hard on the woman's spine but as she reached up to place a book on a high shelf, the man in him liked the resulting curve of her back, the seductive round ass perched high.

From down here, he had a great view of shapely hips, a taut belly, and breasts so temptingly displayed they ought to have a 'for sale' sign on them.

He shouldn't stare. He knew that, but couldn't help himself—torn between the view up her skirt and that of the underside of her chest. He felt like a kid in a candy store, gobbling everything in sight, knowing he'd soon be kicked out and his spree would end.

Sure enough, while he was lost in contemplation of the perfect angle of her thigh, the way it sloped gracefully upward to where paradise lurked, she looked down and caught him ogling. Her face was as sensuous and gorgeous as her body—sleek black hair, creamy skin and plump red lips. For that instant when their gazes first connected he felt as though something mystical occurred, though it could be a surge of lust shorting his brain.

Her eyes went from liquid pewter to prison-bar gray in the time it took her to assimilate that he hadn't been down here staring at library books. What the hell was the matter with him acting like a fourteen-year-old pervert?

"Can I help you with something?"

Since he'd been caught at her feet staring up her skirt, he muttered the first words that came into his head. "Honey, I can't begin to tell you all the ways you could help me."

The prison bars seemed to slam down around him. "Do you need a specific reference volume? A library card? Directions to the exit?"

The woman might look as though her photo ought to hang in auto garages reminding the grease monkeys what month it was, but her words filled him with grim foreboding. He was so screwed.

"*You're* the librarian?"

A ray of winter sunlight stole swiftly across the gray ice of her eyes. "Yes."

"But you're all wrong for a librarian," he spluttered helplessly.

"I'd best return my master's degree then."

"I mean . . ." He gazed at her delicious top to scrumptious bottom. "Where's your hair bun? And bifocals? And the crepe-soled brogues and . . . and the tweeds."

If anything, her breasts became perkier as she huffed a quick breath in and out. "It's a small mind that thinks in clichés."

"And a big mouth that spouts them," he admitted. God, what an idiot. He'd spent enough time with books that he ought to know librarians come in all shapes and sizes, though, in fairness, he'd never seen one like this before. He scrambled to his feet, feeling better once he'd resumed his full height and he was gazing down at her, where he discovered the view was just as good. He gave her his best shot at a charming grin. "I bet the literacy rate among men in this town is amazingly high."